J.B. 2015

W9-CNA-050

# Conquered Heart

## Lisa Samson

**HARVEST HOUSE PUBLISHERS**
Eugene, Oregon 97402

**CONQUERED HEART**

Copyright © 1996 by Lisa Samson
Published by Harvest House Publishers
Eugene, Oregon 97402

Library of Congress Cataloging-in-Publication Data

Samson, Lisa, 1964–
    Conquered heart / Lisa Samson.
        p.   cm.
    ISBN 1-56507-448-3 (alk. paper)
    I. Title.
PS3569.A46673C66   1996
813' .54—dc20                                              96-6121
                                                            CIP

**All rights reserved.** No portion of this book may be reproduced in any form without the written permission of the Publisher.

**Printed in the United States of America.**

96  97  98  99  00  01 / BC / 10  9  8  7  6  5  4  3  2  1

The Abbey series is dedicated to the man who
gave me my start and has believed in me
from Day One, Bill Jensen.
Thank you from the depths
of a heart forever filled with gratitude.

This book is dedicated to
my big sister, Lori Chesser—
a special woman who walks
hand in hand with laughter
and makes each day a party.
You're beautiful, babes!

# About the Author

Lisa Samson has always had a keen interest in history. During a time of study at Oxford University, she fell in love with British history, and out of that love grew *The Highlander and His Lady*, her first novel. A graduate of Liberty University with a degree in telecommunications, Lisa lives in Virginia with her husband, Will, daughter, Tyler, and son, Jake.

# Acknowledgments

Bill Jensen, my gratitude for your belief in me and your editorial expertise cannot be adequately expressed. Thank you.

To Lori Chesser—thanks for accompanying us to England and making the research trip many times more amusing than it would have been without you. Huzzah!

To Betty Fletcher and Margie Brown of Harvest House, thank you for the hours of work you put in on behalf of this book.

For all those who were instrumental in my research—Dr. Homer Blass of Liberty University, Sean Church at Westminster Abbey, Thorskegga Thorn (whose knowledge of ancient weaving techniques and demonstration of tablet weaving proved invaluable)—I give my thanks. Much appreciation also is due to Nancy Sattler for the Latin translations. And to those on the Internet who helped me garner information, I say thank you, but especially to Iain A. Fraser for his helpfulness in providing botanical information for the region of Oxfordshire.

To all my friends and family, your encouragement is priceless. And lastly, my gratitude to my very own little family must be expressed. To Will, Tyler, and Jakey, thank you for making my life rich with hope and blessed beyond all imaginings.

Praise God from whom all blessings flow.

# Author's Note

"The Abbey" takes us into southern England and spans many centuries. *Conquered Heart* begins in the year 1050 with the founding of a new church. That church is affectionately known by the world as Westminster Abbey.

The full name of the monastery of which that church was a part was the Monastery of St. Peter's at Westminster. At times the Westminster Abbey will be referred to as the Church of St. Peter's. During the time period in which this book takes place the last Saxon king, King Edward (canonized later as Edward the Confessor), rebuilt the church and the monastery buildings of St. Peter's. He did so to redeem himself from a vow to make a pilgrimage to Rome. The church was Norman in architecture and is not the structure that stands in the city of Westminster today. There are many books available detailing the history of the abbey, and I would encourage you to peruse them for yourself. The history of this time-honored, venerable, ancient monastery and church is more exciting and tantalizing than any book of fiction could ever claim to be.

Also, on the following pages you will find diagrams of a typical monastery and church. I hope these will be of help to you as the story unfolds.

I have striven for historical accuracy, but there are several areas which I changed for the sake of the story. Most likely the master mason who designed and built Edward's church was a Norman and not a Saxon. There is no Roman fortress near Oxford as my book describes. But a castle mound, or motte, built by the sheriff of Oxneford after the Norman invasion, still stands in the city of Oxford today. As far as the battle of York, the particulars have been lost to time, so what you will read is written to enhance this story. William the Conqueror was referred to by the rebel English as "The Bastard" due to his illegitimacy. I have used this term in this book to be accurate and to adequately show the defiance of the English and their refusal to recognize his overlordship.

All of my main characters in this book are fictional. Lilla quite often quotes Scripture taught to her by her uncle, the village priest. This goes far beyond what a simple woman like herself would have known and understood during this time period. But the main purpose of my writing is to bring others to know Him, and her knowledge of Scripture is a tool I have used to point the way to the Savior. You will notice also that I refer to Jesus in the Latin, *Jesu* (Yay-soo).

Enjoy, and may Jesus Christ be praised.

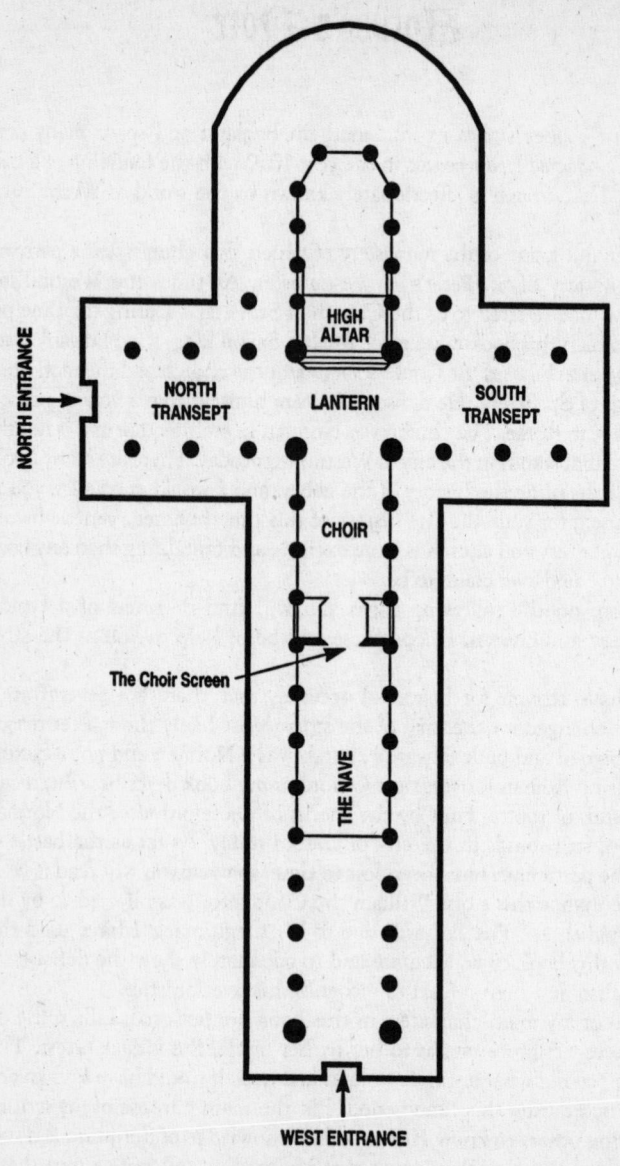

NORTH ENTRANCE

NORTH TRANSEPT

HIGH ALTAR

LANTERN

SOUTH TRANSEPT

CHOIR

The Choir Screen

THE NAVE

WEST ENTRANCE

Typical Church

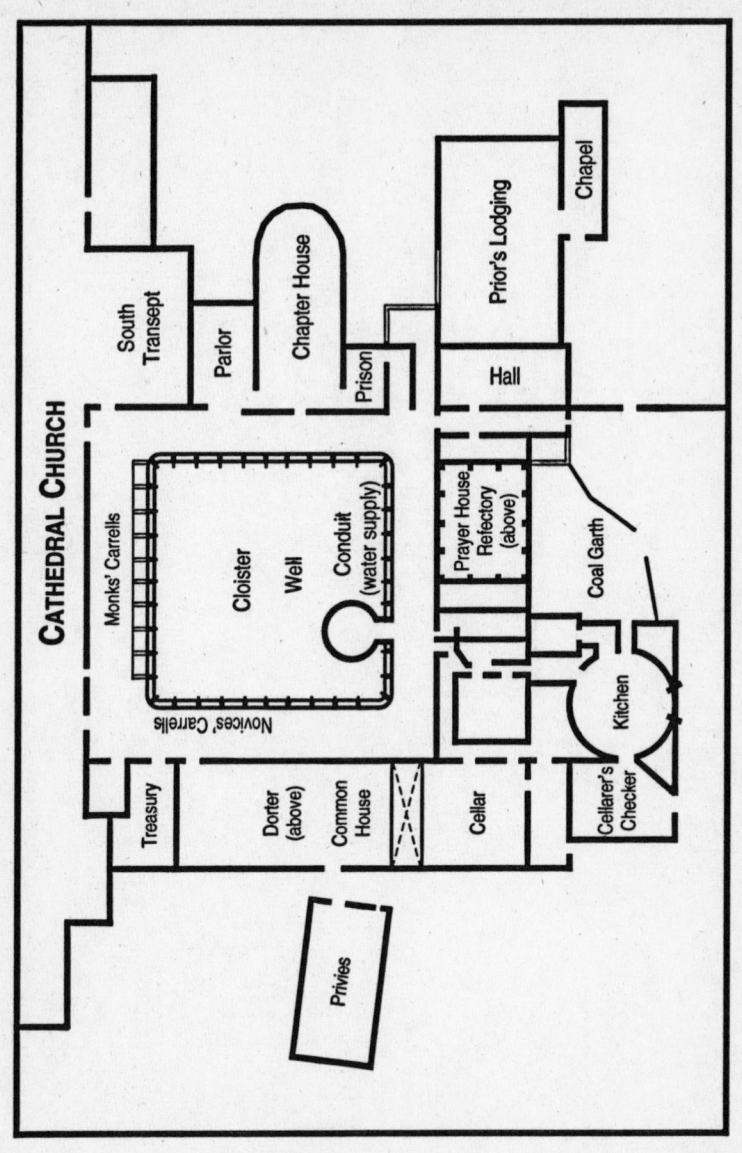

Typical Monastery

---

## Prologue
# The Noble Lord

---

h er roughened fingers curled round the cool, silver amulet. In the fire's light the amber stone, a smoothly polished dome, caught the reflection of the blaze. Outside a spring snow fell out of the waning daylight.

"It's lovely." Her words could not describe such beauty, her heart could not overcome its sadness.

The man sitting across from her looked tenderly into her eyes, searching, searching. For a brief moment she returned her lord's gaze, knowing that she would never love more strongly or more futilely than she did at that moment. A calm shyness overcame her, and she dropped her gaze to stare at the necklace she had just been given.

The winter had been the severest anyone could remember. He had come for shelter three months ago.

"This necklace I have given to you, Bronwyn, for your protection and provision. You need only show it to my steward."

"Will he question . . . ?"

His strong mouth smiled gently in the light of her sweet consternation, and the hand that he had placed on her cheek moved further back, the strong fingers thrusting into her straight brown hair. "Nay, child, he is my most trusted man."

"So you will not be coming back to me?"

"No. My bride arrives from Nottingham on the morrow."

The farewell kiss he gave told her he wished it need not be so. But their love was made to end, as such loves mostly do, and well they both knew it. She placed a hand on her still-flat belly. "Do you wish to know when the babe is born?"

"'Twould be more than I could bear to hear of it and not seek you out."

She nodded mutely, forbidding the swell of tears to draw nigh to the corners of her eyes. Time mercilessly kept its semieternal pace as she stared helplessly at her hands. The warrior lord in front of her knew he should go, and wished with the entirety of his heart that she would bid him stay. She didn't.

"Farewell then, my lord." In dignity she raised her head and gave him a telling look that both loved and refuted.

"Farewell, child. You have served me well."

He left, his warm purple cloak the last snippet of him to leave her tiny house which huddled only a few miles from the shadow of his castle. Lying now on the pallet they had shared, she remembered him well, refusing to yield to time's destruction one crease in the weathered soldier's skin, which tightly covered his large, yet patrician features. Nor would she forget the white-blond hair, silky smooth, which rested on his shoulders. Or his body, long and lithe, and the survivor of many a skirmish. The feel of the scars which crisscrossed his arms and legs, and the ragged round scar which marred the right portion of his chest—the kiss of a Welshman's arrow—were committed to the deepest chasm of tactile memory.

But more than these she would remember best what she could not see—a heart as equally massive as his frame. He had loved her well. Had given her himself for three months when he could have returned to his home. And he would always love her. But his people came first, and the well-being of those who lived on his lands. Benevolently she wished to remember his parting, for her own sake. For nobles did not follow their hearts as other men.

Yet hate was but a minute turn away from love—Bronwyn knew that well. She was used. She knew that, too. But bitterness would do no good.

Her home was empty. The noble lord was gone. And it didn't matter that she knew he loved her in the deepest way a man like him knew how.

Bronwyn would never love a man again. When the spring rains ceased a month later, the lonely young maiden left her town, gathering his gifts, her belongings, and memories which would needs last her the rest of her days.

The babe was born.

Bronwyn was never lonely again. She raised her child to live pure and upright, and wished that her mother would have done the same. Yet still she prayed and hoped against even the dictates of her heart that one day her lord would return . . . if not to her, then to their child.

# Book I
# The Student

## ONE

# Emma

The day King Edward laid the cornerstone of the abbey, hewn by my husband's own hands, was the day my son, producing a dauntless squall, was laid in my arms by the midwife. I laughed—from exhaustion as much as humor or happiness.

And my husband, Eadric, cried.

Even years later I remember it well as Eadric stood there, the dust of stone turning his brown leather apron gray, his hair shedding powder and bits of the God-made stuff he lovingly crafted every day. The sun was shining that afternoon in July of the year 1050 as my husband stood silhouetted in the golden rays flowing through the open window. His thin, sprouty yellow hair shone bright in the heavenly backlighting. Our son he held high in his massive hands, and the motes of his toil—toil on a house of God no less—formed a dusty halo about the two men in my life. One newly given, the other comfortably loved for years. Truly God had consecrated three things that day by my window: the abbey, my husband's talent, and my newborn son.

Eadric of Bath's round, gray eyes refused to ease up their sudden flow of tears when he lowered the babe to his burly chest. The salty drops fell onto our naked son's alabaster skin, and as he wriggled against the tears, he reminded me of a living statue of the Christ child, carved from pure-white marble and exhibiting muscles not usually seen on a babe.

Eadric lifted one of the wee legs and kneaded the longish limb with his callused fingers. Our babe pulled his leg free, his face reddening with exertion. "Look, Emma. Already he promises to follow after his father and become the royal stonemason. Already he is strong."

I pushed back the blanket with a smile and, reaching for fresh rags down by the floor, I began to get out of bed. "How could he not be strong? He moved within me at all hours of the day building up the strength needed to abide in this world of toil, Eadric."

"Are you sure you must get out of bed so soon, my lamb? You must rest."

"My sweet husband, this lad is our eighth child." I held out my arms, already aching to hold this dear little boy whom I somehow knew would be the last child I would bear. Only two of the previous seven had survived. And both were girls.

Eadric handed the baby over reluctantly. "Here he is. I must ready myself for the baptism."

Just then our eldest daughter, 13-year-old Mary, rushed in. Her tiny slippered feet slid over the stone floor, and Eadric had to slow her down before she crashed into the bed. "The king! Father, Mother! King Edward is here!"

Eadric easily lifted me off my feet and carried the baby and me to the bed. "Quick, Emma, back into bed with you! Get well under the covers."

I couldn't help but feel somewhat annoyed at the ill-timed intrusion.

Footsteps approached. And when good King Edward appeared at the door, so humble, so filled with the charity of the blessed Christ, I felt nothing but awe. And truly, for one of the first times in my life, I was humbled.

Eadric bowed. "Your highness."

I bowed my head as well and said the same, adding, "And

what good fortune has befallen the home of Eadric of Bath that we should be so honored by a visit from our sovereign lord?"

King Edward walked softly into the room I had just given birth in and, as a pious man who had taken a vow of celibacy, he felt out of place, unable to comprehend such commonplace domesticity.

"When I heard that the building of God's church was abandoned on the very day that the cornerstone was laid, I came to inquire of my royal stonemason why he left off the work of God." Smiling at Eadric he said, "Truly, I came to see the babe."

Fine white hands stretched forward to receive my son. And I stole a peek at the face which hovered above my own. It was a beautiful face. A long, thin patrician nose, well-formed lips, and eyes bluer than the cornflowers which grew wild on Thorny Isle, where the new Westminster abbey was being erected. His hair was quite fair and was short, yet full, beneath the crimson hat which circled his brow. All in all, King Edward at 46 possessed a pale, ethereal appearance, yet from those eyes a strength emanated—a strength of character that was unmistakable to even the most simple citizen. He was a man at peace with God, more suited to cloister than crown. Upon his request, I handed him the child now wrapped snugly in a warm blanket. The babe's crying had ceased as soon as King Edward stepped softly into the room.

The king smiled into my son's eyes, the blue of his echoed by the babe's. "So you're the sign from God, are you?" he whispered softly to the babe. His words, though spoken in English, held a strong Norman-French accent, belying the fact that he grew up exiled in the safe haven of Normandy in the court of his mother's brother, Robert, the Duke of Normandy.

"I beg your pardon, your highness, but what do you mean?"

"He was born at the same time I laid the stone, madam. A strong, fine, healthy boy. As the abbey grows, so will he. It is a sign from God that the future of the new church at St. Peter's will be bright with promise, even as this little boy's future lies ahead of him—a future of greatness, of earthly glories and heavenly rewards."

Eadric's eyes opened wide with delight. "Do you really believe that, sire?"

"Yes, Eadric of Bath, I do. Truly he is a son of the abbey that I envision and you will build, and I will do all within my power to ensure that he increases fine and strong. And educated. What has taken place is more than a coincidence, and I have taken an interest in this child."

Tears filled both Eadric's and my eyes. "Thank you, your highness," my husband said with great emotion. Our son's future was as secure as any human's could be. And an education was something which was afforded only to those who would enter the church and a few enlightened noblemen. Even some of the powerful earls could neither read nor write.

King Edward traced his gentle fingers topped by large almond-shaped nails across the child's cheek, and as he did so a little hand made its way out of the blanket and grabbed hold. I could see the small tapered digits redden as they gripped soundly the right index finger of the king, and our babe respired one brief yell. He quickly ceased, but did not let go. The king was greatly pleased. "Oui, it is a fine, strong son our Lord has given you, Eadric. You must teach him your artistry even as he is taught to read and write. For when you are gone, my trusted royal mason, he must carry on our work of building churches to the glory of God the Father."

"Amen." Eadric crossed himself reverently. And I did the same, although we weren't in any church just then. The king had that affect. Whatever room he occupied became somehow sanctified.

"And now, the child must be baptized. I will be his godfather," the king pronounced. "Is his godmother present?"

Eadric nodded. "Yes, my liege. It is Rachel the midwife, Emma's good friend. She is downstairs."

"And a godfather?"

"Well, sire, Joseph, my fellow guildsman, should be waiting already at the church." Eadric wasn't concerned. Many babies were blessed with two godfathers.

"Good," King Edward informed us. Both Eadric and I were so overcome we could not speak. We bowed our heads down low and held them there.

"Come now. Let us be going."

As the purification rite of Jewish tradition was still observed by the church, I was not permitted to attend. Until six week's time had elapsed, I wouldn't be allowed to darken the door of our parish church. Reaching down beside the bed for a little parcel, I handed it to Eadric.

"Here . . . it is the christening robe."

Eadric nodded, and they left the chamber. I hastened to the window to watch the royal procession slowly negotiate the small street of London. Members of Edward's court, absent from our bedchamber, now walked in close proximity to the king. That was my baby, carried in the King of England's own arms. Who had ever heard of the like? Eadric told me all about it when he returned a while later.

The abbot of St. Peter's monastery at Westminster—a thin, drab man with soft brown eyes—met them at the door to our parish church, which was a small, austere building of stone. Taking the child from his close friend, the king, Abbot Edwin placed his large, gangly hand upon my child's head. Our parish priest looked on with pride.

"What is the sex of this child?" he asked in rounded, holy tones.

King Edward answered. "It is a boy."

"And has it been baptized yet?"

"No."

Abbot Edwin blessed the child with a gracious smile upon his lips, the Latin words spoken not in a monotone litany but with heartfelt wonder at God's continued work of creation. He then took a wee bit of salt from the cellar which the novice standing by his side held in cupped hands. Placing a pinch of it on the baby's tongue, he said, "May you receive the wisdom of God throughout your life even as you receive this salt. Jesu said, 'You are the salt of the earth.'"

Next the abbot drove out any demons that might be lurking in the child, then turned to Rachel, Joseph, and the king. "Do you promise to aid in the spiritual well-being of this child? To teach him the Pater Noster, the Ave Maria, and the Credo?"

"I do." King Edward answered firmly.

"I do." The others answered after him rather more softly.

After that the abbot tested their own knowledge of the prayers, and the three godparents recited them in unison there on the steps of the church. Happily for my son, it was a July morn, no cold winds whipping the swaddling off his fresh, new, puffy skin.

The party then moved into the dim recesses of the church to the baptismal font—a stone basin lined with lead and filled with holy water. My baby boy was anointed, immersed, and finally named.

"What will be the name of this child?" Abbot Edwin asked the godparents.

Rachel and Joseph looked to the king, who did not hesitate. "The child's name is Alfred Edward Griffin."

Eadric's eyebrows raised. Griffin? He had heard that name before, once. And afterward we both wondered what possible import that could have to King Edward. But, of course, Eadric didn't ask just then.

The king lifted Griffin, for that is what we would come to call him, out of the font, and Eadric supplied him with the white crysom I had embroidered the first year of our marriage for the baptism of our first, and soon-after deceased, boy-child. Griffin wriggled and squalled loudly, renewing the king's delight in him as he wrapped the robe around his wet, slippery body with Rachel's help. Although later she told me, her green eyes finding the humor as always, "Being in the presence of the king himself made me so shaky, Emma, that I fear my help 'twas not much help a'tall."

And back they all came to our home, except for King Edward and his courtiers. Neighbors and relatives had prepared a goodly feast, with varieties of fresh fish and summer vegetables. Griffin was passed around from one set of arms to another. Gifts were given by generous hands, and blessings poured from the happy hearts of our community family. I blessed this day, the day my Griffin entered the world, from the depths of my soul.

The next day was filled with thunderstorms and rain so heavy and thick that the only people who ventured forth were those with pressing business. Eadric stayed in the lodge all day, working on the base for one of the pillars that would line the nave. All the masons were assembled, crafting at whatever task my husband set before them. It was a secret place, the lodge. Only masons were allowed to enter. And one could only be a mason if his aim was one and the same with the guild. To serve with simple truth, to do well, to charge fairly, to avoid usury, and to deal honorably alike, worker to worker, and with the community. They were a closely knit brotherhood, guarding the secrets of the lodge, ensuring proper training of workmen and apprentices, accepting responsibility for the integrity of the trade.

Soon we would be moving closer toward the building site, right on Thorny Isle itself. An old legend maintained that at one time a Roman temple to Apollo, the sun god, stood on the island. An earthquake had seen to its demise. But then, I suppose God didn't take kindly to having a pagan shrine atop land He had consecrated as His church's even before the first man stepped onto the greater isle of Britannia.

"Emma," Eadric told me two months before Griffin's birth, "I suppose I am now a most worthy royal mason."

My embroidery needle ceased to perform its decorative musings. "And why is that, dear man?"

"The king says my house should be near the abbey. In three months' time we shall move our belongings over to the isle."

Naturally, I was overjoyed at the prospect of living so close to the place Edward inhabited faithfully when he was in the region of London. What woman isn't excited about moving into a new home? Not that we were poor, mind you. Eadric made 12 denarii a day. In addition to that, we were given a loaf of bread, meat, and ale. And although my fingers plied a needle with ease, our gracious King Edward provided Eadric with two new robes a year—one in the summer and a fur-trimmed one in winter. We lacked nothing. Our small house in London was more than ample for our little family. And certainly it was more comfortable than the wattle-and-daub home I grew up in near Bath. Bath . . . how Eadric and I still miss walking around the ancient Roman baths of Aquae Sulis. I remember the day he asked me to marry him like it was yesterday.

Eadric's wide hands, knotted with muscle and sinew, had just ceased a shy caress over my brown hair. The memory has always pulled at my heart—the way he was aware of his superior strength and how he overcompensated for such. His touch was so gentle that day, so reassuring and wonderfully comforting. It still is.

"Emma, my lamb, I'm not a rich man."

My blue eyes sparkled underneath his love. "Yes, you are, Eadric."

"How is that so? I'm but a journeyman mason. That hardly makes me a man of wealth."

"You have me."

"Ahhh. That is so, Emma. You are the one treasure of my life."

"And since there is only one of me, that makes you even richer than you first realized."

He ran a sweet hand over the deep crimson sleeve of my gown. "Nay. That is not what makes me so rich, Emma dear."

"What then?"

He bowed his head. "You love me."

"Aye, Eadric. That I do."

Two weeks later we were married.

But I digress. This tale does not concern myself and Eadric of Bath. That is for another day. This is Griffin's tale.

Griffin was a lusty nurser. He latched on from the first try, and my task was set before me. And my contrary little son did not even have the courtesy to sleep the day away like the usual newborn. No. He fed every two hours for the first four months of his life. Large and strong and heavy he grew, like a little white bear.

Mildred, my eight-year-old, was besotted with her brother. When impatience tinged my voice (due to lack of sleep, more than not), she would say with compassion, "But Mother, he's just a wee baby." After her chores were finished, she would cuddle him in her arms and entertain him with the silliest sounds I had ever heard a little girl make. Her black curls would spill down over the blond downy hair on his head, and I would thrill that God could give two parents such different children. Unlike Griffin, Mildred had slept all the time until she was four months old.

Mary, brown-haired like I am, was different. Having lost three siblings whom she could remember, she loved Griffin in a peculiar, distanced way. Rarely would she pick him up or play with him. But she would faithfully wash his soiled nappies or fold them. No one else could fetch me the soap or a clean garment. Mary voluntarily became his menial servant and self-proclaimed nursemaid. But in truth, Alfred Edward Griffin had enslaved us all.

And yet, though demanding, Griffin developed a side to him that was painfully endearing. He would cock his head to the side and stare up through his long, light lashes when he was pleased. And he was happiest when clad only in his nappy, exhibiting that sweet baby body for the family to worship. We knew that Jesu had plans for this child. We said as much the day after his baptism.

Eadric had just returned from the lodge, the twilight subduing the first-floor hall of our home. Mary, standing by the central hearth, was stirring the evening's meal of pheasant stew with root vegetables, and she had just brought home several loaves of barley bread from the baker's oven down the street.

He sniffed in so deeply I wondered if there would be air left for the rest of us. "Ahhh. And what is our sweet Mary cooking up for the household this fine night?"

Mary brought him a piece of warm bread. "Father, 'tis one of your favorites."

Mildred laughed. "Everything's Father's favorite!"

"'Tis true. 'Tis true." Eadric smiled and bit down into the crusty warmth.

Forever I would look back at that moment as the happiest, most content moment of my life. My husband sat at the bench by the table with the telltale markings of hard, ingenious toil upon his clothes, face, and hands. Mary was bustling about in a dither—a state in which she thrived most heartily. Mildred sat at my feet, constantly pushing her head against my hand so that I might glide my fingers through her hair. And with my foot I pushed down on the rocker of the cradle made by one of the abbey carpenters. Griffin lay inside. His face wore the pure, smooth beauty of infantile repose. My heart was so incredibly large at that point I could hardly breathe. Tears welled up inside the pink rims of my eyes. Just then Eadric looked at me, his eyes joyfully feeding upon my thoughts. He understood.

In a way, I realized then, it was the feeling he would one day have when the abbey was done. But although we hadn't built a church together, we had built a family. Just me and Eadric. I wanted to fly, for truly I was soaring upon the wings of happiness, my praise and thankfulness circling up as a living offering to the Father God.

Eadric was suddenly solemn. "Jesu has special things planned for this little one. Surely good things await him someday in paradise."

"Aye, Eadric. Griffin is His child."

"Well, of course he is," Mildred laughed, turning her face back and upward to look at me. "We had him baptized yesterday."

"That is true, Milly."

Our faith in the church was everything. We attended Mass each day, and how many candles I lit over the years I couldn't begin to count! And Griffin would share in our faith. The circumstances surrounding his birth attested to that. He would be a worthy son of the church, of that I was certain. If Eadric hadn't been so committed to having him be a mason someday, I would have encouraged him to become a priest. Yet in the deepest recesses of my mind, even back then, I knew Griffin's destiny was far greater than even Eadric and I could have foretold. I truly believed he was destined for a special life. A pathway trod to greatness. And yet, my motherly fears reminded me, the road to greatness is invariably paved with many stones of pain.

When I looked down into the cradle, Griffin awoke. The sleepy crescents of his eyes achieved a full circle of blue and white. Slowly the pink, full lips spread in the sweetest smile I had ever seen.

My heart broke.

# ❧ TWO ❧

**H**e walked like Saxon royalty that day.

Griffin, the boy king of Thorny Isle. Everyone knew him. There wasn't a free moment the 11-year-old had that wasn't spent out-of-doors. Even King Edward himself realized with good humor that regarding popularity around the sparse population of Westminster, he took second place.

Out the door on a misty morning, Griffin trod over the soppy grass with his head held high and his long, thick blond mane blowing back from his face in the autumn breeze. The colors of fall were softly muted in the haze. Smoky greens and dull browns. The reds of the sedum became a dark, dusky pink, and the hue of the asters became a bluish gray. Griffin's tunic, the color of a mustard seed, faded to a muddy brown the further on he trod.

He was tall for a lad of 11. And accompanying his father to the mason's lodge every day had already given him a head start on strength. Now, however, he was off to learn at the abbey, as he had been doing for the past five years. King Edward had kept his promise, and Griffin's education was an ongoing activity. The king wanted Griffin to get a running start on Eadric's craft, so much of his time was spent in the lodge as well. There was no doubt he wished to please his godfather. The two were greatly fond of one another, though they were in each other's presence rarely. Many times, however, King Edward's hand would lift in greeting from the window of his solar when Griffin ran by the palace on his way to or from the abbey. Blue eyes would lock into blue, and from far away their hearts would quickly fill with affection like deep pools beneath a thunderous waterfall.

It wasn't long before he neared the door to the new monastery finished only that summer for the monks. The abbey church was still progressing rapidly—more rapidly than any other building of its time.

Griffin loved the isle. No doubt the Benedictine monks who first inhabited Thorny Isle in the seventh century were attracted to it by the pure springs, the gravelly soil, and the fishing provided by the rivers Tyburn and Thames which surrounded it. The calm, sweet beauty of the land, where cattle once roamed unattended about the thornbushes, fed Griffin's impassioned soul.

Through the cloister he walked, looking over some of the brothers' shoulders as they worked in the golden daylight. Some copied precious portions of Scripture borrowed from another monastery. Some studied manuscripts. And two or three darned worn vestments. Suddenly a stone the size of a large beetle hit him squarely on the back of the head. Griffin whirled around.

"Hmm," he muttered, a bit perplexed but not at all hurt. Seeing no one, he turned back around with a shrug to proceed around the corner.

Another stone made its mark.

If the monks noticed, they made no pause in their work.

Griffin turned again, and there before him stood a lad about his own age. His feet were placed widely apart on the stone floor—a stance of challenge if Griffin had ever seen one. He sighed. Didn't this boy, dressed in fripperous finery, whoever he was, know that he was the strongest lad around? No matter. He would dispatch him quickly enough.

"Who are you?" he asked forthrightly but quietly.

The other boy, noting with inner dismay that Griffin did not even so much as flinch when his stone made contact, answered likewise. "I am Simon. And you?"

"Griffin. Son of Eadric of Bath."

Simon shrugged now, his black eyes challenging. "Aren't you going to do anything about the stones, Griffin Eadricson?"

"Do you want me to?"

Simon puffed out his chest. "I wouldn't have thrown them if I didn't."

Griffin laughed. "True enough."

"So, what are you going to do?"

"Nothing."

Simon looked disappointed. "Nothing?"

"Nothing right now. This is hardly the place, Simon son of . . . ?"

"Leofric."

Griffin's eyes raised. "The thane?" Leofric the Fox was one of King Edward's favorite members of court, though not nearly the richest. Still, he was well received and was a strong adviser to the king in the crafty matters of war. Between the troublesome Welsh and the overactive house of Godwin, Lord Leofric was a busy man. He was also a valiant warrior, training soldiers for the king's housecarls—something which interested Griffin immensely. He would be sure not to lay too heavy a hand on Leofric the Fox's son. He would, however, teach him a lesson.

"Yes, my father is Lord Leofric."

"Well, lord or not, this is not the time or the place to fight, Simon Leofricson," Griffin repeated. "I will not fight you here. Besides, we wouldn't want to dirty that fancy tunic you're wearing." His wide mouth smirked.

Simon's black eyes sparkled as he purposely reached down and tore some of the trim from the hem. *Hah!* he thought. "Coward," he said, running a hand through his raven hair, making it stand on end.

Griffin admired Simon's finesse. "Nay," his voice challenged softly. "If you want a fight, you'll not be disappointed." He pointed across the Tyburn. "Do you know of the clearing across the river, where they're draining the swampland, near the Widow Urfried's farm?"

Simon nodded from side to side. "I have only just come to stay at the palace. For my education, you know."

"Never mind. I'll show you the way after we finish inside."

"And when we get there, I'll show you the way, Griffin son of Eadric."

"Perhaps," he nodded. "But I severely doubt it, Simon. You may be the son of a warrior, but I am the son of the royal stonemason, and swords will not be deciding this battle—strength will."

Simon studied his newfound adversary. Griffin stood at least four inches taller than he, and he suddenly wondered if he had been a bit thoughtless when he cast that stone. *Perhaps Mother was right*, he thought ruefully, remembering her exasperation at his high-spirited behavior, *that I really will learn a thing or two here*.

"Did you know," Simon caught up to Griffin, "that the King of Wales, that troublemaker, is named Griffin as well?"

"Aye. Troublemaker he may be. But he's strong and ferocious, too. Remember that, Simon. Strong and ferocious. I have much in common with the man."

Now just around the corner on a stone bench which bordered the cloister, dear Brother Adam—a tall, skinny young Norman of 22—had heard the majority of the conversation. His tonsured head shook as he laughed. Brave words, he admitted, but said in the strident tones of 11-year-old boys made it extremely comical. How much they had to learn!

They strolled to the priest's work space like short emperors, and Brother Adam cleared his throat of all traces of merriment and stood to his feet to greet his charges in a quiet voice. In front of him a small table was laden with books and scrolls. A wooden bench faced the monk.

"Welcome, lads," Brother Adam smiled warmly, resting his large, bony hands on their shoulders. "Please sit down."

They did—making sure as much empty space as possible was left between them. Brother Adam took note of the juvenile hostility. But he knew the two boys would be the best of friends by tomorrow, no doubt.

"We are waiting for the final pupil who will make our little sessions complete, Griffin. Until he arrives, I suggest you bow your heads and say silently a Pater Noster."

"Our Father," Griffin began to mouth the words silently, but his mind took over and he began to pray his own words as he always did. "Who art in heaven, hallowed be Thy name. Let victory come, Thy will be done, by the Widow Urfried's place as it is in heaven. Give me this day Simon's head, and lead me not into humiliation. Amen."

He stole a look at Simon and then at Brother Adam, suddenly feeling guilty for changing the prayer. But he had meant the words. And if a lad couldn't tell his wants and needs to Jesu, who could he tell them to? Still, he knew Mother would not approve of his presumption.

"Again," Brother Adam commanded, catching Griffin's furtive glance his way. Griffin bowed his head again and squeezed his pale blue eyes shut tight. He said every word just right, and felt not one bit closer to heaven. However, he soon heard the sound of a leather-soled shoe scrape across the floor.

"Lads," Brother Adam caught their attention, "this is Godfrith."

A small boy, not more than seven years old, sat down between Griffin and Simon. His hands were small squares, and they fidgeted with the simple green trim of his gray gown. An angular bag of bones, this one. And Griffin couldn't surmise in much detail regarding the personality of this new lad. But he did appear as nervous of what lay ahead as Griffin had felt years before. It was a silly fear, for Godfrith was the only one seated before Brother Adam that day to whom the gleaning of knowledge would prove a natural and cordial undertaking.

"And now, students," Brother Adam began, running a hand over his bald head and into the smoky-brown hair above his ears, "we will begin with the basics for you two."

"Latin?" Simon asked, his tone not at all enthusiastic.

"Yes. Latin."

Godfrith's eyes lit up. And as for Griffin, he knew his brain would be aching by the end of the day—not only from going over his declensions, but from hearing the other two chanting as well. But it would be worth it, he had decided long ago. And whoever knew when one's education would literally save one's life?

ৰ্জ্চ ৰ্জ্চ ৰ্জ্চ

Griffin's eyes blazed with a base combative passion as he tensed his leg muscles and sprung at Simon. A primal, joyous cry escaped his lips. His head made contact with Simon's abdomen, sending the brash son of a thane reeling backward into the long grass which grew by the Tyburn. But Simon was not a lad to be easily dispatched. In a moment he was back on his feet, ready for Griffin's next charge.

It came.

And this time Griffin took advantage of the momentum, falling to the ground with Simon, twisting in the air to pin him to the meadow floor. Simon escaped Griffin's hold yet again. They fought furiously, throwing punches—some wild, some right on their mark. Blood seeped from the corner of Griffin's mouth and trickled out of Simon's nose. Black eyes would be sure to follow on the morrow. Simon was fast, but the future soldier was no match for Griffin's strength. Finally, the stonemason's son pinned Simon utterly against the earth. So, as a cornered boy will do in times of desperation, the raven-haired lad reached for a rock with his left hand.

But a mother's intuition prevailed that day.

Griffin's initial yell—a sound heard regularly about Eadric of Bath's domicile—had brought Emma running over from Widow Urfried's home and her weekly visit to help with the cleaning. Emma's creed had always been to let children fight their own battles. And certainly, Griffin could fight them quite well enough, she had learned countless times in the past two years. But a rock is a rock, and she wasn't about to let some strange boy do damage to her son's beautiful face.

"That's enough!" she shouted into cupped hands, hurrying across the meadow on her short, thick legs. Her coverchief fluttered about her face, and she pushed it away, her fingers snagging in her warm brown hair.

Simon stopped within an inch of Griffin's temple. And two heads suddenly turned her way. It was all she could do to keep from laughing as the boys, who in coloring and form were complete opposites, wore the same fearful expression. That expression which comes only when a child is caught unawares in naughtiness. A second later, anger was hers. Griffin was the only son she had. And life, she knew, was infinitely precious.

Both sprang to their feet.

Inwardly, she admired their athletic grace, but her stumpy forefinger wagged at them most spiritedly, and she breathed heavily from her exertion. "Shame on you, Griffin. Shame on you both! Who are you, anyway?" Her eyes had Simon pinned for a second time that day.

"Simon, son of Leofric," he stammered, his father's name bearing no weight under the firm glare of an angry mother.

"Well, Simon, you go home and make trouble there. What would Leofric the Fox think if he saw his son using unfair advantages in combat?" Emma pointed to the rock he had dropped by his feet.

"Were you going to use that?" Griffin asked.

Simon nodded mutely, obviously embarrassed.

Much to his mother's surprise, Griffin began to laugh.

"What is so amusing, my son?" Her question was crisply asked.

"Hah, Mother. He couldn't subdue me by speed or strength. He resorted to a rock. I'd say he did what he had to do!"

Griffin threw his shoulders back proudly and looked at Simon haughtily. Emma's anger heightened. Pride would never do.

"You go home right now, Simon. And you as well, Griffin. Tomorrow you will spend an extra hour at the lodge with your father."

"Oh, Mother!" he wailed. He hated being cooped up in the lodge.

"You heard me well. Now go!"

Griffin gave Emma a well-practiced glare but knew better than to utter a word of defiance.

"'Bye, Simon," he said in surly tones, then walked swiftly and purposefully across the meadow and over the bridge toward home.

Simon stared at Emma with his mouth open, and yet deep in his black eyes there sparked childish indignation. Her reprimanding Griffin had placed the stonemason's son as firmly in the recesses of Simon's heart as if Emma had stolen a pot of Eadric's mortar to bind the two lads together.

"You go on, Simon!" She gave him a little push forward. "You shall see Griffin tomorrow at the abbey."

From that day onward, Simon and Griffin were inseparable.

🙟 🙟 🙟

Brother Adam's voice hushed itself. Every tone which whispered forth from the dark hollow of his throat was coated with the love of intrigue, a solemn respect for history, and the joy of retelling the glorious victory of the greatest Anglo-Saxon king who ever lived.

"The Savior of our heart is Jesu, blessed Lord Christ. The savior of England was Alfred the Great."

Immediately the three boys leaned forward. Griffin's left braid slid around his shoulder. Simon rubbed the sleep directly from his eyes. And Godfrith swept a square hand through his curls and licked his cherubic lips in anticipation. Each pair of eyes glimmered much the same. For there wasn't an English youth who trod the isle of Britain who did not revere and honor the Saxon warrior king who drove the Viking raiders from the kingdom of Wessex once and for all.

"Tell us, Brother Adam," Griffin begged unnecessarily.

Simon and Godfrith drew in their breath. Outside, a summer rain beat upon the crops and fields. The boys heard nothing but the lowered voice of their teacher as he began the tale.

"The longboats sliced through the fog, cleaving the water with their bows. Inside the main boat, each muscle hardened with tension and expectation, the war band waited. Blue eyes moved at any noise which soaked through the silence. Large hands tightened about the handles of sharply honed axes— blades sharp enough to behead a man with a single cursory blow. The Danes had come before, many times, to burn farms, kill men, defile women, and enslave their children.

"For this was before the warrior king had driven away the terrible Danes. The Saxons were living as fugitives in the woodland and marshes near Somerset. Last Epiphany the Danes had come to Chippingham, where the king was residing. Somehow, Alfred and his family managed to escape. Scattered about were his thanes and courtiers. The Danes had occupied Chippingham for the winter. Far and wide from thence they plundered the countryside. Those left behind were reduced to servants and beggars. Chaos reigned in the kingdom.

"Now Easter was almost on the calendar. And the king and his closest advisers had formulated plans to rid himself and his people from the tribulation of the godless horde from the north. The time to move was soon."

The three lads held their breath.

"But until then, a warrior, entrusted with great responsibility by Alfred himself, had a job to do."

❧ ❧ ❧

The Saxon warrior crouched low in the bushes. Waiting. Waiting. His heart beat loudly within the confines of his skull, and his fingers curled about the shaft of his spear. King Alfred had given him orders: "Find food."

His muscles wept hollowly from lack of movement. Still he waited, eyes sharp, ready to pounce on his unlucky prey. A supply cart was rolling up the road, laden with cheeses, flour, and salt pork. A Viking warrior was its sole escort, and that made the Saxon grimace. *To think they are that unafraid of us.*

Ah, but the Saxon was an Englishman. And an Englishman refuses to be beaten.

Any moment. Any moment now. The creaky cart was almost in front of him. Just a few feet further, and he would leap on the Dane from behind. He breathed in deeply, held his breath, and in a single move roiling with a feral instinct, he leapt. The war cry sprung forth loudly from his lungs and echoed off the leaf-laden trees.

Wheeling around, the Viking brandished his ax. But the Saxon was larger and stronger. The Dane was on the ground in an instant, with the point of a Saxon spear held tightly against his jugular vein.

"I've got you now, Viking dog!" the warrior growled, his voice filled with triumph. His family would eat tonight. The entire encampment would fill their hungry bellies because he, Aethelred, was faithful to carry out the commands of his king.

Anger replaced the sudden fright in the Viking's eyes. "How come you always get to play the Saxon?"

Griffin rose to his feet with a hearty laugh and pulled Simon to his feet.

"Because I'm bigger than you are."

"I'm a better fighter," Simon parried.

Griffin grinned heartily. "We'll just see about that, Simon the Mouse."

40

Simon hated the nickname Griffin had christened him with during their first conflict. And soon they were back on the ground, fighting, fighting, and happier than they ever were at any other time.

# THREE

Servants, perspiring profusely in the summer heat, scrambled back and forth from the kitchens outside to the tables inside the palace great hall. Crisp-skinned pigs rotated stiffly on spits. Venison, veal, and various manner of fish—freshwater mostly, and snared by hook and line that morning in the Thames—cooked over a great pit outside. A capacious, black three-legged iron pot stood over a bonfire, its concentrated fire bubbling up a mutton stew. And the kitchen tents percolated with servants paring carrots and parsnips, shucking peas, or crushing blackberries and raspberries for the stewed fruit compote every Saxon who attended would enjoy at the end of the meal. Ale, mead, and wine were ready for the guests to consume. In fact, the king's steward had been full of business for many strenuous days making sure eggs, flour, meats, cheeses, vegetables, and spices were available in marked plentitude for the king's table. Here was manifest God's plenty. The bounties of His created world profusely displayed for the feast of celebration. Truly, King Edward had called for a time to rejoice. And all the guests did just that. .

Proudly alongside his esteemed father, Griffin entered the room of grand proportions. He eyed two open places along a bench underneath a window—one that would afford a breeze during the lengthy meal.

"Eadric of Bath!" a voice heartily hailed his father from just behind.

"John!" Eadric greeted the royal carriage maker with delight. "How progresses the abbey?"

"You've seen for yourself, old friend," Eadric smiled. "What think you?"

John winked at Griffin. "'Tis a wise man who saves the praise of his handiwork for the lips of others." He turned back to Eadric. "It's magnificent. How much longer until the roof goes on?"

"By the end of summer it will be well on its way. Mid-autumn should complete that portion. And then," he sighed with anticipation, "we can concentrate more fully on the interior."

Another man joined them—a thane from the region of Circencester. "'Twill be almost sad, Eadric, when the scaffolding is taken down. For I must admit that my visits to London and Westminster were most assuredly punctuated by my desire to see the church's progress."

"Thank you, Lord Ethelbert." Eadric bowed respectfully, although in truth his position as royal stonemason was every bit as illustrious as the thane's. "Have you ever met my son?"

"No, Eadric. Who is this strapping young lad?"

"This is Griffin, my lord."

"He is a giant! Has Edward already recruited you for his housecarls?" Lord Ethelbert asked unwittingly. Eadric sighed inwardly, but kept up a smile.

"Heavens no. Edward has designated him to follow after me someday."

Ethelbert raised his brows and remarked, "A worthy future. Would that all lads had the blessing of God, the king, and their father upon their future vocation."

"Thank you, my lord," Griffin, now 14, nodded.

The three men continued talking. Others joined in the conversation: high officials, noblemen, and a bishop or two as they made their way to a seat nearer the dais where the king himself would sit forthwith. Griffin watched every man, heard each word said, and Eadric grew larger in his mind as each second progressed. Impressed he was that such a man came home each evening to him and his mother and sisters, humbly breaking bread by the hearth, saying prayers, and voicing his concern over their daily struggles, rejoicing in their small triumphs. A respect, deep and profound, wrapped itself around Griffin's heart, and he suddenly viewed Eadric not simply as his father, but as a man—a competent, respected man who performed his job better than any other mason could ever claim to perform his.

Once a year the king ordered a great feast given for the prominent citizens of London. Eadric, as the royal stonemason, was ranked within such a group. Seeing his father measured against men as important as he was and found not wanting, but clearly superior in most aspects, made Griffin eagerly look forward to tomorrow when he might enter the abbey yet again.

Was it the craft or the abbey itself which excited Griffin?

For to be certain, not a day passed that Griffin could not be found somewhere within the rising structure. The walls had risen higher even as he grew in stature, and when he could persuade a workman to let him climb the scaffolding, he felt an exhilarating joy and unbounded freedom he experienced nowhere else. Breathless, he would relate the tale of his vertical travel to his father, the blue eyes illumined with pleasure at the invigorating remembrance. Eadric was hopeful that Griffin would be a fine mason.

But, in truth, the scaffolding represented more than the building of the abbey itself. It became a highway of possibilities, signifying the need of Griffin and countless humans before him to climb ever upward. And with feet planted on the wooden board some 60 feet high, he looked out over the world around him, his heart bursting with emotions he didn't understand. The abbey provided him with vision. Dreams yet unvoiced as he viewed the lush countryside and the swollen rivers were imbedded in his soul forever. A deep pride became his as he grew to love the beauty that was England. The land which stretched before him magically became his own from such a heightened vantage point. And when they would descend to the ground, Griffin would lean against the sun-warmed stone, hewn by Eadric and his men, and a peace would envelop him, hope would enfold him unto her bosom. His father was building a house to Jesu. And that was cause for hope as well. So Griffin would wander among the workmen, joke with them, inquire of their families, for they all knew him well. But always his eyes would return to the men aloft, and he hoped that tomorrow Egbert, Thomas, or Alfred would take him skyward, up to the high places. Perhaps beyond.

The striking youth and his well-esteemed father found a place at one of the long trestle tables along the sides of the room. At the head of the hall a raised dais supported the king's table, set with golden plate and drinkware. Its occupants were garbed in robes of silk brocade and linen, their deep jewel colors transforming the scene into a living tapestry, its grandeur eclipsing the very hangings which graced the walls.

Griffin breathed in deeply. The smell of baking bread and roasting meat, not to mention the heartwarming perfume of cinnamon, cloves, cardamom, and ginger—smells that only those who feast with kings enjoy—caused his young stomach to ache with hunger. Emma, in her routine manner, had forbade him to eat even a crust of bread before he had ventured forth with Eadric. Griffin found it hard to believe that his mother, so caring and sympathetic in other situations, had forgotten from the days of her youth how gnawing the hunger of a child could feel. An hour delay of supper seemed a fortnight to a boy who had run across fields and through woods all morning and fought with blunted sword and spear all afternoon with his closest friend.

Simon, proudly seated next to Leofric the Fox, his father, nodded from across the room with an uplifted hand. He sported a black eye from yesterday's skirmish in the woods. Its blue-black hues coordinated with the bruises hidden under Griffin's tunic. But the young men were quite satisfied with their friendship. Their battles were toughening them, teaching them to manage physical pain. They would one day be strong men and loyal citizens.

The meal was well underway when Griffin felt a tap on his shoulder. He had just put a piece of veal into his mouth with his fingers, and as he turned around he wiped his mouth on the edge of his sleeve. "Yes?"

A palace servant leaned forward. "The king summons you to his presence."

Immediately, Griffin rose from his bench, and without so much as a glance in his father's direction, he squared his shoulders and walked forward to the dais. King Edward sat with his wife, Queen Eadgyth, who looked not a little miserable. Her husband had sworn a vow of celibacy before becoming king of England. And the fact that she was the daughter of Earl Godwin, the man responsible for the murder of Edward's brother Alfred, did nothing but seal shut her womb with the finality of a tomb. She would never know the joys of holding a child of her womb in the loving, aching circle of her arms. As for the king, he looked as fair as ever though, at 60, age was comfortably upon him. On his head rested a crown fashioned in gold, and his slim fingers wore but a solitary ring, and that his seal. The plain crimson tunic which cascaded below his knees was girdled about the waist, and his short purple cloak was fastened at his right shoulder by a fibula. Long stockings, pulled up over short breeches, were cross-gartered with linen bandages and covered his slender feet shod in soft leather shoes. His hair was still remarkably hueless, and the difference between the white hairs and the blond was not easily ascertainable.

Griffin reverently entered the royal presence, his head submissively bowed. Once before the dais, he knelt down before his godfather.

"Rise, Griffin."

Griffin obeyed the royal behest, regarding the kind eyes of good King Edward.

"You grow fine and strong," the king observed. Eadgyth turned away, the monstrous pain in her heart too great to bear.

"Thank you, sire."

"And at the abbey, is Brother Adam treating you most graciously?"

"Yes, sire. He feeds us most abundantly with the milk of human kindness."

"But do you learn?"

"I try to, sire."

The king laughed. And, of course, those around him did likewise, although they didn't know why.

"Et facit plus eruditionis virum sapientiorem aut ineptiorem?" he asked.

"Sapientiorem occupatione sed ineptiorem foci," Griffin said without a moment's hesitation.

Edward laughed. "Bene dictum, Griffin. Well said. Show me your hands, lad." His fingers curled around his cup, and he took a small sip of the red French wine.

Griffin complied, reaching upward as Edward leaned over the table a bit. Already present in the well-formed muscles of Griffin's hands and wrists was an uncommon strength, exceeded only by that of the royal stonemason himself.

"Ah," the king sat back, "the son is truly taking after his father. Have you yet begun your apprenticeship?"

"Yes, sire. A year ago."

The king looked a bit wistful. "The years pass mercilessly, do they not? My abbey should be finished soon, Griffin. It seems but yesterday that you were born, along with my dream of a house to honor God. There will be other churches to build, much work left to be done before I die."

"May you live a long life, your highness."

"You will work for me and so fulfill the purpose that was

given to you on the day you were born. That is my fondest wish for you, Griffin, son of the abbey."

The king's attention was suddenly taken by the man beside him—the troublesome, thorny earl from the north country, Tosty Godwinson. Griffin was dismissed, but not utterly forgotten. The king's heart burgeoned with an elated pride. His deed of years ago was proving to be most prudent.

All the way home, Eadric's excitement could not be tethered. Times out of number, Griffin was forced to parrot the conversation, even the Latin which Eadric could not understand. And, of course, Emma's jubilation was as uncontainable as Eadric's. Truly, Griffin's future was anchored in a long-becalmed harbor, unthreatened and protected by the king himself. Publicly, Edward had made his wishes known. Whereupon their son would assume his father's mantle. Griffin would be the royal stonemason.

୬ଡ଼ ୬ଡ଼ ୬ଡ଼

Winter had fallen. A lenient one, with a courteous cold. No stiff breezes marked the day as bleak, and the sun had shone through clear, generous skies, delighting all those who inhabited the isle of Thorny. But now a mellow, chilly darkness had settled over river, field, and palace. A silent respect for the chill of night caused hearts to tumble and yearn for hearth and wife as the workmen deserted the newly roofed church. Eadric of Bath was no exception.

Awarding his cheek with a soft kiss as he entered his home, Emma smoothed his fading blond locks away from his element-pickled cheeks. Eadric smiled down at the annular, sweet-featured face beneath his. Yet a sigh cast itself adrift from its previous moorings.

"Emma, my lamb, walk with me."

"'Tis time to sup, my husband."

His careworn brow furrowed yet more, and he shook his head wearily, heart well-burdened and hollowed by sadness. "That matters not, Emma. We must converse privately."

49

Mary was now 27 and married with three children. Mildred, 22 and very particular about whom she would someday join herself to, stirred the broth.

"Griffin has yet to return, Father. I'm the only one here," she assured him. "I'd be happy to leave the room, if you'd prefer."

Emma smiled. "Thank you, Milly, but I do believe some fresh air would be of great benefit. I'll get my mantle."

Easily enough done, they were soon walking along the Thames. The abbey could be seen rising behind the palace, its transepts parallel with the river. Eadric didn't sense the cold. Only a month before, he had received his winter robe. The brown one he wore presently was trimmed about the sleeves and neck with shadowy brown wolf fur. And the woolen mantle secured atop his right shoulder bullied out the chill of the night air as well.

"I do believe," Emma joked, imbuing the troughs in the conversation with small talk, "that we will have Mildred with us always. Young John alighted upon our home again today."

Eadric did not seek a supplemental account, but continued walking, his pace accelerated. Emma persistently sought to bury the silence, content her husband would speak his heart in his singular time and so solve her own much-peaked puzzlement. "She did what she does with all of her suitors: gave him a cup of ale, and ten minutes later handed him his hat and informed him it was time to leave." She chuckled, quite consciously, to herself.

The night air betrayed its demeanor as a living organism as they trod beside the Thames, approaching the river Tyburn. Eadric's aggrieved mind shifted mercurially, like the moonbeams on the water. Just where to begin eluded him, and so he paced still, cradling the petite, pudgy hand of his wife in his imposing, muscular one. His love for Emma was great. She was so soft, he had always thought. Soft skin, a soft voice, and a soft heart. Important qualities to a man who worked with stone from sunup to sundown. Her mahogany eyes melted him inside when they would sojourn with his, displaying a love to which, in the long-concluded days of his youth, he had never fancied a man might be privy.

"What is troubling you, my Eadric?" Emma's soft voice emanated out of the darkness beside him after a time. She realized he was experiencing trouble liberating his inward reflections.

"It's our son." A sigh.

Emma smiled, notwithstanding Eadric's existing cast of soul. Griffin was perpetually questing his way out of one quagmire or another. Periodically, his temper threatened to commandeer a more prominent footing in his range of emotions now that he was physically becoming a man. Emma preferred to view it as passion, but even she, on occasion, was exasperated by her son's strongmindedness and introspection.

"Griffin? What has he done now?"

The royal stonemason's parlance did little to enlighten his wife. "He has opened my eyes."

"Do you wish to explain, my love?"

Eadric drew in his breath, striving to give voice to the jumbled cords of his heart. His head shook with a despair Emma had not thitherto seen. "I must admit what I've refused to see since our son began accompanying me to the lodge. Emma, he has not the soul of a stonemason."

Emma's heart plummeted. For two years Griffin had been apprenticed at the lodge, and this was the first time Eadric—hopeful, optimistic Eadric—had mentioned his son's shortcomings. "Perhaps he is preoccupied with his studies."

"No." The singular word was glutted with anguish. "No, would that was all it were. But I must acknowledge what I've known deep in my heart for many a year."

"What happened today?"

"I gave him a simple enough task: smoothing the carving on a boss. His mind began to wander, and before any of us realized what he was doing, it was too late. Most assuredly, he has the strength, and possesses even the sensitivity when he wants to. The carving was worn down so far the entire piece was destroyed. We'll have to bring in another one from Jumieges, and with winter now upon us, who knows how long that will take?"

"Surely you can make one yourself, can you not, Eadric? Why must you rely on the work of Normans? After all, you trained in Normandy yourself!"

Eadric sighed. "It is the king's wish that the abbey at Westminster be similar to the now-rising cathedral at Jumieges. Henceforth, much of the work is arriving from Normandy already finished, or almost so. Frankly, the reason I gave Griffin the job to do was because the piece looked a bit rough."

Emma responded with that brash confidence most women have regarding their husband that comforts at times and discourages at others. "Well, if you make your own, King Edward will not know the difference."

Even though Edward's eye missed nothing, Eadric knew he was as adept as any master mason across the channel. It would take additional time, but Emma was right. The king wouldn't notice. And the piece was destined for the ceiling, anyway.

"So," queried Emma, drawing her cloak to enclose her more tightly, and staring at the veneer of the water. "What happened then?"

"He fled when he realized his mistake."

"Oh, Eadric, were you cross at him?"

Exasperation skirted across his face. "No, Emma! I did not yell at Griffin. He was gone before I realized what had happened. When did he get home?"

"About two hours before dark. But he left again shortly thereafter."

Eadric of Bath desisted his ambulation. His eyes met Emma's with a raking frankness. "He's not a mason."

Emma said nothing, her intake of breath the only communication necessary.

Eadric shook his head sadly. "No. He has the talent, to be certain, but he has no vision, no love for stone."

"Are you sure? He's still so young!"

Eadric nodded, concentrating on the barren branches to his right. "I wish in age an excuse could be conjured, Emma. But no, that intuition, that love of feeling a substance give way beneath your chisel, the glory of a leaf or a face appearing from what was once a very part of the earth, that is something that is born into a man. Besides, he's already 14."

"Can it not be learned, my love?"

"That is what is so frustrating. He could do it if the desire was present within. When I compare him to some of the other apprentices . . . in inborn ability . . . the others fall far short of our son. But the love isn't there, Emma. Being a good mason, or carpenter, or painter is more than just doing a job and going home at the end of the day's toil. It's taking pride in each chip of stone removed, each stroke of the brush. It's true love, Emma dear. It feeds the heart as well as the family. It fills the soul as well as the hours in a day. It's what keeps us going when our hands are bleeding and our eyes are watering from exhaustion."

Emma said nothing again. The words he spoke surprised her not.

"What do you suggest we do, Emma?" His heart was bruised.

"I suggest we give him time. Besides, dear heart, I'm not sure we have that great a say in the matter."

"Hmm?"

"Forget not who is his godfather. King Edward makes plans for our son to someday build churches to the glory of God and the edification of mankind. So loving the craft or hating it, Griffin will be a mason."

"God help him," Eadric whispered, "for no man should live his life attending to that which he manifestly despises."

Emma rested her head against her husband's Herculean shoulder. "God will succor him, husband. Let it be so."

Meanwhile, Griffin reclined on the lea at the back of Widow Urfried's hut. The same place he had battled Simon almost four years before. His blue eyes were round as they stared unseeing into the sky. Truly, he believed himself a failure. Two years as an apprentice, and already irreparable damage on a precious piece could be charged to his account.

Frustration was his. He knew that to do better must be his calling. For everyone involved. The king. Father. Mother. But especially father.

*How can I ever tell him that merely to pick up a chisel makes me feel as though I am caged?*

Hands behind his head he lay, eclipsed in a musing befuddlement. The darkness reinherited entirely its appointed place, until the mists rose slowly from the undulatory waters of the Thames to hang wraithlike above the river as the atmosphere rapidly cooled yet more.

*It was too much to live up to from the beginning,* Griffin pondered. *Indeed, my future was decided the day I was born. No chance was given me to prove myself where I excel the most, no thought was given for innate ability or learned preference.* And Eadric's confidence in his inborn talent was not shared by his son. He saw himself as fumble-fingered and inept. As much as he loved King Edward, he was shackled to a life and a profession he abhorred, simply because of his birthday.

"Why?" he asked. "Why did I have to be born on the day the stone was laid?"

He rose to his feet and walked home.

Neither son nor father thrashed out the event. Neither knew how. And beginning that day, a silence saturated their relationship—a chasm of wished-for expression that would last for years to come.

# ❧ FOUR ❧

**B**rother Adam believed that to certain men a calling was distinctly apportioned.

The others, he wasn't particularly certain about.

"Take, for instance, each man here at the abbey," he discoursed to his students one morning during lessons. The new monastery buildings were completed two years previous, and the studious group, clustered in their habitual pattern of assemblage, sat upon the sunlit grass inside of the cloister. "God called us out from the world, and here we are. Cloistered and relying upon the Divine for our very survival."

Simon, his cheek resting heavily on his left hand, his elbow balancing on his knee, asked the question he had wanted to put forth for years. "How do you bear it?" His tunic felt much too warm, making him even sleepier than usual. A fine young man, skilled in the arts of war, loyal and stouthearted, was emerging from the Fox's once foolhardy son. His propensity to effectively banter with all manner of weapon: sword, spear, dagger, and ax, did little to alleviate—in truth greatly exaggerated—his boredom with much learning. Yet, despite his lackadaisical approach to the accumulation of knowledge, Simon was content with his present, and his future lay before him at the end of a road paved by his father, shining golden with the promise of great rewards.

Brother Adam's composure was not dismantled the slightest measure when the normally unassuming Godfrith gave answer to the sour inquiry. "How could a man do anything else? Practically all recorded knowledge is cradled within the bosom of a monastery. Think of it! Being privy to the wisdom that has passed down through the ages. It isn't all chanting and singing and praying, Simon. Being a monk is a quest—a lifelong quest."

As the third male child of a well-to-do London spice merchant, Godfrith's destiny for the church was drawn indelibly in turgid, impenetrable delineation. For generations it had been such. His family was a close-knit trust that tradition bound together, procreating a comfortableness with the present and a surety respecting the future. To this generation of spice merchant, God had entrusted a son to whom the calling was more soothing than a warm house imbued with smells of cinnamon, clove, and saffron, more comfortable than even the tradition which bade him enter the church from the day his lungs first expanded with the breath of life.

"That's right," Brother Adam nodded. "So to you, Godfrith, being a monk will enable you to further benefit your mind. Is that all it means to you?"

"No." The lad looked sheepish, heavily aware of the monk's well-intentioned rebuke. The subsequent words were swiftly put. "I love the church, her institutions, and her tenets." He swallowed deeply, his large Adam's apple sliding down, then up.

"Good. But is that all you love, Godfrith?" Brother Adam continued to prod.

Confusion flared on the young man's face. And Griffin suddenly felt compassion for him. He nudged him in the ribs with his elbow and whispered, "Jesu, Godfrith. Jesu!"

"Oh yes." Godfrith quickly sought to redeem himself, his voice cracking embarrassingly as he did so. "'Tis not merely the church that I will serve, but ultimately our Lord and Savior, Jesus Christ."

"That's right," Brother Adam smiled compassionately.

During their sessions over the past years, the learned monk had garnered much information regarding his pupils. Simon, destined to be a soldier and to then assume his patrimonial inheritance upon Leofric the Fox's death, was well suited to the climate of his future. Perhaps Godfrith—quiet, studious, and complacent—was achieving his destiny through the back door. But he would make a faithful, industrious monk. Brother Adam was certain that one day Godfrith's faith, bud-like and closed, would flower, blossoming under the nourishing light of God's love.

But Griffin's story seemed vague, lacking a foreseeable ending, despite the fact that his future was royally planned down to the finest detail.

*'Tis a pity*, Brother Adam thought as he imagined the lad inside the lodge, blue eyes gazing with longing at the outside world framed by the constricting doorway. The monk inwardly crossed himself. After all, who was he to judge the plans God had in regard to another of His children? Still, Griffin was a curious patchwork of conflicting particularities. Truly, out of all of his pupils, only Griffin's heart was already turning to God, as well as his mind. Because of this, he seemed more suited for the monastery. Yet, domiciled in an inner fortress of the soul was a quality that drew others to him—a quality that offered solutions and the will to avenge their possibilities. Even strong-willed Simon had always played their games Griffin's way—games Griffin had ransacked out of an uncircumscribed imagination. Certainly, a sharp appetite for military history had become preeminent in his exploration of mankind's exploits. Wanting to know how each battle was fought and won, how each man stood or rode upon the field, the detail was never magnified enough for him. Indeed, it was like gazing at the abbey from far across the Thames, close enough to see but never able to set a foot inside. The adventure triumphing in those clear blue eyes attested most effusively that the lad, promising and gallant, would

never be satisfied with the quiet monastery life. And being wholly donated by king and father to the profession of masonry was hardly better. Griffin was a being with a need to roam unfettered. He required flight. And whether confined by monastery or the building of such, he would only yearn to be free.

Was there perhaps another calling?

Brother Adam often suspected Griffin deeply pondered such. But he directed his question to Simon instead. "And what destiny has God singled out for you, Simon?"

Simon barely shifted his position, though asked a question. Now leaning quite heavily into his hand, his words came out slurred. The middle of his cheek was somewhere just under his temple; his right eye was squeezed shut. "My future duty is to be a good thane: kind to my subordinates, loyal to king and country, answerable to God."

"And said with such conviction," Griffin muttered with a smirky snort.

"Well, do better then, Griffin," Brother Adam challenged, wondering how the now-towering youth would answer. "What is your God-given destiny?"

Griffin's face hardened. Only slightly. But the monk could see the change. "To be the royal stonemason."

"Are you certain?"

"Yes." The word was spoken through clenched teeth. And Griffin continued. "Brother Adam, with much respect, I implore you. Why torture us with this talk? From man's dawning he has been left with little choice. Each of us here must relent to the wishes of his father. We must follow the path they have cleared for us. And that," he shrugged, "is that."

"The ways of our Lord can very often confound even the wishes of the most well-meaning of sires, Griffin. Remember that. And never forget to seek the will of the Father."

That portion of the discussion being closed most decisively, Brother Adam changed the subject to one that would interest his pupil much. He cleared his throat and began to speak without aid of book or scroll.

"Today, lads, we will be resurrecting the wondrous deeds of the great Roman general Gaius Marius."

Immediately, Griffin leaned forward, that enthusiastic gleam vaulting back into his now-expectant eyes. Brother Adam leaned back on his stool and began to relate the epic adventures of a man who beat the odds, dumbfounding all of those who were born to be what he eventually became.

❧ ❧ ❧

Hot. The day was surprisingly hot. As the swords clashed mightily, the discordant tones of tempered steel battering against another portion just like it, sweat poured from their brows. The shields vied to push each other aside, seeking to pry open a wider corridor of vulnerability.

"Push, Griffin! Push! Harder!" Simon bellowed.

Griffin did his friend's bidding, and soon Simon's shield no longer played sentry to his body.

"Good!" Simon maneuvered himself back into such position that he might employ his shield to cast Griffin's balance awry. "Always remember: A shield is not just to defend, but to attack as well."

The meadow behind the Widow Urfried's hut was again their battlefield of choice. But no longer pretended they to be Alfred, or Charlemagne, or Alexander the Great. Such imagery in play belonged to boys. Simon was mastering the art of battle. His formal military training was now full-dress. Each of the housecarls knew him by name and sought to impart to him their own personal tricks of play with sword, spear, and ax. And like a good friend, he was faithfully teaching Griffin everything he knew.

From the distant abbey the bell for vespers tolled through the steamy twilight. Griffin quickly handed over his dull sword and makeshift shield to Simon. "I must go. Father will wonder where I've been."

Simon looked on as his friend ran through the meadow. Over the past year Griffin's frustration had become his own. Never would they fight together, defending each other's back. Never would they swap much-exaggerated stories by a campfire or secretly admit only to each other they missed mother and hearth. Griffin was destined to be a mason by the royal decree of the king, and there was nothing he or anyone else could do to change that.

❧ ❧ ❧

Like a broadly woven tapestry, the world spread beneath his eyes. Primitive greens, misty browns, and the reflection of the sapphire sky upon the river gliding upon its murky bed. Sometimes hours would saunter by before he would take an accounting of the sun's latest position in the sky.

Two hours had passed since he had climbed the remaining portion of scaffolding where the glaziers were working on a magnificent window which told all those who looked up that Jesu would one day come again to judge the living and the dead.

Here he felt most at peace. Here he felt most at war with himself. For even as the building was reaching ever upward to the heavens, groping to the very fount of the Almighty, his soul lifted in the structure's presence. Here he would imagine the dying Christ. Arms stretched wide, he would stand on the scaffolding in the predawn dimness, wondering unconsciously what crucifixion entailed. Wondering why the Father would subject Jesu to such a torturous death. The mind pictures often became so real that the horror would pull down the very essence of his empty soul. Then, as the sun appeared in the eastern horizon, he would remember the resurrection with a hopeful gladness. The warm rays of morning lightened his pale features with a golden hue, and he would imagine the world without Christ as dark and thick. Incapable of sustaining life at all. How many Masses had he attended, how many prayers had he uttered, and yet he still could not make sense of it. Yes, Christ was the light of the world, the sustainer of all things, but Griffin felt an emptiness when he thought of the King of heaven. To but meet Him, to find out what it was like to really know Him seemed an impossible blessing. But he knew that somewhere Jesus could be found—found without doubt and with an obstinate security. Find Him he would, for neither King Edward nor father had a say in what the Almighty might do with his soul.

The abbey, the building so linked with who he was, called to him irresistibly. It was his destiny. He knew that wouldn't change. But the fields called him, bidding him escape his prison.

*Flee, Griffin!*

*Be all you ever dreamed you could be.*

He shook his head.

*I cannot fail my father or the king.*

He leaned back against the rough stones behind him and felt a despair sink deep within him. There was no way out. Yes, his skills had increased a bit, and if he worked hard he would succeed. But his heart was not to be found in the ministrations of his hands. His carvings had not the life—the sweeping, representational beauty—that the work of other carvers displayed. Even as he stood, his vantage point that of the angels, he eyed the intricate carvings that centuries of humble citizens would never view from the ground. He was not possessed of such a span of love in his heart to painstakingly create such work to be seen only by the heavenly hosts and winged creatures.

Already his left hand itched along its calluses. And climbing carefully but swiftly down from the heights, Griffin went to seek out Simon.

❧ ❧ ❧

"You look saddened, my son." The king laid a thin, bluish hand upon Griffin's ever-broadening shoulder. Attired in a robe of deep blue trimmed with gold thread, he was utterly regal. Yet his eyes, paler blue with age and clothed with authority, accompanied the statement with tenderness. "Are your studies proceeding adequately?"

"Yes, sire."

Griffin's honor of standing in the king's presence had been going on for almost 15 minutes. They had spoken of nothing but the abbey, which at first was not at all an unpleasant conversation. For Griffin's love for the building was as genuine as the ruby on King Edward's finger. But for the past five minutes they had talked exclusively of masonry. Once again, King Edward noted with delight the calluses on his godson's hands. He talked knowledgeably of the craft and its methods, while Griffin sought with all his strength to appear enthusiastic. But it finally proved too much, and his eyes dropped in melancholy distraction. Hence the question.

"Do you wish to confide in your godfather, Griffin?"

"Sire, your servant wishes not to speak of what brings sadness to his heart and so risk bringing sadness to the heart of his lord."

With an imperious wave, the king motioned to all of the nobles. "Leave us," he commanded.

Knowing the special place Griffin occupied within the heart of the king, the room was quickly abandoned.

"Tell me, my son."

Griffin drew in his breath, remembering to whom the abbey was built, to whom his life had been dedicated, and asked for Divine forgiveness. "It is being a mason which saddens me, your highness."

Edward's eyes widened in surprise. "And why is that?"

Griffin thrust his hands forward, their roughened surface definably contrasted by the smooth gilding of the throne, the silken garments of the king, the splendor of all that was royal. "You see here calluses, sire. But they are not just from lifting stone, handling pick and chisel. Do you see this band of calluses, my lord?"

Edward nodded, tracing his own finger upon the roughened skin at the top of Griffin's palm, just beneath his long fingers. "They are the markings of one who uses a sword."

"Yes." Griffin bowed his head in shame, even as an anger for feeling such sparked in his subconscious.

"You wish to be a soldier? One of my housecarls, perhaps?"

"Yes, my king."

A sigh escaped Edward's lips. "Oh, my son. You do not know what you ask. Before you lies a peaceful path—one of hard work and many rewards. What you seek instead is a life of uncertainty, of hardships and pain—pain which lasts far beyond the day of battle. Being a man of war is not all that it seems. It is a life of waiting, Griffin. Battles consume but a few minutes in the hour of a soldier's life. The rest is waiting. For the next skirmish, the next battle, the next war. Can you honestly tell me that is what you truly want from the one life our Lord has given you to live?"

The king clapped his hands, and a servant appeared momentarily to tend to his liege's command. "Bring me my sword."

He arose from his throne and walked over to a window—a window from which the abbey was clearly visible. Griffin followed.

"Look upon that building, Griffin." He breathed in, overcome by its beauty, the majestic arches, the stalwart towers. Griffin's eyes were affixed upon the tableau as well. Autumn had alighted upon England, and the sky, a fathomless azure, contrasted with the crisp brightness of the yellow foliage. And the pallid hue of the stone structure attributed yet more to nature's diversity. "Tell me it isn't everything a church should be," he whispered, more possibly to himself than to Griffin.

Griffin shook his head. "It is the most beautiful place God has blessed England with."

"Yes. God inspired it, Griffin. Can you so easily leave that behind? To build a church is the most noble of callings, my son. Some of my ancestors would have said that to be a monk is only second to being a soldier. I disagree with them. To live only for God is the highest calling. But for the blood which flows through me, I would have done just that."

That was no surprise to Griffin.

Just then the servant reappeared. A sword was loosely held in his unskilled hand.

Edward's sword.

Forged in Normandy, its blade was double-edged, tempered steel, a living thing, with blue lights reflected up and down on the polished shaft. Carvings down the blade proclaimed it the sword of the king. The hilt was simple in form, meant to be bound by leather straps during the day of battle, but the carvings upon it were exquisitely rendered by a strong, loving hand that had mastered the intricate, exacting art of sword-making. The pommel was inlaid with smooth, precious stones.

Edward took Griffin's left hand and placed the sword in it. "Give it some more time, lad," he said kindly. "You are young, and now you cannot bear to see Leofric the Fox's son leave you behind. But that is his destiny. Still, I believe in my heart that it is to the very man whom God reveals His purposes. If He calls you to be a warrior someday, then well-fitting it is that my own blade is cradled in the hands I so sought to be used for His glory. Take this sword. But if God reveals to you that you are to follow after your father, use this to defend your family and those you love, and to remember this moment when you stood at a crossroads."

Griffin lifted the sword and he couldn't help but smile at the feel of the weight of it in his left hand. King Edward noted his godson's expression. He yearned to set him free. *Be a soldier then, my son!* he longed to say. But he could not. For as surely as he knew years ago he must build an abbey to St. Peter, he knew that Griffin had more lessons to learn before he was free to fly.

# Book II
# The Outlaw

## FIVE

# Emma

The abbey was consecrated in the year of our
Lord 1065.

My heart quickened at the arresting cast of the resplendent building which quelled the majesty of the others on our island, even the palace. Eadric's work was without parallel. Yet at the same time, a chapter in our lives—one which took 15 years to write—was pursuant to an indisputable close. A small sadness that life never ceases to change circumferenced my daily toil when I sought to envision our future. Another church elsewhere? A new palace? And trying to imagine such was like picturing what lay round a sharp bend of a path hitherto untraveled. It proved a bit disconcerting and altogether futile. No matter how hard I sought to force the wonderings from my mind, that fact of imminent change depressed me. Perhaps I felt the cool winds of change more keenly than most. But I couldn't have possibly foreseen, nor yet could any loyal Englishman, that the change was to be far deeper, soaking into the very fabric of the kingdom itself, like heavy, staining blood into the finest of silk.

"The first Norman church in the country," King Edward had proudly remarked to Eadric long ago when the abbey had first begun to rise against the backdrop of the heavens.

Because of the king's vision and faithfulness, the abbot and the monks now experienced a comfortable existence within the great cloister—complete with dormitory, refectory and kitchens, chapter house and scriptorium. As was common, a sanctuary of refuge for the distressed could be found at the Monastery of St. Peter's as well. Thorny Isle was still as comely as before, and the monastery enjoyed the life-sustaining harvest of its orchards and gardens—nature's bountiful tribute to diligence and service. Coupled with the estates bequeathed to them by Edward, the brothers also had reaped the benefits of a vineyard, a mill, and granaries. Completely self-sufficient, their community ran on a scheduled discipline, solemn and serious to the vows which the monks had made with lips as well as heart. But in the midst of it all rose the abbey church. Eadric's church.

The yawning foundations were laid with large square blocks of gray stone. Facing east, the entrance was rounded, and in the center rose a lordly, pinnacled tower. Two more towers, noble and imposing, soared above the western front. Nested therein were the sonorous bells that would call the monks to prayer and the citizens of Westminster to worship. Their musical offerings were as sweet to our ears as most assuredly they were to divine ones. The timbered roof, rising some 60 feet above the ground, was masked with lead. Inside and out were pillars and entablature. The bases and the capitals of the pillars were grand and royal in their workmanship. Tempera paint was copiously applied for decoration. A vast nave with lofty arches, a stone vault, and the storied windows attested to my husband's and the king's perfectionism. The choir was beneath the lantern, and the presbytery had two bays with a rounded apse and an ambulatory. The triforium arches were a fitting background for heavenbound, contemplative eyes to rest upon.

A series of chapels graced both stages of the transept ends. And though the king's good friend and advisor Robert of Jumieges had left England over a decade before to return home to Normandy, Eadric was faithful to the vision that had been set before him so long ago. The church was a masterpiece of Norman architecture. Masons, carpenters, painters, joiners, plumbers, and smiths had come together for a single purpose: employing their God-given gifts. They took pride in their accomplishment. And now the fruit of their labor was born. Surely the Lord was pleased with their strenuous toil as they employed the talents He had given them.

I know Eadric was pleased.

Anticipated for well over a decade, the time for the dedication was approaching rapidly. King Edward and Queen Eadgyth had prepared rich gifts for the church from their hearts, to the One who created and sustained not only themselves but the land over which they ruled.

"Emma, my lamb," Eadric reported one evening following a day at the lodge, "the gifts the king and queen have bestowed upon the church are a sight to behold."

I put down my darning needle. "Truly? And what are they?"

"Well," Eadric's face soaked up the firelight in the chilly December night, "today they arrived with the treasure. Gold and silver plate for the altars. Vestments of silk for the priests that the queen herself embroidered. Jewels . . ."

"How fine was her majesty's needlework?" I interrupted, leaning forward. Being overly fond of embroidery myself, I was perhaps a little too vain when it came to my talent.

Eadric smiled that knowing grin which told of my transparency. "Very fine . . . but not as fine as yours, Emma dear," he hastened to add.

I sat back with a hidden sigh of relief. And the queen had more time of leisure to ply her needle than did I!

"Relics were given as well," he went on. "I wonder whose leg bone it was this time?"

Horrified, I dropped my needle onto my lap and quickly crossed myself. "Eadric! You are nigh unto blasphemy!"

"And you are not God's voice in this home, Emma," Eadric retorted quickly and with irritation. Immediately, like a good wife should, I bowed my head in submission. More than once my mouth had gotten me into trouble over the years.

Tenderly, Eadric leaned forward and circled me in his arms. "Forgive me, my lamb, for speaking so forcefully."

I nodded and nestled into his strong chest. I loved the broad, forceful hardness of his body and the strength that lay therein. But I digress, and if distracted by particulars of Eadric and my love for him, I should go well past the boundaries of Griffin's tale.

So the abbey was finished. The laborers no longer milled about the site with their wheelbarrows, the carpenters no longer sawed and hammered, the masons ceased hewing and chipping. All was quiet. Too quiet.

The king fell sick.

It was the Godwins again, the ultimate bane of Edward's reign—and, some said, the family that truly ruled England. Tosty, the queen's own brother was, suffice it to say, an oppressive lord. Consequently, a revolt ensued in the wilds of Northumbria. The king was weighed down with sorrow for he had pardoned the presumptuous Godwins, noble Saxons notwithstanding, many times before. His soul was sick and weary and, as the weeks progressed, so did his illness with them.

Griffin's heart was broken. For the greater his learning at the feet of Brother Adam, the greater became his gratitude and love for his godfather. He grew silent, sullen, and neither Eadric nor I could help him. We sought to do such, but he pretended to be engrossed in his studies. And in the lodge, so my husband said, he went about his work quietly and without sport. Each evening after supper, whether skies were fair or foul, he would walk the countryside until well after Eadric and I had retired to our bed. Neither of us asked the reasons for his ramblings or tried to curtail their frequency. But surely he walked, even as Adam did in the garden, with God. Was he pleading for his godfather's recovery? Was he finding God out in the cold evening wind? Did the breeze whisper to him of God's care and concern for not only Edward but for himself as well? I knew not. But I could only hope God was with him. My heart agonized for him as closer the day of the dedication drew and the king fared no better.

A ray of hope glimmered on Christmas day, even as the sun shone upon the snowy fields and sparkled on the icy Thames. Edward struggled bravely to fulfill his duties. Invested in heavy royal robes and crown, he presided, according to custom, over the festivities of that day and the two following. The abbey's consecration was scheduled for the next day, December 28, Holy Innocents Day.

For the first time in weeks, Griffin's eyes resembled those of my precious son once again. And much of his time was spent near the palace in search of a good report. But his hopes were confounded when it was told that King Edward could endure the pain no longer. His white head was perpetually bowed in weariness. And with a keen amount of disappointment, I am sure, the king summoned Queen Eadgyth to his chamber. His nobles and all those assembled from far and near at court for such an auspicious occasion were to proceed with the ceremony as planned. Solemnly, Eadgyth agreed to take his place, such as she could. If it was any consolation to Edward, Eadric had the notion that the queen loved the abbey—yea, revered it—almost as much as did her husband. Perhaps it was the only love of which their marriage could boast.

The day dawned cold and fair. Eadric and I donned our finest robes. Fur-lined, our mantles swaddled our bodies inside their cumbrous warmth. And Griffin was nowhere to be found.

Early the church received us into its cavernous interior. Eadric had never failed to escort me every week to view its progress. And I could hardly say its beauty was a surprise. But

I knew that today my joy would not simply be found in what my eyes had beforehand been well acquainted with, but in viewing those who had yet to experience God's blessings upon the talent of the craftsmen who resurrected the imposing structure.

Naturally, I stood in the back. Many of England's some 5000 thanes would gain the choice positions near the front of the nave. The choir would be filled with holy men, and the arms of the transepts would hold as many of England's highest officials and noblemen as possible.

They began to arrive. And as each man stepped inside, I watched.

The open wonder upon even the most hedonistic of nobles' faces filled my heart with an even deeper love and respect for my husband. The vivid colors of the interior assaulted them vigorously, and the sun shining in from the high windows illuminated both the faces of the entrants and the glories of the building. Their personal trappings could not compare. Suddenly, all the nights spent alone while Eadric was at the lodge, all the meals taken in the chilly darkness to refresh him, all the soothing ointments I had rubbed into the tired, knotted muscles of Eadric's arms and back became a living sacrifice. For these moments alone—these gifts of wonder to each snippet of mankind who entered—the past 15 years were worth it.

The abbey was finally filled. And the processional began to the music of the great organ, the old Saxon one—a cumbersome wooden structure now replaced with a newer one. The archbishop was the last to walk up the aisle, following the high officials of the church, all clad in magnificently embroidered vestments. But before any of these, the monks of St. Peter's Monastery at Westminster filed in. Highly contrasted were these humble servants when compared to the finery around them. Yet they, above all men present, would enjoy on a daily basis the fruits of the labor of hundreds.

Seeing them in their black robes, heads bowed in humility . . . remembering the reason this church was truly built . . . well, I felt the familiar melancholy once again invade my previous high thoughts. And all I could perceive thereafter was the stark absence of the king and my son. After Eadric, they loved this building more than any two men in the kingdom. And in a reign consumed by internal troubles, this abbey was one of Edward's only joys. Yes, my heart surely was sore and aching for both of them. How could I have known they were together during the dedication, where amid the ceremony, prayers were offered for the well-being of the king.

Later that day, Griffin entered our home, his eyes redrimmed, his newly matured voice deep and harsh from solitary weeping.

I laid a hand tenderly on his arm. "Where were you, my son?"

He cleared his throat. "With the king. At least, that's where I was during the ceremony. I've just been wandering about since."

"Did he call for you?"

Griffin nodded from side to side. "I asked for an audience. He gave his consent. And when I appeared, he asked me to bide with him, saying it was but fitting that 'the son of the abbey' should be with him on the day of its dedication."

"'Tis true," I nodded, "if he could not be at the abbey, he could at least be with the babe who was born at the same time as the church."

"He said as much."

"And does the king fare any better this day?"

Griffin's gloomy expression said all that was necessary. He could not speak more.

I turned to the fire, ladled out a bowl of broth, and pressed it in his hands. "Take it to your bed, my son, drink it, and retire soon afterward. You must rest."

King Edward respired his final breath eight days later.

The echo of the workmen's hammers still hung heavy on the air; the prelate's voice consecrating the great church had hardly hushed before the Church of St. Peter was used for the lofty purpose for which it was commissioned. Behind the high altar, Edward's body was laid to rest.

Within the massive structure the funeral rites of its founder were held. So long the object of Edward's thoughts and prayers, and the saintly king did not live to celebrate even one Mass within its solid walls. My hope was great that kings and princes and millions of worshipers would come to this spot one day, would seek throughout the centuries to pay their respects to the king whose heart was fully given to God.

The last royal son of Woden died on January the fifth in the year of our Lord 1066. It was a year in history that would change the face of England forever.

The next day as the sun's first beams pierced the atmosphere, I sought to waken my son, but the loft was empty. Good King Edward's sword still sat by the fireplace. To the abbey Griffin had gone. And when he returned that night he informed us of his decision.

At peace with Edward's death, he wanted to know better the God whom the king served with all his soul.

"King Edward will turn to dust." His head was bowed and his hands were folded quietly in his lap. "And yet, there is a God who is full of mercy. There must be. And if He is to be found, I will find Him at the abbey."

Eadric and I both knew, however, that it was more than that. Griffin was following Edward. His connection to his loving godfather somehow unseverable, even in death.

Later that year an unnatural portent appeared. Many feared the long-tailed star which blazed across the sky by day and by night. And well it was a fearsome harbinger, for it told us all that disaster would surely strike.

In October during the year of our Lord 1066, the duke of Normandy, forever to be known as William the Conqueror, landed at Pevensey. King Harold, a Godwinson no less, fought bravely. The flower of England—our bravest noblemen and warriors—stood to the last man. And as the sun set upon the bloody field of Hastings, William set his supper table upon the crest of the hill and ate beside the fallen standard of the English, the fallen king, and all those who sought to protect their homeland from the Norman army.

Even his most loyal knights were sickened by the callous gesture.

And so we became a conquered people.

And so continues the tale.

## SIX

Poverty. Chastity. Obedience.

The abbey monks practiced all three, achieving stability. Or so St. Benedict believed would be the case when he founded Monte Cassino around the year 520 and thereby firmly established Eastern monasticism in the West. At that time there were many itinerant holy men wandering about the Christian world in rags, seeking holiness through deprivation and sacrifice. But within the peaceful confines of a monastery, a man who desired a life lived solely unto God could still experience community. For it was as true then as it was when God created Eve that it was not good for man to be alone.

Because of their black woolen habits, the Benedictine brothers became known as the Black Monks. And St. Peter's Monastery at Westminster was but one of many where Benedictine rule was practiced. The day was divided into seven times of prayer.

"Orare est laborare: laborare est orare," one of the monastery inhabitants muttered on his way to Compline, the last prayer time of the day at which all the brothers would be present. "To pray is to work: to work is to pray."

It was nine o'clock in the evening.

Upon hearing three psalms, a lesson, and another reading, he was free to leave the monastery. The wind, as if unaware the calends told of spring, was chillier than he expected an early May wind would be and, with a balled fist, he gathered the collar of his robe up under his chin. In the distance the light of home shone dimly under the door. The windows spewed forth no light at all, their hide coverings securely in place against the cool spring night. Truly, the old lantern resting on the table—the one his mother refused to relinquish—would be a sight most welcome. With a frame constructed of wood, the lantern's side panels were of thin-shaven ox horn, which let through the light of the candle in a mellow display of warmth. The recollection of its pleasing light soothed his troubled mind. For he was a most melancholy sort these days.

A three-quarter moon danced garishly above with some rain clouds sidling across the eastern skies. No wonder the chill now pervaded the close weave of his habit. To weather out the hard rains in the confines of his loft, surrounded by things once familiar, was a most pleasant prospect.

He placed his hand on the latch and walked inside.

"Griffin!" Emma rose immediately from her seat near the hearth and rushed forward. Eadric followed likewise.

"Mother, Father," he received their fond embraces.

"Son!" Eadric's smile was wide, his voice festive. "Sit down, son, and warm yourself by the fire. Emma, my love, fetch our son a cup of wine."

Griffin willingly complied, as did Emma, and soon they were discussing the changes in their lives that had taken place since they had last met. The abbey had housed Griffin for over three years. William the Conqueror was now the king, and yet life in Westminster Abbey had remained relatively unchanged.

"We received good news yesterday, my son." Eadric took the cup Emma offered him as well.

"Ah, yes." Emma, not imbibing with the others, sat back on her bench and took up her sewing. "'Tis of Simon."

"Simon?" Griffin sat forward. "What of him?"

"He's alive. He survived Hastings after all."

A relief besieged him, as well as the self-congratulatory remembrance that he alone thought Simon still alive. "Thank God," he uttered. "Yet at the same time it must be difficult for him to see his patrimony taken from him. I assume he has not bowed the knee to William?"

Eadric nodded. "Nay, I assume not. I have not personally conversed with him."

"How do you know for certain that he lives?"

"I've been working on the new house for one of our Saxon lords who swore fealty to William, Lord Ulfric. He's rebuilding his home not far from Charing Cross. I saw Simon with my own eyes of an evening when I tarried later than usual."

"Did you speak to him?"

"Alas, no. He took no note of my presence in the mason's yard, and upon my questioning Lord Ulfric the next morning, he denied Simon's presence."

"Are you sure it was he?"

An emphatic nod. "Oh yes, my son. Several times during the walk from the stable to the house he picked up a pebble and aimed it for an oak tree that grows nearby."

Griffin grinned involuntarily. "Then it was Simon, most assuredly. Always aiming to hit something. He could hit the trunk of a sapling from a hundred feet away. I suppose he has yet to dispose of the habit of continually trying to better his record."

"And at least this time his target was neither boy nor beast!" Emma could laugh about it now.

A cheerfulness at past times of boyish delight gilded Griffin's heart, set a torch to his soul. It was the first time since Edward's death that he truly felt a sublimation of his disposition. Indeed, life at the monastery had not afforded the peace of soul for which he still hungered. And in spite of Brother Adam's exhortations to leave and fight or take the vows, he found his ability to make a firm decision decrepit and harried.

When the explosive news of Hastings spread across the land, Griffin had become even more agitated than before. And not having the pleasure of fighting beside Simon was a too-keen respite from his normally brooding state. But at the same time, he was cloistered away and couldn't have possibly realized the extent of the danger in which England had found herself. Yea, even afterward, as King William preferred the fortress at London to the palace of Westminster, life was little changed on the isle of Thorny. For surely the Normans were a Christian people who would not have marauded the monasteries as the Vikings had done throughout the previous centuries.

"Will you take the vows?" Emma asked kindly, reaching out to rub a motherly hand over his still long, golden hair.

Griffin sighed. "I have not yet decided. I suppose I keep hoping the future will somehow be decided for me. I can hardly imagine swearing my sword arm to the new king. But the time is soon coming upon me when I shall have to choose one way or the other."

A knock exploded on the door.

"Open up in the name of the king!"

Momentary expressions of bewilderment passed between them before Emma rose to lift the latch. As soon as the latch was freed from the catch, the door was thrown open from without, and Emma was shoved aside.

Into the room flowed a number of men—all Norman, all soldiers. But one shone far above the rest.

"Eadric de Bath?" the leader demanded, a knight in goodly costume, his fine armor polished and shining in the firelight, his booted feet spread as wide as his broad shoulders. Plain and coarse was his face, and his short brown hair was mostly hidden beneath a conical helmet. But the brown eyes fired with delight at the imminent plight of this family of "backward Englishmen."

Eadric, already on his feet, replied. "I am Eadric of Bath."

The knight made no pretense at polity. "Then you are the master mason on the fortified home of Lord Ulfric." He spoke the Norman French of his homeland. Griffin, having learned the language from Brother Adam, translated for his father.

"Fortified?" Puzzled, Eadric looked at Griffin, then turned back to face the Norman. "That is no . . ."

"Are you or are you not the master mason in charge of the project?"

"Why, yes I am, but I don't . . ."

"Enough!" He pulled out his dagger. "Though Ulfric swore fealty last year to the king, he has secretly been involved with the rebel forces, supplying many men and even more gold to the cause of the English. You of all men should know of his sympathies. You are a traitor, and this night shall you breathe your last."

Griffin folded his hands in front of him and, looking as holy a man as he could, he stepped forward. It made sense. Why else would Simon have disappeared for so long, only to show up later at Lord Ulfric's estate? Obviously, Simon was involved in the rebellion as well. But to blame Eadric for this? To forfeit the life of so fine a man for something he knew nothing about?

"Please, sir," he implored softly, calling up three years of quiet at the abbey. "This man built the abbey itself. Surely your sovereign, good King William, would not wish for such a man to be destroyed? My father is a peaceable man who cares nothing for the pottering of kings and political sycophants. If his home is warmed by a well-fueled hearth and his family is fed, he is grateful to God and at peace with himself. As my father has said, he knew nothing."

Far beneath the blue of his irises, a fire ignited with a molten anger, waiting for the instant when the great plates of tension that were momentarily fusing the situation together would shift.

"So he claims. . . . But I do not believe him!" The knight finished the statement in a self-important rush.

"Emma, go to our chamber now and shut the door," Eadric commanded his wife and, when the door was snug into its frame, he turned back to face the knight. Griffin continued to translate between the two men. "My lord," Eadric held out his hands, "after William was first crowned at the abbey, I willingly offered my services, knowing that England's sins were great and that perhaps your duke was our judgment from God. I've accepted him as my liege lord. The house I'm building for Lord Ulfric is not fortified. And as far as subversive activities, I swear I know nothing. I'm a simple man."

"Hmmm." The knight looked around him. "'Tis a fine home you have here, mason. Did you build it yourself?"

"Yes."

He eyed it with the flat stare of a jackal, a covetous twist distorting further the narrow mouth. William would be most happy to extend to him this bit of property. *My leman will be housed here before tomorrow's sunset*, the knight decided. "Well then, you shall build no more," he said.

Griffin stepped closer to the knight. "Good sir, have mercy, I implore you!"

"Oh, I've decided not to execute him. As you say, he built the abbey. And let it never be said we Normans are not Christian. But when he is turned away from his home this night, I will make certain he won't be aiding the resistance any longer."

"But sir . . ." Eadric began.

The knight held up an impatient hand. "Silence! Take hold of the traitor!"

Eadric resisted. And Griffin ran toward his father. But he was taken by the arms. It took three men to contain the impossibly strong once royal mason.

"His hands!" the knight barked. "Place them flat on the table. You there, Jean! Hold them out flat."

Griffin didn't need to translate. Eadric knew exactly what was happening.

"No!" he yelled in a language they didn't understand. "My livelihood. My life. You'll take my life from me!"

He resisted with the brute force of a bulldog. His eyes seethed with a fury Griffin had never seen. But in a matter of seconds the hilt of the knight's dagger descended forcefully upon his knuckles. The swell of popping sinew and crushing bone, alarmingly loud, was heard momentarily before the great man cried out in excruciating pain. Around the room the Normans laughed, with a cruel edge twisting the corners of their mouths from a smile to a smirk.

After that, the forged muscles of an iron colossus could not have held Griffin in check. With the force of ten men he wrenched his arms free of the constraining grasp of the soldiers. A whirlwind of black he became as he turned to the hearth and grabbed King Edward's sword, leaning exactly where he had left it three years before. That his past sequestration in the monastery had done nothing to quell the fire inside him was immediately evidenced, and in that moment of Eadric's culminating agony, Griffin became oddly whole. His heart rocked and quaked, and the volcano of long-suppressed anger and unrecognized hostility burst open the seams of an arrayed calm.

"Will not any of you fight?" he challenged. The cowl fell down around his neck, and his untonsured hair spilled over the garment as he wielded the sword with brute strength. His eyes were hideous chips of blue ice and simmering lava.

The first to respond to Griffin's challenge was the largest of the crew: a burly redhead with a wide, infected grin. He extricated himself from Eadric's side, swaggered most assuredly around the table toward Griffin, believing himself up against a man only religious. And his courage snaked its vaporous way into his compatriots' cankered hearts. "At him, Goliath!" yelled several Normans, cheering their hero on. "Here's what you've been waiting for: your very own David!"

His laugh soured the air between them, and he poised his blade in midair, ready for an easy strike. None moved to his aid. To them the Saxon novice's death was more certain than the coming rainfall.

Eadric cried out again as the other hand met the same fate as the first.

*Father shall not be the only man to lose his wherewithal this day,* Griffin promised himself with the grim smile of a lunatic.

Goliath's sword came crashing down. Griffin met the blade with his own, pushing it to the side. And his sword hacked down, smoother than a thought, quicker than a dying man's prayer. Before anyone could move, Goliath's sword plummeted to the ground, his severed hand still wrapped around the hilt.

A howl of pain erupted from his cavernous throat, but Griffin instinctively went for the kill before realization battered the others into action. Swiftly, he thrust his blade, shimmering scarlet, into the heart of the once-laughing giant. The blood from the cruel man's wound spread in a sanguine puddle across the stone floor. The sight of it fed Griffin's need. And the scarlet lust of justice, of dreams fulfilled amidst the agony of his father's torture, coursed like thundering oxen through his veins, heart, and lungs.

Mouths opened in disbelief, astonishment. Confusion erupted as the knight bade two of the four soldiers left to go forward. "At him, men!" the knight bawled, his forceful command tearing to pieces their ambiguity. "Which one of you will receive an extra share of the booty tonight?"

A cry went up, and even as the knight's promise fed their courage, so did their shout spur Griffin to an even greater and more glorious madness. They rushed on Griffin as their champion's eyes closed in death. Griffin extricated his sword and, with a swift shove of his leg before the dead man could crumble to the floor, he forced the body into the advancing men. They fell back, and with a loud, angry cry, King Edward's sword was raised into the air again. All technique taught by Simon was lost within the rage, and Griffin hacked and hacked, employing his superior strength to a deadly advantage. The soldiers were dead before they had time to rise to their feet.

Two more soldiers were left. One advanced forward, seeking to draw nigh to the blond berserker. He died as well. His own blood spewing from his devilish mouth, cursing Griffin as the spawn of Satan.

Mesmerized, Eadric watched his son, though his mind threatened to close off the portals of consciousness against the pain which raped his hands. The knight was filled with an anger as he pushed the final soldier, a mere boy, aside. This was a man's job. He should have dispatched the Saxon giant himself. Four of his most trusted men lay in pieces on the ground.

Griffin sought to pull his sword out of the soldier he had just killed. It was lodged in the spine. Too late. The knight was advancing quickly, sword raised, a grim smile on his face.

"Thou art no man of God," hissed the knight, face-to-face with Griffin, whose eyes blazed with a passioned hatred. "Your disguise hides you not. You are an outlaw and a devil."

"As thou sayest." Griffin grated the words quietly.

He thrust at Griffin, but the younger man reeled away, reaching behind him to grab Emma's bench. It swung through the air like a deadly pendulum, aimed straight for the knight's head.

He quickly ducked, but the bench caught the sword. It flew from his hand and under the table.

The dagger was redrawn in a split second.

Surprise registered in his eyes as Griffin waited not for him to advance, but with a cry leaped across the room, grabbing both of the knight's wrists. He cried out in pain as the stone-mason's son forced his wrist back. The popping of tendons was heard, and the dagger clattered to the floor. In his pain he dropped his shoulder slightly. Griffin took advantage of the momentum, pulling in on his wrist so the knight now faced outward. A half-second later his hands were up around the man's jaw, and he said softly in his ear, "Remember your sins, and the grief you brought upon the house of Eadric of Bath.

And if this be Satan's justice, then indeed he has disregarded the prophets and deserted the forces of evil."

And with the strength that helped to build the abbey, he twisted with a gigantic force.

The knight's body went limp, and Griffin threw him on the table.

Still standing by Eadric, the young soldier looked upon him with fright.

"Will you, too, be slain this night?"

All the energy rapidly abandoned Griffin's muscles, and he looked upon the lad with compassion and even a little envy. His breathing was labored. "Hasten to London and tell your bastard king what he has wrought this night in Westminster. Tell him may he be accursed forever for the black order he issued from his tower."

With a needfully respectful nod and a dart of the eyes, the youth ran out the door. The hoofbeats of his horse were heard soon after, beating a macabre melody against the night atmosphere.

Emma was already by Eadric's side.

"Did you hear?" Griffin asked.

"Yes." She lifted her husband's arm to examine his hand and fell on her knees, burying her face against his thigh. "Oh Eadric, oh my Eadric! That someone should have done this to you." Her hot tears baptized the hands which were starting to swell to monstrous proportions.

"Please, Griffin," Emma pleaded, looking woefully into the eyes of her son. "Get back to the abbey at once. Find sanctuary. They cannot touch you there."

Eadric nodded, unable to voice his agreement through the veil of pain which separated him from the situation at hand, but which allowed the conversation around him to filter through.

"They will be back in seconds. You must go," she prodded.

Griffin turned tearfully to his father.

"But, Father. What about you?"

Eadric shook his head, trying to unwrap the tight swaddling of pain which constricted his consciousness, if only momentarily. "I'm . . . still alive. And I . . . want you to . . . be the . . . same, my son. Go! It doesn't . . . matter where. Just . . . go."

"I will. But not back to the abbey. First I shall summon the doctor, then I shall run." He dislodged the bloody sword, wiped the blade on the knight's cloak, and slid it into the ornate scabbard which lay on the hearth. Walking toward the door, his gait strong and purposeful, he strapped it round his waist.

"Where will you go?" Emma asked, torn between comforting her husband and kissing her son farewell.

Griffin's mouth had become a straight, willful line. "To find Simon. Only one path stands before me now."

"Wait!" Emma cried, rising as quickly to her feet as her now-rotund frame would allow. She hurried over to the fireplace and opened a small carven chest. "Take this!"

An amulet bearing a large topaz stone swung from its chain. On the back a crest was carved—a bear and a dragon. "This necklace belonged to an ancestor of mine who fought under King Alfred. It was given to him by the king himself in honor of his valor and his bravery on the field of battle. Perhaps it will bring you luck." She crossed herself.

Griffin felt the weight of it descend into his palm, and he immediately pulled it over his sweaty head. The cold, hard weight of it settled next to his heart. He had seen the amulet many times when mother had gone out and he had looked at her private possessions, but its significance had remained a mystery. Until now.

Emma's eyes teared. "It is in your blood to fight. I've always known it. But I think it's only fitting to give this to you now. For you will never be a stonemason, will you my son?

"Mother . . ." Griffin began, but was cut off by Eadric, whose hands began to go numb.

His voice was tinged with desperation caused by the pain, yes, but also by concern for his son's well-being. "By all that's holy, Emma, let him go! Of course he'll not be a mason. If you had seen the lad fight, you'd know as well as I do that for battle he was born."

"Father . . . I . . ." His eyes met with the man's who had loved and cared for him since the day he first held him in his arms by the sun-strewed window.

In a wince of time, eternal reconciliation between father and son was made.

Eadric breathed in, and with an iron will, forced down the pain, seeking to impart some of his own extraordinary strength somehow to his son. "It's all right, my son. Go! Go fight. And remember who you are. The son of Eadric of Bath. And an Englishman."

No one could bear to say more. Several seconds later, after Emma had shoved an old tunic, a loaf of bread, and a skin of wine into a knapsack and handed it to him, Griffin mounted one of the soldier's horses and receded into the dense rain which heaven had just let loose.

Emma ran to the door.

"Ride for Oxneford!" he heard her call through the rain. He didn't even notice the gaping slash in his thigh as he hastened first for the surgeon then over the river Tyburn, across the field behind Widow Urfried's hut, and out into open countryside.

The necklace bounced against his chest—a reminder of who he had been, who he now was, and who he would become. And even as his nameless ancestor had fought bravely at Edington to rid the Viking raiders from their shores, his destiny was the same. Griffin Eadricson would not rest until William the Bastard and his Norman horde were forever banished from the rich brown earth and verdant fields that were England.

※ ※ ※

Dragging heavily from his shoulders, the torrential rain imbued its cold, wet drops into the black woolen fibers of his habit. His hair was plastered against his head, its long strands snaking about his neck more and more tightly as he continuously turned his head, looking for those who would find him. Impatiently, he reached up to his neck and removed the constricting yellow locks. Beneath him, the horse's hooves thrummed a monotonous pattern into the black rain. His mind stole back to the confusing agony of the past three years at the monastery. The only consolation was his proximation to the abbey church. But even there his heart yet opened in a yawning, aching chasm of emptiness and despair that the church herself was incapable of filling. At the abbey he had felt closest to God, and at the abbey he felt the most removed. Torment. Inner fragmentation. Both were his. The chains of his decided future had become even more astringent after the death of King Edward. His benefactor was gone, and so ended his education. Memories of the arguments regarding his future that had ensued between he and Eadric thrashed around in his mind as the scenery blurred around him.

Well, no matter now.

He was finally escaping. Would that he could do it some other way, but ironically, the heavy weight of the habit felt good, the rain on his face was ecstasy. In becoming a wanted man, he had gained his freedom. Or an earthly semblance of such.

The night wore down and, without warning, two hours before sunrise, Griffin felt a pain in his leg so sharp that he gasped. The wound throbbed louder and stronger than his thoughts.

The rain ended.

Immediately, he pulled the great, black Norman war horse to a glade of twisted oak trees to the right of the meadow across which he was riding. When he dismounted, his injured leg failed to support the weight, and he crumpled to the ground. His eyes darted to and fro. Were they following him, or had they been thrown off course? And what of Mother and Father?

Griffin lifted up the robe to examine his thigh. The blood shone black in the moonlight which beamed through the now-dissipating clouds. An owl hooted from the tree overhead. When he saw the extent of the wound, his heart failed him momentarily. There wasn't help around for miles, Saxon or Norman. Oxneford was still a ways to the west. Pulling the knapsack down from his mount, he slapped the great beast's hindquarters and sent him galloping back to London. He would find shelter in the dark shadows of the forest, get some rest, and then find some food when daylight arrived. Again his leg flared with an angry, enlarged pain as he put weight on it. Finding a large stick several hundred agonizing yards away, Griffin leaned his great weight upon it and, weaving through the trees and brush, trod deep into the dripping woods. Griffin hastened to pick up his pace.

Flight.

He had never run from any man before—only himself. And never was his very flesh at stake. The fear of capture impelled him. The unknown spurred him on, and he gripped his sword in his bloodied hand. What was he seeking? Where was he going? Oxneford. Oxneford. Emma's bidding was clear. But whom should he find in the small market town?

The sword fell from his hand and into the brush.

The exertion proved too much for his flight-weary body.

Pain clouded his vision, and blood loss caused his head to spin. Gold and purple spots of brightness milled like ired gnats beneath his corneas and covered the dark scene before him as he slipped into oblivion and collided horizontally with the forest floor.

L illa jerked closed the door to her small hut. The knurled bottom scraped abrasively across the worn doorstone as she ventured into the fledgling dawn. The forest air was fresh with the previous night's rain and the promise of a fair day at market. Her small terrier, tail high and wagging, set out beside her, escorting her to where her pony was tied. She breathed in deeply.

"Gather yourself, then, Soot," she commanded in her musical, low-toned voice to her black canine companion. For though she lived alone, a companion was all poor Soot could claim to be. He couldn't have been much protection with his diminutive proportions. But it mattered not. Lilla was perfectly able to fend for herself, anyway.

Most of the time, leastwise.

A shaggy pony, tied in a small stall attached to the side of the hut, could be heard crunching his fodder. Bracken pulled at his rope, bobbing his contrary, rounded little head in anticipation. Obediently he allowed Lilla to harness him to the small, dilapidated old cart—her sole means of transportation. And Lilla was grateful to the little brown pony for the service he extended. For each step she took was accompanied by great pain—a perennial reminder of the day she had fallen from high in a tree when she was nine. On some days it eased a bit, but others weren't nearly so kind.

But Lilla had learned to live with the pain of it even on the worst of days, and the looks of it . . . well, her gown took care of that. At least she had convinced herself that was the case. Unfortunately, after the rain and the humidity that accompanied it, today wasn't a good day.

Grabbing the sides of the cart, she pulled herself up using the great strength of her long arms. Already loaded were the yards and yards of fine woolen trim she had woven the past month for market day in Oxneford. As she threw her knobby oak cane into the back with her wares, Soot bounded up beside her in anticipation, his little pink tongue tasting the sweet spring breeze which shifted the leaves overhead and the brush around them.

She snapped the reins gently. "Get along, Bracken! First the stream, little one, where you and Soot here may wash away the night's thirst."

The brooklet, providentially, was only 20 yards from her home. But to lead Bracken down and back as she usually did each morning before harnessing him would have meant extra use of her leg. And the wee pony never seemed to mind this arrangement they had on the days they journeyed to market. Lilla's two cats, Simon and Peter, stretched their backs, condensing and expanding like gypsy accordions, then lay gingerly down by the door to await her return. Before the two wheels of the cart began to turn, they were already slumbering peacefully. Lilla knew that quite possibly, and most probably, they wouldn't awaken or desert their post until her return almost 12 hours later.

When the cart stopped at the creek, Soot hopped down eagerly and began drinking the hyaline water which eventually harmonized with the Thames. Of course, the river was much less grand up this way. But as Lilla's mother had always said, "The Thames is the Thames no matter where it flows, sweet Lilla. I wouldn't want you to think those fancy Londoners have anything on us!" And with the foxglove, wild iris, and bluebells which bloomed in the wood, she knew there wasn't a sweeter place to be just then.

And yet, London was a fascinating beast. A great behemoth that drew because it repulsed. Crowds of people. Animals. Kings. Queens. Foreigners. Food. Shoes. And London men especially intrigued her with their fine tunics and caps. Men. They were as foreign to her as city life. And just as intriguing. Secretly, she loved to watch them from her little stall where she displayed her goods. The way their hands moved. The way they nodded their heads soberly or rubbed their chins when the conversation turned grave. The way their eyes deepened in anger. Especially, however, she liked to watch men laugh. They laughed comprehensively, with their whole body—not like women, who used their shoulders only. There was not a sight lovelier to lonely Lilla than a man rocking back on his heels in mirth. The fact that no man would consider her to wife made their very existence even more captivating, and ever a thorn.

Before she realized it, they were on their way and again, as one who has lived alone for far too long, one who had been banished by her fellow peasants to a life of reclusive solitude, Lilla's mind began to wander. Back to the days when they had called themselves a family. Father. Mother. And Lilla. Three completely different people who loved one another with intensity. Father—a gamekeeper for Lord Uhtred, the thane who owned the quarter-hide of land upon which they lived. Mother—weaving on the tablet loom Lilla herself now used with an even greater skill. And Lilla—carefree and coddled by her parents, but prone to solitude. After the accident, they sheltered her from all things menial, her time gentled by thoughtful silences that stretched too long for one so young. Her uncle, the village priest, took a little pity on her and taught her several portions of Scripture. He couldn't have known the comfort the Sermon on the Mount would give his niece years later after he was dead, and she was all alone. But she knew she had been loved and adored. She had a brother once, but he had been away for years and when she tried to remember his face it proved to be time ill-spent. But in her dreams she saw him below her . . . dark and screaming with eyes of terror.

Mother, unable to overcome the chill of a particularly harsh winter, had passed on eight years previous. And Lilla had grown up quickly after that. It was a joy to take care of her father, a wiry, strong, quick man with hair as red as a cock's comb and a temper equally as fiery. She had learned quickly how to sew and clean and cook. And she took to the loom soon after Mother lay buried beside their home. Looking back, and she could laugh about it now, the tangled mess she had made at first was just cause to quit right then. Determination won out, however, and Lilla learned to weave a braid so intricate in pattern, so fine to touch, women stood in line on market day to gaze at her artistry even if their purses forbade them the purchase.

But the Conqueror had come. Entering the land as though he had received a deed to England from God Himself. Father had fought valiantly at the battle of Hastings, as did Lord Uhtred and the rest of the flower of England. But whereas the Lord of Oxneford had died upon the carnage-strewn field with a host of others, the grievously wounded gamekeeper was brought home to die.

The cart stopped.

Lilla's brows knit, and she urged Bracken forward. The pony locked his little knees and tried to back up, his bony posterior rearing into the front of the cart. He made a good stand of it—a stolid statement for a creature so menial and small.

"Bracken, what trouble are you beckoning our way? Oh Lord, blessed are the poor in spirit. For that is what I am this day. I shall be late to market again this week," she sighed. The stall fee had been raised again, and Lilla despised it when she failed to get her money's worth from such a steep, albeit necessary expenditure.

Soot jumped to the ground, yipping his insignificant, tiny dog bark up at the indifferent foliage. Leaning forward, Lilla looked toward the place the terrier had gone, and there, off to the side of the pathway, lay a darkly clad form.

Bracken wasn't going anywhere, Lilla decided, so it was best to alight from the rickety old trap. Grabbing her walking stick from the back, she edged alongside the man and was surprised to see the dark clothing was a monk's robe, soiled with blood, caked with grime and leaves. The sun had warmed the air a bit by now, but still Lilla could see the man had experienced a cold, wet night.

Her long fingers curled into his shoulder as she tried to waken the Black Monk.

No response.

She reached out, felt his forehead. It was warm. Much too warm. A fever raged. His eyelids appeared paper-thin, and his lips were a purplish color. Flushed in bright-red patches were his cheeks, like a babe in summer.

Lilla was a woman of scant talk and corpulent action. Market day entirely forgotten, she planned exactly how she would transport this sick stranger into the back of her cart.

She sat down with a sigh, gathering strength and feeling somewhat overwhelmed at this drastic surprise, this unforeseen change in her normally regulated life. "He needs our help, Soot." The terrier settled his bottom beside her and looked up at her with his sparkling brown eyes. Her own eyes navigated the length of the stranger's long body. From beneath the robe a leg protruded, visible only from the knee down. The blood on the skin was brown and crusty, dry and completely devoid of the life-giving sustenance it once carried to its owner's heart and lungs. The blond hair of his calf was matted into the dried blood.

"He's wounded, Soot. That is why he is so warm. We must get him home. I would see to him quickly."

She leaned forward and examined the calf. No wound there. Lifting the garment above his knee, she saw the wound clearly scrawled across the corded muscles.

She rose to her feet. Painfully. Biting back a cry.

Working slowly but with the strength that had come from years of spinning and weaving, Lilla dragged Griffin to her cart. Her right leg cried out in agony, and she tried to put as little of her weight on it as possible. She knew by her very actions, quite impossible under normal circumstances, that clearly heaven was championing her small crusade.

A moan escaped his lips, and his eyes opened.

"Can you hoist yourself into the cart?" Lilla asked, knowing full well this man would never remember this moment. His eyes were fiery with the beginnings of delirium.

He nodded, rising onto his knees and clumsily crawling up into the back of the trap. Lilla arranged his limbs, his legs hanging over the side from the knees down. Her fingers wound into the thick hair at the nape of his neck as she lifted the heaviness of his head. Under it she placed his knapsack.

"Let's get back, then," she said to her animals, breathing heavily as she limped to the front of the cart. "The market will have to wait until next week. We must help this man, my little friends. Remember, blessed are the merciful."

But before they rolled on, she took a length of deep-blue cloth, almost a week's worth of toil, and laid it on top of the wounded stranger.

Lilla prayed the entire way home.

❧ ❧ ❧

*Soon you will be mine! I will feast upon your agony and delight in your cries of pain as your flesh burns but is not consumed. You will seek after God, but He will not be found. For no matter which way your head shall turn, all you'll see is me . . . me . . . me . . . .*

"I'm not ready to die!"

Griffin screamed at the hellish specter which danced before his eyes like a war mask. Its mouth, opened in grotesque putrefaction, leered and laughed at his plight. Its nose exhaled flames of eternal torment. And eyeless black sockets spoke of a torturous eternal void . . . the created separated from the Creator.

And Griffin was spinning, spinning, spinning into a scarlet darkness.

❦ ❦ ❦

Simon and Peter lay on Lilla's pallet, languidly observing their mistress's ministrations upon the stranger whom she had unexpectedly dragged into their home just moments before. The slanty golden depth of their eyes focused upon the large form with feline disdain, even as Lilla's eyes frowned with worry. The fire she had lit upon entering was now blazing, and its light warmed the gray fur of the cats' coats.

The wound was worse than she had thought upon initial observation.

The black robe was dew-soaked and heavy. Bits of broken grass littered the raven surface, and Lilla brushed away the fragments along the simple rope-like sash which nipped the garment in at his slim waist. With confident fingers she untied the knot and undressed her God-given patient, covering him as she went with her own woolen blanket.

Gripping the handle of a battered wooden bucket, she limped down to the beck. Her leg was beyond pain now. It was numb with exhaustion. "It matters not," she said to Soot, who followed her everywhere. "How dare I complain about my old infirmity when he lies there in such state as that?" Soot cocked his ebony head, looking as though he, too, sought to understand the stranger's plight.

Back inside, she cut off a small piece of the newest, softest fabric she had woven for a new and much-needed gown. Fresh water warmed over the fire. It was time to clean him up. First the grime and sweat from his face, neck, chest, and arms. The burgundy wool of the blanket she rolled down to Griffin's waist. Despite her usual placid certitude, she involuntarily drew in her breath at the sight of his body. Arms, thick and hard, lay limply by his sides, and his chest, wide with corded strength, tapered down to a flat, muscled stomach. Almost a warrior's form. Yet without battle scars. And clad in the robe of a monk. Puzzling indeed, she thought, as she began to bathe the stranger with the cloth made of her own two hands. She scrutinized him as she did so.

His face could be described as handsome, yet she had seen handsomer at Oxneford. Rather broad-bridged, his nose sat high upon his face. He appeared quite young, perhaps 21, she thought. A firm chin, cleft ever so slightly, jutted below lips that were on the thin side, but appeared in no way sly or displeasing. Even in repose, it was evident he was a thoughtful, introspective person, his brow, neither high nor low, already lined from much pondering. Around his mouth were no deep smile lines carved from galing laughter.

The flesh of his face was smooth and white. In some ways he appeared an alabaster effigy of the man he must truly be. Except for his hair—the sunny hair which grew down to the middle of his back was matted together more thoroughly than the nest of a falcon. But easily Lilla imagined it would be like a shimmering, straight curtain of light gold when clean and newly dry, winking with sunlight, moonlight, and starlight.

Gently, she returned the blanket to rest warmly over his chest and began to cleanse his legs. By the time she had finished, the water from the fire was quite warm. With compassionate hands, she cleansed the gaping slash, careful to leave as few fibers behind as possible. His legs, slimmer in proportion than his upper body, told her he used his arms with more frequency. She knew not that this man on her floor could heave blocks of stone which most other men would be unable to budge.

Without warning, tears flooded over the rims of her eyes, dropping in heavy splatters onto the backs of her hands, sliding, leaving wet trails along the protruding blue veins lying just under the papery, dry surface of her skin. "He looks so sad," she whispered to the faithful terrier, who whimpered softly in response to his maiden's gentle sympathies.

After cleaning the raw slash as best she could, Lilla realized the manner of care this stranger needed was beyond her limited healing capabilities. She would fetch Father Andrew right away.

For a second time that day, Bracken was hitched to the little cart, and Lilla left her handsome charge upon the floor to battle the raging fever alone. Her leg smarted terribly, but she said with a very weary smile to Soot, "We're laying up treasure in heaven this day, to be sure, little one."

❧ ❧ ❧

Griffin's appearance gripped women's eyes hard and held them spellbound thereafter. Only he didn't know this. Almost 19, and a man by anyone's standards, he had experienced a marginal amount of contact with women. Mostly older ladies—friends of his mother. The Widow Urfried knew more about him than almost any female he knew. It seemed she was always turning a blind eye to the fights, real and mock, which went on near the woods behind her dwelling.

He didn't seem to notice the young ladies of Westminster and London who gazed on him with large, syrupy eyes whenever he walked past on his way to the lodge. Of course, once the monastery swallowed him whole, all thoughts of girls, no matter how sparse they had been before, were banished within the masculine walls of St. Peter's. The lasses of the neighborhood soon forgot their Saxon youth and were fawning over other eligible males, Simon included, soon after Griffin had quit the streets for the sobering abbey.

Lilla would have had no trouble sharing their admiration. In fact, as she rode to the small parish church, the memory of Griffin's white face haunted her disturbingly. But there was no time for daydreaming on this journey. She had to get to Father Andrew quickly before it was too late for the man who lay unconscious on her floor.

The village church was fixed a scant mile west of her hut. Its timbered frame and thick wattle-and-daub walls exhibited only peculiarities compared to Eadric's abbey. But here could God be discovered. Here the daily magnification of His Son was the consequence of the devotion of many who arrived, cloaked in humility, seeking but a glimpse of Him. And here Lilla came to worship and pray.

"Father Andrew!" she shouted, her voice tight with strain.

It wasn't the normal, carefree greeting he was used to, and he rushed over, his white habit swinging behind him. "What is it, Lilla, my child?"

"It's a matter of extreme urgency, Father." She began to get down.

"No, please, Lilla," he touched her elbow gently, his voice lowered and familiar, "stay where you are. Tell me what concerns you."

"Soot and I were on our way to market day in Oxneford when Bracken suddenly stopped. A man lay unconscious by the side of the road. He was wearing a black monk's habit, Father. But his hair has seen little of the shears. He is wounded, and although my knowledge is limited in such matters, Father, I would cast a bet that a sword it was which scored his leg so grievously."

A masculine voice shouted from inside the church. "Everything all right, Andrew?"

"Aye, Father John!" he called back to reassure the aging priest who was the chief shepherd of the village flock.

"A black monk's habit?" The red-haired priest was puzzled, and a fabulously large hand rubbed his prominent chin—a mannerism Lilla had always admired.

She nodded. "I've bathed him, given him water, and cleansed the wound. But it needs stitching, Father. And treatment with one of your healing salves. Already his fever rages."

"He is feverish?"

"Frightfully so. His skin feels quite hot to the touch." In spite of herself, Lilla blushed and looked quickly away before the priest noticed.

"I'll fetch my supplies."

"I shall wait here for you."

Watching him recede back into the small church, Lilla's mind for the first time voiced a feasible conjecture as to who the young man was. Was he a member of the English rebellion? Positively not! Not in a monk's habit. But then, he certainly didn't wear comfortably the mien of a holy man. Not at all. And yet, if it wasn't for Father Andrew's garb and his manner of genuine humility, he wouldn't look like a priest either. He seemed, well, too large for the church. His eyes were a dazzling blue. An intense blue that held a casual glance and turned it into a look of meaning. His great laugh could be heard clear to the village, and his wide, warm smile summoned others to join him. But the most inviting quality that Father Andrew maintained was his compassion for the people.

A few minutes later he was back, a pouch containing small pots of ointments and a needle and thread slung over his shoulder. The look of concern worn earlier had deepened, and he displayed an agitation, wanting only to hurry on their way.

He took the reins she held between her fingers and led Bracken along the path. "Let us hasten."

The hut, once insignificant, but that no more, waited for them to cross its threshold. The priest was through the door and tending to the needs of his new patient ere Lilla had placed one foot on the ground.

❧ ❧ ❧

The dark blossom of night released its dark perfume of quiet into the cool, early May. Lilla tugged a blanket closely about her thin frame and paced outside to partake of the fresh forest air. Crickets, now roused from their winter slumber, chirped. And slickly armored beetles buzzed their discordant hum into the duskiness of the timber. Inside the hut the fire warmed the room to the point of discomfort, and Lilla had tossed upon the floor for almost an hour. *Soon*, she thought, *soon the air inside shall cool down a bit and I shall find sleep.*

Griffin lay, still submerged in a sickened slumber, mumbling at times, deathly still at others. His benumbed state proved a blessing. For Father Andrew had swabbed the wound again, stitched the incised skin together, and applied a poultice which Lilla had concocted according to his directions from herbs and salve. Lilla prayed fervently on the young man's behalf. And a peace settled over the room as if some heavenly guard had been sent to accompany them during her vigil.

"I suppose I must lift him into the cart now," Andrew said as the sun dropped beneath the horizon.

"He must stay here with me, Father," she persuaded quietly, the firelight casting its orange warmth upon the soft lines of her face. "Just until he is well enough to move."

"I fear I must agree with you, Lilla." He nodded his red head and looked down at the sleeping form. "For now, we'll tell no one of his presence. And when his healing permits us, I'll remove him to the church. For propriety's sake, of course."

"Of course," Lilla responded, pushing down an unexpected twinge of disappointment. But she knew that whoever the stranger was, his presence seemed more like an appointment than an accident.

Hours passed.

&#x2767; &#x2767; &#x2767;

The fire curtailed its blaze, diminishing itself to a mound of winking red coals. It was the sole agent of light in the darkness of the diminutive room. Lilla's pallet was near the fire, and Griffin lay upon it, deposited there by Father Andrew.

Beside him on the hard earthen floor Lilla lay in repose, shivering despite the layers of blankets which sought to shield her from the cold, weighty air which descended with the wee hours of morning. Still, she slept. Every half hour or so she would stir, just to listen to the stranger's breathing. And when the fire would burn down too much to benefit from its warmth, she would stoke it to ensure the patient's warmth. As well as her own.

୬ଈୢ ୬ଈୢ ୬ଈୢ

Misty gyrations, receding, thickening, receding again. Patches of consciousness flourished then faded. Red sparks, blackened hues—at variance within.

Until . . . finally . . .

Griffin sluggishly emerged from the checkered trance. Consciousness had come, but his eyes declined to engage in their calling. Was he in his cell at the monastery? Was he by the fire at home? Was he in the woods? Was he still where he had fallen? Was he alive?

His eyes opened, dispelling any question of being locked in the world of eternity.

A fire. A small room.

His eyes made a darting movement, taking in a small bit of the mysterious vista before him, the unfamiliar world which he had unwittingly encountered. Someone lay beside him.

A woman.

*Who?*

And though confusion held unquestionable sway, Griffin wondered how he came to be in the home of a stranger.

His eyes became accustomed to the gloom. And when he looked upon the woman whose face was only two feet from his own, he forgot all previous quandary. For the young, recent warrior had never before witnessed anything so lovely, so truly pure and unaffected. Indeed, the peace prevailing upon her face was more comely than all the alluring beauty the ladies at court had to offer, and contrasted directly with the raging scene he had left in Westminster. Her brow was clear and smooth, devoid of the stain that city life wickedly and subversively bestowed upon its inhabitants. And her tranquillity attracted him to her like the face of a sleeping child captivates even the most hardened of men and makes them smile.

He did the same.

Her eyes were slumberous crescents, and short, thick, curled lashes rested peacefully on cheeks that were slightly full, almost babyish in their innocence. A tendril of light-brown hair fell across her downy cheek—hair that was as curly and looked more delicately soft than the winter coat of a rabbit. Above the slightly crooked, pale pink lips sat a somewhat prominent nose that gifted her with the bearing of royalty. Her beauty was warm. Approachable. Home.

He shook his head at the thought of royalty.

King Edward.

His sword!

The nature of his true circumstances ripped through his foggy consciousness, and the blinding reality of the plight that brought him to this humble hut surfaced with the force of a leviathan.

He had to leave.

Right away.

Whoever the fair damsel was, she was in danger. His presence made it thus. Surely the Normans were close. They had to be.

They were bloodhounds all.

Griffin attempted to roll over onto his side when a pain, uncommon and ferocious, barraged his heated leg, prompting him to suck in harshly, all thought of Norman manhunters immediately dispelled.

Green eyes opened.

And the maiden sprang to a sitting position.

"You're awake!" she cried. "Sit still. Lay back. I shall fetch you a cup of cool water."

He watched her in mute fascination as she reached for her walking stick and pulled herself to her feet. Instinctually, Griffin reached out to help her. A soft cry of pain emitted from him.

Lilla pretended not hear. Men despised others' weaknesses. Their own they abhorred. That she knew right well.

In several moments she was back sitting on the floor beside him. "Here, my stranger," she smiled into his eyes, and thought that she had never seen a more handsome man. "Drink deeply. You need it much."

"Thank you." Griffin lifted his head and gratefully accepted the cup she offered. The pure water was soothing as it tunneled benevolently down the parched wasteland of his throat. And the sight of the lass before him, after three years in the monastery, was surprisingly refreshing as well. He realized it was more than just her peaceful ways which charmed him, or even the quiet beauty of her face. The feelings were new to him.

An awakening of the body.

"Who are you and how did I come to be here?" Griffin whispered, handing her the cup. His small store of strength was rapidly deteriorating, but he tried to hide it. The sudden sweep of emotion was yet another stone laid atop the edifice of exhaustion which was threatening to eclipse his desire to find out more about her, to learn more regarding the current predicament.

"My name is Lilla, and this is my home. You lay unconscious this morning in the forest whence I found you. Good sir, you are most welcome to abide with me and heal until you are ready to be moved."

"Has anyone inquired of me?"

"No, sir. Why would they?"

"How long have I been here?"

"You've passed the night here."

"Truly?"

"Aye, truly." Unexpectedly, she reached forward, then shyly dropped her hand. "And as long as you . . . have need of me . . . I will care for you."

A mellow, unexpected sense of well-being overcame him, and he smiled. A certain rarity for the stonemason's son. His eyes closed once again, despite an overwhelming sense of curiosity. Lilla's heart glowed at the gentle smile upon the sad, youthful face. She had looked in his eyes. Lifted his head. Heard his voice even as he had listened to hers. And still she didn't know his name or why such a one should steal softly into her life.

# ❦ EIGHT ❦

Lilla's emerald eyes expanded with concentration as she diligently dabbed at the wound with a clean cloth and fresh water. She reached behind her and mixed the poultice, preparing to slather it liberally on the stitched laceration. The quiet stranger had wakened over an hour before, had taken a little more water, consumed a scrap of bread. He had also confided to her his name—a name which delighted her exceedingly. A Griffin was part eagle, part lion. The name became him like a fine tunic. Truly this man was not a Black Monk. "Were you persecuted for righteousness' sake, Griffin?"

"Pardon me, madam?" Griffin, more alert than before, had become more guarded.

"Please, I have no husband. As I said last night, my name is Lilla. And I invite you to address me as such."

Griffin nodded.

"You forgot to answer my question, sir."

"I'm not certain what the meaning of your question was." He winced as she rubbed a tad too heavily.

"Forgive me," she whispered. "When Soot and I found you, you were wearing a monk's robe. A Black Monk's robe. 'Tis true I've not known many monks in my lifetime, but you look no more like a Benedictine than I do!" She gave a light, self-conscious laugh.

107

"No, Lilla. I was not persecuted for righteousness' sake. What I flee from is not, I am sure, what our Lord had in mind when He spoke the beatitudes upon the Mount of Olives."

"So you are not a monk?"

"No. I am not."

"I was right then." Lilla sighed with relief, then turned quickly away. "Is the wound from a sword?"

"Yes."

"Father Andrew said that you should regain full use of your leg once it heals. You were fortunate."

"That is a relief." Inwardly, he was alarmed. "Who is this Father Andrew?"

"The village priest, and a very good friend. Aye," she wistfully looked down at her own leg, which lay twisted beneath her gown. Griffin could not see it, but he had wondered why she limped so. "You are blessed that you have broken no bones."

Griffin thought of his father.

She continued her healing ministrations. "We shall have to pray for your healing, Griffin."

"There is one who needs a far greater healing than I do, Lilla."

"Who is that?"

"My father."

"Has he been taken by illness?" Her forehead wrinkled with concern.

"Something like that."

Silence ensued as Lilla gingerly began to wrap Griffin's thigh. He was able to bend his knee this time, thereby giving her hands room to maneuver. *'Tis a good sign*, she thought, hopeful his recovery would be complete.

"This priest of whom you spoke, who is he?" Griffin had to find out what side the man's sympathies lay on. Was he Saxon or Norman?

"It is Father Andrew. He has helped to minister to the needs of our small parish since Hastings."

Lilla was obviously a Saxon woman—she would under-stand. "Was he invested by the Normans?"

The woman before him smiled widely and, much to his surprise, ran a tender, comforting hand over his sunny hair. "No, Griffin. A truer Englishman I've never known. Besides, I would rather die than bring a Norman into my home."

"Will he be back today?" he asked.

"Yes. He was here all day yesterday to see to your good."

"Yesterday? Do you mean an entire day I passed in your home without wakening?"

Lilla nodded.

"You are a good woman. You deserve my thanks."

"'Therefore all things whatsoever ye would that men should do to you, do ye even so to them, for this is the law and the prophets.'"

"Easier voiced than carried out," Griffin remarked. "But you, Lilla, must be most pleasing to the heavenly Father."

"That is my reason for living," she said simply. "Rest now, Griffin," her soft voice invited him to repose. "There's much to accomplish this day, not the least of which is tending to my garden so that we shall have food to eat. And then I shall have to set to my weaving. I trust the loom will not bother you."

"No. I am simply grateful for the shelter you have afforded."

"You are welcome, sir. 'Tis glad I am that you are here. My heart has been lonely for quite some time. And a wounded companion is much preferable to none at all."

Griffin closed his eyes. *My heart has been lonely for quite some time.* Her words piloted him to the land of sleep, and his hollow soul echoed her sentiments. Lonely she was . . . yes . . . it was evident. But not empty. Her eyes were full and luminous when she voiced the words of Jesu. How effortlessly they slipped off her tongue.

ᵔᵔᵔ ᵔᵔᵔ ᵔᵔᵔ

The sun pressed its rays between the doorposts and bur-nished Griffin's hair. It was matted, tangled with the dried sweat of the chase. His scalp began to itch most annoyingly. He knew that Lilla had bathed him; she told him so when he asked. But being embarrassed was pointless, as there was nothing he could have done at the time. Still, he craved a visit to the stream Lilla had previously mentioned.

Just then, a shadow tumbled across the doorway, and Soot scampered inside. Griffin leaned back to see who was visiting.

"How is our patient today?" A huge face appeared before his own. A lively Saxon face. The face of Father Andrew. Griffin eyed him warily. Andrew laughed. And Griffin almost jumped out of his skin at the volume.

"So sorry," the priest patted him on the shoulder. "Perhaps, my son, you wish nothing to call attention to your presence. I mean, your wound . . . the habit you were wearing . . ." His voice trailed off, and he hoped Griffin would supply some details. The young Saxon obliged him not. He merely shot another suspicious glance in the priest's direction. Andrew laughed again.

"No need to fear, my son. No need at all. My ancestors came over in the very first Saxon raid upon the Britons centuries ago. I would not do you harm."

The breath Griffin had been holding was let loose slowly. "It is as you evidently surmise, Father. I am an outlaw, most assuredly."

The priest crouched beside him, scrutinizing him.

"I see. Did you fight at Hastings then?"

Griffin nodded no. "I was at the abbey of St. Peter's at Westminster at the time."

"Were you seeking refuge? I can see by your hair you were not one of the brothers."

"I was seeking refuge. From myself."

The father gently exposed the wound.

Griffin, used to exposing his soul to one priest or another over the years, decided to do so now to Andrew. There was something about the priest that could be trusted. All he knew was that, as Lilla's confessor, perhaps Father Andrew could bestow on him as well that assurance, that peaceful cohabitation with the things of God that Lilla experienced. Certainly Lilla's humble hut awarded him with the same feeling he knew during solitary moments in the abbey.

"Leastwise," Andrew encouraged him further, "if you talk it might steal your mind away from the pain."

Griffin began, explaining who his godfather was, his education at the abbey, his apprenticeship with his father.

"The son of the royal stonemason, eh?" Andrew's brows lifted in surprise. "And King Edward's godson as well. You are only a tad shy of being nobility." The father held his fingers slightly apart. "Perhaps it was King Edward's wish to one day make you his thane. You're probably better educated than most of them."

"That's not saying a great deal," Griffin chuckled, which pleased Andrew greatly.

Meanwhile, at the door of the hut, Lilla listened to the hushed, whispered tones of the two men inside. The word *outlaw* she had overheard from the stranger's own lips. What if the Normans came? She felt confused and not a little frightened.

*If God feeds the sparrows and clothes the lilies of the field, so shall He care for His Lilla.* She prayed for a greater faith and sought God's forgiveness for her previous lack thereof. Just then, Father Andrew walked out the door.

"Where did you find him?" he asked, bending down on his haunches in front of Lilla.

She pointed yonder. "About a quarter of a mile down the path there. I was on my way to market."

Without further utterance, Andrew marched in that direction. Lilla asked no questions just then; her concern was only for Griffin. Clambering to her feet, she penetrated the serene, midday dimness of the hut. The hearth bore no flame, as her patient had grumbled against the heat. *Another good sign*, she thought. But now he sat straight up on her pallet staring absentmindedly at his hands. She couldn't know how strange they appeared to him, their calluses all but faded from his three years at the abbey. Invisibly stained with the lifeblood of five men. His left hand, his sword hand, was raw and scabbed from the unwrapped hilt which had torn open his palm. *Soon*, he promised himself, *soon I will bear the scabrous patches of a man who wields a sword.*

Lilla pulled a crude stool from across the room and sat down. "Did Father Andrew bring you any comfort?"

"He said my leg should be healed quickly enough. Tomorrow I might even get a little exercise, walk around a bit."

"I should like that! I'll help you myself." She glimmered with expectation.

Without thinking, Griffin stared at the knobby stick which rested against her thigh.

"Oh that!" She waved a hand. "I'm stronger than I look. I got you in here, didn't I?"

Griffin's eyebrows arched in surprise. "Father Andrew didn't help you?"

"No. I'm not completely helpless. Aiding you in a few circles around the room should prove a leisurely task."

Embarrassment reddened Griffin's face. "I didn't mean to offend, Lilla. 'Tis only the overprotectiveness I inherited directly from my mother."

"Your talk with Father Andrew has loosed your tongue a trifle. And indeed I am glad. But tell me about your mother. Do you miss her?"

"A little."

"When will you be going back home? And where is home?"

"Westminster. And I shall not be returning anytime soon. My fate was sealed two nights ago when I killed five Norman soldiers."

A fire, small but very visible, kindled in Lilla's eyes.

"They destroyed my father's hands, Lilla. My father was the royal stonemason to King Edward."

Her eyes widened. "I'm sorry."

"So am I. But I shouldn't be telling you these things. The less you know about me, the better it is for you." Clearly, he became uncomfortable with the topic. "Tell me about yourself, Lilla. What of your parents?"

Her soft voice quickly retreated to another season, its tones wistful, wanting. "Father died at Hastings. Mother went long before that. I've been living on my own, weaving and selling my wares for nigh unto three years now."

"But surely you took care of things after your mother passed away?"

She nodded. "Since I was 15."

"Fifteen?" he looked surprised. "How old are you?"

"Twenty-three. And you?"

"Almost 19."

"Well, then. You see there, we are practically the same age," she joked. "And I for one do not feel a day older than I did at 19!" Then Lilla laughed. It was as musical as her voice, and it covered Griffin's heart like a silken swath. However, he did not share in her mirth. But Lilla took note that his eyes sparkled a little more than they had before.

He grew very serious. The side of him that Brother Adam had become so accustomed to emerged. "And the Normans . . . do they bother you greatly here?"

"I doubt very much that they know I live in these woods. For surely the new lord, Baron Stephen de Chauliac, would have taken advantage of my services long ago. Have you ever been covered by a more finely woven blanket?"

Griffin ran his hands over the blue fabric that rested around his waist and over his legs. "No, Lilla. Your children will be most fortunate to be wrapped in such fine material."

For the first time she saddened, and he noticed. "That troubles you?" he asked. "Surely you mean to someday marry, do you not?" *Actually*, he thought, *23 is past marriageable age. But she is possessed of such a sweet loveliness.*

113

"I used to, but I live a quiet life here. I'm happy this way."

He couldn't imagine the woman before him happy in this solitary, albeit peaceful and pleasant existence. Her laughter was too throaty, her voice too deep. Her hands moved too smoothly and purposefully. To think they would never please a man who called her "wife."

Lilla arose from her chair and sat at her tablet loom. Although she admired men greatly from afar, she shied away at any close contact. Certainly some touting advances had been made the first few times she vended at market. But her infirmity was noticed. And shortly thereafter, the admiring looks vanished and were replaced with ones of pity.

Lilla despised that.

Life was hard for the common man. She knew that well. Only a man of strength and fortitude, a man possessed of a heart with room enough to contain the love of a thousand men, would embrace someone incapable of strenuous toil from sunup to sundown.

The loom shook as her fingers flew. In fascination, Griffin watched, mesmerized by the rhythm of her work. His admiration for Lilla grew. And a chastening was suddenly his. For years an inner war he had waged. A bright future as an esteemed mason had stood before him, and he dared yearn for more. He yearned for glory and valor. Instead, he was accompanied everywhere by misery. But before him now sat a woman whose parents had been early claimed by death, whose lot in life was never questioned. A woman who weaved, worked her garden, and lovingly saw to the daily care of her creature companions. Who quested after the wisdom of the Scriptures. Who prayed most fervently with no thought to self, with no anger or mistrust of the Divine One.

He was ashamed.

But now the path of his future stood before him, leading only in one direction. Beneath the weighted agony of Eadric's hands, Griffin received the desires of his heart. He would fight. Yet the emptiness and the misery still clutched its ravenous fingers around his soul. He watched Lilla's arms move back and forth as her fingers worked the woolen thread. Her brown hair which escaped from the long braids she wore frizzed around her face. And her cheeks were flushed and warm. She had the answers. She knew peace.

Father Andrew bolted through the door like a full wind encased in white woolen.

Griffin's eyes devoured what the priest held in his hand. Edward's sword. Clearly the man had been running. Without a word and with a gallant hardihood, he threw the sword to Griffin. Speeding across the room, he bent down and picked up the wounded man in his massive arms. The sleeves of his robe slid down to his elbows, and a crew of scars on his arms flashed their slick surface in the light.

"Soldiers—they're coming hence."

His breathing was heavy.

Lilla naturally started to rise.

"Stay where you are!" Andrew commanded, his voice forceful. "Pretend nothing is amiss."

Griffin began to protest. "I'll fight them."

"I'm sure you would, but in your condition I wouldn't advise it. They won't hurt Lilla. I'll see to it myself."

"Where are you going?" Lilla asked.

"Deeper into the woods, up near the waterfall. Light a fire in the hearth when all is safe, and we shall return when we see the smoke."

"All right."

They were only gone a minute when the sound of horses reached Lilla's ears. Her fearful heart, swollen in fervent prayer, became calm. She placed her hand unquestioningly in the Master's, knowing He would not fail her in this most harrowing of hours.

A shadow loomed large across the floor.

## NINE

The Norman captain's English was crude and heavily accented. "You haven't seen anyone like we describe?" His eyes were flat, unsympathetic.

"No. It's quite peaceful here in the *vale*." Lilla alluded to the Norman atrocities at Oxneford and around the castle of Beam-Dune Maur with a proud tilt to her chin. Lilla arose from her bench, lifting the skirt of her dark green tunic higher than was necessary to extricate herself from the table. It was a well-calculated move on her part. The captain, like any red-blooded Norman man, eyed the exposed leg.

A jagged scar, beginning at the ankle and as thick as a strong cord snaked over the shin. The lowest branch of an ancient elm tree, which helped to break the fall, had also torn open the tender flesh of her lower leg. The tibia had fractured below the knee when she finally impacted with the ground. The break ruptured the skin and had left a scar the size of a child's fist. Although the injury was now 14 years old, the deep red crevice carved across her limb appeared ghastly and fresh with pain.

She heard their quick intake of breath and raised her chin yet more proudly, meeting the leader's black eyes. In them she saw a grudging look of admiration. Not sexual admiration, but the admission that she was a survivor, like himself. Instead of feeling the humiliation she well expected to experience at baring her leg for the first time to a stranger, she praised Jesu for the diversion and felt an inward strength flux from her soul to her extremities.

"We must be going, madam." Another man assuming she was married. "If you should come across the man we are looking for, Griffin Eadricson, tell the commander at Beam-Dune Maur. The man is a dangerous outlaw and can fight like the devil himself. Be wary."

"Thank you, I shall be careful. But I wonder if I have more to fear from those who now inhabit Beam-Dune Maur?"

"Your infirmity loosens your tongue, woman. But be sure that one will come along to whom your suffering will mean no account."

Lilla raised her chin. "Indeed, you are a Norman that speaks the truth. I thought none existed."

He ignored the remark, and they turned to go. But at the door, the captain turned around and looked at her. "You are a weaver woman."

She nodded.

He pointed across the room. "Give me a length of your cloth and that piece of trim you've just finished there on the table. Baron de Chauliac will be pleased to know that someone such as you is living on his land."

Lilla knew better than to refuse. Englishmen died for less nowadays. So she chose a swath of soft black from the shelf near her and limped across the room to hand to the captain what equaled three day's worth of work.

His callused fingers stroked the woolen swath, and his eyes admired the trim she had extricated from her tablet loom only that morning. "Ah, it is fine work you do. At least as fine as anything I've seen in Normandy."

"Well, we English do have talents if you'd care to take the time to recognize them," she replied. But inwardly she was pleased, as any artist is, for the recognition of her expertise.

The men had been gone several minutes when she began to light the fire. But Father Andrew walked into the room.

"Where is Griffin?" she asked the priest.

"At the waterfall. He bade me come back and hide in the brush nearby to make sure you weren't harmed, instead of relying on my ears to hear from afar."

Lilla blushed and turned away. Heaven help her, but she had blushed more since Griffin came than she had done in her whole life. "Perhaps you should bring our patient back."

"He said to wait a while just to make sure. He's a man of the outdoors, Lilla. Most assuredly he is more content sitting under the canopy of the forest with the music of the waterfall flowing peacefully beside him. You could see it in his eyes when we exited the hut."

"You don't think the Normans will journey in his direction, do you?"

Andrew grinned. "Even if they do, they will not find your Griffin."

*Your Griffin.* She said nothing about it.

"Griffin could be your son, you look so much alike. Have you noticed?"

Andrew laughed. "We could very easily be related, Lilla. He is a Saxon. Not a Celt, not a Norseman. But in truth, we are both Englishmen. True Englishmen. And perhaps what burns so much alike in our hearts is what makes us appear likewise." He paused.

"Perhaps we can find out more about him. But there might be a chance that his past is something he doesn't relish discussing."

Father Andrew bowed. "As for me, I'll go back now to fetch Griffin."

"There's no need." Griffin leaned with exhaustion against the post. "I've come myself."

Father Andrew quickly crossed the room and helped his patient onto the pallet. A meaningful look passed between

Andrew and Lilla—a look of satisfaction. "Get that fire started, Lilla. And hand me a cup of water. With the loss of so much blood, he still needs plenty of liquid."

Griffin drank gratefully from the wooden cup. "Thank you."

"How did you make it back here on your own?" Lilla sat down next to him.

With eyes closed, Griffin explained. "One of my greatest trials to bear these past three years has been that I didn't fight for England. When I thought of King Harold, a broken arrow protruding from his eye but fighting on, when I thought of his brother Gurth, a warrior with a monk's heart, standing firm till the end—the last man to go down before our standard was claimed by William himself, how could I not play the man and ignore my wounded leg?"

"The youth and their bravado!" Andrew sighed. "Here, my son, let me look at your leg. We can only pray you didn't open it up again."

The priest unwrapped Griffin's thigh and breathed a puff of relief. "You heal more quickly than a babe, Griffin. Everything is as it should be. But for now," he rose to his feet and got ready to go, "you need to rest. I'll be back tomorrow to change the dressing on that wound again."

He said a few more words to Lilla regarding Griffin's care. "Do you have the dye?" he whispered.

Lilla nodded and handed him a stone flask of one of her many colors.

"Thank you, Lilla." And by the time he was out the door, Griffin was already asleep.

Lilla tried to accomplish much weaving that afternoon. But her eyes stole across the room to the large, beautiful form of the sleeping man near the fire. Her heart recalled the lonely hours and days of solitude she had borne for far too long. And though she knew little about the outlaw who graced her pallet, she loved him well.

✧ ✧ ✧

*The rain beat down upon Lilla's face. Around her the land was wilderness, pocked and scarred by fire and devastation. The trees lifted their stunted, charred branches in mute, tormented supplication toward the heavens. A hollow wind whispered deridingly around her head.*

*But in the distance, far off in the distance, a green hill, smooth and lovely. Sparkling like an emerald, the motte protruded from the desolate hardness that was the earth. The sky opened, a small lens looking into the heavens, shining a ray of sun upon the verdant dome. Flowers bloomed. An eagle soared. A lion rested peacefully. The two became one.*

*The rain beat down upon her face. She pulled with all her might at her leg, the ankle held tight in a crevice. It held her back, and she wondered if she would remain in that solitary wasteland forever.*

The earthen floor received the brunt of Lilla's tormented dreams. Griffin's breathing was even and deep. A healing sleep was his blessing from Jesu that night. But if he could have dreamed, his dreams would have been much the same as the woman who shared the dark room, the woman whose eyes had beguiled him into manhood. Yet they caused him to yearn with an innocent passion, a pure wanting of beauty and its essence always by his side. Her heart, on the other hand, reached out to his in a way like nothing before. Father's heart had been much like Lilla's. At times he had seen the love of Jesu shine out of the man from whose loins he had sprung. But too many stiff silences in the confines of the lodge had occurred for Griffin to be drawn to the love of his father's soul as he was being drawn now to Lilla's. Before he fell asleep that night, he promised himself that tomorrow he would inquire of Lilla just who she knew Jesu to be. And he was completely confident that she would tell him the answer.

Years later Griffin would tell his grandchildren his love for Jesu and Lilla flowered at the very same moment. It was his third day at the hut when the truth ravaged him with a tender fury. Jesu could be known intimately. Griffin had always known that the Christ had sacrificed Himself upon the cross for the sins of mankind. But that day, viewing Lilla's humble servitude, her honor of God, he realized that the Son of God had died for him.

"How can you speak of the Christ so freely, as if you know Him?" he asked Lilla that night. They shared a meager repast of bread and cheese.

Lilla looked at him, a bit puzzled by his question. "How could I not know Him? Griffin, He came down to earth from the heavens and took my place at Golgotha." She pointed to a crude wooden crucifix which hung over the table. "Surely, if someone sacrificed His life for you in such agony, and for all eternity, wouldn't you wish to know more about Him?"

"I learned the Scriptures at the abbey."

Lilla sighed. "'Tis wonderful to have had that opportunity. I suppose my loneliness has prompted my desire for Him. For a simple maiden such as I, it could never be a quest of the mind, but a quest of the heart."

"But that's it exactly, Lilla. I want to know Him the way you do." Griffin swallowed his last bite of brown bread and leaned back in his chair. "My father built the abbey, as you know. And I believe he knows Jesu as you do. He is a man of few words, however. I'm not sure he could explain what his heart feels, even if he tried."

"What of your mother?"

"She is a most devout member of the church, faithful in all its requirements. But her eyes do not shine as yours and father's do when the name of Christ crowns the air."

"And do you not hear glory at the sound of His name?"

Griffin pushed out his chair, rose slowly to his feet, and walked to the door. He gazed out on the twilight searching through the foliage for a glimpse of a star. At the same time that Lilla thought he was the most beautiful sight she had ever seen with eyes or heart, she prayed for his soul. Surely, that might be why God brought him here, mightn't it? To lay his life and his soul at the feet of the Son of God?

He turned to face her. "Have you ever been in a great church, Lilla?"

"Only the church of St. Frideswide's in Oxneford. 'Tis a humble church by your standards, I'll warrant."

"One day," he promised her, his eyes shining, "I shall take you to the abbey at St. Peter's." Her heart skipped a beat. "I was born on the day the first stone was laid, Lilla."

She walked over to him and laid a gentle hand on his arm. "Tell me of the abbey."

They sat on the doorstone together, and Griffin began to describe the magnificent building that had claimed his heart long ago. The pride in his father's skill and vision was evident, and always there was a love for the King who founded it, the king who loved Griffin almost as a son. Lilla was breathless, rapt with attention as Griffin told her of his life. How he grew with the abbey, how the church called to him—that part which no one else sees or ever knows. How it brought him peace at some times and left him aching at others.

"Only in the abbey, when no one was about, did I feel God." He looked into her eyes. "Isn't that odd?"

"I don't think so. Many people feel that way in a building built purposefully for God's glorification. 'Tis why they're so faithful in the rules of the church, darkening the door every chance they receive. It brings about that warmth of soul they never feel at home or in the marketplace."

Griffin rested his chin on the heel of his hand. "You're right, I am sure. So why do I feel so close to Jesu at some times and so far away most others?"

Lilla chose her words carefully. "I believe you revere that building, and rightly so. In it is housed the genius of your father, the spiritual commitment of your godfather, and the happy days of your childhood. Mixed in the mortar that holds it together are all your hopes, dreams, and expectations. It is a part of you, Griffin. That much is easy to tell, for when you speak of the abbey, your eyes shine with the brilliance of your heart. Your voice warms itself like the healing sun of early spring. And those good things make you feel closer to the Creator of all good things, Jesu Himself. But what happens when you leave the abbey?"

Griffin didn't speak right away, for he knew Lilla's question was rhetorical. The evening breeze wandered down through the treetops. Lilla shivered, crossing her arms to let her hands rest on her shoulders. Echoing the tenderness Griffin witnessed each day in Eadric toward Emma, he rose up, his leg stiff in front of him, and retreated into the hut to retrieve the soft blue blanket. Gently he placed it around her shoulders.

They smiled into one another's eyes.

"Better?" he asked.

"So much better, Griffin."

Griffin had never kissed a woman. And just then, he wanted so badly to feel her mouth beneath his. But this desire was new. It could wait.

He cleared his throat and answered the question asked minutes before but remembered as if it had hung in the air only seconds. "I leave God's arms as soon as my foot crosses the threshold of the church. How I long to find His presence somewhere else as well. I've looked for it, you know. In nature, at home, everywhere. I see it in others: you, my father, Brother Adam. You walk in peace. You pass each day in a cathedral of the heart, Lilla. Tell me how to construct one for myself, dear maiden." His voice lowered with emotion, and he felt older than usual and terribly, terribly vulnerable.

"You can have that, Griffin. You can be full with the love of Jesu. And no matter what mankind or the earth we inhabit brings to you, peace is yours and the assurance that God is watching you, guiding you, and loving you."

Griffin turned to Lilla, his face imploring. He took both of her strong hands into his stronger ones. "Give me the tools to chisel away the stone which holds captive my heart. Build for me a scaffold to raise my soul heavenward and look upon the Christ as my own. Show me what it means to love God with all my heart."

"Oh, Griffin," Lilla's voice held an intense excitement. "Simply trust. He is the cornerstone, the foundation of all things. Lay your fears and your emptiness at His feet, and He will fill you with all the riches He has to offer. His power and His graces and the very love that sent Him to the cross will be yours."

"You make it sound so easy, Lilla, to put away the fear, the emptiness. And you are right. It cannot be so difficult, for I've been seeking to do such all my life."

"Then do so, Griffin. I realize you've never been driven to Jesu by loneliness and pain, the way I was—"

"No. I'm driven by desperation."

"Does it matter why we come to God, as long as we do so?" She took his hand.

He turned and gazed at the crucifix on the wall—a symbol he had seen all his life. Yet, Jesu had come down from that cross. There was hope in that—supreme hope.

Griffin had always been old for his years. But on that evening, as the twilight turned to darkness, with Lilla at his side, he became a child again. Lilla prayed, her lips moving silently, and Griffin, his eyes now on the heavens above him, opened his heart unto the Savior, believing finally, without a doubt, that the Christ died for him.

# ❧ TEN ❧

The primeval wood caressed them in windy whispers as they walked hand in hand over the leafy path. Ceaselessly alert and watching for Norman soldiers, Griffin mentally assured himself of several options of escape open with each new vista that spread before him. Just yesterday his very presence had once more attained a precarious footing. This time by the shire-reeve—an ignoble Englishman who exploited the misery of his countrymen for exclusive monetary gain. Griffin, after bathing, was down at the stream drawing water for Lilla when he observed the corpulent man mincing up the pathway to the hut.

His fleshy fist, fat on the toil of shire's inhabitants, rapped on the door. Lilla opened it up expectantly, and Griffin had been a little surprised at the undisguised loathing, the utter scorn which blistered her expression. Her brows almost met in the middle she scowled so.

"What do you want, Egbert?"

She glanced up, spotting Griffin. And with an almost imperceptible nod from side to side, she assured him the hoggish man would render no genuine trouble. He kept himself from view and watched Lilla, just to be sure. Certainly, the shire-reeve was regarded more as a pesky vermin than a dangerous beast of prey. Still, the tolls and taxes he harvested lined the king's purse, and no one dared step too forcefully on the toes of one of the many men responsible for the oppressor's wealth.

"Come to collect the toll, Miss Lilla. For your booth at the market. Didn't make it last week, eh?" With grimy fingernails, he scratched his large belly as he let out a flatulent belch.

"No. I'll be returning next week. You'll get your money then."

The shire-reeve shook his head and sucked noisily at a snippet of the pigeon meat that had annoyingly remained in his teeth since his dinner. "No. No. I'm thinking that you'll do the courtesy and pay me now."

She began to argue. "But—"

Egbert held up a hand to let her know right away he was hearing none of it. "No. No. I'm thinking that King William will not favor his people shirking their responsibilities to the crown."

Her green eyes flashed when the king's name sullied the air. "I suppose he wouldn't, being the illegitimate son of a tanner's daughter."

*Careful, Lilla,* Griffin thought.

But the fat man laughed and sucked some more, not put off at all by her remark. "That may be, miss, but wherever he made his start, he'll die the king of England, so what is past is past. Just don't let the Conqueror hear you mention his humble matronage. Now, now. Go get your toll like a good lass."

Lilla withdrew inside to procure the required coinage. Emblazoned on the front was the customary royal rendering. A metallic portrait of William. The face was clownish and coarse, and had provoked many a scathing jest from the conquered English upon its minting and distribution. Banished from the land were the Saxon faces of Harold and Edward.

The shire-reeve trumpeted in, "And how about a horn of ale while you're up and about, eh?"

"No!" Lilla shouted. "You pilfer enough of my money without depleting my larder as well, Egbert. You should be giving *me* ale!"

Griffin had never heard so many nos in a single conversation. Nevertheless, he had a suspicion that Lilla saw a bit of humor in the situation. And indeed, Egbert, with his overlong legs and short, pumpkin body, was a comical creature. Despite his power and position, he evoked pity in those who knew him. His deathbed would accommodate a rich but lonely man.

Soon the coins were deposited in the man's eager hand, and off he went to harass the next unsuspecting person, anxious to collect the devil's dues. Griffin emerged from the brush.

Lilla shook her head in exasperation. "Egbert is the bane of my existence, the foul fellow! And it is the same with the others. Taxes. Taxes. And always William wants more and more! I hear that castles are springing up in profusion over all England. I am paying for the subjection of myself and my people."

"Aye," Griffin walked in and set down the bucket upon the table. "So many terrible changes to our way of life. And yet, it is always the common man who suffers for the greedy nature of the powerful few. I should be completely discouraged, seeking only to leave England, but I know a king can be good, Lilla. I knew King Edward. He was a kind man and a good king." Griffin was silent for a while after that, remembering with sadness his benevolent godfather.

But now, in the cool woods as he walked next to Lilla, his mind was at peace. To their left, on the other side of the stream, a fawn stood still, waiting patiently for their passage.

"I feel new," Griffin confided to Lilla. "No longer am I the melancholy boy who roamed Thorny Isle."

"You have found Jesu, Griffin. Your happiness is mine."

"I know that. Your face belies all of your thoughts, Lilla." His meaning was evident. And she blushed, adding further credence to his observation. He laughed and pulled her closely against his side, careful not to jeopardize her delicate balance. "And the face that tells me all is the most appealing I've yet to see."

Lilla looked up at him sharply. "Surely not. You are from the city. I hear there are many great beauties in London."

"Perhaps. I never noticed. Not really."

"Why not?"

"You are the first woman I've ever really looked at. And having seen you, I need never see another woman again."

She laughed nervously. "You are young yet, Griffin Eadricson. There is ample time for you to see what beauty really is."

"I've seen more beauty than one lad has a right to view."

"Oh Griffin." She stopped walking and lifted a tender hand to brush a tendril of hair away from his cheek, "I am an old maid. Twenty-three years I've borrowed from God's earth, and since I was nine, you are the only man who has said such knowing that I am crippled."

He was silent, realizing for the first time how Lilla's affliction continued to be just that not only physically, but upon her heart as well.

Deeper into the weald they walked. Slowly. Both had much to ponder as the sounds of the forest, the birds, the stream, the leaves, swashed over them peacefully. Griffin was filled with wonder that such an extraordinary woman could possess a full heart for him. Love was so new. And declaring such feelings was something he knew little about.

Lilla walked along, leaning heavily on her crutch, aware of each step she took. Ungraceful. Irregular. Each week she admired the dancers in the marketplace, whirling gracefully, their legs extended, toes pointed. The way their backs arched and their necks followed the fluid line was as exquisite as a psalm. And she became excruciatingly aware that she would never appear graceful like a swan, or regal and queenlike. She knew Griffin's heart had opened to her. The way his light blue eyes searched her face, looking for her reaction to his words, begged her to deem him of import. Obviously, after what he just said, he realized she cared for him. But did he know she loved him? And could he ever truly love her, scars and all?

She doubted it seriously.

❧ ❧ ❧

Father Andrew awaited their arrival. Soot scurried forward on his wee black legs to greet the priest, who sat at the door with Simon on one leg and Peter on the other. Both animals slept with a feline smile upon their pointy little faces. And when Andrew shooed them off to rise from the bench he had dragged outside, they gazed into his merry eyes with unmistakable effrontery.

"Walking, eh?" he asked the wanderers.

"Yes," Griffin said, approaching. "And just about now that lowly seat appears like unto a king's throne."

"Then sit. I'll get another from inside. Lilla, will you join us?" Andrew invited.

"No thank you, Father. I must needs tend to the garden, or I shall not be eating well come winter, if at all."

She disappeared into the house to change into her old brown gown. And soon she and Soot were situated at the back of the hut where her garden plot was positioned. Her mind was still whirling with Griffin's words. Remembering also what Father Andrew said: *"Griffin requested I come back to make certain you were safe."* A tear escaped her eye.

No one had cared that deeply for years.

"I am indeed placed in a most precarious position, Soot." Unable to kneel in the dirt, she sat on her bottom beside the row of turnips. But she was speaking not of her physical coordinates.

Her voice whispered huskily, full of new emotions. "You see, little one, either way I am doomed for heartache. Even if Griffin truly loves me, which I doubt he does when he has not yet looked upon all of me, he remains an outlaw. His season here is short, and soon he must go. As soon as his leg is healed even a little more, my time with him must end. Danger lurks nearby. And the longer he tarries with me, my little black friend," she reached over and patted the dog's head, "the greater his risk of being captured by the Normans."

Involuntarily she shuddered.

She had heard tales from some of the villagers. Some of the peasants had been killed just because they were Englishmen and their new overlord's son was having a bad day. The Normans were just as cruel to one another, vying for the king's favors, posturing themselves at court at others' expense for more land and more prestige. *They are a violent people*, she thought, *reaping where they have not sowed, gathering where they have not strewed.* She would suffer more herself to spare Griffin's capture by such men.

"And if he does not truly feel a lasting affection for me, my heart is yet his. He will leave eventually, forget Lilla, and I shall be left alone."

But the fact was, and Lilla knew this all too well, that Griffin could not stay. When she recalled his face, the eyes which caressed her when he thought she wasn't looking, the hands which curled naturally around the hilt of his sword, yet slid her curls between their fingers absentmindedly when they conversed in front of the fire, she made a decision. However long he was here, she would love him.

※ ※ ※

The following days their hearts entwined naturally, like vines beautifying a hillside or smoke trailing from a homey hearth. Their hands touched as often as was possible, and more often than necessary. Their eyes met and locked a thousand times a day. And the beating of their hearts was quickened and light, heightening the smallest of tasks, magnifying the simplest of pleasures. Griffin prized her maturity and her strength. Lilla relished Griffin's youthful adoration. To the people of her village she had become a maiden most pathetic—unmarriageable and aging with each daybreak. But beneath the delight-filled gaze of Griffin's blue eyes, she became a woman. Not someone making do with life as it was handed to her.

A decision crystallized the morn Griffin arose from the floor without wincing. Father Andrew pronounced him healed. Outside, the rain pummeled the ruggedly thatched roof of Lilla's hut, the drops rhythmically hypnotizing the animals as they basked before the fire Griffin had kindled upon awakening.

The priest left a while before, having conversed with Griffin privately for quite some time.

"We cannot stay on as we are, Lilla," Griffin said softly but firmly an hour later.

They were perched before the fire. Soot slept by Griffin's feet, and the cats curled around each other near the blaze.

Lilla looked up from the tunic she was sewing for Griffin. Obviously, the monk's robe was useless, and the old garment packed so hastily by Emma before his flight was much too small.

"What mean you?"

"We cannot live here with one another now that I am whole."

"Yes. 'Tis unseemly. But no one knows you are here."

"It matters not. Besides, Father Andrew knows. And he is a man of God."

Lilla set down the garment and clenched her jaw tightly, while her green eyes went all soft. He was saying good-bye. In his gentle way, he was telling her he must go as she always knew he would.

## ELEVEN

T hen you leave in the morning?"

Sudden agitation rendered her flustered. "I must sew more quickly. There's so much to do to prepare. I wanted to gather food for your journey to . . . where? You don't know where you'll go, do you? Oh, so much time I thought I had! Off you're going to battle the Normans, and you've not even a coat of mail or a leather gambeson! What shall happen when another's sword swings your direction?"

"Lilla, hush, my lamb. If you talk any faster, I fear for the both of us!" His eyes were twinkling.

"Oh, Griffin," she could take no more, and the tears fell like the rain outside. "I knew the time would come. But I deluded myself these past few days into thinking it wouldn't."

He held her close to his broad chest. "'Tis true that I must leave eventually. But I had it in mind to put that off for a while."

Her gaze told him she was clearly confused as she pulled away from him. Undaunted, he continued. "I want to be your husband, Lilla. I am young—I know this. But I love you with an ageless affection."

Unable to speak, Lilla's tears flowed more freely. Griffin reached out and took her chin in his hand, fastening her gaze to his. It was brimming with tender devotion. "I realize that what I ask from you is great, Lilla. To be married to an outlaw, our union must remain a secret for your safety even more than my own. That I must leave you is predestined. And our final reunion mayn't occur until years from now when William is driven back to Normandy. But will you love me now? For just a little while. It is all I ask. I love you, Lily."

Lilla's tears dried as his declaration drowned her with its consequence. But he had never seen that which others could not bear to look upon. "Griffin," she began hastily, her strong hand reaching up to slide over his golden hair, "I cannot. I'm not whole and strong. Were I more of a woman, I would marry you gladly and live with you daily, running from the Normans by your side. But you know that is impossible. Love you now, for a little while, you ask? Nay, it is not possible. I can only love you forever. And that love must be from afar. I will not drag you down or hold you to a promise made when you look upon that part of myself which I abhor. I love you so, Griffin. Believe that if you believe nothing else."

Griffin dropped his hand from her chin, then raised it to cradle her cheek. "I will discern whether or not your leg will bother me, Lilla. You look upon yourself through the eyes of the agony you've been forced to bear for 14 long years. I'm sure it is not as horrible to others as you believe it should be."

Lilla shook her head wildly, her voice raised in frustration. "You don't understand, Griffin! When the Norman soldiers came, I could tell advances would be made. It only took a simple lift of my gown a little too high, and I was safe."

"I'm not a Norman, my lamb. I'm an Englishman—an Englishman who looks more deeply than most. Have you ever looked upon yourself, Lilla? You have the grace of a doe, despite your broken limb. Your hands, though strengthened by your craft, move like two doves in flight. Your face rivals the most beautiful rose in King Edward's gardens. But your heart is most lovely. And it is that which I prize most dearly."

"Then you must promise me you'll gaze upon my leg before we marry, Griffin. And know I give you leave to depart tonight and never return. It's what I expect." Her sigh was deeper than Frideswide's well.

Griffin's heart broke. True, they had not known one another for more than a week, but had she the privilege of watching him grow from the stripling boy to an oak of a man, she would have realized her words were unfounded. A more loyal young man existed not in the enslaved kingdom of England. "I shall not look upon it yet, dearest Lilla. You've given me a heart for God and the love of a woman. Because of you I feel a flooding of my soul and a joy in my heart merely by looking into your green eyes. Your leg matters not, my lamb. Trust God, Lilla, and know that when I do look upon it, I shall only love and adore it, because it is part of you. It has made you who you are this day as you sit next to me, strong and capable, a woman of valor and hope. And for that, I love your affliction. Do you agree to my terms then, dear Lilla?"

She nodded, wondering how she had lived for so many years without this wonderful feeling in her breast. The blood pounded in her ears, and the sweetness of his words assaulted her with the force of a battering ram.

Griffin leaned forward, and his lips brushed hers ever so softly. "You may not realize it, my love, but your greatest affliction is your love for me. Our separation will bring you more pain than your leg ever has. And for that, my grief is great. But I cannot stop myself from asking for your love, from giving you myself."

Lilla's eyes opened wide, seeking to reassure him, to let him know she wanted him now and expected nothing from the future. "But I would risk that pain, my Griffin, for a time of ecstasy in your arms. To be your wife for but a season will make worthy each tear shed in your absence."

Griffin's arms encircled his beloved. Did he long to kiss her just then? Yes. But it could wait. Although they had not much time to learn the ways of love, he was content to simply hold her in his arms. It was the first time for it. Many firsts would be theirs before the sun set over the tiny hut.

He wished to savor each one.

❧ ❧ ❧

An hour later, after Griffin had placed more wood upon the fire, Lilla asked him a question. "Will we be married by agreement, or shall we go to the door of the church?"

"'Twill be binding either way I know," Griffin answered. "However, let it be at the church, in the presence of Father Andrew." He looked into the fire, and his eyes became wistful and heavy with a thought Lilla couldn't identify by his expression.

"What is it, my Griffin? What troubles you now?"

"'Tis nothing of import. Always I believed that if I did choose to marry, I should do so at the abbey."

"I'm sure you would have if you weren't marrying a peasant such as myself. Surely, your mother would be upset if she knew you were deigning to marry so far beneath your station."

Griffin nodded. "Beneath my social station, perhaps. But that matters not to me. Besides, I have no social standing now, Lilla. It has been stripped bare since the Conqueror came."

"We are all equal in the sight of God," Lilla said.

Griffin agreed.

"When shall we be married?" Lilla rose to look out the open door.

"Tonight."

"Tonight?"

"Under the cover of dark shall be so much safer."

"'Twould be safer if we merely made an agreement right now and were done with it, Griffin, and so much easier."

Griffin smiled. "'Tis true. But I don't believe for one moment that our life will be easy, do you? Why start off on falsely secure footing?"

Lilla laughed. "I do love you so, Griffin."

"How could I have known that there was a woman waiting just for me? A woman so right, so perfect, and so loving? Truly God is merciful, my lamb."

Griffin smiled into her eyes.

৵৵ ৵৵ ৵৵

Under the cover of nightfall, they journeyed to the church, Griffin leading Bracken and the cart so that Lilla might be comfortable. Neither would forget the vows they made. Vows that could have easily gone unsaid but for Griffin's desire to pledge his body and his love to Lilla before God.

Father Andrew's eyes looked upon Lilla tenderly and almost paternally as Griffin's strong voice repeated the words Father John spoke from his small book.

"I take thee, Lilla, to be my wedded wife . . . to have and to hold, from this day forward . . . for better for worse, for richer for poorer . . . in sickness and in health, till death us depart . . . if holy church it will ordain . . . and thereto I plight thee my troth."

Lilla's throat, nervous and tight, hushed her words to a shaky whisper, but her whole being radiated with the love she bore for this once stranger. It seemed ages ago that she came upon the youth in the monk's robe. Beside her stood a man. A man of great potential. And he loved her as much as she loved him.

"I take thee, Griffin, to be my wedded husband . . . to have and to hold, from this day forward . . .for better for worse . . . for richer for poorer . . . in sickness and in health . . . in bed and at board till death us depart . . . if holy church it will ordain . . . and thereto I plight thee my troth."

Andrew's eyes shone with happiness that one so worthy loved Lilla.

Their love had erupted so quickly, their life together would be fraught with foreseen and unforeseen difficulties, but Andrew knew as Father John married them together that night in the now softly falling rain, that Griffin and Lilla had been meant to be together since time had begun.

His heart ached when he thought of the future.

❦ ❦ ❦

The rain continued falling, and the chill of the May midnight settled upon the land as Griffin lifted Lilla from the cart and carried her in his strong arms to the hut. The pallet still lay in front of the fire, which had burned to a low mass of crimson embers. Griffin crouched in front of it, added more wood, and soon it was dancing brightly in the darkness, providing light by which to see.

Lilla stood with her back to him, pouring homemade blackberry wine into two simple drinking horns. She had been relieved when she had walked in and seen the fire so low, shedding a dim, scarlet light. But when Griffin began to restore the blaze, she held her tongue. Perhaps if she didn't mention that she would rather not let her leg be seen so clearly, he would forget about it.

"Lilla."

She turned to face him, anxiety written upon her green eyes. The shadows eclipsed his face from plain view, but she knew his clear eyes were glittering with anticipation of that which was to come. He stretched forward his hand, his body a dark silhouette against the fire.

"Come to me."

She reached for her walking stick and, with head bowed in shame, she obeyed. Once in front of him, he tilted her head up. His eyes bore into hers. "I could have carried you, my Lilla, but I wanted to watch you come. And I wanted you to realize that your movements are beautiful to me, so very lovely."

"Oh, Griffin," she breathed quickly. "I'm so frightened and ashamed."

"After this night, my lily, you shall never feel shame again."

He knelt in front of her, and in full firelight rolled up the hem of her long tunic. Lilla shook as she stood, realizing that this was the moment she had dreaded since she was old enough to want a life with a man. The woolen material of her gown brushed against her shins as it rose up to her knee. Her face and neck turned to flame as she waited for his rejection. She should have been more wary, she reasoned, bracing herself against the inevitable. But she was in love. Her head was addled over the young stranger, so much so that she couldn't have thought properly when he proposed a life together. The seconds seemed to flow like thick minutes, and time protracted excruciatingly.

Griffin took a deep breath, not worried about repulsion, but feeling deeply for his new wife. Before gazing upon her infirmity, he looked up at her face. She would not meet his eyes, and her expression, for the first time, was stony. And still she waited for him to make a move.

His hand moved slowly forward as his eyes lowered.

"Griffin," she began, her voice finding it hard to speak, but to her surprise she felt the smooth wash of his fingertips as they caressed first her ankle, then her shin, finally her knee. He left no scar untouched, no raised area disregarded. The caress was so gentle, so kind, so compassionate. And devoid of pity. His lips tenderly followed the trail left by his hands. Lilla shuddered.

He looked up again, but before doing so he placed a tender kiss upon her other knee. "So you know I love every part of you."

Lilla still could not look at him. Griffin rose to his feet. He cradled her face in his smooth hands and looked at her intently. "Do you still love me now that I've seen you?" His gaze held all the love she would ever need. And for the first time since they entered the hut, Lilla smiled. "Of course I do."

"Then show me, my lily. Let us learn the ways of love together."

With her own, she covered his hand upon her cheek. Sweetly their mouths met in the purest of earthy passions, as love experienced its first awakenings in a holy way, blessed by God from the beginning of time, from the Garden itself. They reclined together upon Lilla's pallet, spread with a newly woven blanket of crimson, and soon they were lost to the feel, sight, sound, and scent of one another. And as their love was completed, pure and a gift from God to those who love in Him, a gust of wind swept in from the murmuring forest to cool them. Seconds later a nightingale . . . raised his impetuous, sweet song, and the trees ceased their sighing as though pausing to listen in wonder to the little bird's love song.

⋘ ⋘ ⋘

"When you were at the abbey did you ever seriously consider taking the vows?" Lilla asked much later, her head resting upon Griffin's broad, smooth chest. The necklace of his ancestor rested under her fingers.

"Yes. After King Edward died, and his wish with him, I was like a ship which had lost its way in a mist. I knew that I would never be a worthy mason, only succeeding upon my father's name and reputation and not my own skill. And owing most of who I am to my godfather, I felt that to become a fighting man would dishonor his wish for me. For if I could not serve God with my hands, I felt I could serve Him with my heart."

"But your heart was not in that either, was it?"

"No." He ran a caressing hand over and through her tresses. "How could it have been? My heart did not even know the One I sought to serve. So, because of the skirmish at my father's house, I have no way to serve Jesu now."

Lilla raised her head and looked at him in earnest. "But that's not true, husband." *"Husband," how nice.*

"What mean you?"

"God is all-powerful, is He not?"

Griffin nodded.

"Well," she continued, "perhaps He is planning to use you in the way you most desire."

He looked doubtful. "All I have left to me is the sword. How can an outlaw serve our heavenly Father?"

"Did you ever think that you would end up as such?"

"No."

"Was it not circumstances beyond your control which made it so?"

"Presumably."

"Then our sweet Jesu has a purpose in it. Of that I am most certain. You've learned to love Him, Griffin. Now you must learn to trust Him. He brought us together, didn't He?"

Griffin smiled. "Of that I have not one doubt."

"'Tis true then that He will make his purposes known."

Griffin's love and admiration for Lilla, although he would have thought it impossible five minutes earlier, grew tenfold in the nourishing light of her childlike faith. For how could he have known that she had been praying ever long for a brave young man just like her husband? Surely, he had a job to do, and Lilla knew exactly what it was.

# ⫷ TWELVE ⫸

The summer heat was fully established as Father Andrew buckled a hauberk beneath his habit. Cloistered in the ply of his robe, a large knife waited, its bejeweled handle dulled by the darkness therein. He touted a prayer book for all to see. Pulling the cowl up over his head, he closed the door of the church and began to trudge toward the massive fortress on the great hill that overlooked the road to London and the river Thames.

It was a menacing fortress, his destination. And when the horizon dipped and the castle rose from the green landscape, he inhaled sharply, for to him it was beautiful—a commanding spectacle of defensive strength and power throughout centuries. Beam-Dune Maur had dominated this site under one name or another, one people or another, for 2000 years. Originally a "hill fort," the extensive earthworks were erected by ancient Britons. Although their warriors preferred to wage their battles in front of their forts, inside the walls the townspeople were safe from the raiders. First the Romans, then the Saxons, then the Vikings, finally the Normans.

To repulse Saxon intruders, the late Romans had raised up massive stone walls in the fourth century, even as their empire was crumbling. At the twilight of the fifth century, the Saxons made Beam-Dune Maur their own. The ancestors of the late

Lord Uhtred constructed several great, low, timbered halls since that time. Fire had destroyed the first three. And the one which remained was now inhabited by Normans.

The great Roman walls were strung with eight drum-shaped flanking towers. Andrew's destination was one of these very towers. The gatehouse overshadowed him. Built by Lord Uhtred, the late lord of Oxneford, the double entrance, protected by two giant portcullises, was flanked by two semi-circular towers.

Andrew breathed in deeply, letting the fresh air blowing off the Thames nourish his lungs, feeling the air revive every particle of him, down to his fingertips. A guard called down to him in Norman-French. "Well, if it isn't the priest!"

Andrew, proficient in languages and well-educated for a man of his time, called back. "Come to see the prisoner. Will you take me there, or must I see the baron's son first?"

"I'll warrant you must see my master first. Come into the courtyard. I'll take you to him myself."

Through the gatehouse Father Andrew trod. The outdoor kitchens scented the air with the smell of roasting lamb and onions, and a flurry of activity milled about him like a snowstorm. Soldiers tended to their arms. Several smiths called to one another over their bellows as one repaired swords and arms, working side by side with the de Chauliacs' armorer. The others were shoeing horses and fashioning great iron hinges. A bowyer was busy with his craft, and a fletcher was intently making arrows. There were various craftsmen in small huts all around the great timbered hall of Lord Uhtred. Obviously, Baron Stephen de Chauliac was a wealthy lord—fantastically wealthy. Andrew never remembered such a flurry of activity as a child.

But those were merely everyday activities in a castle that must assure its garrisons were well-equipped and ready to quell rebellion of any kind. A macabre reminder to those who would hunt their lord's game or fail to show up to labor on the new stone keep being raised in the southeast corner of the courtyard hung from the prison tower in grim decay. Several Englishmen, wanting only to feed their hungry families, would never provide for them now.

Father Andrew shook his head wearily. One of the victims of the swift and oftentimes cruel Norman justice that hung there was Frithuwulf, a simple churl. Forced to work on the new keep, he had had no time to raise his crops. His capital crime was successfully hunting a pheasant. Inside Andrew, an anger gathered like waters in a tidepool. But he quelled the rush immediately, knowing in all things he must keep his mind cleared of all emotion.

"Wait here," the soldier commanded. And he turned to walk into the hall, his sword bouncing in its scabbard against his thigh as he hastened to his lord. Soon the eldest son of Baron Stephen de Chauliac appeared at the doorway, and with a purposeful, arrogant stride, he came to meet Andrew.

Even in middle age he was a pretty man. His short black hair bore no trace of gray, and it curled in softly around his large brown eyes. Small and straight was his nose, and his mouth, easily twisting itself into a cruel slash when opposed, most often was found by women to be shapely and sensual. There was no better-looking man at court than Odo de Chauliac. And he knew it.

A large man? No. Powerful of body? Yes. A braver warrior, a more fierce fighter was not to be found among William's knights. In battle his sword became as a forged snake, hissing as it sliced quickly and gracefully through the air, almost always making its mark. Skilled in all manner of war Odo was. Ruthless in the ways of life . . . that, too. Extravagant, yes. Cruel . . . sometimes. When the situation at hand was tinted black by desperation.

Andrew studied him as he drew closer. The blue robe Odo had donned earlier that morning fell to the middle of his calves, its neckline embroidered in fine gold and silver thread. His undergown, the tight sleeves of which ended below the wide sleeves of his robe, was of plain, dark gray wool. Andrew scrutinized the garments and knew that the material could not compare to Lilla's. Gray hosen and black brogues completed the costly ensemble.

"Father Andrew!" Odo called pleasantly. It had been a good morning for him. Two more rebels had been hung.

"Father Andrew!" Odo called pleasantly. It had been a good morning for him. Two more rebels had been hung, and the evening before he had exercised his *droit de seigneut* upon a most-fair Saxon wench. Her tears of shame as he handed her back to her new husband were like nectar to him. But the lad had stolen two horses. Of course, it couldn't be proven, but Odo wanted to make certain that the groom or any other Englishman with delusions of a fruitful rebellion would cease their foolishness. He would continue to slam the English into submission. Heaven knew, they asked for such measures by refusing to succumb to the authority of the new regime.

"What is the reason for your visit to Castle Chauliac?"

"I've come to visit the prisoner, to hear his confession."

Odo nodded. "How is the father this morning?" he asked genially as they walked toward the prison tower.

"As ever." Andrew's answer was noncommittal. "And your father, Baron Stephen, has yet to return from Normandy, I presume."

"You are correct. He is busy doing the work of our Lord." His words sounded pious, but his eyes were anything but reverent.

"And when will his church be finished?"

"He hopes to return within six months. Perhaps sooner." Educated in Paris, Odo shrugged like a Frenchman.

Father Andrew said nothing to that. From all accounts, Odo's father was a righteous man who ruled his people with kindness. If he knew of his son's ironfisted ways, he would be furious. Or perhaps he was a parent who chose to ignore his offspring's evident shortcomings.

"The keep progresses." Father Andrew observed the storm of activity.

"Oui, nicely. No timbered halls for us, father. Stone is the only material from which to build. This so-called castle was in grave need of improvement. How Uhtred and his sons could tolerate living in such rudimentary conditions is quite beyond my comprehension. But I suppose even pigs appreciate their sty," he drawled.

Andrew's hands balled into fists. The knife felt good where it sat against his stomach. *Steady, man, steady*, he warned himself, lest all be lost.

"Is all well at your parish?" de Chauliac inquired. He was actually quite generous with the parish, knowing if Baron Stephen showed up sooner than expected, his neglect of their family's ecclesiastical responsibilities in the region would be unpardonable.

"Yes. In fact, it is due to your magnanimous donations that those who work all day on your keep can lay a bit of food upon their table. And the church itself, under good Father John, continues to lay food of a heavenly sort before them as well. With your many sins, my lord, it is a good thing a man like you has much money to give to the church. Perhaps it may buy you a bit of mercy come the day of judgment!"

"Spoken like a true man of God," Odo said, but not without seeing the humor. But he was more concerned about his earthly father's goodwill, than the heavenly Father's. If Stephen de Chauliac decided to disinherit his eldest son, the younger son, Hugh, would be only too happy to step into the position. But then young Hugh, the son of Stephen's second wife, was another matter altogether.

As for Andrew, he experienced no small sense of satisfaction knowing that Odo's money went to finance Englishmen's needs of a different sort. If only the Norman had more to give to the rebellion!

"How fares the prisoner?" Andrew asked as they marched toward the prison tower.

Odo laughed and looked Andrew squarely in the eye, albeit Andrew was a good eight inches taller than de Chauliac. "Leofwine's an Englishman. How good can he possibly be?"

"Is he comfortable?"

"He should be. He's home, is he not? 'Tis a pity Leofwine wouldn't submit to King William. All this might still be his." He swept his hand in a sweeping arc over the Oxfordshire countryside.

Andrew held his tongue.

"I'll leave you now to visit Lord Leofwine. His imprisonment will not last much longer. And I'll tell you why, seeing it is not entirely due to his illness. The raids upon the castle must cease, father. No more cattle lifting. No more ambushes of my hunting parties. No more defiance. If this continues, the matter is simple: Leofwine will die."

It was what Andrew expected.

A guard led him up a spiral staircase and unlocked a heavy wooden door. Father Andrew stepped inside the circular room, and the door was shut behind him. A second later, it was locked from without.

The prisoner was sleeping on a bed of old straw piled in the corner. But when the lock mechanism clanged in place, his eyes opened wide. "Brother?" he asked, trying to sit up.

Andrew hastened quickly across the room. "Stay as you are."

The prisoner's bloodshot eyes were wide. "Does anyone suspect you?"

"No. I am quite safe now. You've been here for over a year and a half. No one suspects a thing."

The prisoner coughed and wiped the blood from his mouth and nose with a soiled rag. Andrew pulled down the meager blanket and examined his older brother's legs. From ankle to calf on his right leg he could see more internal bleeding had taken place since his last visit a week ago. The other leg was worse, and the cough was progressing rapidly as well. It wouldn't be long at all. The man was surely dying.

"Any news of the rebellion?" Andrew's brother asked weakly.

"No. Nothing new. We have to get you out of here. Odo is starting to threaten. I'll not let you die in chains or at his hand."

He shook his head, his white-blond hair skimming his shoulder blades. "It's too dangerous. Besides, my job is done. You are firmly entrenched, with no Norman the wiser. I can die in peace, brother, and with confidence that you will restore Beam-Dune Maur to us. Father would have expected no less."

"Father would have expected us to storm the fortress by now and to have driven the invaders from our shores within two weeks of Hastings!"

"'Tis true. He was a most dynamic man. Being a son of Uhtred wasn't an easy task, was it?"

"No, but it was most rewarding. His was a fierce love, but we never doubted for an instant in its existence."

"So many memories," muttered the dying prisoner. "So many fond memories. It is all my life is now made of. I have not much time until our Lord sends for His servant. And for that I am most grateful."

Andrew held his brother's hand tightly. "You'll not die here, my brother. That I promise you. If I have to kill every Norman soldier garrisoned here first, I shall get you out."

"No. No. You mustn't do that." His ravaged eyes were wide with concern for his brother's safety. "I shall be dead within a month no matter where I am. Be at peace, brother. Jesu has us where we are for a reason."

Pulling out a vial of holy water, Andrew bowed his head and handed it to his brother. "Bless me . . . please."

The prisoner dabbed his thumb into the water and made the sign of the cross upon Andrew's forehead. And placing his two almost-fleshless hands upon his brother's head, he breathed a prayer heavenward. Andrew looked earnestly at his brother, holding back the tears. His older brother sighed. "Go now. I tire."

Andrew leaned forward and kissed his cheek. "I shall. But I shall return. I promise you'll not die alone and in captivity."

Knowing better than to argue with his headstrong brother, the dying man nodded simply and closed his eyes. As Andrew knocked for the guard and was gone, the prisoner raised his hand and promptly fell back asleep.

❧ ❧ ❧

Outside the hut, Griffin rubbed a piece of stone in the summer starlight. Finally, he had a reason to pour his heart into the craft he had been learning since childhood. Two forms were slowly emerging from the single block. One a man, the other a woman. Father would have been proud to see his son and his as-yet-unknown daughter-in-law in effigy.

Griffin himself was surprised. For so long he deemed himself of little talent. But time and patience and desire were proving otherwise. Edward had known all along that he was capable. And father had done what he could to encourage his success. But before now, Griffin hadn't wanted to succeed. Besides, he had a reason for wanting this carving to be beautiful. And he almost dreaded when it should be done. For no anticipation of what he wanted to render next existed within him.

Lilla exited the hut and sat down beside him. She traced her forefinger along the stone personage of her husband. "It's beautiful. But, I must say, I am a bit jealous."

"Why?" Griffin looked at her in surprise.

"When I married you, I thought I was the only artist between us. Now I find I have to share the glory with you!" she laughed.

Griffin joined her. "To be honest, I never knew I could carve such a work."

"It's a wonderful piece!" she encouraged. "You've been working on it diligently now for several weeks."

"I must do something, Lily. Certainly, I'm no help to you at the loom."

152

"No. You're right. But since I've not had to draw water, fetch wood, and tend the garden, I've produced more braid than ever before. So in that way, you've been much help."

"It's nice to know you don't just want me around for your plaything," he smiled.

"Oh yes," she laughed, "there's that, too!"

But when the conversation might have gone whimsical and led to other things, Lilla looked at him solemnly. Her eyes were grave. "Do you trust me?" she asked pointedly.

"You know I do."

"Then we must hasten."

Griffin set down the small statuette. "Why? Where are we going?"

"I can't tell you yet. You shall find out soon enough. Take your sword."

Under the cover of night, they slowly retired into the deep hollows of the forest. Unexpectedly, for Griffin, they ventured upon the ruins of an old Roman villa. The half-moon shone down in eerie strands upon the crumbling structure.

Long ago the red roof tiles of the villa had been stolen by severe winds and rains. Leaves from many autumns littered the rooms, and there was no sign of it having been inhabited for centuries. It was easy to see which rooms were which. Through a narrow, crumbling entrance they entered the atrium. At one time a compluvium would have been present to let in the sun, and the falling rain would have been collected in the impluvium below the opening in the roof. But now the entire dwelling sat beneath the open sky, and the night stars winked as Lilla and Griffin walked through the tablinium, where the owners would have entertained guests. On the floor, in amazingly good condition, was a mosaic of Neptune, the god of fresh water and then of the sea. The paintings of other gods, goddesses, and their activities which adorned the walls had long since perished.

Their final destination was the peristyle. A hooded figure awaited them in the column-lined area, a soft carpet of long grass hiding the bottom of his tunic.

"My lord?" Lilla whispered.

"Yes. It is I. Come closer."

Griffin stood still. His fingers curled round the hilt of his sword, the hair on the back of his neck bristled.

"Do you trust me?" Lilla asked him again.

"Yes."

"Come forward, then. My lord Leofwine will do you no harm."

They walked the remaining ten feet left between them and the cloaked man. In the light of the moon, Griffin could see the warrior's form in front of him.

He removed his cloak. The silver moon glinted off his ring-woven corselet, and a round shield ornamented with a dragon and a bird in flight leaned against his leg.

"Father Andrew?" Griffin gasped and turned to Lilla. "What means this?"

"Sit down upon the grass, Griffin." No longer was the voice which issued from the henna-haired man one of a priest. It was commanding, strong, and Griffin automatically obeyed. "I have much to say to you this night."

Griffin helped Lilla onto the grass and, in the ruin of a civilization extinct, the stonemason's son was told a tale the likes of which he had never heard. Sitting in front of him, back straight, body strung more tightly than a Welsh bow, the rightful lord of Oxneford spoke.

"On October fourteenth I fought at the battle of Hastings."

Griffin leaned forward.

"My father, Lord Uhtred, died beside me, and afterward I was struck unconscious. My faithful servant somehow dragged me into the surrounding forest under the cover of darkness, and for several months we lived as fugitives, mostly here in these parts. After what seemed a short span of time, the de

Chauliacs were given our lands and all our possessions. But Odo wanted more. He was hunting me, making sure that I would not incite rebellion against him and his family. I would have done the same. One day I was walking in Oxneford in disguise when I overheard the conversation of several Norman soldiers. They talked of the capture of Lord Leofwine, how Odo de Chauliac had tracked him down to a small priory near Bath . . . that he was claiming to be a monk. My brother Edmund was thrown into the prison tower at our castle Beam-Dune Maur, where he remains to this day."

"So he is pretending to be you? And is he truly a priest?"

Leofwine nodded. "He realized that if he sacrificed his own freedom, I would be hunted no longer."

"So why do you wear the cowl of a priest?"

"It is the perfect disguise. With the help of Lilla and her dyes, I make my hair red. With a softened voice and gentle gait, I beguile my people into keeping my presence among them a secret. And so, because of Edmund's sacrifice I am able to rally my people—or try to. De Chauliac is a hard master—they fear greatly, and for the most part are unwilling to lift a hand against their oppressor. When they do, they are almost always caught and hung."

"How did you manage to set yourself up at that parish?"

"That was easy. Father John is a loyal Englishman, and knowing I would not be offering communion, hearing confessions, or saying Mass, he willingly aided in disguising my identity. He's an aging man, and could use the help besides. I simply cut my hair, donned a habit, and moved in. No one has asked questions. And those who suspect are smart enough to keep their mouths closed." He went on after a brief pause. "I was educated in the monastery of St. Albans. I knew the right words to say and when to say them. But more than that, Griffin, you must remember that these are my people, and I love them."

"But to impersonate a priest is a grave offense. Is it not?"

"To some, yes. But these are desperate days, Griffin. And I

am not like my brother. The blood of too many men stains my hands, son. I've stopped trying to beg for God's favor or His forgiveness long ago."

Despite Leofwine's words, Griffin thrilled at the events he was just told. The very person who brought him back to health—yea, befriended and protected him—was the true lord of Oxneford. He wondered how he couldn't have seen before that this man before him was a noble lord, a warrior possessed of a hideous strength and a will of granite. "So the humble priest is actually a noble warrior. Why didn't you tell me, Lilla?" He turned to his wife.

"To compromise the identity of my lord could prove disastrous for the rebellion."

Leofwine nodded. "William has been on our shores for far too long. It is time to move forward. I cannot rely on the people around me, living in such great fear as they do, to aid me effectively any longer. I have many plans. Not the least of which is making de Chauliac's life an earthly torment. But there is a more pressing matter at hand. For that, I need your help."

Griffin looked sharply at Lilla. "Is this the purpose you were so certain God had for me?"

"Perhaps." Her expression was solemn.

Griffin straightened up considerably under the assessing gaze of Leofwine. "'Tis true that I cannot be any more wanted than I am right now. Speak, Lord Leofwine. I will listen."

Leofwine laughed, exhibiting shades of Father Andrew for a fleeting moment. "Believe me, lad, you can be more wanted than you are right now. And if you do what I've requested, you'll be more wanted than you can possibly imagine."

In listening to Leofwine's hushed tones, Griffin realized his calling was sure. He would not fail the lord of Oxneford. He would not fail Lilla. Because he felt most comfortable with Edward's sword in his grasp. God had made him thus, and now he finally had seen the reason why.

## THIRTEEN

L eofwine trekked in priestly garb toward Lilla and Griffin's hut. The young outlaw was a godsend, most certainly. Edmund would be rescued and assured of a peaceful death. His only reluctance was that by putting Griffin in danger, Lilla might experience heartache. But Lilla was strong—she'd had to be for so long. And Leofwine was convinced that a wise woman like Lilla would have counted the costs before she agreed to wed the stonemason's son, would have envisioned the possible outcome before she brought him to the villa.

The August morning was warm—uncomfortably so. He breathed in deeply, a warm smile settling on his mouth and in his soul, and called through the open door.

"Greetings, friends!"

Lilla was weaving, and Griffin worked in more detail on his almost-finished carving, utilizing tools procured by the influence of Lord Leofwine.

"Come inside, Father Andrew!" Lilla called, as always being careful to keep his identity safely hidden. Who knew when the soldiers might return or Egbert might come doddering by? Griffin raised his eyebrows conspiratorially, but was grave and ready for instruction when Leofwine joined them at the table.

"Have you broken your fast, Father Andrew?" Lilla asked, breaking off another piece of bread.

Leofwine nodded. "But a bit of bread should prosper me well, fair Lilla. I must garner my strength, and you must provide the same opportunity for your husband."

Griffin leaned forward. "Has the time come?"

"Yes. Tomorrow night."

Griffin arose. "I'll shut the door."

"No. Do not bother, Griffin. We must meet tonight where it is safe to discourse freely."

Lilla's eyes widened, and her pulse raced with excitement and sorrow. "The villa?"

"Yes, the villa. Meet me at the eleventh hour of the evening."

"Will you be alone?" Lilla asked meaningfully.

"No. Ebb shall be with me."

Lilla's eyes brightened, but her look of hope soon was quelled. "No, Lilla." Leofwine's words were stern. "I want Griffin to come alone now that he knows the way."

"Perhaps he is right, my love," Griffin said as he placed his dusty hand upon her arm. "The last time we went you could barely walk for the next three days." He turned to the rightful lord of Oxneford. "Who is Ebb?"

"He's my personal servant. He's been with me for many years. He fought beside me at Hastings."

"The man who dragged you off the field?"

"Yes."

Lilla's words were soft. "He is my brother."

"What?" Griffin turned to her. "You have a brother?"

"We haven't spoken for years. The last time I saw him was when I was nine years old. But we'll talk of him later. Can you bide with us for a time, Father Andrew?"

"No, thank you." Leofwine stood to his feet. "I've said all I've come to say. We shall see you tonight, Griffin. Any second thoughts?"

"No." Griffin didn't have to consider his answer at all. God's hand was clearly evident.

"I should be getting back to the church—there's much to be done today. And Father John has several needs I must attend to as well."

"How do you continue to play the priest, my lord?" asked Griffin, wondering what the holy church would do if it found out. Secretly, he couldn't help but wonder what God thought as well.

"I don't. I assume I'm Edmund, even as he is assuming to be me. In an odd way, it brings me great comfort. Till tonight, then."

He left the hut.

"He's a lonely man," Griffin whispered after Leofwine disappeared down the leafy path.

"Aye, a lonely man."

"Does he have a wife?"

Lilla shook her head. "No, he never married. He fights to win back the lands of his father, yet there is no heir to assume his title once he passes on."

"'Tis strange," Griffin muttered, not understanding the ways of the noble, and not really wanting to.

"Tomorrow will be our last day together, most probably, for quite some time," mourned Lilla. "I shall miss you, my husband. But I believe you are doing what Jesu requires."

"I must leave you, and that pains me. But since it is inevitable, let's spend today not thinking about it."

"Yes. Let's make every minute a moment of heaven." Her green eyes sparkled into his.

"How do you propose we do such a thing?"

"Oh," she grabbed soft handfuls of his hair and pulled his face down to hers, "I'm sure we'll think of one thing or another to occupy the time."

His eyes closed as his lips descended, seeking the sweetness of her own. But Lilla looked at him as his face dipped ever closer, and she fastened the vision of his loveliness into the far corners of her heart. Never to be forgotten. And to be recalled when the nights would become lonely, cold, and strange.

❦ ❦ ❦

A hot August wind flustered the grasses of the peristyle. And Griffin waited. His ears were pricked to intense alertness, and his eyes scoured the darkness around him unceasingly. He was learning the ways of war. Waiting.

Waiting.

For some reason, the abbey and its glory penetrated his thoughts. It had been over three months since Westminster was left behind. Lilla's presence helped, most assuredly, to quell the ache which the remembrance of the church wrought inside him. Yet, still the great monastery called to his heart. And now that he knew the One for whom the illustrious building was built, its whispers plunged more deeply into his soul, bringing with them a yearning he failed to understand. Hadn't this been what he had always wanted? To fight with sword against the enemies of England? He quickly turned his thoughts to other matters.

Without warning, an arm encircled his throat and the blade of a knife pressed itself under his chin. "Don't forget to look behind you, lad. Never forget to look behind you," a soft voice whispered menacingly into his ear.

Leofwine appeared.

"Unhand him, Ebb." Looking at Griffin, Leofwine said, "Ebb could sneak up on the devil himself."

Ebb now stood before Griffin as well. The moon was large, full, and hot, and in its bright golden light Griffin could see he was under scrutiny. He returned the stare. This was his heretofore unknown brother-in-law. And he couldn't have been more unlike his sister. Where Lilla was tall for a woman, Ebb was small. Compact strength he owned. A ferocious fighter, quick as the wind, his stature belied his manliness and the

160

courage of his heart. His black, straight hair grew long and hung down in his face. And his eyes were fiery orbs of brown intensity. He was crafty and cunning. A man of agile mind. Always in control. A more devoted servant had yet to serve his master.

Tortured inwardly he had been for years. Through violence he had sought to expel the demons which haunted him.

Ebb straightened himself, cocked his head, and observed a moment longer before pronouncing his benediction. It was a simple one.

"You'll do."

Griffin said nothing.

"Come sit," invited Leofwine, pulling out a skin of wine. "I've much to tell you, and you'll need to hear each detail, Griffin." He offered some wine to Ebb, who shook his head no. Griffin declined as well.

"Do you know of Hereward the Wake?"

Griffin nodded. "He was banished by King Edward at the wishes of his father years ago. I remember he was thought of as crude, a bit of an upstart, and yet he may be the bravest Saxon warrior of our time."

"Aye. He returned quite some time ago from exile. Much of that time has been spent in Cornwall. But now the north country has called for his military prowess. It is a land ripe for rebellion, Griffin, but 'the Wake' is from the fenlands, and the people of the north will not follow only him. They need a leadership which extends to their hearts as well as their enslaved wills and hungry bellies." He took a sip of wine. "Even as we speak, Waltheof, the earl of Northumberland, son of the great Siward, is imprisoned by the Bastard."

"How so? I thought he had sworn fealty to William."

"He did. But each day that restlessness flowers more openly up north, William the Norman becomes the more uneasy. Waltheof is entertained at court, fed, clothed, housed, and given most everything a man of his stature could possibly need. But he is not to leave William's fortress in London. He is a prisoner, no doubt. But more than that, he is a hostage. For as long as he is in the clutches of the Norman, his people will not do that which William most fears."

"So what must happen?"

"Waltheof must be set free. He must escape William's confines. And once he does, our forces will gain in might and strength under his banner."

"Why are the forces gathering to the north?"

"William has not crushed it under his heel like he has the south. He is erecting many fortresses down here. But his finances, I suppose, have limited his ability for such extensive domination in the north country. Besides, they are a hardened lot, not taken with the idea of submission, and willing to lay their own lives down before they would recognize the Bastard's kingship. And his end is that they do just that."

"So where may I serve, other than by helping to free Edmund?"

"Once Edmund is liberated, you must take him to Northumberland to the castle of Earl Waltheof. He will be welcomed there. Perhaps by the time you arrive, Waltheof will have already made his escape. Such plans have been set in motion, or so I trust. For Waltheof will do all he can to make Edmund's end as easy as possible."

"And after that, I shall stay in Northumberland and offer my services to Earl Waltheof and Hereward the Wake."

Leofwine shrugged his wide shoulders. "That, of course, is your decision."

Ebb stirred.

Griffin breathed deeply. "Yes. I must. As much as my heart belongs to Lilla, I cannot stay hidden forever and without a purpose."

"She will take care of herself," Ebb stated flatly.

Leofwine agreed. "Yes, she will." He paused and drew from his tunic a mellowed patch of parchment. "Now. Let us review the plan for tomorrow night's raid." He unfurled the scroll, and a diagram of Beam-Dune Maur—drawn from Leofwine's memory—was illumined by the moon. As the former lord of Oxneford's explanation commenced, Griffin realized the plan was daring, almost foolhardy—but it just might work. And gazing at his newfound compatriots in rebellion, Griffin readily placed his life in their able, battle-scarred hands.

ぐふ ぐふ ぐふ

Edmund sat up in the corner. He was feeling a trifle better that day. The warmth of summer served to lessen the effects of the cold which had settled in his lungs back in February. Respite was his.

But briefly.

He knew the soon-coming winter, advancing hand in hand with death itself, would surely be his last. He feared for his brother. With each visit, Leofwine had renewed his vow of rescue. Such an attempt was futile, Edmund knew. Yet hope abided somewhere within, though he failed to recognize it.

The door to his cell opened. Leofwine entered, his back slightly bent, his head slightly forward—a posture of submission. Once the door was closed, he hurried to his brother.

His tones were hushed. "You look better today."

"Yes. The summer heat continues to fare me well, Leofwine."

Leofwine looked around, making sure no one was near the door. He whispered so softly Edmund was forced to read his lips. "Tonight you'll be free."

Edmund looked alarmed. His whispered answer was harsh, almost reprimanding. "What? Leofwine, you can't possibly mean—"

"Oh, I do, Edmund. The plan is in place, the right men are prepared."

"Griffin? You've spoken much of the lad."

"Yes."

"He's young, Leofwine. Unskilled and untried in the art of war. This isn't wise!"

"Untried, yes. But not unskilled. He learned much from Simon, the son of Leofric the Fox."

"God rest his soul." Edmund crossed himself.

"Aye, and all who died at Hastings."

"Does Simon live?"

"When the battle turned late in the day, his men were caught in the thick of it. He was believed dead. And although no one I know has seen nor heard of him since that day, Griffin's father swore he saw Simon at the home of Lord Ulfric."

"No one has seen nor heard of you either, brother," Edmund smiled, displaying a row of pleasingly crooked teeth.

"Thanks to you." He placed a hand on Edmund's bony shoulder. "There's something I've been waiting to tell you concerning Griffin, brother."

"What is it?"

"He wears the amulet."

Edmund's eyes widened. "Truly?"

"Aye. When I first came to Lilla's hut to tend to the young man, I saw it. Not certain how he came to be the possessor of it, I didn't want to come to false conclusions. He could have stolen it, for all I knew then. After he healed, I inquired of his parents' lineage. Both are from Bath. His mother never knew her father. The only item she had of his was the necklace. The physical similarities to our family are great as well."

"What is his mother's name, then?"

"Emma."

"After all these years . . . I can hardly believe we've found her. Does he know of his . . . position within our family?"

"No. I wonder if his mother is aware that she is our father's illegitimate daughter? When I asked concerning his grandparents, Griffin said his grandfather died before Emma was even born. He did say, however, that Emma bade him ride for Oxneford the night he killed the Normans. Perhaps she knows more than she will reveal to her son."

"Have you told him he is our nephew?"

"I don't think it is wise for him to know at this time, brother. I believe Griffin to be an upright man, but how can I be sure after only knowing him a few months? This mission I have set out for him will tell me much."

"If only father could be alive right now to see his only grandson."

"Aye, father was beset with locating our half sister, we both knew that—had known it since Mother died."

Edmund sighed. "He seemed to be trying to atone for past sins. And if Emma knows and has hidden it from Griffin, we might do ill to tell him. She may have reasons we could never understand."

"Do you wonder what she looks like, our sister?" Leofwine asked.

"Yes."

"She doesn't sound at all like us. Griffin says his mother is sweet-faced and round."

Edmund laughed at the description, then quickly sobered. "I doubt I shall ever have the opportunity of meeting her. But you must, Leofwine. She is, after all, the daughter of our father."

"Perhaps you shall meet her too, Edmund. After tonight—"

"So you are determined then?"

Leofwine nodded and turned to look his brother in the eye. "Edmund, you're my brother."

The true minister of Jesu put his arm around his brother's strong shoulders. "So be it."

Leofwine rose to leave.

Edmund called to him. "How will I know him when he comes?"

"Oh, you'll know him, Edmund. You'll recognize him as you would recognize your own face."

## FOURTEEN

D awn stood two hours distant. Soon the languishing summer sun would impel the dark shadows of night to flee in the face of its fervent rays. But for now, the minutes which strained before them were ebony-hued. Blacker than a stygian night. Denser than a tomb. The atmosphere compressed about them, tightening around their lungs. Tension. Pressure.

The skiff slid over the somber waters of the Thames toward Beam-Dune Maur. It moved in silence, as quiet and unobtrusive, as dark and unnoticeable as the men whose powerful biceps sliced the oars through the water. Their ears were honed, their eyes severe, their expressions grave, centered.

Still.

Battle gear was strapped to their bodies, each man possessing a shield, sword, and knife. The plan was well-rehearsed, each tactic committed to memory.

All had stained their skin with berry juice, and they appeared as warlike specters, the whites of their eyes contrasting with their blackened skin. Ebb had sharpened their weapons only an hour before. They were ready to do their job—a job of revenge, rebellion, and most ultimately, love.

Leofwine steered the skiff, slowing it against the portion of the fortress walls which had received the watery caresses of the

Thames for centuries. The three men stared at each other for a brief second, and the lord of Oxneford nodded.

The time was now.

Slowly Ebb lowered himself over the side of the skiff. Griffin did the same, feeling the cool waters surround his limbs with a thick wetness. Ebb handed him the other end of the rope he had tied round his own waist.

"Ebb," Leofwine whispered, his voice little more than a mouthing of words, "you remember the way?"

Ebb nodded. He was a man who forgot little.

The disparate men filled their lungs with air and submerged under the inky depths. As Ebb made his way to the drain, his knobby fingers feeling for the opening in the wall, Griffin swam behind, careful not to let go of the rope as they descended further down underneath the roiling river.

Leofwine, certain they would not be coming back up, paddled the skiff further down the river to the corner of the fortress where wall ceased and embankment began. Lithely and without sound, he removed himself from the boat and moored it to a shrub which grew near the wall. Through a dense thicket of alder he walked, oblivious to the branches which brushed his face, neck, and hands. At the base of the nearest drum tower, his fingers felt along the curving wall for that irregular bit of stone shaped almost like a child's hand. This passage had been built during the Viking raids two centuries before. Leofwine's intimate knowledge of his home had made this mission possible. No tunnel, no drainage ditch, no passage was unknown to the man whose family had occupied this castle for centuries.

His breath caught in his chest when his sensitive fingers realized the protrusion. With a gentle push, the stone moved inward and fell on the passage floor. He pushed in the remaining two, low to the ground, and crawled through the small hole on his belly.

He was inside.

❧ ❧ ❧

Griffin thought his lungs would burst. His only attach‑
ment to the world now seemed to be the rope which he had
wrapped several times around his hand. He felt alone in the
thick, watery silence, unable to see so much as Ebb's outline.
The innermost tissue of his lungs burned for air, and when he
thought he must let go of the rope and rise to the surface, he
felt his shoulders brush against a chiseled stone corner. For‑
ward they swam, enclosed now in a tunnel. Still no light reg‑
istered upon his waiting retinas, and Griffin wondered if Ebb
had led them into an abyss—an endless, watery grave.

Ebb continued swimming. Griffin followed—a wildness
assaulting him, his eyes bulging, his lungs convulsing.

Finally, the rope slackened as Ebb's movements ceased.
He was through, his dark head bobbing up to the surface.
Griffin followed, and gratefully they gulped in the ancient air
around them. The stench was horrific, thick and putrid, and
even as he greedily filled his lungs with oxygen, Griffin
quelled the sudden lurch of his stomach. The drain led up
into the very tower they sought. The prison tower. The ver‑
tical shaft was narrow, as dark as the river and the drain
through which they had come—a well which hadn't been
used to draw water for years.

"Hand me the rope," Ebb whispered, his voice an airy echo.

Ebb coiled the woven hemp and attached it to his belt.
After Griffin pulled his blond hair into a cap, the climb
began, Ebb leading the way through the odoriferous shaft.
Griffin didn't know that Ebb had been here the night before,
preparing. Leofwine was a man who left nothing to chance,
and Ebb had learned early that to assuage his lord's fears and
worries made his own life much easier to negotiate.

They worked their way slowly up the shaft, their feet and
hands pressed against the walls, rising out of the abyss. No
light appeared. But after a while he felt Ebb stop. As quietly as

possible, Lilla's brother removed the heavy wooden cover above his head. And Griffin knew the time for waiting would begin. He breathed a prayer for Leofwine, whose task loomed large and dangerous. And even as he prayed, he felt a strength consume him. He sensed that Lilla was at that moment in prayer for their safety before the throne of heaven.

All was at stake for her.

Even as Griffin realized that thought, he vowed he would return to her, and the power that had stored itself in his great muscles since he had lifted his first block of stone was called to attention, ready to uncoil at its master's call.

They entered a room by climbing over the rim of the well. A low torch burned, and visible to their adjusting eyes were implements the like of which Griffin had never seen. Devices which would tear a man's reason from his body. Torturous implements of pain and death littered the blood-stained floor and hung from the walls. Pulleys held ropes which arched through the air like the proud handiwork of a deranged and bloodthirsty arachnid.

❧ ❧ ❧

By faded starlight, Leofwine peered at the expanse of ground before him now within the mammoth courtyard. His feet temporarily declined all movement as in his mind's eye the sun detonated its light onto the fortress that was once his home. He clearly saw the green grass inside the perimeter of the great walls, and the brown dirt trodden low by the many horses and soldiers garrisoned by his father, always ready for the king's summons. The distant sound of a minstrel strummed through his mind, his voice trilling and his fingers plucking as his mother relaxed with her women in the garden. If it had been happening that instant, Leofwine wouldn't have seen it any more clearly. Two white-haired boys on spindly legs raced to their mother, screeching with delight then disappointment as she proclaimed the contest a tie. Father, the Lord Uhtred, marched by with several of his men at arms. Leofwine could still recall in detail the tiny cracks in his leather boots as his feet passed him by.

"Sons!" he called, and they straightened their shoulders and stuck out their chins.

"Father!" Edmund and Leofwine rejoined martially. Just then, Uhtred stopped and walked back toward them. Playfully, he banged their heads together. "Carry on!" his voice boomed. To their mother he gave a rare smile. "You too, ladies!"

How could he have known that he would be so thoroughly dispossessed of his patrimony because of a man whose kingship went against all English law, all royal tradition. A man who crossed the sea from Normandy, usurped the crown by military force, handing out stolen lands freely to those who fought for him, giving large guerdons in gratitude for robbing a people of their country, a nation of its heritage. The de Chauliacs were among those so enriched, believing they deserved his, Leofwine's, inheritance for risking their lives for William. A savage hatred filled Leofwine that was neither Christian nor beneficial, but he felt powerless to stop the empowering feeling. Indeed, he fed upon it, willing revenge to fill his muscles with strength. He would use this hatred, channel it to his arms and legs and into his sword—the sword he now held in his hand as he inched against the wall, lost in the sonorous shadows, toward the timbered hall.

Boldly, he walked into the open door where the de Chauliacs' servants and many soldiers slept on benches if one was lucky, or on the rush-strewn floor. A single torch slanted from the wall. Snores vibrated the air, and for a brief moment Leofwine felt a stirring grief. He had slept many a night upon that floor, having convinced his father that to be a successful soldier he must learn their ways and habits. Uhtred had been only too happy to concede to his son's wishes. He looked around him one last time, and his grief fled. If I cannot abide in this hall here with my people, neither shall the Normans.

A grim satisfaction sidled up next to his regret. Two conflicting emotions. Hand in hand and leading him onward.

Turning on his heel, he stalked to the outdoor kitchen that was so prevalent in all great castles. The fire in the great oven was banked for the night, the coals shining bright-red eyes through the cinders. Grabbing a scoop beside the clay oven, Leofwine reached in and took some fire. Back to the great hall he raced. With a heave of his right arm, he flung the burning coals onto the roof of the hall.

He waited.

The wooden shingles, dry and brittle from the summer heat, caught more quickly than even he expected. Running back to the tower from which he had emerged only minutes before, he quickly disappeared down the steps. A shadow.

"Fire!"

The cry erupted, but Leofwine was back in the boat before a single soldier had issued forth from the sleeping quarters.

Having sneaked past the prison guard, Ebb had seen it all. Upon hearing the cry from outside, the guard leaped to his feet, only to be met by the point of Ebb's knife. His yell was quickly replaced with silence as he crumpled to the stone floor, his hand against his gaping throat. Ebb the Silent stepped over the speedily dying man and raced back down the steps toward Griffin.

"Come quickly," he ordered. "We must move before the fire is brought under control."

Griffin said nothing. His sword was out. He was prepared.

Ebb ran up the circular staircase. The keys were in his swarthy hand, and in one quick motion he thrust the iron implement into the lock and turned. Edmund was on his bare feet, ready with anticipation.

"I'll wait for you at the entrance." And Ebb was gone, ready to kill anyone along the way that he had to. He used the key again, and again, and again. Three more Englishmen were free by the time he was done. He showed them the way to the watery tunnel.

"Bless you, stranger," one said solemnly—an old man—and disappeared down the passage with the others.

Griffin rushed into the room. Sheathed his sword. "Put your arm around my neck," he commanded gently. Edmund complied. It was as Leofwine had said—he was unmistakably descended from the loins of their father, Uhtred.

Griffin swept Edmund into his arms. How light the man was despite his height! They were free from the prison tower and, with his back to the great inner wall, he made his way in shadow to the drum tower through which Leofwine had gained entrance.

ぐ⁂ぐ⁂ぐ⁂

The courtyard was in a state of utter pandemonium as Odo de Chauliac rose from his bed. He rushed to his window in the newly completed stone keep and gazed out. His men hurried to and from the well with buckets of water. To save the hall itself would have been an exercise in futility. They were dousing the stables and other feeble outbuildings with water.

He cursed God for several seconds and watched the activity suddenly with a change of heart. Leofwine Uhtredson would be watching his home burn from the tiny window in his cell. He smiled. But even as he did, another thought entered his active military brain.

"I do not trust the way that fire burns," he said, turning from the window.

"What, mon cherie?" a voice came from the bed. It was not the voice of his wife.

"I shall be back. Elaine, do not move from this room!" he severely commanded the pretty Norman serving girl.

Odo de Chauliac was possessed of a suspicious mind, having an insider's view of how devious mankind can be. This was no doubt the work of the rebels. And long ago he had decided he would extend no mercy to such. There was a reason the people of Oxneford were too frightened to rise up. Even King

173

William trusted him implicitly to extract from various members of the rebellion information regarding the whereabouts of their hideouts and plans. And the room at the bottom of the prison tower had heard the confessions from Englishmen all over the island.

He pulled on his hosen, grabbed his sword, and dashed down the steps to the first floor and out the great doorway.

"You there!" he shouted to one of the soldiers. "Where did it start?"

"The rooftop, sir." He pointed up.

"Carry on!" de Chauliac shouted above the din. He ran toward the prison tower. More than just the Uhtredson was locked inside. This act was surely planned to do more than merely burn the hall.

The leering throat of the jailer greeted him with its gruesome smile. De Chauliac cursed as he raced up the stairs to Edmund's room. It was empty. Quicker than lightning and a thousand times more angry, Odo de Chauliac sped down the stairs and out into the courtyard. He didn't know who to look for, but someone was leaving with his prisoner. In a glance, he saw that the drawbridge was up, the portcullis down. All defenses were as they should be.

Good.

But a movement caught his eye over by one of the towers which flanked the gatehouse. Griffin's cap had worked its way off and, in the shadow of Leofwine's tower, his white hair reflected the firelight.

"Seize them!" Odo screamed, and he started to run. But in the exigency of fighting the fire, the roar of the flames, and the men each shouting to one another, no one noticed their lord running alongside the wall, his sword brandished in the air.

No one but Griffin, having grown up in the din of a rising church.

He turned around, and Ebb, too, saw de Chauliac running toward them.

They were almost at the door.

"Hurry!" Griffin shouted as they entered. "Get Father Edmund down to the skiff. I'll stand against him!"

At the entrance to the passageway, he set down Edmund. The passage was narrow and low. "Can you walk from here?" he asked Leofwine's brother.

"Aye. I can." Courage firmly gripped his heart.

"Come," Ebb held out his hand, "I'll show you the way." Ebb took Edmund's arm and looked at Griffin with a harsh encouragement. "Now's your chance, lad. Fight the Norman, and fight hard. Prove yourself." They disappeared into the darkness as Griffin pulled his shield from behind his back, slid his right arm under the straps, and ran back outside.

Face-to-face with Odo de Chauliac.

Griffin's sword—Edward's sword—slithered from its sheath. A moment later, both hands wrapped firmly around the hilt, Griffin blocked the hacking force of Odo's blade. The fight was hot, hard, and seconds turned to minutes as they battled in the shadows of the wall, moving back, back toward Edmund's tower.

*This child will be dispatched easily,* the seasoned soldier thought with a smirk. He hadn't been involved in a fight for a very long time. He would play with Griffin a bit before burying his sword in the lad's heart.

They circled one another in a dance of death, Odo gaining the advantage, then letting Griffin have his way for a bit. His bare chest heaved with the movements of his arms, and he smiled with delight. More potent than Elaine was a good sword fight.

Suddenly, Griffin realized he was caught in the nobleman's game.

&#8766; &#8766; &#8766;

"We can't wait any longer," Ebb said. "He could be dead by now. Surely Odo will be sending out men."

"We cannot leave without him!" Edmund said.

But Leofwine knew Ebb was right. And he pushed the skiff off the bank and into the water.

## FIFTEEN

With the giant roar heard all too often by Simon and Emma, Griffin pushed forward with his shield, taking Odo off guard and forcing him to the opening of the prison tower. Griffin's sword thrust in and out like a tongue of fire. Odo's did the same.

But Griffin's sword leapt out further and left its mark—a gaping slash upon the cheek of Odo de Chauliac. The rage which won the day in Westminster was not present. Instead, Griffin remembered all Simon had taught him.

The Norman screamed as an anger flared to life inside him with a hellish vengeance. "You'll die, English pig!"

The time for play was gone.

Griffin fought hard, parrying each violent thrust of de Chauliac's blade. They circled round, each seeking footing to his own advantage.

"The stables!" A frantic shout was heard. "The stables are on fire!" Odo's concentration was stolen.

Griffin was halfway down the steps toward the well when he turned back around.

Odo gave pursuit, but it was halfhearted, for he knew this rebel was the least of his worries with the stables ablaze.

Griffin stood on the edge of the well, amid the torturer's devices. He shoved King Edward's sword into its scabbard, held his arms close to his sides, and before Odo's eyes he stepped off, falling down the shaft and into the watery abyss.

"Adieu, Englishman!" Odo called down, his voice echoing off the side of the well. "I promise you you'll be back in this room someday."

But Griffin was already submerged under the waters of the Thames.

❧ ❧ ❧

As dawn broke, footsteps entered the church, and Lilla turned. Leofwine entered. Her smile was one of broad relief, and she put a shaky hand to her hair. "You're back!"

Edmund came next.

She stared at the door expectantly. "Where's Griffin? With Ebb?"

Leofwine came quickly to the front of the church. "Lilla . . ." he began.

"He's dead, isn't he?"

"No. No. He was fighting Odo de Chauliac when Ebb left him. He put himself between Edmund and Odo. It gave Ebb time to get Edmund down the passage."

"Didn't you wait?"

"We waited as long as we could, Lilla. I swear to you. But if we didn't leave soon we wouldn't have gotten Edmund back here before the alarm was sounded."

Lilla said nothing, but all she could think was how unjust it was to sacrifice a healthy man's life for a dying one's. She looked back at Edmund, ashamed of such thoughts, yet unable to stop them. He spoke as if he knew what she was thinking. "I bid them stay, Lilla."

She nodded and turned to Leofwine. "Is there hope, then?"

"There's hope. Griffin can take care of himself. Come, brother, I'll take you to my cell where you may rest before the journey."

Edmund made his way down the aisle and through a side door that led to the priests' quarters.

"Then all I can do is wait for his return," Lilla said to herself and knelt back down to pray.

"Whose return?" Griffin walked into the church, clothes still wet from his swim up the Thames.

"Griffin!" She started to get up, a relieved smile upon her face, but Griffin ran forward and knelt down beside her.

"When a man has a smile such as yours to return to, my Lily, he makes sure he does just that!"

"What happened?"

Griffin shook his head. "I escaped by the same route I entered."

Leofwine walked back into the room. "Thank God, you're all right! What happened, then?"

Griffin explained about the fight, the stables catching fire, Sir Odo's new facial wound. "Where's Edmund?" he asked. "Is he all right?"

"Edmund is back in my cell. Thank you for bringing over the bread and cheese, Lilla. He is in bad need of proper sustenance."

Lilla smiled, her relief evident as Griffin helped her to her feet. "Will he be all right for the journey?"

"Yes. He says he'll make it fine." There was pride in Leofwine's tone. "He did well tonight, didn't he, Griffin?" Griffin nodded. "We couldn't have done it without you, Griffin. He is a strong man, your husband." Leofwine finished the sentence looking at Lilla.

"'Tis true. He can lift me with ease."

Griffin smiled, sweeping her off her feet. "You, my lamb, are as light as Soot." He turned to Leofwine. "I'll be back at sundown."

An air of celebratory relief saturated the atmosphere.

"Edmund will be ready. Ebb found a cart two days ago. All is ready to go. Till sundown, then."

With Lilla still in his arms, Griffin walked back to the hut. She stripped him of his wet garments, laid him on the pallet, and poured him a cup of water. Griffin's exhaustion rose even as did the sun. But love was felt as true and deep as ever and, in the sweet circle of his loving wife's arms, Griffin, home from his very first rebel mission, slept with the innocence of a babe.

❦ ❦ ❦

"Look!" Griffin pointed out the door of the hut.

"What is it?"

"On the poplar tree there. The first change of foliage I've seen this fall."

Lilla smiled. "I remember looking for the first patch of yellow when I was a child."

"Me, too. Then I knew the time was coming when my tunic wouldn't weigh so heavily upon me, and my longing to run about the isle without clothes would leave."

Lilla's chuckle was warm. "I'd like to see that."

Griffin pulled her close, and they walked toward the stream, his arm a steady support. "So many changes, my Lily. Can you bear it?"

"I must. At least I won't be alone."

He agreed with a nod of his blond head. "Yes, Leofwine will be here to protect you. And, of course, there's always Soot for companionship!"

"Somehow, he just isn't enough anymore. I'm afraid you've spoiled me, husband. But I wasn't speaking of Leofwine or Soot. I do believe you've left a little piece of yourself behind. In eight months' time, Griffin, we two shall become three."

Griffin was happy and alarmed at the same time. How would she keep their marriage a secret now? He didn't reveal his reservations to Lilla. He simply pulled her tight against him and kissed her soundly. He would have to place her in the hands of Jesu. "It gives me even more reason to come home often."

Lilla caressed his face. "I was hoping you'd say that. But come into the hut, husband. There's something I must do before you leave."

He carried her back and set her gently down on the bench. "Would you get me my comb, Griffin?"

"Aye." He reached overhead to the shelf that hung on the wall near the table. "What for?"

"Here, sit in front of me."

"On the floor?"

"Yes."

He did so, his back facing her. With nimble, quick fingers she began to run her comb through his thick white hair. A leather strap she used to confine it above his shoulders. Then she braided the silken mass he had washed in the stream a few hours before. Another leather strap tied off the ends grown down almost to his elbows.

"Are you ready?" she asked, reaching for her shears.

He turned his head, his eyes grown so round and so blue she laughed out loud. "Are you about to do what I think you are doing?"

She nodded.

"Why, Lilla?"

In one swift movement she grabbed the braid, wrapped it around his neck, and pulled.

"Cut it off," he commanded.

She did.

❧ ❧ ❧

Above the dense forest burned a gloaming sky. Its sanguine hues faded eastward into a bloodless purple, then a deep, star-speckled blue. Scattered over the riotous, graduated backdrop were ever-changing cloud-scapes traversing the sky like a celestial parade. Inside the church, four people waited for the darkness.

"I told Edmund about your necklace. It is most extraordinary." Leofwine was talking to Griffin.

"Yes," joined Edmund. "May I see it?"

Griffin reached down into the neck of his jerkin and

181

pulled the topaz strewn amulet over his head. "Here." He handed it to Edmund.

Edmund studied it carefully, turning it over and over with a thoughtful expression on his face. He caught his brother's gaze, and a wordless conversation erupted—a thousand words unvoiced in the blink of an eye.

He smiled and passed it back. "It's a wonderful piece," he said genuinely. "You must be careful not to lose it."

"Thank you," said Griffin. "I have no intention of losing it. I shall keep it here," he patted his breast, "next to my heart." He turned to Lilla and whispered softly in her ear, "If only I could keep you there as well, Lily."

They exchanged the secret smile of lovers.

Leofwine cleared his throat. "You'd best be off. I'll get Edmund settled so that you can say your good-byes."

Lilla and Griffin fell into each other's arms. But an uninhibited, passionate parting was not theirs. They simply stood together, feeling one another's closeness. Drinking in the reality of one another. The loving summer had come to a close.

"It's time." Leofwine appeared at the door.

A tender kiss was their good-bye.

The cart rolled forward, with Edmund sitting beside Griffin, who held the reins to a tattered-looking donkey. Through the dark forest it rolled, and although Lilla could not see Griffin turn and wave, she knew that he did just that.

"Well, Lilla," Leofwine said in tones of happiness mixed with grief, "we did it. Edmund is free and on his way to Northumberland. God speed their journey."

"Aye, my lord. God protect them on their way."

As Leofwine pulled his cowl up over his head and entered the church, Soot bounded up beside Lilla. She clicked to Bracken, and the rickety cart started back to the tiny, empty hut.

Tomorrow was market day.

# ❧ Sixteen ❧

The capital of the north rose cold from the ashen marshlands. An ancient city whose walls had welcomed and repelled for centuries, York was sturdy and built to last millennia. It eyed them suspiciously. A wounded child. Grim-faced and bleary in the autumn mists. Undefined.

Under Norman rule, the inhabitants of the city and its surrounding regions had shouldered much suffering which would have transferred a weaker, lesser people into slaves. Nevertheless, York seemed to say by its sonorous silence, that he who would enter in would do well to cast all hope aside.

Already a castle built by the Conqueror rose in its midst. Already the Saxon forces had overtaken it, but not before the fleeing Normans set fire to the wooden palisades and the donjon atop the castle's motte. The overall structure hulked forlornly, attesting to the power of natural elements over a strong will.

The Roman road which led through the forest gave way to the great gate of the exhausted city which stood before them.

To Edmund, fighting . . . fighting each day to live just one more, the haggard town before them was paradise found. Mortal exhaustion had eclipsed his sunny ethos a week before, and the final joint of the two-week journey Edmund made entirely in the back of the cart. Stopping frequently along the way at the whims of the Normans lengthened their travels considerably. But when the Norman soldiers' eyes flickered over the cart's occupant, realizing his condition, most waved them forward hastily enough, crossing themselves in prayer that the sickness was not contagious. A few of hardier constitution sought to further probe by what occasion two men should be found traveling the lonely road north. Griffin well remembered the prayers of his youth during the tense confrontations—words uttered from the heart, not repetitious pleadings. And when perchance his tongue failed to gain them safe passage, his sword did not.

Waltheof had escaped. York was now dominated by the rebel forces. And so the weary travelers were spared the venture further onward to Northumberland.

The arduous, protracted journey was finally over.

From atop the smoke-stained city wall, a man in ring mail called down, his head appearing over the top of the embrasured tower which flanked the left side of the gatehouse.

"State your name and your business."

"Griffin Eadricson, bringing Edmund Uhtredson for sanctuary. I've come to join the English forces."

The man disappeared. Shouts echoed in the street behind and presently, by a mighty crank, the great drawbridge was lowered and the iron portcullis raised, its rope neatly coiling on the massive beam above the passageway inside.

Griffin clicked to the weary little donkey and checked on Edmund. "We've made it, Father Edmund. You're finally safe."

Edmund's eyes closed in relief. For the first time in two years, he felt a true smile of the heart ignite within. And he tried to sit up, but could not for want of strength.

"Be at ease, father," Griffin commanded, his voice firm yet kind. "You shall be out of this cart soon enough. 'Tis sorry I am the journey took as long as it did."

Edmund's smile was truly of good cheer. "You were most brave, Griffin Eadricson. Leofwine would have been proud."

Griffin's attention was then arrested by two men who called him in greeting as the city's defenses once again slowly returned to their secure moorings.

One man was darkly hale, his black hair tumbled robustly to his shoulders, and he was dressed most finely in a tunic the color of wine. Not overly tall, Earl Morkar, Waltheof's brother, stood sturdy, invigoratingly potent, and at home in whatever habitat he would find himself, be it cave or court. His invincible appearance—windblown, yet majestic—bespoke of the wild, yet hauntingly beautiful moorlands in which he had grown to manhood years before. Griffin recognized him immediately as one who had sojourned from time to time southward at the palace of King Edward at Westminster. An admirer of the abbey as well, he often inquired extensively of Eadric of Bath as to the continuing progress of the house of God. And though he never said as much, he admired the brutal strength the royal mason possessed. Morkar was impressed as well by Eadric's artistry, as one who grew among the heather and gorse in bloom would naturally be.

The man striding beside Morkar was tall, his massive frame wired tightly together by knotted muscles. There wasn't a superfluous bit of flesh to be found on this man who stood waiting patiently (except for the tapping of one hand against his thigh) for the cart to halt. His hair, the color of Griffin's, blew about his face in the autumn breeze. Intense eyes—one blue, the other gray, both darker than Griffin's—echoed his stormy past. They missed nothing and were ever vigilant. A practicable, intelligent twist to his mouth assured a ready answer to any military problem. Already a legend in his native countryside, this son of Lady Godiva was Hereward the Wake.

He stepped forward. "Griffin Eadricson, welcome. The Normans didn't pester you too greatly?"

"Only minor skirmishes, my lord," Griffin said, not willing to tell the Wake that ten more Norman soldiers would not oppress another Englishman. Such a number was a pittance to the warriors the Wake had felled in his 29 years of living.

"You've brought Edmund Uhtredson." He leaned closer to Griffin. "How is he?"

"Last winter his lungs nearly breathed their last, but summer proved a respite. The bleeding disease progresses slowly, but it is the coming cold which makes me fear for him the more."

The Wake nodded, his hard eyes softened without apology by sadness. He walked to the cart and sat down on the back. Edmund again tried to rise, but the Wake held up a hand. "Nay, good father. If any man deserves rest, before God, it is you."

"Bless you, Hereward."

The military genius smiled. "It has been overlong since we last met."

"Yes, and now the circumstances upon which we are doing so are most grievous."

"And that dog Leofwine, how does he fare?"

Edmund chuckled despite his weakness. "Physically, he's fine. But in his soul he is weary, Hereward. The people of his realm are not willing to rise up. I fear that he may have to shed his disguise soon and join us here."

"That, my friend, would be most welcomed. A sword arm like that found on your brother is rare, indeed. What of Ebb the Silent—is he still faithful to your brother?"

"Yes. He and Griffin aided Leofwine in my delivery from Beam-Dune Maur."

"Ahh," the Wake's eyes were heavy with fond remembrance. "I remember well your castle. And the daughter of your father's steward, Eva, is she still there?"

Edmund laughed. "Nay. She married a merchant years ago, and off she went to London."

"'Tis a shame," the Wake puffed out his chest, "when she could have had me. But never mind the past. 'Tis glad I am that no woman binds me to herself now that William has come."

"Leofwine and I knew long ago, Hereward, that no woman would have you!"

They stood in the bailey, where tents littered the flat space of ground. Smoke roiled up from braziers in front of the kitchen tents, and over a bonfire a caldron bubbled up some manner of stew or soup. Griffin couldn't tell which it was, but as he had not partaken of a hot, proper meal for two weeks, it didn't matter what it was as long as a portion of it made its way into his empty belly. The rebel soldiers trained in the bailey—some wielding spears, others axes. All shouted to by several commanders, once Harold's thanes, who answered only to the Wake or the earls. Halfway up the motte, in front of the charred, almost nonexistent donjon keep, sat a solitary figure: Earl Waltheof himself. As fair as Hereward and Griffin, but possessing a smaller heart and not as fair a share of wisdom. *He is a figurehead in this campaign,* Griffin thought. He had bowed the knee to William easily enough before, and now had scorned that vow with a disconcerting facility. And yet, when the battle would rage in its bitterest of angers, Waltheof was as fierce a fighter as any man within the compound.

The Wake and Edmund continued to reminisce as Morkar strode toward Griffin, who was gazing at the palisades, mostly consumed by fire, which surrounded the bailey. That he and Waltheof were sired by the same man was the only similarity between the two brothers and seemed to be an almost-surprising coincidence. He held his arms wide. "Griffin Eadricson, the years fall away at the sight of you."

Griffin bowed slightly. "Earl Morkar, it is as you say. Many years have come and gone since I was last afforded the honor of your presence."

"What of your father, Griffin? Now that the Conqueror has come to wreak havoc upon our country, has he fared well? I've thought of him many times and prayed that the only upright tradition of the Bastard's heritage has seen him through these dark days."

"'Tis true they have built more than their needful share of churches in Normandy," Griffin agreed.

"Has he been engaged in the services of William the Norman?"

Griffin shook his head. "Have you not heard, my lord?"

"Heard what?"

"After finishing the abbey, and the subsequent troubled reign of King Harold, he was commissioned to build a fine house for the Lord Ulfric. William did not call him into his service."

Morkar laughed a gritty, sarcastic "hmm." "Certainly, William's loss. It proves we are fighting against a mudlark indeed! Crafty and strong, but a mudlark nonetheless. What is your father working upon now?"

Griffin cleared his throat and became uncomfortable. The Wake walked over, having heard the question. "Did I hear Morkar say your father was the royal stonemason to King Edward?"

"Yes, sir."

"Then are you he who killed five Norman soldiers singlehandedly?"

Griffin nodded but said nothing.

"If the report I heard was accurate, you did them in most handily. And no wonder, after what they did to your father, those sons of the devil!"

"What did they do, son?" asked Morkar, disturbed at the possibility of ill tidings.

"A Norman knight crushed his hands, my lord, with the hilt of his dagger."

Morkar hissed through clenched teeth, controlling a righteous anger. "They shall live to rue the day."

Hereward the Wake slapped Morkar on the back. "No, my friend, there's where you're wrong. They're all dead—every soldier that broke in upon them that night."

"Every one?" Griffin asked. "What of the one who ran for help?"

"He was killed several days later by a band of rebels. It appears the honor of Eadric of Bath was a concern to many. But all that is past. You are here now, Griffin, and we are most happy that you are."

"Thank you, sir. Now tell me please, my lord," he turned to Morkar, "where shall I take Father Edmund? Lord Leofwine instructed me to see firsthand to his comfort."

The Wake turned and walked back over to the cart. Gently, he lifted Edmund from the cart. "He shall stay in my tent. It is the least I can do for my friend Leofwine."

Edmund began to protest, but the Wake would hear none of it.

"I am most grateful, sir," Griffin said, following the Wake and Morkar as they walked past the kitchen tent to Hereward's saffron-colored tent. They were accompanied by the sound of workmen's hammers. A homey, pleasing sound to Griffin.

"We're building barracks," the Wake explained. "October is soon here, and the cold will be upon us."

Griffin only nodded as Hereward bid him pull open the flap to the tent. A small brazier, cold and lit only in the chilly evenings, sat in the middle of the canvas shelter beneath a small vent in the roof. He deposited Edmund upon his own bed and called for one of his men. A soldier appeared seconds later.

"Food and wine for this man," he instructed. "And a sentry is to be posted at the door to his room all hours of the day and night. If he falters yet more, I am to be notified right away. Light the brazier as well."

"Yes, sir."

He turned to Edmund, but the noble monk was already fast asleep.

The Wake turned to Griffin as the stonemason's son covered Edmund with a blanket woven by Lilla. "Find some food for yourself before journeying back to the ravaged south."

"Sir?" Griffin stood straight and tall, his eyes boring firmly into the Wake's.

189

"Speak your mind, son."

"If you would accept my services, I would swear them to you, earls Waltheof and Morkar, and England."

The Wake nodded. "You would be a most welcomed addition to our forces, Griffin Eadricson. Gather yourself a space of turf with the others outside. But first, take that weary donkey to the fold. If we cannot use it for burden-bearing, perhaps his meat will do when winter is upon us." He turned on his heel and, without polity or dismissal, he strode toward the motte and a melancholy Earl Waltheof.

Toward the fold Griffin walked into the autumnal sunshine. As much as the small battle in his home had aged him, the trip north matured Griffin even more. Many of his fears were overcome. He had learned to trust Jesu more fully. Surely, he would give his all for the battered, ragtag army of which he was now part. It had to be so. For Griffin was now possessed of an honor he would have never understood within the walls of a monastery.

It wasn't merely fighting that had made him so. True, the small battles he fought for Edmund's safety had honed him to a sharper, more deadly point. But sitting around the fire in the chill, golden-hued forests at night, discoursing with the saintly man, growing in the knowledge of Jesu, that is what deepened him, made him more like his wife, more like Jesu Himself. Caring for the dying man's needs taught him well that he had been living in a self-serving manner. Others must be considered and served.

And in this he found a surprising joy.

Now, back in some semblance of civilization, Griffin was tired and hungry. But he pushed down those feelings and grabbed the reins of the donkey. King Edward's sword gently bounced in its scabbard against his thigh, and he realized that he was where he had always wanted to be. He was who he always wanted to be. He was a soldier.

And an outlaw.

The abbey loomed large in his mind. And that small whisper of discontent once again was heard. He firmly pushed the feeling aside.

Toward the stable he walked, shoulders back, head proud.

Without warning, a stone the size of a large beetle hit him squarely on the back of the head. And a familiar laugh caused his head to turn.

❧ ❧ ❧

"The rebels of the north have taken York from the Conqueror's men," Leofwine whispered in the confines of Lilla's hut. Two weeks before, Father Andrew had mysteriously disappeared and gone to London for news. The man who stood before her now was back to being fair-haired and dressed as a warrior lord.

"My lord, what will you do?"

"All men are needed. All Englishmen must go to York if they want to destroy William and see the blood of his army dripping from the city walls. The men of the north are united, Lilla. Waltheof escaped over a month ago. Earls Morkar and Edwin are with the forces. The Etheling is there as well!"

"Prince Edgar? But he's so young!"

"As Alfred Etheling's son, he has a blood claim to the throne as well as William. They have taken York—in a bloody battle, I might add—and William will soon be on his way to regain the capital of the north. But from what I hear, however, he has other rebellions to quell along the way. Such is the plan. We must keep him occupied elsewhere while we join with the Danes."

Lilla's heart thudded forcefully in her chest, and alarm claimed her. "Will Griffin be all right?"

"Aye. There has been no activity since the city was taken. I don't know when William will arrive, but there's nothing more I can do here in Oxneford, Lilla. I must get there before William cordons off the town and there is no way in or out."

"Will he set out a siege?" she asked, eyes wide with fear. There wasn't a person alive who had not lived through or heard directly the horrors of a town under siege. The slow starvation, the sickness, the terror of dying by inches.

"I'm not sure. I imagine he will order an all-out attack first."

Lilla clasped her hands together. There was something she had to know. "My lord, did you see Griffin fight Sir Odo?"

"No, but Ebb did for a brief moment."

"Can he wield a sword well? Will he be a noble soldier?"

"Ebb believes so. Griffin has a timing, a sensitivity that one is only born with. And if that should fail him, he is possessed of an incredible strength garnered over his many years building the abbey. Even now the Wake must surely be training him. And I am not unhandy with a sword. I will aid him as well. He will certainly hold his own most competently on the field of battle. As you would tell me, Lilla, trust God."

"Thank you, my lord. 'Tis always so easy to trust in Jesu's care when life strolls before me in dull predictability. But now that each day could lead to sorrow or, most probably, more questions, 'tis not so easy."

"'Tis in the face of the unknown when faith truly becomes faith, and trust becomes more than thankfulness.' Edmund told me that once. I must go. Ebb waits at the villa. Trust in God, Lilla, for both of us," he said again, taking her hand, "and pray that when I see you next the man who stands before you will be the lord of Oxneford once again."

"As God wills," Lilla said, squeezing his hand, her eyes seeking to impart a bit of strength, some encouragement to exist upon during the long journey north. "Take care of my Griffin," she whispered, bestowing a kiss upon the warrior's leathery cheek. "Tell him I fare well and that he need not worry."

His eyes softened. "Your Griffin is indeed most blessed to have you for a wife, Lilla. I will do all I can to watch over him . . . for you."

Then he was gone.

Lilla stared into the future as the forest absorbed him, his form a dark outline against the foliage and then part of the forest itself. Ebb stood far away, drawn to the hut in spite of his refusal to set foot in the little building. In a futile gesture, she lifted her hand and waved to her brother. It was unnoticed or ignored. Lilla didn't know which. Ebb turned without expression and walked away.

She limped to her pallet and shed many tears. Some for Griffin, some for Ebb. Some for Leofwine, and some for England. All, in one way or another, for herself.

## ❧ SEVENTEEN ❧

After Griffin made the journey north, Lilla made a journey of her own. In late September, it happened of an early morn when the mists rising off the stream curled their witchy fingers round the camberous trunks of the ancient oaks that guarded her hut like living pillars.

The sun had just begun to cast a faraway, golden hue on the atmosphere.

Lilla had not yet risen from her pallet when the door shivered under the vicious rap of a gauntleted fist. Not waiting for an inner response, Sir Odo de Chauliac and two of his father's knights stormed into the room.

"Get up!" he commanded forcefully, pulling the blanket off Lilla. Soot barked in high-pitched protectiveness but was ignored.

"What is the meaning of this?" she cried as the morning chill skittered across her flesh. Reaching out, she snatched the blanket from his grasp. A fire danced in Lilla's green eyes. De Chauliac noted it with pleasure.

"Do you know who I am?" he asked, proudly pacing in front of her, hands clasped behind his back. Lilla, noting the raised purple scar upon his face, newly healed, knew the answer, but did not say so.

"No?" He pulled her quickly and easily to her feet. "I am Sir Odo de Chauliac, the master of Castle Chauliac."

"For now," Lilla retorted. "Until your father, Baron Stephen, returns."

"Ah, so you are well acquainted with your new lords?"

"How can I not be, sir, when the broken bodies of my people swing in chains from your towers?"

His eyes flashed tempestuously, brown storms kindled with lightning. "If you learn not to hold your tongue, woman, you will find that fates much worse can await someone so fair. There are many lonely men within my garrison, and they are not as giving as myself." The tempest left as quickly as it had come, and he looked down to examine his meticulously clean fingernails.

"What do you want of me?" Her green eyes looked at him straight on as his anger faded and he took control of his emotions.

He walked over to the shelf which held her skeins of thread and cloth. "These."

"Take them, then. They're yours."

He laughed a humorless "Ha!" "Of course they are mine." He swept an arm around the room and walked back to her side. "All of this is mine. You are mine."

Lilla winced. "No, my lord."

His smile was disarming. "We shall see about that, pretty madam. I'm sure you led Griffin Eadricson on a merry chase before you lured him into your bed."

Lilla said nothing.

"Surprised at what I know? Don't be. The prisoners that escaped along with Edmund were captured easily enough the next day. One exchanged the whereabouts of your husband's domicile for his own life. He told all that he knew, and now he abides once again with his wife and child. A free man."

"How magnanimous of you. But I'm sure Egbert had a thing or two to say as well," she surmised dryly.

Odo de Chauliac raised his brows. "Ah, yes. Surprising, isn't it, how a flabby buffoon such as Egbert can round up many bearers of supposedly secret information? Apparently, you weren't as careful as you should have been. No matter. Now you must come with me. Back to the castle."

Lilla grew afraid, raising her chin in feminine defiance and looking lovelier to the aggressive knight than she would ever have wished to appear. "Why can I not weave from here, my lord? Of what possible advantage to you will my presence have?"

"Your husband, my enemy, will return to you. I want to make it that much more difficult for him, and that much easier for me."

"Does your new scar burn that much, my lord, that you now live to get revenge on a 19-year-old?"

"Revenge?" Odo began to laugh. "Oh, my dear woman, you English do bring everything down to a personal level, don't you? The scar means nothing more than the discomfort it brings, which will fade in time even if the mark does not. I seek the Griffin purely for political reasons—to learn the whereabouts of the rebels, to find out their next move. This mark means nothing when compared to the crushing of this godforsaken people. King William will know that I, Odo de Chauliac, am most loyal, and that, unlike my father, I support the merciless domination of an inferior nation."

"Griffin would never reveal the secrets of the rebellion."

"No? Then you are as naive as you are fair, madam. Griffin will talk, as surely as the dead cowards who revealed your presence to me. Pain opens wide the mouths of fools."

Lilla said nothing. It was useless to argue, anyway.

"Gather your belongings, Lilla. My men will use the utmost of care when transporting them. And you will find that Castle Chauliac—it is Beam-Dune Maur no longer—is not without its creature comforts. You will be well looked after. I shall see to it personally."

"That, my lord, is what I am afraid of." She limped to the table to get her cane, but Odo, taken aback by her infirmity,

197

hurried on ahead and handed it to her. "Here," he held it out. "I would offer you my arm, but I sincerely doubt that you would accept a kind gesture on my part." Clearly, with a limp like that, she wouldn't be a real threat. But it proved her to be a survivor. Like myself, he thought.

Lilla snatched the stick away from him. "I must warn you, my lord, I can but favor you with my weaving. My leg keeps me from other laboring."

A softness shone in his brown eyes, a grudging admiration. "Did you think that would make any difference, madam? What you look like from the knee down matters not when your eyes shine with that queer, green beauty." De Chauliac lifted a gloved hand to her face. "I am not a less-principled man than your lover. Your injury will be taken into account, madam, and you shall not be asked to do that which you are unable."

Odo de Chauliac turned on his heel and barked orders officiously. "Men! Gather the loom, the yarn, all her belongings and bring them to the castle!"

"What of my animals, sir?" she asked.

"What of them?"

"May I take them to Father John to keep in his care?"

"You may bring them with you if you'd like. Your imprisonment may be lonely without them. The pony will stay in the courtyard, as will the dog. But you may keep your cats with you in your room." His face assumed a look of distaste. "I shall expect you in no more than two hours. Your room will be prepared for you. And do not attempt to flee before then. Robert here," he pointed to a younger knight, "will accompany you back to Castle Chauliac."

Lilla lifted her chin. "So, I am to be your prisoner?"

"Most certainly. Merely by being in my keep you will create a nest for the Griffin—a nest to which he will surely fly home soon."

❧ ❧ ❧

Sweat covered muscle. Grunts peppered the air. And steel rang against steel.

Griffin had never fought so hard, so long, or so well.

"By the gates of heaven, man!" the Wake yelled, advancing toward Griffin with a wildly swinging ax. "You've the strength of ten men!"

Griffin parried, and the shafts of the ax handles came together in an ex between them. Each pushed against the other.

"But I've the strength of 15!" the Wake shouted triumphantly as he shoved mightily with a giant growl. Griffin was on his backside in the dust.

An instant later, a hand was held down to him. Griffin took it and was pulled to his feet by Hereward. "One day, son. One day you will prevail against me."

"Never, my lord."

The Wake shrugged. "You are young yet. But you are your father's son. Even I was impressed at the weighty blocks of stone Eadric of Bath could lift. You've inherited his strength, and it will grow even as your body reaches its final stages of maturity."

Griffin breathed in and out heavily, his breath forming soft clouds of steam in the cold air of the forest. Only he and the Wake were present in the clearing. Hereward walked to his horse and pulled down a skin of water. "Here."

Griffin drank. Hereward threw his gambeson to him, discarded as the training had become heavier. "This, too."

The stonemason's son donned the quilted leather garment.

"Let's go! The day is young, and our task lies heavy before us."

"My lord?" Griffin's blue eyes were dulled by the gray sky.

"We've a lady to rescue."

"Who?"

"The Lady Aethelwine. Her father was the thane just north of here. The Normans have taken over his holdings. She marries on the morrow to a man she loathes." Jumping onto his horse, he motioned for Griffin to mount the other.

"Who is she marrying?" Griffin asked as they began the journey northward, galloping into the brisk wind which barreled down from the Humber.

"It doesn't matter. He is old and cruel. And Norman. Aethelwine was always kind to me at court, despite the fact that berating me was the popular mode of the day."

"I see. Where will we take her?"

"Scotland. She has relatives there. But we won't be journeying with her. It is merely our job to free her from the confines of the castle."

Griffin smiled, and Hereward looked at him sharply. "You find this amusing?"

"Oh no, my lord, not amusing. I just never thought I would end up an expert in freeing prisoners."

ംഃ ംഃ ംഃ

Lilla had never before experienced such luxury. Already five new kirtles and undergowns hung in her room. Each one embroidered with silken thread. A sheer wimple covered her curly hair and was held in place with a gold circlet. At first she protested when the fine garments were brought to her, refusing to don them. Odo threatened to put them on her himself if she dared argue further. It seemed but a small concession when compared to her virtue, and she grudgingly complied. How she prayed each night for Griffin to set her free from this ivory tower.

In the southwest tower of the keep, the large room which had housed her for almost two months now was circular. Two windows—one looking over the river, the other affording a view of the bailey—punctuated the walls. Over the stone walls hung several parti-colored tapestries. Fanciful works of art, sporting maidens, unicorns, dragons, and lions. Even a prince bowed chivalrously amid the silken threads. The tablet loom sat upon a table, and her supplies were organized on a shelf above it. Her bed was simple yet delicately carved of maple wood, and over its feather mattress lay a deep-blue coverlet. At night, however, Lilla preferred to warm herself with her own blankets. On the deep sill of one window, Simon and

Peter lay sleeping in a shaft of sunlight which shone through an opening too narrow for even a child to pass through.

Daylight hours inched slowly by. No longer did she weave the fine woolen cloth. Her time was filled by creating intricate braid for Odo de Chauliac himself. *How many tunics can one man need?* she asked herself each day, knowing that he sought only to keep her occupied. Fine as her handiwork was, it couldn't compare to the rich silk embroidery or the bejeweled trims she had seen him in before he went down the hall to sup each evening. And yet, her imagination was sparked by the expensive, rich threads he obtained for her use. She had never woven a finer braid before coming to the castle.

Having her animals nearby proved to be the only food for the heart of which Lilla partook. Each day she saved a crust of bread or a bit of cheese from her breakfast and her luncheon. The sharp whistle she always employed when calling for her canine companion would sound from her window after each meal. And Soot would come running! A little black shadow racing across the courtyard from the stables.

"Soot!" she cried, when he grew close, his tail wagging furiously. "Catch!"

From the window the bites of food would fly, one after the other, Soot racing toward the arching culinary projectile. Lilla would laugh at his leaps and turns, clapping her hands in delight when the tiny terrier would actually somersault in the air. It became a daily pleasure for all the workmen and soldiers to watch the two, though separated by proverbial prison bars, play and banter with one another.

"Go, Soot, go!" The craftsmen, cooks, and even a soldier or two would shout their encouragement, having peeked out of their tents upon hearing the loud whistle that came from between Lilla's lips. And when, perchance, the little tike would catch a morsel before it fell to the ground, a hearty cheer would erupt. 'That's the way, boy! There you are!'"

Most afternoons and each evening her noble jailer, Odo de Chauliac himself, visited her on the pretense of inspecting her work. The appointments were characterized by stiff, stilting conversation. Pleasant interrogations they were—nothing more than Lilla answering Odo's bounteous questions with a severe verbal frugality. This day in late November was no exception.

"I see we are busily going about our day," he chimed as he let himself in with a key. For her sake, he was speaking a very stilted English. And if she didn't resent him so greatly, she would have found much amusement in his mispronunciations and unorthodox word choices.

"Yes."

He bent over her and examined her workmanship. "I thought I had seen all the beauties the world has to offer, and yet, here in Oxneford of all places, an artist lay hidden in the woods."

"My lord, the embroidery on your tunic is many times more fine."

"Not so!" he argued. "Yours has a freedom and a quality that is so . . . so . . . ." With a graceful gesture of his hand, he fought hard for the right word, but owned no victory thereby. So he chose another mode of description. "It is a dance. A wild, joyous dance of pattern and color. Anyone can learn to embroider flowers, birds, and such nonsense, but you have a very rare ability, indeed."

Lilla dropped her eyes at his effusive compliments and resumed weaving. Nevertheless, she was pleased that the subtle nuances of her work were appreciated and duly noted.

Odo leaned against a massive blanket chest underneath a window. He crossed his arms over his chest. "And how do you feel?"

"What mean you?" Was her pregnancy becoming noticeable?

"You look a bit pale, Lilla. Would you be of a mind for some fresh air?"

The wind blew in cool gusts around the castle, but truly he could have offered her nothing she would have liked more. "Yes, sir, I would."

"Good." In his hand he held a black mantle. He put it around her shoulders. "I shall escort you myself."

Lilla made no response as he placed the fine cloak around her shoulders, his fingertips lingering a bit longer than was necessary upon her neck. It was easy to see how such a charming reputation among the female members of William's court was so obviously earned. Shutters of warmth and caring he snugly closed over eyes that were naturally hardened and unforgiving. Every move of his head, each wink of the eye was carefully calculated. He was a purposeful man, not given to excesses of diet or unsporting varieties of recreation. Keeping an iron control upon any debased propensities, save a pretty wench now and again, only his love for clothing caused other nobles to regard him frivolous. This, too, was a calculated move on de Chauliac's part. He could prove to be a formidable adversary with no one the wiser. And none of his sworn enemies lived to tell who was responsible for their demise. He was an invisible player at the games of court—invisible, strong, and altogether deadly.

They walked down the stairs, de Chauliac aiding Lilla's descent. "Am I correct in assuming all your needs are well taken care of?" he asked in that solicitous manner.

"Yes. All needs except for my freedom. My lord," she placed a hand upon his arm, "this confinement pains my heart. Please let me serve you from my home."

Her eyes pleaded up into his, and de Chauliac felt his darkened heart tumble. He quickly pushed the foreign feeling aside. "If your only purpose was to weave, madam, I would certainly extend to you your freedom. But not only do I seek the Griffin, you aided Leofwine Uhtredson in the escape of his brother as well. For such a crime my punishment is gentle. For such a crime most would not be left alive to weather another winter." The mild wind off the Thames blew the curls around his well-formed head as they stepped outside. And in his eyes Lilla beheld a spark that caused a shiver to snake its way out of her spine and down through her appendages.

Turning away from him to look about, she whistled sharply. Soot ran across the courtyard at the sight and scent of her and bounded happily into her arms. Pressing her face into his dark fur, she kissed his little wet nose, then looked up, refusing to set the little fellow down. Before her eyes a world of humming activity unrolled. Interesting it was to take in all the happenings she had come to know well these past months from this lower, closer vantage point.

Bracken was tied up near the kitchen tent, grazing on what little grass there was. But the scene which interested her the most was the great wooden vat in which two people stamped down their feet in a quick, heavy-footed dance of seeming aggravation. They weren't aggravated in mind, however—just in body. Their conversation ebbed and fell as they spoke the trivialities of castle servitude.

They were fullers.

Lilla watched as a length of undyed cloth was pummeled beneath their feet. Such forceful agitation would expand the thread and soften it, so making the fabric more suitable for wear by a nobleman—or any other person, for that matter.

Abruptly, they stemmed the tide of their conversation when they noticed her staring at them with great interest. That she was with Sir Odo, and walking with a stick, told them who she was. Assuredly, the tale of her abduction had been the main topic of conversation for a week following her arrival. Bets were cast as to who was really the prisoner—Odo or Lilla. Some resented an Englishwoman's presence in the new keep, being clothed so beautifully, bathed so regularly, fed so well. She was a source of extra work in the eyes of the maid-servants, but to the menservants, soldiers, and even Baron Stephen's knights, she was clearly an enchantress. How else could she have convinced Sir Odo to lavish her—a prisoner and the wife of an outlaw—with such luxuries? Would their master succeed in bringing the outlaw to heel, the rebellion to a halt?

Of course.

And if they knew their master, he would win the heart of the rebel's woman to seal the bargain with aplomb. There was no doubt it would be so. For though they thought Lilla an enchantress of sorts, they knew Sir Odo possessed his own magical charm. Tougher sorts than the Englishwoman had been beguiled by Odo de Chauliac. And as they resumed their toil, they smiled secretly to one another and resumed their talk of matters simple.

Lilla took note of their expressions.

"I'd like to go in," Lilla said as the sound of the portcullis being raised in the gatehouse reached her ears. A handsome carriage, drawn by two chestnut horses, rolled into the bailey. Digging the end of her cane into the loamy soil of the courtyard, Lilla, seeking the anonymity of the keep, turned. At that moment, de Chauliac turned in the opposite direction, and they collided. Her leg buckled beneath her, but Odo, nothing if not showily chivalrous, scooped Lilla into his powerful arms. Soot hopped to the ground but stayed nearby. Odo smiled a grin of secret origins that Lilla failed to see from her vantage point.

The carriage halted as he began walking toward the keep.

Lilla strained against his arms. "Please put me down, my lord."

De Chauliac said nothing and kept walking.

"Odo!"

A feminine voice called from the direction of the carriage. It was a voice that expected nothing and everything all at the same time. A voice of bitter wine that was oddly capable of quenching the thirst if one was only allowed a sip.

"Odo!" A bit more forceful this time. He sighed heavily, angrily, but checked his rubicund temper as he turned. And when he did, Lilla saw a woman whose exquisite beauty was so rare, so perfect, Lilla forgot to even compare herself. Which may have been a good thing. For although Lilla had an earthy, rustic beauty, she couldn't begin to compare to the refined, cool beauty of the woman alighting from the carriage.

She was possessed of a royal demeanor with a crown of honey-colored hair hanging in braids down to her calves. The ends were tied with golden twine, and bejeweled ribbons wandered through the thick plaits. A fine wimple fluttered delicately about cheeks which were peachy-pink and unravaged by pock scars or blemishes. Indeed, the velvet skin appeared to have never felt in full the harsh rays of the noonday sun. Deep blue were her eyes, reminiscent of larkspur, yet infinitely more beautiful in their round, wide stare. Her mouth, full and red, was the only feature which belied the seemingly tranquil air she sought to give herself as she hurried over to her husband.

Even as she felt a shiver, Lilla's cheeks burned from Ida's stare, which held just the right amount of disdain, just the right amount of indifference.

"Odo, time has indeed moved along quite remarkably. It appears, once again," she looked meaningfully at Lilla, and looked at her no more, "you forgot that I was arriving from Normandy. No matter. I assume my room is prepared?"

"Your room is ready and waiting, madame." He bowed as best he could. Lilla's mortification was heightened. Failing to understand what was being said, she realized, nevertheless, by the looks which passed between the two Normans that they were man and wife.

Ida breezed forward and was halfway up the stairs to the keep when she turned back around. Her eyes were a frozen river, and the beautiful face measurably hardened. "It would be appreciated that while I am in residence you restrain from parading with your slattern in front of the people. As for me, you can sequester yourself with her all you want, but I will not be scoffed by the servants. I hope I've made myself clear."

Although Lilla had no idea what was being said, the final frigid glare in her direction gave a clear indication.

"Utterly, madame." De Chauliac bowed again. "How long did you say you were staying?" he asked in a most smooth voice, keeping Lilla close against him.

"As long as it takes to make your life miserable. Has Hugh returned?" Ida spoke of Odo's younger brother.

"Not yet."

"And Sylvia . . . will he bring that insipid little wife with him?"

"Yes. Naturally. Wherever he goes . . . she follows."

"Imagine that," Ida's tone was sarcastic. She turned on her softly slippered heel and disappeared, a flutter of blue silk and velvet, through the massive doorway. But her face peered back through, and she smiled with an acrid sweetness. "Your cheek, my lord, most becomes the man I know you to be." And she was finally gone.

De Chauliac set Lilla down immediately at the foot of the steps. And suddenly, it became clear. "So, my lord, I see you could not bear for her to think that you are bedding a less-than-perfect woman."

"Ida is perfection enough for all here at Castle Chauliac," he said dryly. "I have no wish to speak of my wife again. She is no concern of yours—or of mine, for that matter. And she isn't half the woman you are, Lilla."

"As you wish." Lilla bowed her head. "But in the long run it matters not to me what a castle full of Normans believes me to be. I know the truth, as do you. You will never approach me in a way befitting a trollop."

"Madam, if I wanted you in those regards, I would never have to resort to force."

"Perhaps where Norman women are concerned you need only soft words and heavy wine, but I'm an Englishwoman, and when I give my heart, I give it for life. Force would be the only way you would ever have me, my lord."

De Chauliac smiled his odd smile, and his brows raised as though a revelation had come upon him. "Most commendable. But now it is time to go back to your room."

As she gathered her skirts, Lilla hoped as well that Ida would leave soon. It would be foolish not to realize that de Chauliac remembered exactly that his wife was coming that day. Perhaps the lookout had warned him of her approach. Why else would he take her down to the courtyard—a courtesy extended without precedent?

"Lilla, just so you know, I've never needed wine to beguile a woman."

"How silly of me to suggest it, my lord."

Nevertheless, she sighed as she painfully started up the steps with the baron's son behind her.

"Let me carry you," Odo said.

But Lilla held up an impatient hand, refusing his offer.

Into the circular room she was led, and when the lock slammed in place on the outside of her door, Lilla's relief was profound. True, she could not leave. But inside her little room she was not alone. All she needed presently was there: Jesu, recalling the Scriptures her uncle had so faithfully taught her, and memory's sweet rendering of her beloved's face. She fell on her bed in fervent prayer, feeling the heavy, heady weight of communion with the Holy Spirit descend upon her head and shoulders.

"I will never leave you, nor forsake you."

The words resonated inside her heart as a pain shifted through her lower abdomen and blood rolled down her inner thigh.

# ⚜ EIGHTEEN ⚜

The wind, pauperized of the scent of blooming heather and golden gorse by mid-autumn frost, blew in linear gusts off the moors. Slow was the going to York as Leofwine and Ebb forsook the highway—an ancient Roman road which led first to Lincoln and then on to York. As Griffin had done before them, they avoided the scrupulous Norman soldiers when possible, and fought only when absolutely necessary. They much preferred to lead them on a merry chase through the dense forest. Near Nottingham they came close to being gibbetfare, but nature had graciously taken them into her leafy bosom, cradling them in a dark, small cave.

York stood before Leofwine. A friendly city, this one. An English-hearted town, with brave-hearted men willing to forsake hearth and family for the only thing a man could ever truly call his own: his freedom.

Leofwine's heart accelerated its faithful rhythm as the sentry shouted down the expected inquiry. Afraid he was not of being welcomed. Afraid he was of what he might find. Or, in this case, whom he might not find. Leofwine wanted only to look upon his brother once more. And if the God whom Edmund served was as kind as he claimed, his brother would still be living. But Leofwine trusted Him not.

❧ ❧ ❧

"My God, my God, why hast Thou forsaken me?" Burning tears of vacancy flowed as Lilla lay spent and pale upon her bed. Three hours previously her pregnancy had become a shading of the past, and the wee babe which was perfect in form with perfect fingers and perfect toes now rested in the Thames, wrapped in a length of silk.

Her tear ducts seemed to be finally desiccated of all they once held, and her eyes no longer held tears but merely a glassy stare.

"I was pregnant, and now I'm not."

It was such a simple statement, but within was permanently inscribed a hollow, futile yearning, a feeling of premature cessation that only women who miscarry can know. Her now-dry eyes screwed shut against the agony of incompletion. The torture of the only tie to her husband in the bleak solitude of her imprisonment was suddenly gone, never to return. She would never know the tiny boy-child who fit entirely into the palm of her blood-stained hand. Would never hear his cry, see him smile, or one day feel his chubby, soft baby arms hug her neck.

Lilla knew miscarriage was a natural thing, a work of God. And as some women can do, she took a small, grudging comfort in the sovereign love of Jesu. For He knew so much more than she did what the future held. But even such thoughts could only come about through intense concentration, for all she really wanted to do was scream out, "Why?"

*Surely God could have prevented this! Why did I become pregnant at all if this was to be the outcome?*

She felt abandoned by Him whom her soul loved greatest.

The tears came again.

For two more hours, wrenching sobs wracked Lilla's body and rung their knells of an earthly passing. Untimely. Permanent. What would he have looked like? Would he have loved her devotedly? What kind of a man would he have made?

Futile questions. All futile. But asked nevertheless. And she knew that in two years time, four years, five, eight, twenty, she would picture that child in her mind as he would have been had she been given the privilege to raise him, love him. Love him? Nay, she already did that, though she had been just on the verge of feeling his tiny limbs move within her body. Love that child she would. For the rest of her life. She would never forget, and at the most odd times of the day would she recall that she had mothered another child, for four brief months, who was with the Father in heaven. One brief moment, when a tiny heart stopped, would affect the rest of her life.

Perhaps someday the pain would fade down to a small, fond ache for what might have been. But until then, she would remember the blood, the fear, and the sudden barrenness of her womb. Empty. Always the blood. The blood.

Lilla embraced the pain that filled her from womb to heart, turning her organs heavy and sodden with grief. The pain was all she now had left to remind her of Griffin.

It was all she had.

The walls of her prison room were no substitute for life, love, and happiness. And the peace which she had come to take for granted had flowed out of her with the waters of her pregnancy, the blood of her womb.

*Why?*

God had always seemed so just, so benevolent. Even in the death of her parents she had never questioned His care. Now the room was empty, gray, and cold. Griffin was gone. So was the child. And what of herself . . . gone, too? And for just how long would she be forced to suffer in silence, alone and without even an ear to hear her cries of disillusionment?

Anger bolstered her suddenly. At God. At Griffin. At the black hearts of men who conquered and killed. She threw off the covers, limped to the window, and pulled back the hide. A brisk breeze, conceived in shadow, ushered itself into her darkened room and over her naked, blood-stained body. It dulled her emotions, bequeathing strength.

Finally, shrouded by a fresh tunic, Lilla called for hot water. By the time her supper was brought around at eight o'clock that evening, the room was just as it had been. The only thing that had changed was Lilla.

c⅌∾ c⅌∾ c⅌∾

Edmund lingered yet.

His form was skeletal, and the consuming disease which was devouring his mortality promised him a fair field and no favor in his battle with bodily dissolution. Griffin bided with the dying priest, who now was kept tonsured, clean-shaven, and robed in the black habit of his order. It was actually Griffin's robe, which Lilla had so thoughtfully laundered and mended and sent with them on the journey north.

Griffin gently dabbed at the blood which slowly trickled from Edmund's nostrils and mouth. They had tried many treatments for this incurable disease which sickened Edmund's blood, but they were of no help. The gentle man was nearing the end.

Edmund was glad of it.

He looked upon Griffin, his eyes the overbright, glossy eyes of the dying. Though considerably weakened, with barely the strength to raise his arm, he nevertheless reached out and placed a pale, bony hand over Griffin's rosy, youthful one. The startling resemblance that Leofwine had seen between Griffin and Edmund was completely gone. Yet, it was comforting to Edmund to look upon Griffin and remember what manner of man he had once been, would be again in the kingdom of heaven.

"How much longer?" he whispered, swallowing the cough which threatened to erupt. "Do you think Leofwine will come?"

"Aye, father. I do. Jesu will not bid you leave us until you may do so in the arms of your brother."

"Soon . . . he must come soon. For most truthfully, my son, I am ready to go on, to meet Him whom my soul loves greatly. Would that I could go now."

Griffin smiled gently and added more wood to the brazier. "And meet Him you shall, Father Edmund. Of that I have no doubt. It will be so much better for you when the new buildings are finished. A tent isn't the choicest of lodgings for a man in your condition."

"I'm grateful for it," Edmund contradicted him. "Leofwine realized how important it is to die a free man. It doesn't matter where the dying is done."

Just then the tent flap shivered, and it was pulled quickly aside. Leofwine filled the opening.

"You're alive!" He was overwhelmed with joy.

Edmund smiled weakly. "You came."

He hurried over to the pallet. "Of course I did."

"The Normans terrorize England, Leofwine. And yet, we prayed, didn't we, Griffin?"

Griffin nodded and backed away from the bed.

"'Tis true, Edmund. But I am here."

"Yes. And now I may depart."

Leofwine's heart shattered. He wanted to protest. But indeed he could not. His brother had wasted away so. His great misery was evident. Jesu would be most kind to welcome him into His loving arms before the cold settled more firmly into Edmund's lungs.

"Yes, my brother," he whispered, holding Edmund's hand in his own, ready to ease him into the mysterious journey which man has made since time's beginning. "I will not leave your side. We will watch for Jesu together."

"You must rest, Leofwine. Take a little food."

Griffin, who was still standing by the door, spoke up decisively. "I shall fetch some victuals and a pallet for the floor."

"Thank you, Griffin."

Half an hour later, after notifying the Wake of Leofwine's arrival, Griffin appeared carrying a wooden trencher laden with roasted meat, cheese, bread, and a large beaker of mead. He set it quietly down upon the wooden table. A pallet was brought in and laid next to the bed. Leofwine would have no use for it. The stool upon which he sat would cradle him well enough for the death vigil. Still holding Edmund's fragile hand, Leofwine watched his now-sleeping brother, his brows knit in concentration. He turned his head toward Griffin.

"Thank you, Griffin."

Griffin bowed slightly. "It was an honor, my lord."

He walked around to the other side of Edmund's bed, and with a tender hand he touched his friend and confessor's cheek for the last time. Leaning forward, he kissed the noble brow good-bye. Both knew that when morning would grace the skies, Edmund would be gone.

It was just as they thought.

When the moon hung low, Leofwine felt the sudden stillness.

He crossed his brother's hands over the silent chest. "The Lord giveth and the Lord taketh away," he whispered the words, knowing Edmund would have been pleased by them. "Blessed be the name of the Lord."

ir Odo de Chauliac slipped into Lilla's room. The scrape of his slippered feet on the floor caused her to sit up in bed with a start. She grabbed the covers around her, forming a soft, ineffective defense.

"What are you doing here?"

She wanted to stand up, get out of the bed, but when she moved her legs, they felt watery and weak from the blood loss she had experienced earlier that day. Simon and Peter lay next to her, seeking her warmth and imparting their own.

"Your maid told me you seemed unwell." He held the candle close to her face. "Indeed, you are paler than death, Lilla. Something is amiss."

Lilla forced down the tears so well that Odo saw not one trace of her grief. "'Tis merely my cycle, my lord." She dropped her eyes in mock embarrassment.

"Ah, so the Griffin has not left you a part of him, eh? Surely, I thought you were carrying a child. You had that look about you."

"You are mistaken. I carry no child." Suddenly removed, she felt as though she were a spectator of the conversation at hand. Some other Lilla was saying the words. Someone who bore no pain, no anger. Someone complete.

"'Tis a pity."

"My lord?"

"Well, certainly if your husband thought you were carrying, he would seek even harder an avenue of rescue."

Lilla laughed harshly through the gloom. "Thank you, sir. For a brief moment I thought you actually possessed a heart."

"Ha! That was destroyed long ago."

"No doubt. But 'tis a pity you don't have a child or two. Perhaps your life would be more than warring and dressing well."

Odo became silent, brooding in a past time that Lilla knew nothing about. The room was cold, and the light from his singular candle did little to cheer the chill darkness.

"I'm sorry, my lord." Certainly she didn't wish to experience the dark side of him which lay just beneath the surface—the side which slaughtered those who thwarted his plans, stifled his ambitions. "I did not mean to upset you. Of course you would want a child and an heir."

He looked up, eyes clear again, and shrugged. "What man doesn't? But, as you see, I've survived. Something, I can easily see, you know much about."

Lilla shifted her position in the bed and winced.

Odo noticed. "I fear your exercise in the courtyard might have aggravated your injury further."

"Oh no. My infirmity is not recent."

"Let me see it. I want to make sure you need no further care."

Her face burned. "Sir Odo . . ." She hesitated, wondering if this wicked day held any more foul surprises. No verses of Scripture came to mind just then.

"I order you to, Lilla."

She shoved the covers from over her leg and hid her embarrassment behind an angry facade. "There!"

Holding the candle close to her leg, Odo de Chauliac's face remained impassive as his brown eyes examined the calf. "Hmm. I've seen many battles, and my body does not bear such a mark." He traced his index finger along the hideous scar.

"Thank Jesu then." She pulled the covers back over with a snap.

He looked up quickly. "It pains you still?"

"Aye. Some days 'tis worse than others. But I've learned to live with it and try not to dwell on it."

"And your husband—he doesn't mind?"

"Mind? No. He cherishes it, adores it because it has made me who I am."

Odo realized then that his enemy was far from a fool, far from a child. He sat back on his stool. "It's very true that what pains us forms us into who we are. I used to be a happy, almost contented man . . . until Ida came into my life."

Lilla found that hard to believe. But she was glad to get the conversation's topic off herself. "How long ago were you married?"

"Ten years."

"And no sons?"

"Oh yes. Plenty of sons, but none by Ida."

Lilla looked down at her hands. "I see."

Odo chuckled. "No, you don't. You don't see in the least."

"Then perhaps you wish to enlighten me," she suggested, interested in knowing further her adversary.

"You saw Ida. She is chillier than the channel during midwinter. Our marriage, of course, was arranged. On our wedding night, I entered the chamber, and she sat upon the bed, still in her bridal clothing."

"Was she frightened?"

"Frightened? Ida? Not in the least! She had nothing to be frightened of, leastwise me. Especially in those days, Lilla. I thought her beautiful, and though I was in no wise an innocent schoolboy, I believed Ida and I could be as happy as we wanted to be."

"A noble outlook. What happened?"

"She told me as she sat there, still in her finery, that our marriage was a farce, that she went through with it only because her father threatened to lock her up if she didn't. She would never bear me sons or daughters. It would be a marriage in name only."

"Did she love another?"

"Ida wouldn't say. The only information she divulged was that I sickened her and that I always had."

"Did you know each other for a long time then?"

"Yes. But not well. Our fathers visited each other once or twice a year. That sort of thing. Anyway, I couldn't bring myself to take her then, or anytime after. She's a frivolous, silly woman who was given everything she wanted by her parents."

"So . . . you sought love elsewhere?"

"Ah, you do see." His smile was disarming. "There have been many women, both peasant and noble, who were only too happy to lure me into their bed."

"And your children—do you care for them?"

"No. I will not pretend I use women for anything other than playthings. There is one child, however, whom I have watched growing from afar. I care for her financially, anonymously so. And visit the village in disguise. At least I did when I was in Normandy. If her mother found out where the moneys came from, she would be constantly asking for more."

"A girl? You are attached to a girl-child?" Lilla was surprised.

"Yes. Marie is one whose way will be rough in the world. She has always been a sickly child, but her eyes . . . they're much like yours, Lilla. They sparkle with life, and it's easy to see, though she's only eight, that her happiness is found within, not from the performances or gifts of others. She is a pure soul."

Lilla looked down. She didn't feel like a pure soul just then.

"And you cherish that?" she asked.

He nodded. "Funny, isn't it? I know I'm a cruel man, Lilla."

"That's obvious," Lilla replied bitterly, but Odo grabbed her hand, her implications not lost on him. The conversation changed instantly.

"The peasants have to die, Lilla." His cruel words were unspeakably gentle, and the candlelight distorted his comely features. "That is the way of a conqueror and a conquered people. It's about power and wealth. Two things peasants have no understanding of."

"And yet they are the pawns in the wicked game of the rulers," she said knowingly.

"Yes. It is the innocent who always suffer, isn't it?"

"I dislike that things should be that way."

"But they are, and have been since Cain killed Abel. As I've said before, Lilla, I am a survivor. I was born to a high position and am afforded not the luxury of a simple life, a simple outlook on myself or those around me. And so I seek to raise myself ever higher. It's the way of things. The only way I know."

"What of your father?"

"He's so wealthy his power is laid out for him, more sturdy than a Roman road. And he is strong enough to maintain it. Whereas I . . . I still have my way to make in the world. And make it I will, no matter how it must be done."

Lilla pulled her arm out of his gentle grasp. "Do you enjoy the killing?" she asked harshly, refusing to look at him.

"Enjoy it? Hmm," he looked thoughtfully at the hide-covered window. "No . . . no." He nodded from side to side. "No. I don't receive the kind of enjoyment you speak of. It's a necessary evil, that is all."

"So you do admit 'tis evil to treat people in such a way?"

"Yes. I'm a man of many sins, but hypocrisy isn't among them. It is an evil, to be sure. But I do it, anyway. My world is not like yours, Lilla. Only the strongest survive and live to play the game another day." He got up to restore the fire, crouching down and placing more wood carefully upon the glowing embers. The cats jumped down, interested in the prospect of a blazing fire. "It's not about battling the weather or the elements. It's dealing with crafty, sly men who would rather pierce your heart with their dagger than have you gain the pre-eminence. And if I oppress the English to gain favor with my king, so be it."

"But what do you have to gain personally from your actions, other than William's favor?"

Odo turned around and looked at her in utter disbelief. Norman women were duplicitous, self-serving—at least the ones he knew. How could this simple peasant not inherently know that a wise king never took the loyalty of his subjects for granted? That loyalty was a luxury, bought at a high price—high enough to maintain a throne. "William has been handing out large guerdons to many who fought at Hastings. I fought well and hard for my king, Lilla. And yet he delivers not on his promise of land and title. If he sees that I am most loyal to his purposes, I will receive my guerdon and be out from under the heel of my father, once and for all."

"But you will not receive all the wealth of the de Chauliacs upon his death, sir?"

"Yes. But I am 40 years old and my father is 60. He's strong and will be going for another 20 years, if I had to guess."

Lilla shook her head sadly. "'Tis not in me to understand how you can justify taking a man from his family forever, leaving little ones to be fed this winter and no one to hunt."

Odo de Chauliac, satisfied with the now-blazing fire, resumed his seat beside the bed.

"I know you don't, Lilla. And it is that innocence of heart which draws me to you in a way even I don't understand, much like I am drawn to little Marie. But as far as my treatment of the English, Lilla, you must understand the ways of men. When a man deliberately enters my forests, he knows that he may be caught. He knows that it is he who is responsible for feeding his family ultimately. And when he sets foot inside the boundaries of my preserve, he knowingly commits an act of war, of rebellion."

Her eyes filled with rage. "By seeking to feed his family? You kept them working on this cursed keep from sunrise to sunset. They had no time to work their land! You came into our villages and picked and chose the strongest men, even the not-so-strong! Your men have killed entire families and have stopped at nothing to make our lives a hell beyond description! And you do this all for a guerdon?"

"I do it because I am a man. It was the same with Leofwine. He refused to bow the knee to William. The king waited two weeks at Pevensey to be recognized, to give the English the opportunity to choose a merciful domination. They came not, and chose the wrath of Normandy instead. Leofwine refused to bow, to relinquish his power . . . at the expense of his people. He knew what manner of man William was. But he did what he had to do as a man. He wanted his life to be on his own terms, not a foreign conqueror's. So much so that he let his own sickly brother take his imprisonment for him so that he could find a way to regain his patrimony. It was the same with Elfwine who hunted a pheasant in my woods—he did what he had to do as a man. What power he did have, he used. He said, 'I'll make my own way, de Chauliac be cursed.' It is what we all say to ourselves at many points in our lives: 'I shall make my way.' And I shall. On my own, without father's help. On . . . my . . . own."

"It doesn't matter how cruel you are in the process?"

"No."

The word hung on the air, simply put and enigmatic to Lilla.

"You don't understand, do you?" he asked.

She shook her head.

Odo stared at her, his expression suddenly placid. "I'm glad you don't."

He rose to his feet and gently pulled the blanket up to Lilla's chin. "I hope you never change, Lilla."

"Then set me free," she pleaded.

"I cannot." He turned and went to the door, opening it and looking back one last time, brown eyes deep and almost sad.

"I cannot."

The door closed, and the bolt was thrown into place.

৵৵ ৵৵ ৵৵

The funeral for Brother Edmund Uhtredson took place under a leaden sky. A light, keen drizzle spattered the faces of all who watched the wooden coffin as it was lowered into a grave dug within the burned palisades. Edmund's body would decay in the bailey of the castle William the Conqueror had built two years previous—the castle the northern forces destroyed only months before. But the city walls still stood firm. And so did Edmund. Unseen and living eternally, firm in his commitment, rewarded for believing.

The chaplain of the resistance, a fighting monk, read aloud passages in Latin chosen by Leofwine. Edmund's favorites. Leofwine stood erect and lordly, Griffin's presence beside him a secretly bolstering force. The Wake, earls Edwin, Morkar, and Waltheof attended, heads bowed respectfully for the brother of Leofwine.

Without explanation, Griffin experienced an emptiness he couldn't have foreseen. A part of himself was being buried. He knew that more surely than most of life's continuous puzzles. But why he felt that way, he couldn't say. He thought perhaps the past two months in Edmund's faithful presence was the explanation. During that period, all his spare time was spent at the priest's side. A great love and a deep respect were inlaid in his heart. Pieces of Edmund, living on within him.

Words of remembrance filled him. Edmund's words. *Jesu never promised that our lives would ever be more than toil and personal heartache, but He promised to bear our burdens, Griffin.*

*Trust in the Lord with all thine heart, and lean not unto thine own understanding. He'll direct your paths, my son, even when the way before you extends itself in the vaguest of mists, the darkest of nights. It is in those times that we rely upon His direction the most, and it is in those times that we feel we cannot see Him through the deep storms of night.*

*Father Edmund, God bless you!* Griffin inwardly rejoiced. And he wondered afresh at God's mercy in allow-
ing him to care for the needs of a man whose service to
Jesu was willing and joyous—a man he would forever remember as the one who showed him the path to maturity,
both spiritual and terrestrial. He gazed upon the set face of
Leofwine. The lord of Oxneford's hair was now back to its
blond shading, cropped short. And Griffin grieved for the
tortured man even as his soul soared with Edmund's.
Edmund—the rightful heir, the older brother. The man
who had forsaken wealth and power to serve God alone, to
gain heavenly riches and an incorruptible fortune which
does not fade.

Despite Leofwine's presence, Griffin felt alone.

Lilla's arms, soft yet strong, called to him. How lovely a
place to lay his sorrowful head would be her bosom. And to
feel her fingers comforting him as they caressed his face and
hair would be all that he as a man could have asked for at that
moment.

But the Conqueror would not ignore York forever.

And Griffin knew he could not return to his wife anytime soon.

Hereward the Wake laid a hand upon his shoulder.
"Come, Griffin, we must hasten. We're raiding tonight."

"Who?"

"The Count de Brisbois is traveling close by. He's a rich
man. Our coffers are lower than makes me comfortable."

"All right."

Griffin ran back to the barracks, pulled on a new corselet
of Norman chain mail procured on a raid a month ago. Simon
was readying himself as well.

"You going, too?"

"Aye," the dark-headed man answered as he buckled his
scabbard around his waist. "I thought surely you'd be staying
back tonight . . . with Father Edmund and all."

"Perhaps the Wake knows what a man needs most when his grieving is most sore."

Simon nodded and strapped his ax to his back. "Let's go."

# ❧ TWENTY ❧

For days Lilla sat at the window of her room, over the cold river, heartworn and weary, feeling as if stomped on by the fullers' flat, heavy feet. But like the fabric she wove, the pressure of tribulation was strengthening her faith, enlarging her heart, and deepening her understanding of Jesu's way with His people. And her fuller was God Himself, knowing how soft, strong, and more beautiful she would become under the pounding of divine feet. The anger was beginning to recede, but the deep feelings of loss pointedly remained.

Mealtimes were still the apex of her day, when Soot would come running, delivering with his very presence a portion of her naive past. It made her recall the faith she once knew in the haven of the forest. And she realized that her hut and the trees which surrounded it weren't the only places accessible to God. Even the stronghold of Castle Chauliac was unable to keep Him at bay. Lilla's simple heart, so unlike her husband's, gave way easily to the will of the Lord God. And while she would never understand the loss she had borne, she would simply trust that it was all for the best. She hoped that she would one day have the privilege of knowing why.

The clinking of the raising portcullis stole her attention away from the courtyard where Soot hopped around, seeking more goodies. Soldiers snapped to attention. The garrison commander came running forward. And a line of servants queued up the steps of the keep. Lilla wondered whose arrival demanded such an uproar at the castle. She leaned forward on the sill, aiming for a better look at the occupants of the carriage which had just stopped. The door was pulled open by a servant, with a bow, a scrape, and an overabundance of pomp.

A foot appeared from the open door. A surprising foot at that, Lilla thought.

It was a fine foot to be sure, adorned with a pair of brown leather brogues. Expensive . . . yes. Frivolous . . . no. They were sensible shoes, Lilla decided, cut from the best, most supple, most durable leather, and bought not to go with the saffron hosen and olive-green tunic which next appeared, but to serve their owner in comfort for the next three years, maybe longer.

The garrison commander stepped forward and held out his hand. A thin, tanned, yet masculine one took the outstretched hand of help. It was loose-skinned with age, the fleshy covering too large for the shrinking muscles underneath, much like a pillow whose stuffing has hardened and shrunk, leaving the cover to meander its folds only so far around its innards. The finely dressed man wore a signet ring upon his forefinger, but no other jewelry—at least on that hand. And when his head finally appeared, it was obvious the man was almost completely bald. The fringe of hair around the sides and back of his head provided a sparse covering for, despite its thinness, it was shorn extremely short in the style so common to the Normans. The man's nose was quite large, but it was a friendly, approachable, calm sort, devoid of sharp edges. And though his lips were thin, they warmed to a smile of gratitude for the commander's help. Deep lines creased around a mouth accustomed to smiling, and a rich brown mole on his cheek, quite large, was pushed further back in time with the grin. His was a life inflated by hardships. He handled them with strength and moral fortitude for the sake of his family, shouldering them with courtesy and humor for his own.

When Ida came running down the stairs to curtsy deeply and kiss the ring of the distinguished gentleman, Lilla knew he could be none other than Baron Stephen de Chauliac, the new lord of Oxneford, courtier and thane to William the Conqueror, and of noble, ancient blood. Despite the fact that he appeared so cordial, so kind, so gentle, Lilla tasted the bitter essence of resentment as she remembered her dear lord and friend, Leofwine. So what if Stephen had dug deeply into his overflowing coffers to build 80 longboats for William's landing at Pevensey? What did it matter that his son Odo de Chauliac had fought with skill and bravery, cleaving many an Englishman through from shoulder to breastbone? This fortress, standing since Roman hands placed one stone atop another, did not belong to the de Chauliacs. It was Leofwine's! And it should have always been handed down to the ancestors of Uhtred, the lord of Oxneford.

Yet, in her heart she admired a man of Stephen's means choosing such stout shoes.

Two more people appeared after the baron—both as clear of countenance and as open of expression as the man who preceded them from the lavish vehicle. The man was on the small side, and thin like his brother. But that is where Hugh de Chauliac's similarities to Odo halted. Odo's curly hair was brown—Hugh's was a wiry, boisterous red. He kept it quite short, but no matter how hard he sought to conform the wayward locks to his wishes, the top stuck up like several impudent flames. His skin was as fair as Griffin's, but his cheeks were covered in freckles—much to his chagrin and his wife's amusement. However, Hugh wouldn't relinquish the sport of falconry and the exposure to the sun it demanded just to bridle the brown spots which danced over his face. And his eyes were magnificent. The deep, long slits of his lids could not hide the brilliant blue shielded therein. Even though the day was overcast, his eyes were still the amazing color of a clear summer lake. His clothes were much like those of his father, though darker in color. They were expensive, yet practical. With a smile of true delight, he helped down Sylvia, his bride of four years.

Sylvia de Chauliac had been born to laugh.

When Hugh reached for the small, plump raven-haired young lady's hand, her heel caught in the hem of her gown. Out of the carriage she tumbled and into his waiting arms. For a brief moment tension stirred through all who stood in attendance upon the small entourage, but when Sylvia's laugh rang out, bouncing against the outer palisades and the great keep, Lilla could hear an audible sigh of relief. And that humorous laugh—so gay, clear, and filled with fun, even at its owner's expense—unexpectedly warmed Lilla's heart.

The young couple disappeared into the keep, following the baron, and for the first time since she had been locked into her gilt cage, Lilla yearned to see what was going on down in the great hall.

৵৵ ৵৵ ৵৵

Odo de Chauliac let himself into her room a half hour later. "Did you watch their arrival?"

"Yes. But you weren't there."

His eyes were shuttered again, like the day he came for her in the woods. "No. There were more pressing matters which needed my attention."

Lilla shrugged. "Your father seemed as if he was a good enough man—for a Norman, that is."

Odo seemed unaffected by her statement. The Normans were in England to stay, and the sooner these English realized that fact, the happier everyone would be. Let them talk all they liked, for William would quell them all.

Lilla pursued the topic. "From everything I've heard about your father, it can be said he is a righteous man. Why, then, did he feel justified in supporting William's expedition?"

Odo sighed. "Lilla, possibly there's much you don't know about the affairs of England before we came. It wasn't just a matter of William saying, 'I'd like to be king of England.'"

"What then?"

"King Edward had named William as his heir years ago. Your King Harold was sent over by Edward to swear fealty to William. That was long before Edward's death."

"Truly?"

"Yes."

"Then how did Harold attain the throne?" Her eyes were wide.

"He coerced a change of bequeathal from Edward's lips. On the king's deathbed, no less."

"But surely Edward wouldn't have agreed . . ."

"He was dying, Lilla. Some who were close to him said he was out of his mind the last couple of days."

"Still," she reasoned stubbornly, "once Harold was king, it should have been left at that."

"But there were others who supported William in his quest for the throne."

"Who?" she challenged.

"The pope himself."

Lilla drew in her breath. "The pope?"

"To many of the Normans, it became a holy war, so to speak. Rome sanctioned the conquest, believing William to be the true heir, not Harold Godwinson. More than just Normans fought for William at Hastings. The pope lent his full support, backed William of Normandy without question."

Lilla sat back in numb shock. The church agreed with William's claim, recognized it wholeheartedly. Had Leofwine known this? Edmund? Griffin? "Still, it just doesn't seem personal enough for a man like Baron Stephen to fall in line with the others like that."

Odo's eyes darkened. "Oh, believe me, Lilla. He had personal reasons, good reasons, to do what he did. In my father's heart burns an utter hatred for the Godwinsons."

"Why?"

"Alfred, King Edward's brother, was my father's closest friend. They practically grew up in one another's company. Have you ever heard what happened to Prince Alfred, Lilla?"

Lilla shook her head from side to side. "The Godwinsons?" she surmised.

"Oui. Earl Godwin, the father of your King Harold, captured Alfred when he himself sought the throne years ago. He sought to blind Alfred, but in so doing protruded too deeply into the eye socket and penetrated the brain. Alfred died a horrible, agonizing death. My father never got over the loss. And in his eyes, the sins of the father truly are visited unto the children. Harold was another Earl Godwin all over again, as far as he was concerned."

"So it was all about revenge?"

"Yes."

"And you?"

"What of me? I came over for the glory and the riches. You should know that by now."

"True," she sighed, then reached for the cat, Peter, who sat next to her. "You've given me much over which to ponder."

"Things are not always all that they seem to be," he said softly.

"No . . . no. Rarely is that the case."

A silence ensued for several minutes as Odo examined a new length of trim and made sure her needs were being well looked to. Finally he turned back to her and cleared his throat. "I have news for you. William is going north, Lilla. He will cordon off York as soon as he arrives." He saw the fright in her eyes and noted the way her skin turned ashen. His hand reached forward in concern. "I leave for York in two days' time."

Lilla's shock ended as fast as it had come. So did the fear when she remembered the mettle of the men who now held York. "I shall pray for you, sir. That my husband and the English rebellion will not extend the same vile courtesies to you and your countrymen when the flower of Normandy falls. It matters not why William came here. His behavior since then has nullified any righteous reasons for conquest. Rest assured: Victory will fall to the English." Her chin rose in defiance, and she prayed that just then she truly was a prophet.

He shrugged in that continental fashion. "Perhaps it will be as you say . . . if they see William coming. Chances are most great, however, that they will not. The Conqueror is most like a jaguar, purposeful in his direction, leaping with bared fangs in a moment of surprise. If the rebels succeed, it will be only because they have nothing left to lose. When all that a man has left is his skin, he will fight handily to keep it." His eyes focused heavily on hers during the last statement.

Lilla could only drop her eyes under his gaze. He grabbed her hand and squeezed lightly, then sprang to his feet. "Adieu, fair one. There is much to be done, so this will be good-bye. I will do my best to ensure your husband's life is not taken away from him at York."

"Will you bring him home to me?"

His eyes were solemn, quiet. "I will try."

The door shut a second later. And where Odo de Chauliac had once been, he left in his stead a roiling tide of confusion.

Odo de Chauliac was falling in love with an Englishwoman.

But York stood before the Normans now, and the rebels must be warned. There had to be a way, she reasoned. There was only one thing to do.

⋇ ⋇ ⋇

Later that evening, Lilla's maid brought in her supper. With Odo gone, Elaine would be Lilla's last visitor until morning.

"Are you busier now that your lord has returned?" Lilla asked genially, for she truly liked the boxy, quiet young woman whose wiry, mousy hair never remained neatly tucked in her plaits past 8 A.M.

"Oui, miss. But I welcome his presence." Odo wasn't easy on his servants.

"Are they dining now?"

She nodded up and down. "Baron Stephen prefers to rise early in the morning, so the evening festivities begin that way as well. Oh, miss, the first night he is back is a sight to see. The cook doesn't miss any chance to impress the baron. He's even prepared a peacock tonight!"

Lilla always wondered how men could kill such a beautiful bird just to eat it, but she didn't want to spoil the girl's enthusiasm. "I'd love to see what they're doing now. It must be quite gay."

The maid's eyes brightened up a notch or two. "Oh it is, madam."

"And is the guard on duty still?"

"Non, madam. He's gone down to the garderobe for just a minute."

Sitting at her tablet loom, Lilla arose with a smile of satisfaction. "Elaine, sit here and tell me what you think of this braid."

"Oui," Elaine easily complied. She appreciated Lilla's work as much as any other woman. With Elaine now on the stool, it was easy work for Lilla, a length of braid in hand, to tie her to its seat, then gag the surprised girl before the possibly-returning soldier would hear her cry.

"I'm sorry, Elaine," Lilla apologized to the frightened maid as she caught the flailing hands and tied them behind her back. "I assure you I mean you no harm."

Lastly she tied Elaine's feet together.

On the bed lay a knapsack stuffed with a blanket and some bread, nuts, and cheese she had hoarded from dinner. After placing her dark cloak around her shoulders and pulling the hood far over her head, she strapped the knapsack over her shoulder, picked up her walking stick, and exited the room. She locked the door behind her, just as Elaine would have done.

Three minutes later, Ralph returned none the wiser.

It would be difficult to traverse the great hall unnoticed. But her worries eased a tad when she recalled that a screen was placed in front of the minstrel gallery.

For just a moment she paused to watch the splendor before her eyes. Odo de Chauliac was already seated with his family. The baron's knights were assembled as well. Lilla had known this would be a good time to escape—this time when fewer soldiers were on duty.

Servants hurried in from the kitchens outside and back again to refill the trenchers, which seemed to empty as soon as they were set down. At long tables the soldiers consumed the feast with vigor, yet they were a bit more concerned about their raucous behavior now that Baron Stephen had returned. The family was attired in their finest tunics and gowns, all of brightly colored silks, jewel-encrusted and embroidered artistically. Baron Stephen's voice—a golden, deep voice—could be heard easily from where Lilla waited. She wondered what it would be like to hear such tones give voice to Scripture.

"The church is finally finished," he was saying.

"It is breathtaking. Absolute perfection!" Sylvia joined in, her hands clasped under her bosom. Ida and Odo shared a private moment of disdain for their sister-in-law.

"Father is right." Hugh leaned forward and placed a hand upon his older brother's arm. "You should take a trip back to Normandy soon. I do believe this house of God is more finely built than even the cathedral at Jumieges."

"Not as large, though, hmm?" Odo asked.

"No. But the workmanship is more detailed. It's a worthy house of God."

"I'm sure Jesu is pleased either way," Odo said.

Stephen saw through his son's seemingly pious remark and changed the subject. "So King William is marching to York?"

"Yes."

"And did Ida tell me correctly when she said you were leaving the day after tomorrow?"

"Yes, sir. The northern faction of the rebellion is, most certainly and most logically, the strongest. William wants to wipe it out as quickly as possible. And I swore my sword arm to him long ago."

"You will be taking our men as well."

"Well, yes, father. It is your duty to the king to provide military assist . . ."

"I know what my duty to the king is, Odo!" Stephen grew impatient with his son's patronization. "Take as many men in the garrison as you think necessary. Just leave enough here for our protection."

"As you wish, father, naturally. William called for them days ago. And with our garrison fighting alongside other brave Normans, I doubt if a single Englishman will be left standing!"

Baron Stephen leaned forward to stare at his son. "Odo, I've lived many years, fought in many battles," he pulled up the sleeve of his tunic and showed off a matted display of battle scars Odo had been shown too many times to still be effective. But he listened like a dutiful son as Stephen said, "You know what I believe is the correct way to subdue England. But we must obey the king. And I pray that the day will come when it will be possible to rule through justice. All I ask is that you help see to it that the justice meted out to the English is swift and to the point. There is too much torture and needless, lasting pain inflicted on the people. As we scar their flesh, we harden their souls for revenge against us. Do you understand me?"

Odo nodded, eyes flat and hard.

"Go and prepare your men. You leave at first light," Stephen ordered.

"As you wish, father. Naturally." Without another word or a response from his father, Odo de Chauliac rose from his feet and hurried across the hall.

"Captain! Knights!" he shouted into the mass of warriors. "Report to my quarters in ten minutes!"

Lilla used the diversion for her own purposes and crossed the hall slowly, trying to hide her limp. The soldiers hurried by her, the knights failed to notice the cloaked woman, and Odo had vacated the room before she stepped foot from behind the gallery. His absence was truly a godsend. She prayed a prayer of gratitude.

Once outside, flattened against the wall of the keep, she crept slowly along. She hadn't been in the bailey often, but she knew that carts of supplies and grain came in and out frequently. Right now, however, the portcullis was down, and she was right in assuming no one else would be coming in or out of the castle until dawn broke the next day. She would have to wait out the night.

The early December wind clutched at her cloak, its cold as sharp as pins. Already her fingers were chilled as they held the warmth of the woolen closer round her body. For a moment her heart failed. How would she get to York faster than the Conqueror?

*There has to be a way!*

Remembering the blazing blue of Griffin's eyes the first time he had taken her, sweetly loving her with his body as well as his heart and soul, she knew she would find it. First she would go into Oxneford. There were many loyal Englishmen who would willingly travel north to confound William. The rebels would be notified before he was north of Lincoln. After procuring a courier, she would set out for Westminster. Surely Eadric and Emma would take her into their home.

Crouching low against the rough wall, seeking respite from the wind, Lilla huddled inside her cape and prayed that morning would soon arrive.

At 3 A.M. the keep door opened quickly, and a dim light shone through the great recess. Odo's voice woke Lilla from her icy stupor with a jolt.

"Find her, men!" he shouted. "She can't have gone far!"

## TWENTY-ONE

My lord!" Elaine wailed behind Sir Odo. "Please, I didn't know she was planning to . . ."

"Shut up!" Odo turned suddenly, and with the back of his hand he pummeled Elaine across the face. The force of the blow sent her sprawling down the steps of the keep.

He stormed further into the courtyard. By this time, several soldiers held aloft flaming torches. Wincing from her hiding place in the shadow of the great wall, Lilla gazed in frozen fright upon Odo. His cloak swirled in the breeze, and he reminded her of a large, menacing black bat.

He called forcefully up to the gatehouse. "Has the portcullis been raised since nightfall?"

"No, sir."

"No one has been in or out?"

"No, sir. We've seen not a soul!"

Robert, the same knight who had ushered Lilla to the castle months ago, stepped forward. "She must still be in the confines of the bailey, sir."

"Obviously . . ." He looked around. "Curse the woman! How could she have thought for a moment . . . with that leg . . . she could be killed out there! Sir Robert, go to the stables and let out that little mutt of hers. If she's in the courtyard or anywhere else within these walls, he'll find her."

Lilla's heart sank. She was as good as captured. The question was, Should she remain in the shadows to be found, or turn herself over right now? It didn't take long to decide when she thought of Griffin at York. If she could just make it further on down the length of the keep, there was a staircase that led to the outer palisade. Perhaps she could jump into the river.

Concealed in shadow, she sidestepped to the stone stairway, watching all the time the progress of the soldier hurrying toward the newly-built stables. He was inside, his call to Soot carried faintly on the stiff breeze.

Almost there. The steps were in front of her.

One foot on the bottom step.

The soldier emerged.

*Up you go now, Lilla.*

Soot barked.

And out of the corner of her eye she saw a little night shadow bounding across the bailey, tail wagging with glee. Halfway up the steps.

All eyes fell upon her.

*Just a little more.*

Soot leaped up, begging for a pet. Soldiers ran in her direction. Odo shouted, "Stop her!"

She hoisted herself up onto the wall with her strong arms.

*Don't look down.*

One drop.

Odo's feet rapidly devoured the steps.

Lilla looked frantically at his approach. Then steeled herself against the fear which began to overpower even her will to escape.

One foot off the wall. Then the other.

"No!" Odo yelled as she stepped off into the darkness. The air rushed up around her neck and through her hair.

"Lilla!" Through the air Odo flew, leaping to grab her. His strong fingers grabbed the collar of her tunic, and Lilla thudded back onto the vertical plane of the wall.

"You fool!" he yelled, his face a wan mask, perspiration clinging to every inch of skin which showed about his collar.

"Let go of me!" Lilla yelled. "Let me free!"

With one mighty heave at her collar and a handful of hair, Odo pulled her up onto the top of the wall and onto her feet. He grabbed her by the shoulders and shook her hard. "The river is over *there!*" He jerked his head over to the opposite side of the bailey. "You would have been killed!" He held her tightly against him for several seconds, then pulled back, eyes once again devoid of fear, icy, distant.

"Better dead than your prisoner," Lilla snapped, glaring at him angrily, wondering how she could have gotten turned around like that.

Her expression cut through the one tender portion of his heart.

"You will find, madam, that your first attempt at escape will be your last. You will be afforded a maid no longer. Your food will be brought in by a guard, and you shall not step foot outside of your room again."

Lilla looked down. "But, sir . . ."

"You are a foolish, silly woman. I've had enough for one night. Robert, take her back to her room and see to it that tomorrow she receives nothing but water. Lilla, I could kill you for this. . . . You know that, don't you?"

She looked back up into his brown eyes. "But you won't."

"No. I won't."

"And you won't reprimand Elaine?"

"That I cannot promise you."

Lilla looked over the edge onto the grass below. Her shaking became uncontrolled—not from the chill of the early morning, but from knowing she had almost died. She gasped and stumbled forward. Odo quickly caught her and held her close, trying to warm her. "Promise me you'll not do anything so foolish again."

Robert took her arm, and they proceeded slowly down the steps back to the keep. But Odo stood upon the wall until dawn broke. Gazing, solitarily gazing over stolen fields and foreign soil.

He departed for York .

❧ ❧ ❧

The next day a guard entered with her dinner.

"Food?" she asked.

"Sir Odo is not without mercy."

"For Normans, perhaps," she said crossly. But she couldn't help smiling at the tray of bread and meat. "Does Sir Odo know you've brought so much food up here?"

The guard winked. "We wouldn't want poor Soot to go without. And he did say we might bring you a scrap or two."

"Looks like more than just a scrap or two," she commented, picking up the small loaf and walking to the window. "Where is Elaine?" Lilla asked suddenly.

"Went home to Normandy for illness' sake."

"Elaine is sick?"

"Her maman."

"Oh. Thank you then," Lilla said by way of dismissal, then turned away and sat on the sill. So Elaine's mother had become ill. It was good of Odo de Chauliac to send her all the way back to Normandy for the sake of a dying parent. Clearly, there were two distinct sides to the Norman nobleman.

But Odo's trusted guards knew the truth. Elaine's mother had been dead for years, and the serving girl was nowhere to be found.

❧ ❧ ❧

The cold had settled in for good. Snow was scarce, and the landscape was brown and dead. Dormant. It told the tale of Lilla's inner heart. She had never known such bleak loneliness. Even having Odo to converse with was better than utter solitude.

240

Always she watched the horizon.

The cold of the air plaintively refreshed her with a vast melancholy. To feel anything was beneficial; to be sad was better than feeling nothing at all. For if she was sad . . . she was alive. If she was alive . . . she loved. Somehow, Griffin's heart seemed to mesh with hers across the vast miles of English countryside which separated the two lovers.

Once—only once—she had seen Griffin from her window. It was a month after she had been taken away by Odo de Chauliac. Hereward had called Griffin to him early one morning. Another loyal Englishman awaited freedom, this time in the region of Oxneford. Due west of Castle Chauliac. The journey was much shorter due to Hereward's knowledge of the countryside and his crafty manner of evasion. Five days later as they rode by the castle at a gallop, Lilla saw him. Though dressed as a royal Norman courier, the massive frame, and the scabbard which bounced against his thigh and sheathed Edward's sword, gave her knowledge of the rider's true identity.

She wanted only to call to him, but fearing his identity would be discovered, she kept her peace. Concern creased her brow. He would go to the hut and find it empty! What would he do? Griffin did, in fact, find the hut empty. But a few questions to Father John told him all that he needed to know.

That night Lilla's extreme, most heartfelt wish was granted when she heard a pebble hit the hide at the window which overlooked the Thames.

She arose from the bed, pulled back the hide, and looked down. Far below in the darkness she saw two forms. One removed his hat, and a mass of blonde hair tumbled to his shoulders.

Her breath caught as with a courtly gesture Griffin bowed, then pressed his fingertips to his lips. He raised his hands up to her, offering the sweetness of his mouth in a single gesture.

She did the same, her arms reaching down.

Hereward nudged Griffin. It was time to go.

He waved, but Lilla motioned for him to stay. She hurried to her table, grabbed a short length of scarlet braid and threw it down.

Seconds later, he was gone.

As for Griffin, he knew she was safe, though confined. He had seen her with his own eyes and realized, with some relief, that he needn't worry about her when winter arrived.

But now, with December newly come, that brief moment shared seemed an eternity past. Just one more flash of affection, to be looked upon with love, to be giddy in Griffin's favor was all she wanted.

Waiting consumed her time when she wasn't weaving the fine trim that Ida de Chauliac ordered of her upon inspecting her husband's new tunics. Of course, her games with Soot still occurred, but she longed to feel the little dog's warmth next to her, not just gaze down from way up high. If she had heard the conversation the night before at supper in the hall, Lilla would have realized that her days of utter desolation were coming to a close.

A more simple meal was laid before the recipients that evening, with only four selections of meats. The bread, fine and light, had turned out especially good that day, and Sylvia de Chauliac reached for the loaf in front of her.

She tore off a large piece, flicking the excess crumbs from her fingertips.

"Why, Ida, your gown is exquisite. The braid on your sleeves—is that woven in real gold thread?" she asked, trying only to make pleasant conversation with her sister-in-law. Ever since Odo had left, Ida had become even more sour. She solely represented those humans truly cunning and duplicitous at Castle Chauliac now, and perhaps wasn't up to the strain. But even then, Sylvia knew, at least Odo wasn't a hypocrite like his wife.

"Of course it is real gold thread." She lifted a beaker of wine to her lips, the silver-rimmed wooden cup clicking slightly against her pearly teeth.

"I don't remember you having it in Normandy, sister." Sylvia liked to call Ida "sister," knowing how much Odo's wife disdained such familial proclivity.

"No, it was made by a woman here in Oxneford."

Sylvia's brows lifted in minor surprise. "Truly? An English-woman?"

"Oui. She is, in point of fact, under Odo's guardianship."

Sylvia knew precisely what Ida meant. "Does she live in the village?"

"No. She lives here."

"At the castle?"

Ida nodded.

"How do you put up with it?" Sylvia realized she was sinning, but she somehow rejoiced in Odo's infidelities in the face of such outward perfection.

Ida shrugged. "The more he is in love with other women, the less I myself must see of him. It's an agreeable arrangement. And," her eyes sparkled, "I am not without my own amusements."

"I don't doubt that." Sylvia said dryly, seeing no humor in Ida's admission. Arranged marriages were often such. "Why haven't I yet seen this woman?"

"She is Odo's prisoner. Her room is well fortified."

"Prisoner? You seemed to imply . . ."

Ida's brows raised. "That they are lovers? According to him . . . yes. But then again, according to him, what woman wouldn't fall prey to his looks or his readily available charm?"

"What of him? Is she just another in a long line of female companionship, or is she finding a niche in his heart?"

Ida looked at Sylvia with a frankness that was unusual. "That is an answer I cannot give. On the day I arrived, he flaunted her . . . was walking in the courtyard with her. But I haven't seen her since. He keeps her well hidden and purely for his own amusement. It makes me wonder. . . . And he goes to her each evening as well."

"Well, then," Sylvia decided, "I shall visit her on the morrow. I am most interested in seeing her work. Mayhap she will grace me with her wares as well. Besides, she must be quite interesting to have such a hold on Odo. I fear I, too, am becoming most bored now that winter is here."

"May fortune smile upon you then, Sylvia. The guard at her door has strict orders to let no one in."

She reached out and touched the trim on Ida's sleeve. "You got in, didn't you?"

"Heavens, no! Odo brought this to me. A sort of peace offering, I imagine. You would think after almost 20 years, he'd stop trying."

"Well, I shall at least try and seek her out. I'm most definitely intrigued by the whole thing. Odo's never brought one of his paramours to stay beneath the castle's very roof, has he?"

"No. Usually if a serving wench isn't meeting his needs, he finds amusement outside the range of eyes and ears of those who live with him. Odo has never been all that choosy."

"Hmm. She must be someone quite special. And his prisoner, too! Goodness, your husband gets more mysterious with each year."

Ida sat back with a secret smile. Sylvia's words didn't wound in the least. In fact, she quite liked the idea of Odo truly in love with another woman.

# ~ TWENTY-TWO ~

The next morning Sylvia hastily dressed and wandered through the cold, stone passages to the southwest tower of the keep. A guard stood by the door.

"Let me in," she ordered haughtily, calling into use the strength of her breeding.

"Forgive me, my lady, but I cannot," the guard apologized. "I have my orders . . . given by Sir Odo himself."

She moved closely within his space of comfortableness, stood on tiptoe, and let her eyes bore into his. "What is your name?"

"Ralph, my lady."

"Ralph, Sir Odo is gone. Lord Stephen is home. Do I need to disturb him?" She crossed her arms and stepped back, waiting for a reply with a tapping foot.

"Yes, my lady. Forgive me, but orders are orders."

"All right." She turned on her heel and returned 15 minutes later with Hugh.

"Go ahead, Ralph, let her in," Hugh commanded. "My father says that it will be all right to do so." He turned to his wife. "There, Sylvia, are you happy now?"

She gave him a quick peck on the cheek. "Yes, Hugh. Thank you."

"Anything to keep you from being bored. If I have to hear you say, 'Darling Hugh, there's nothing to do,' one more time,

I shall go daft. In you go, then!" he said with a cheerful swat on her hindquarters and was off down the passageway.

The key clanked in the lock. Lilla turned her head away from the morning light, fully expecting to see Ralph's face. Her surprise was great when the face of Sylvia de Chauliac appeared from around the door.

"I hope I'm not disturbing you," the young woman apologized.

"You disturb me not, my lady."

"Have you eaten yet?"

"No, madam. Dinner is not until 11:00"

"Ralph!" Sylvia called. "Have a little food brought up. Make sure it's something tasty!"

"Yes, my lady." Ralph bowed, his merry eyes catching Lilla's, and he left the room.

Lilla waved a hand over the end of her bed. "Will you have a seat, my lady? I'm afraid my accommodations are not effusive."

"But hardly those of a prisoner." Sylvia sat down after reaching for a piece of braid. "You do beautiful work."

"Thank you. May I weave whilst you tarry here? Even prisoners must earn their keep."

"Please do. I should like to see how it's done."

Lilla slid down from the window, and if Sylvia noticed her limp, she said nothing about it.

Sylvia stood behind Lilla at the table and watched the young Englishwoman's capable fingers turn the tablets then move the shuttle of thread in between the multicolored yarns. "The Lady Ida wears one of your braids upon her newest gown. It is quite beautiful."

"Thank you, my lady." Lilla's fingers accelerated their methodical actions as the rhythm of her work once more became comfortable.

"If I wasn't so accustomed to Sir Odo's habits, I would think it was she who held you here in this room. Fashion has always been preeminent on her list of priorities."

Lilla said nothing. She had no idea why Sylvia had come.

"He holds you prisoner here, then."

"Yes, my lady."

"Merely for your weaving?"

"No, my lady."

Sylvia began to pace in front of the window. To be sure, she felt an uncommon confusion. True, the Englishwoman was pretty enough, if a bit pale from her months of confinement in the tower. Obviously, she was being fed, and that she wore the scent of rosemary and sported shining curls attested to her cleanliness. Most prisoners were not afforded the luxury of bathing. But then, she needed to be sweet and clean for her lover, Sylvia surmised.

"What is your name?" Sylvia asked, touching the skeins of silken thread on Lilla's table. The colors were arresting: Bright purples and deep blues echoed the hues of a waning day, and gold and silver thread shimmered in the morning sun which streamed in the window. It was cold in the tapestried room, but Sylvia hypothesized that Lilla's need for light caused her to push back the thick hide which normally kept the December chill at a more respectable distance. She pulled her thick robe about her more tightly. Winter was always a chilly season, indoors or out.

"I am called Lilla."

Sylvia smiled. "Lilla. It is a beautiful name. And it suits you so."

"Thank you, my lady."

"How did you come to be in the castle, Lilla?"

"Odo de Chauliac."

"So I assumed. Were you brought by force?"

Lilla looked up without malice. "I am an Englishwoman."

"I see. But now that you are here, it is rumored that my brother-in-law has stolen your heart. Is that the case?"

"Sir Odo has stolen many a heart I am sure, my lady."

"But has he stolen yours?"

Lilla couldn't quite understand why Sylvia was so

adamantly concerned with the feelings of her heart. Was she just a busybody, or did she have a reason? She shrugged and continued looking down at the piece of scarlet and gold trim which was lengthening more quickly than usual.

Sylvia sighed and sat down at the edge of the bed. "I understand your wish to keep your feelings your own, Lilla."

"My feelings are all I have left to me, my lady."

"But surely you are well cared for. You are being fed well, aren't you?"

Lilla nodded. "All my bodily needs are met."

Still no admission of love. Sylvia so wanted something more than this to report to Ida. She couldn't wait to see her sister-in-law's face when . . .

Lilla interrupted her thoughts. "Is there something I can do for you, my lady?"

"Me?"

"Yes. I assume you had a reason for coming."

"Well, actually, I did. I wanted to meet the woman who has stolen Odo's heart."

"Come now, my lady, Odo is a married man."

Sylvia burst into laughter. "That's never stopped him before. I thought that for him to be so taken, you must indeed be something special. Odo's paramours last usually for but a fortnight, if that long. Besides, it's so dull around here, I seek any bit of entertainment I can find during the winter months. That's the real reason I've come." She shrugged.

"That I can understand. At least I have my weaving to occupy the time."

"Yes, at least you have that. I've always despised embroidery, and yet . . . well, it's our station, you know. That's all the men think we're good for. Would you create some trim for me as well?"

Lilla waved her hand over the skeins of yarn. "Certainly. Pick out the colors you would like for me to use."

"Where did you learn to weave?"

"From my mother."

"And does she still weave?"

"No. She died years ago."

"I'm sorry. My parents are still alive, and all my grandparents. I feel so blessed. Poor Hugh—his mother died several years ago. She was Lord Stephen's second wife, you know."

"So Sir Hugh and Sir Odo are half brothers then?"

"Yes."

Another tidbit of information. No wonder Odo wasn't particularly close to his younger brother. The almost-20-year span between them was probably more to blame, however.

"How did you come to be here, Lilla?"

*She's persistent,* Lilla thought. "I'm sure you can find out that piece of information from any one of the guards, my lady."

"Why don't you tell me, then?" Sylvia invited.

"I'd rather not speak of such things, my lady." She didn't trust any Normans. Not yet, anyway.

"Has Odo forbidden you to speak of such matters?"

"No, my lady. I forbid myself. It's my way of not complaining."

Sylvia laughed. "Have the de Chauliacs proved to be so inhospitable?"

This time Lilla laughed and pointed. "What do you call that bolt on the door?"

"You're right. Perhaps Lord Stephen will grant you your freedom?"

"I doubt that very much. In truth, my lady, I'm a prisoner because I've taken a small part in the rebellion. I'm sorry it isn't more glorious than that. Lord Stephen would most probably agree with Odo's decision. But your brother-in-law has been most courteous, sometimes even kind . . . considering."

"Odo?" Sylvia's head shook in disbelief. "Are you sure we're talking about the same person?"

"He saved my life."

"How so?"

"I was trying to escape, and I jumped off the wall. He caught me just in time from falling to my death on the ground below."

"Why would you do such a thing?"

"In my fear during the escape, I got turned around and thought I was at the other end of the wall where the river laps right against the castle walls. After that attempt, I've been more heavily guarded."

"I'm surprised he didn't kill you for that."

"Odo? No. He wouldn't. I'm worth much more to him alive than I could ever be dead."

"Why?"

Lilla laughed. "I told you, ask one of the men. But let me inquire about Lord Stephen. I watched from this window your arrival that first day. He is a good man?"

"Oui."

Lilla nodded. "That's good. I thought it was so when I watched him alight from the carriage."

Their conversation flowed from that point onward. The food arrived, and they ate together. A delighted Sylvia even threw a few morsels down to the excited Soot. Sylvia, spoiled and cosseted, yet strong of character despite such, felt a warmth toward the humble weaver woman. Three hours later, when dinner arrived for Lilla, Sylvia rose to go.

"Truly," she said, crossing her arms over her bosom, "I am almost glad Odo has you here, Lilla. Mayhap this winter will prove to be amusing."

❧ ❧ ❧

"So, you are the wife of Griffin Eadricson?" Sylvia, barely through the door, exclaimed.

"Yes."

"Well, I am relieved. Then you are not Odo's lover?"

"No. Nor shall I ever be."

"Ida swears he is in love with you."

Lilla could hardly believe Sylvia said the words.

"I'm no more than bait. He needs me alive. A lure to my husband."

"But so far your husband has not returned?"

Lilla turned to face her loom, biting back the tears. "No. I saw him once from afar. But he is most probably now in York," she said quietly, "waiting for William to arrive."

"And Odo," Sylvia reminded her.

"Yes. God help them all."

"And do you believe your husband will come for you, victorious?"

"With all my heart."

Sylvia kept silence. She had seen the Norman war machine in action. But the last thing she wanted to do was frighten Lilla.

"Your husband has already garnered quite a reputation, Lilla."

Lilla's eyes widened. "How so?"

"The night he killed those soldiers in Westminster, well, according to the tale it was like watching a Viking berserker of old. Already his fame has spread among the Norman camp. What is it like to married to such a man?"

"I know not the Griffin of which you speak, my lady," Lilla said softly. "To me he is loving and tender, so gentle, sweet. What you say doesn't surprise me, for I've seen his strength. But, well . . . we wives have a special view of our mates, wouldn't you agree?"

"Oui. Hugh does well enough on the battlefield, although I'm not so certain he could best your Griffin, as he was a stonemason and is known to be a giant of a man. But Hugh also has an uncompromising, formidable sense of business. Yet to me he is all fluff and feathers."

"I believe that's the best part of being a wife, my lady. We get the tender side of them all to ourselves! By the way, will Hugh be going to York as well?"

"No. The king realizes that my father-in-law needs one of his sons close by. And to be quite honest, Odo is the better fighter."

Lilla grew silent, thoughts of York and what lay ahead storming her mind. Sylvia followed suit and drew out her embroidery, halfheartedly plying her needle in the silence.

# ~❧ TWENTY-THREE ❧~

William the Conqueror strode before his pavilion. His royal banner fluttered overhead: two golden lions with menacing claws, one over the other on a field of bleeding crimson. The wind plucked at his russet hair, and his piercing eyes surveyed the quiet city. Gray stone walls stood silent in the December light, pale and silver as the snow fell upon both the English within and his encampment without. Norman warriors, fierce and loyal to their king, sat around bonfires scattered about, seeking warmth from the winter chill. Many of his men had died in this very place—victims of English wrath months before. But it had all come down to this, and they would rue the day they ever set about defying him.

Nine days before Christmas, William had arrived, wrapped in a blanket of night, and when the rebels awoke, they knew they could not flee the massive Norman army. No one had been able to warn them of his approach. The city was cordoned off. For a week now, no one had gone in or out.

William stared intently, almost willing the ancient walls to crumble beneath the heavy animosity of his gaze. Subduing the rebels would not be easy—he had known that from the start. But subdue them he would. Because William had never given up on obtaining anything he desired. And he had never disappointed himself.

Already he had quelled the western rebellion under Eadric the Wild. Chester had fallen to him as well as Dorset. And on the way to York he had left a wake of devastation so bleak it was a wonder the rebels of York did not flee before his arrival. Sparing no males, he destroyed everything which could support life for the northerners.

A messenger rode into the encampment and up to Robert Montgomery, a noble of high standing. With a salute he handed the Norman nobleman a scroll. "A message for the king from Lady Matilda."

William's sharp eyes missed not the messenger's arrival, and he strode upon his massive, muscular legs over to Robert.

"A message sire," Montgomery bowed. "From Lady Matilda."

"I heard."

Montgomery wondered what William *didn't* hear. For truly his ears were as sharp as his eyes.

William procured the scroll from Montgomery and hurried to the tent. There was only one man he trusted to read this message from the woman he adored. In their years of marriage the Conqueror had not so much as eyed another woman in an unseemly manner. Matilda owned his heart utterly, and though she favored their eldest son Robert even more than she did her husband, William could not betray his feelings for her. Their courtship had been fiery, and truly it took him longer to subdue Matilda than England. But she had proven a worthy prize.

The thought of her pretty face brought a smile to his lips.

With daylight streaming in from the opened flap of his royal pavilion, he broke the seal and handed the scroll to his half brother Odo of Bayeux, an educated man and a bishop.

The dark-haired man scanned the message in a moment before he read the words of his sister-in-law out loud to William. In that brief span of time, he was already dreading the news he was bidden to give.

"What is it?" William asked impatiently. "Come, come . . . read it!"

"It concerns your eldest," Odo of Bayuex began.

William gestured impatiently. "What trouble is Robert Shortpants finding now?"

Odo grimaced inwardly at the disdainful nickname of William's short-legged son. "He has squandered his funds yet again."

"Sweet heaven! I've never seen a young man so eager to please those around him. His excesses are shameful. It's a wonder Matilda told me of this."

"She fears for him."

William the Conqueror rubbed his smooth-shaven chin. "Ah. Probably she pictures him starving in Rouen." He paced before the door of his tent, thinking of the next step. He looked out and spied a man walking nearby. Just the man he needed. "Guard!" he beckoned loudly to the sentry on duty nearby. "Get Odo de Chauliac there. Right away."

"Yes, my liege." The chain-mailed soldier bowed and called for a soldier by the campfire. In less than three minutes, Sir Odo stood before his king. By this time, William sat in his carven chair, a table spread with maps in front of him.

"You summoned me, my lord?" Odo bowed respectfully, wondering what this could mean. Perhaps he was finally receiving his guerdon from the king. Heaven knew he had fought hard enough for the man at Hastings, and he had yet to receive so much as one hide of land for his valiant effort. Wisely, he chose not to remind William at that moment. The Conqueror's face bore a distinct resemblance to a storm cloud.

"I need you to leave for Normandy right away. Shortpants is having difficulties."

"Will all be well?"

"He has emptied the purse yet again."

"And what would you have me do?"

"Leave for London, find my exchequer, and procure the needed funds. Tell him we are aware of his financial irresponsibilities, and if he stops this ridiculous, pandering display, we will forgive him."

"As you wish, my liege. But tell me, will I miss out on the battle?"

William grinned and slapped Odo heartily on the shoulder. "Ah, de Chauliac, you fail me not. I will wait at least another month. Their bellies are not emptied enough for me yet. What we have before us is a city filled with the finest English fighters that once littered the isle. They have gathered from far and wide, and they have the advantage of the defensive position. We need more than just a battle cry and battering ram to defeat them."

William had never underestimated his enemy before, and he wasn't starting now. "You must hurry, and pray that the channel is kind. But you should be back in time."

Odo bowed and was riding out of the camp 15 minutes later.

❧ ❧ ❧

"What's this?" Lilla asked, reaching for the parcel Sylvia held between her hands.

"It's something for you."

"And what is the occasion?"

"No occasion other than that I'm thankful you're my friend."

Lilla began to undo the twine, and she thought back to the past two weeks. Surprisingly enough, Sylvia truly had become a friend. Having never before experienced the close friendship of another woman, Lilla was enjoying the heartfelt, surprisingly deep conversations they had begun to share shortly after their initial meeting. "It is the way with women," Sylvia had assured her. "We seem to bare our souls much more quickly than our male counterparts." But Lilla knew their friendship was special.

The twine gave way, and the woolen bag opened to reveal several handfuls of old rags. Sylvia laughed at the perplexed expression on Lilla's face.

"That's not the real present!" she chimed. "Dig deep!"

In between the scratchy clods of fabric, Lilla's fingers touched metal. When she pulled the unexpected gift out of the bag, she gasped with delight.

"How beautiful!" She held up the intricately made cross in the light. It was formed of silver, its metalwork exquisitely rendered. Interconnecting curves and swirls proclaimed it an ancient piece, probably from Scotland or Ireland. "Where did you find it?"

"In London. Do you like it?"

"Of course! I've never owned anything so costly. How can I possibly thank you enough?"

"There's no need. There will come a time, Lilla, when the world will be set to rights again, and you will depart this keep. I hope you'll wear it always and remember me." Her words sounded slightly sad, for she knew Lilla's imprisonment had enabled them to cross over social boundaries into spheres normally inaccessible to either of them. Their friendship could not last forever. And Sylvia knew this, even if Lilla did not.

The cross hung from a long chain. Sylvia belted it around Lilla's waist so it swung just above her knee.

"Does Baron Stephen know you purchased such a costly gift?"

Sylvia nodded with a broad, closed smile. "Of course. Even Lord Stephen thinks it is a good idea."

"He knows about me?"

"Naturally. Odo isn't one to sneak about when he does something."

"Then perhaps he may set me free?"

"No, Lilla. As you told me the first day we met, you played a part in the rebellion. And it wasn't as small a part as you would have liked me to think. Aiding Leofwine Uhtredson for as long as you did was no mean feat."

"Perhaps, but a friend will do all she can to aid her loved one."

"Yes, especially when she deems it in his best interest."

"What if she doesn't really know what her loved one's best interests are?"

"Oh," Sylvia shrugged, "friends see more than they may let on."

They both knew Leofwine was no longer the subject of the conversation.

"Perhaps," Lilla replied, "but maybe they only want what's best for them."

"I don't think issues of safety and well-being can ever be construed as selfish."

"What do you mean?" Lilla asked.

"Oh, dearest Lilla. Winter has come . . . and you are alone. Too many strangers roam the land. You must realize that Castle Chauliac is the safest place for you now."

Lilla sat in silence, the cross held tightly in the palm of her hand, the recipient of her thoughtful stare. Sylvia spoke again. "If you were in my position and I in yours, tell me you wouldn't do the same as I."

Lilla still said nothing.

"I know. I couldn't possibly understand how you feel, Lilla."

"'Tis true."

"But you must admit, my motives are not sullied by selfishness. I cannot help you escape. Besides, my loyalty first and foremost must always be to Lord Stephen. Surely you can understand that, can you not, Lilla?"

Lilla looked up. "Yes. I understand where your loyalty must lie. I wish it didn't have to be that way," she smiled softly, "but I understand."

They embraced in a fond hug and Sylvia pulled back. "I have another surprise for you."

"So many surprises! I believe I shall swoon from the excitement of it all. What is it?"

"Tomorrow is Christmas. And you will be allowed out of

your room to hear Mass! I convinced Lord Stephen myself!"

Lilla drew in her breath. "Oh, Sylvia. How long it has been since I've been to Mass!"

"I know. But that's not all. If you're a good girl at Mass, you'll get to take dinner with us in the great hall."

"Praise be to God!" Lilla threw her hands up in the air with joy. "Thank you, Sylvia. Thank you!"

Another hug. Several tears. A departure.

The rest of Lilla's day was spent in almost merry anticipation.

ళ్రీ ళ్రీ ళ్రీ

The next day, Mass was solemn, yet the joy in Lilla's heart at receiving communion could not be denied. Lord Stephen looked at her from across the aisle, taking note of her expressions. After Mass was said and the final blessing given, he hurried to Lilla's side.

"You will feast with us?"

"Thank you, my lord."

"Good."

That was all she heard from him for the rest of the day. But in the great hall, a simple meal was set before them, and Lilla heard Sylvia chattering at her elbow the entire time. When Odo appeared on his way to London, all were surprised.

He coolly took note of her presence, spoke privately with Lord Stephen, and ushered her back up to her room.

"Sylvia should know better than to go against my wishes," he said as he gently saw her into her chamber.

"It is Christmas, sir," Lilla pointed out. "She was only being kind."

"Why did you not try and escape?"

"Sylvia made these arrangements out of the fullness of her heart. I would never betray our friendship in that manner."

"Hmm." Odo walked over to her table. "You've been busy, I see."

"Yes. And you as well, my lord. Going back to Normandy?"

"Oui. But I will return. York is under siege, Lilla. I won't miss the battle." He turned to face her.

"I'll pray for your safety," Lilla said, and truly meant the words.

"Will you? Why?"

"Oh, sir," she said, walking to him and placing her strong hand upon his arm, "because I sought to leave this place in no wise means I despise you. It's only natural for a creature to push against that which binds it so. Wouldn't you feel the same way if you were held captive against your will?"

"That is the difference between you and me, Lilla." A bit of warmth was back in the brown eyes.

"What is, Sir Odo?"

"I would have succeeded in escaping."

She laughed. "Yes. Yes, you would have. No doubt."

He smiled purely. And she mourned inside that expressions such as that were rare. "I must be on my way. There are still a few hours of daylight left. The next time I see you, it will all be over. One way or another."

"Good-bye, my lord."

Odo lifted her hand to his mouth, bowed, and was gone.

From her window, Lilla watched for quite some time as the small entourage disappeared far over the horizon.

# ◈ TWENTY-FOUR ◈

Three weeks later the lanterns in the barracks shone in the early winter darkness, doing little to brighten the gloom. Men lazed on their forlorn pallets. Some dreamt of home, their eyes shining shamelessly as they found themselves outside the walls of York adrift in a skiff built of memories. Their first kiss, their wives, their sons and daughters, the smell of the springtime earth between their fingers, the satisfaction of a good harvest—such remembrances returned to aid them in their lonely plight. Others played games, gambling moneys they possessed not. And outside, several bonfires belched black smoke into the starlit sky which canopied their isolation and stretched far beyond. They whittled away at small pieces of wood or sharpened their knives and axes, the sharpening stones singing with a raspy twang along the simple blades.

One young lad, a minstrel's son, strummed on a lute. At first a sad song was his choice of entertainment, hollow and echoing the state of the rebels' stomachs. For still William tarried, patiently striding before his pavilion each day, staring without expression at the walls.

"Edwin!" a large man with curly red hair looked up from his ax, "by all that's holy, play us a merry tune! If you keep that up much longer, we may all throw ourselves in despair from the walls and win the Bastard's battle for him!"

261

"'Twill be the only way he'll win!" someone else shouted.

The others laughed. "Well said, Wulf! Do as he asks, Edwin, and so make our hearts merry." And Edwin stood to his feet. His clear, strong voice announced above the crackling of the fire, "I will sing a song of a boy and a dragon."

"Here, here, lad!"

"That's the way!" Griffin eagerly looked up from his sword.

"On you go, boy!" the rebels encouraged him, and the other bonfires were quickly abandoned, men willingly sacrificing warmth of skin for warmth of heart and temporary peace of mind.

The lute was strummed in a singular, full chord, and Edwin's voice floated out into the night.

"Long ago, the sorcerer Gandulf reigned over a land that was not his, and terror reigned with him . . ."

Another chord. Dark and harsh.

". . . a black terror broader than the world itself. A child was born."

Before long the men forgot about their carvings and their axes and stared at the spindly-legged boy, forgetting where they were and the real terror beyond.

The song progressed. His fingers plucked a delicate melody. "The child grew into a mighty man. And all prayed that he would be the one. For no matter his age, the dragon would shun him."

Edwin strummed strongly now. "And armed with spear and an ancient song of victory, his great voice filled the dragon's yellow eyes with fear." The lute ignited under Edwin's fingers.

"Battled they desperately each day for three years."

The strumming became wild, frenzied, and Edwin began to dance with abandon as he practically shouted the weavings of the battles. His eyes fired with the warrior's tale.

The rebels clapped in time to the music.

"The day of the final battle drew nigh. The sun turned

dark as the two raged against one another. Even the dead rose from their sleep, the tumult was so great, and came to watch."

"Thrusting his spear with his last bit of strength, the weapon sung a song of death, burying itself between the eyes of the dragon!"

A cheer erupted around the bonfire.

"The battle was finally won!"

Edwin kept up the wild strumming, feeding the glory of past ages into the veins of his compatriots, and without them realizing it, the melody slowly changed from one of wild fury, to happiness, a frenzied joy!

Then the splendid excitement was sucked without warning into one mournful note.

"But the price of killing the terror was high."

All were filled with anticipation. A somber, yet musical melody floated around them. "The warrior was buried that day, untouched by the creature, but dead nonetheless."

Wulf yelled above the tune. "No more, lad! No more! 'Twas a happy tune we sought."

"Ah, good sir," the lad bowed. "'Tis not over." Another note, in a major chord. "For several days later, the warrior emerged, victorious even over death! And so, the people rejoiced!"

He sang, his body moving in a dance, circles of abandoned joy.

"Peace returned to the land." Then wordless notes issued from his mouth, harmonizing with the melody of the instrument. "Victory was his!"

Wulf jumped to his feet, pulling men roughly to their feet with a great and glorious shout. "Ha! Victory will be ours!" His mouth was wide, and he threw his arms into the air and danced with the boy. The others did the same, the merriment more contagious than the joy of a wedding feast.

And before the bonfire, silhouettes turned and dipped, their axes raised in salute to the boy, to their ancestors, and to each other.

"Ha!" they shouted, their voices ringing through the city, over its walls, and into the ears of the Conqueror.

"Ha! Victory is ours! England forever! England forever!"

Soon the entire barracks were emptied. Men danced with joy, their hearts swelled with love for their homeland.

"England! England! England! England!" Their cries filled the sky above them, above the entire captive land. But more importantly, it filled their hearts.

"England!" Griffin yelled with all his might. "England!"

The day would surely be theirs.

⌘ ⌘ ⌘

The waiting continued for two more weeks.

Ignoring the rumblings of his belly as he threw the three dice onto the backgammon board, Griffin chose to use the die which sported only one black dot and captured Simon's man with a surly shout of triumph.

"You're growing more ill-tempered every day. Do you miss her that badly?" Simon asked suddenly.

"Lilla? Of course. Not a moment goes by that her face is not before me, Simon. And to think I may well have ended up in a monastery."

Simon laughed. "At least you had the chance to marry, to know her fully."

Griffin pushed the dice over to Simon. "Aye, and for that I am most thankful. Jesu was kind to me. Have you heard word of Ethel?"

"She was given to the Norman, just as her father promised the Bastard. She is now his wife, William's reason being to mingle the blood of our people right away. She will bear Norman brats and learn a new language. She will drink their wines and eat their foods. She will die an old woman, forgetting that once she loved an Englishman."

"How do you stand it, Simon? Is your love for her still strong?"

"Aye. And that is why I fight, Griffin. It was one thing when they took my country. Father and I were ready to swear fealty, knowing William would win in the end. But when Ethel was taken to wed a Norman, they took my soul from me and bloodied my heart beyond recognition. They gave me nothing in which to hope. My dreams have faded to naught. And joy is past. That is why I fight, my friend."

"But surely you can find peace in the love of God, can you not?"

Simon closed up the board wearily, having lost the game to Griffin. "There is no peace. I am of little account to Him. Perhaps He created us and left it at that."

"You know that isn't the case, my friend."

"Do I?" The dark-brown eyes sang a melody of infinite sadness—a tragedy in any case, even more so in one so young.

"I shall pray even more rigorously for you, Simon," Griffin promised. "That you shall find God, and that happiness will once again be yours."

"A futile prayer, to be sure. And even though I believe your petition before God is for naught, I know it stems from a true heart of friendship. For that I thank you."

Griffin nodded, but his mind turned thoughtful, and he realized that life had been stripped bare of joy. Even though he hadn't taken his days with Lilla for granted, he felt he did not appreciate them enough when he lived them, that he did not suck the wonder from each word said, each minute gone by in the other's presence. But as Simon said, they were given the opportunity to love and to love well. Jesu was indeed kind.

Not saying a word, Griffin arose from the table and headed to a small church near the castle ruins. Once there, he felt the love of God surrounding him, and he prayed for Emma, Eadric, Simon, and Lilla. Minutes turned into hours, transporting him into the past, and when he at last opened his eyes, he was surprised to find that he was not in the abbey at Westminster. How easily his soul traveled through time and space to the building that was part of himself. He could only pray once more that he would live to pass through its arched door once again.

Night fell. And Griffin walked back to the barracks, a solitary figure on the cobbled streets of the captive city of York.

వళ్ళ వళ్ళ వళ్ళ

All was silent. William had offered one final opportunity to surrender. But it was shunned. The rebel forces were in order and, after celebrating Mass, they prepared even more vigorously for the soon-coming attack. The siege would not last as long as planned. Other rebellions were sprouting up, and the Danes were causing a fair share of trouble for the new king as well. He had to snuff out the northern forces who were aligning themselves with the Norsemen. If William did not act soon and with great fortitude, England might become a divided kingdom as it had been in Alfred's time, with the north a Viking stronghold once again.

Griffin partook of a meager supper. It was simple fare of bread, a small scrap of meat, and wine. And the conversation around the temporary hall ranged in all directions. All managed their fear in different ways. Some boastfully bragged of past soldierly exploits. Some talked of their homes and those who relied upon them. Some joked. Others stayed silent, feasting on the energy of uncertainty, willing it to strengthen the hungry muscle and sinew which would lead their axes and spears to victory or death.

Griffin was relieved that Simon would be fighting at his back. When the battle reached its peak, he knew that his childhood friend would not fail or falter. Both he and Simon left the table early and proceeded to the barracks. Neither wished to hear young Edwin—a poignant reminder of what many of the rebel warriors had left behind. The wandering minstrel who had appeared several days before William's arrival did not pluck at either of their heartstrings. His nasal voice with its twittery vibrato somehow transformed songs of victory and glory into plaintive tributes to man's constant battle with himself.

Not bothering to light a lamp, they settled on their straw-filled pallets. Griffin placed his hands behind his head and leaned back against the wooden wall. "So we battle at dawn."

"Aye. Lords Morkar and Edwin were most adamant when the Bastard's retinue arrived giving us the final opportunity to surrender. Hasn't the Wake himself been telling us there is no other first course for us but to war with the enemy?"

"No. He's right. War we must."

They were silent for a moment, listening to the faint echoes of the strained merrymaking from the hall. The rest would be coming back soon. A good night's sleep was needed by all who inhabited the camp. For surely, the Conqueror would strike at dawn.

"Griffin," Simon's voice filtered from the gloom.

"Yes, my friend?"

"Maybe you're right about God."

"What do you mean?"

He sighed. "So many times when we battled with our swords upon Thorny, I felt cheated that you and I would never fight together. But we're here now. So perhaps God does keep a careful accounting of life here on earth."

"He does, Simon."

The cold of the night snaked in through the cracks, and both wished for sleep to no avail. They lay wide-eyed in the gloomy silence.

"Griffin, are you asleep?"

"Nay. My mind won't bid me rest."

"Nor mine."

"'Tis on a night such as this when men must ponder the state of their souls the most," Griffin surmised.

Simon didn't respond to that.

"Griffin?"

"Yes, my friend."

"Pray for me."

"You know I shall, Simon."

"Yes, I know. And rest assured that tomorrow I shall put your life before my own when we come face-to-face with the devils of Normandy."

"I vow the same, Simon. Your life before mine."

"Aye. 'Tis the way of a soldier, Griffin."

"Simon, 'tis the way of a friend."

Sleep descended after an hour had passed. And the sun continued its journey beneath the belly of the earth, promising to arrive at dawn, promising to shed its light upon the death of thousands.

## TWENTY-FIVE

S ylvia laughed until her sides ached, tears skidding over the rims of her eyes. Lilla joined in.

"So your husband is responsible for the lovely flaw that graces my brother-in-law's now less-than-perfect face!"

Lilla nodded and reached for a tart. Sylvia had come laden with a tray of sweetmeats—something Lilla had only tasted but once in her life.

"He may say it doesn't bother him, but don't believe it. Odo is the vainest man I know."

"I do feel sorry for him, though," Lilla admitted.

Sylvia looked dumbstruck. "Dear me, Lilla. Scar or not, if there's one person alive who can take care of himself—it's my brother-in-law."

"And your husband, Hugh. Is he anything like his brother?"

Sylvia frowned. "He's quite driven, but possesses a softer heart."

"Do you love him?"

"Intensely. Our kind don't marry for love, Lilla. So when we do stumble upon it and with our mates, we're that much more thankful for it."

"Oh, I think I can understand that. I truly believed I was destined for a life of solitude. But Griffin came along, loved me for who I am, and is passionate as well."

The two shared a common, knowing expression, put their hands up to their mouths, and chuckled. But suddenly a look of compassion burst upon Sylvia's expressive features. "How can I giggle girlishly about such things, when I realize now how lonely you must feel? Oh, Lilla, sweet Lilla, forgive me."

The conversation turned immediately solemn. "'Tis true, my lady. At times the separation forces such sadness upon me I wonder how such melancholy can be borne by one mortal woman. But then I thank Jesu that I have known such love. Do you ever feel overwhelmed by the love Hugh has for you?"

"Yes."

"And do you ever feel almost guilty that so many women will never experience such a happy, warm relationship?"

"Yes, often. It is that way regarding children, too. So many of them suffer, if not from the hardships of life, then from the cruelties of those around them. I feel awestruck that my baby will know only a loving home."

Lilla grabbed Sylvia's pudgy hand. "Your baby? Oh, Sylvia, can it be true?"

Sylvia nodded.

"Have you told Lord Hugh yet?"

"No. I wanted you to be the first to know." They put their arms around each other and squeezed in a fond embrace.

Tears formed in watery crescents on Lilla's curled eyelashes. "I couldn't be happier for you."

But after the time of female emotion settled down, they laughed and talked of names and child-raising techniques that mothers—no matter what their station in life, nobility or peasant—handed down to their daughters. All too soon Sylvia realized it was time for her to be going.

"Do you think the battle has taken place yet?" Sylvia asked.

"I don't know. Oh, Sylvia, no matter the outcome, we can never let this come between us."

Sylvia reached forward and embraced Lilla. "Never. It's always been the way with men, Lilla. They fight, and we stay home keeping the peace. That will not change no matter who carries the day."

"More than anything we must pray that Griffin comes home alive."

"Yes, we must do that. And Odo?" Sylvia asked.

Lilla's mouth straightened, but she nodded. "Even Odo. It is he who needs the mercy of Jesu the most."

۞ ۞ ۞

William's blood hammered powerfully through his veins when he woke early the next morning and prepared for battle.

Having dispersed most of the Danes in the Humber, there was no one from without to come to the aid of the rebels within. Ere daybreak bobbed to the surface of the sky, soldiers on both sides of the city wall readied themselves for battle. They were silent, grim expressions pasted on their stony features. Going through the motions. Preparing to fight. Perhaps to die.

The sky birthed a bloody dawn, and the Norman troops gathered on the heath to the north of the city, the red heavens reflecting off their conical helmets, shimmering off their mail hauberks. Cautiously, they moved as a unified, disciplined mass across the frozen heath. Their breath rose in clouds, and their feet pounded the turf. First the foot soldiers with their kite-shaped shields, swords, and lances, then the archers, crossbowmen, and slingers. Only William and his knights were mounted upon great war-horses. When the city walls stood before them, not an Englishman was seen nor heard.

A single cry pierced the air.

On the ramparts above, silhouettes appeared against the morning light. And brave-hearted Englishmen bellowed forth a unified cry, craving only the lifeblood of their oppressors. Even the bravest of Norman soldiers shivered beneath his armor. Before the echo of the shout faded into the frigid atmosphere, the English let forth a barrage of javelins. War machines flung forth a blackened hail of rocks and boulders, crushing the approaching enemy. The Norman machine recoiled, until William's booming voice was heard above the din. "Turn back! Turn and fight! The day does not belong to the English dogs! It belongs to us! Ha! Rou!" he shouted the Norman battle cry. "Forward!"

"Ha! Rou!" thousands of men replied to their liege lord, and forward they went again.

The scaling ladders were thrown up against the blackened stone walls. The arrows which pierced the attackers' mail were mere nuisances of pain. Upward they climbed, swords in hands, facing the swinging axes of the English, wanting only to destroy the man they saw above them.

Down below, William's engineers sought weaknesses in the walls' defenses. Soon a boulder was loosened, then more. Bundles of straw and wood were placed into the cavity and set aflame in hopes that portions of wall would come tumbling down.

A battering ram, made of heavy English oak, was brought into place as the Norman bodies began to pile up at the base of the walls—a gruesome collection of limbs and death masks. William's archers made their mark with numerous Englishmen as well, and many of them fell screaming to their death below.

The morning advanced in rapid strides until finally the gate fell, and a large section of wall crumbled into a heap of torrid stones. The Normans stormed into the city. As the English defended the breaches, the dying lay moaning in their agony, and the dead were piled four and five deep at the base of the city walls before the Normans gained the advantage. The maniacal fighting Englishmen persisted in holding the grounds of William's original castle. But the English were severely outnumbered, and the Normans finally stormed across the bailey shouting "Ha! Rou!" multiplying the destruction tenfold. Around the motte, Griffin and Simon fought. The Fox's son swung his ax in wild determination. And King

Edward's sword, the hilt bound with leather thongs and held tightly in Griffin's grasp, wreaked a circle of destruction.

Still the Normans advanced.

Up the mound the two young Englishmen fought, their countrymen falling around them like victims of a violent plague.

Finally, at 9 A.M., Earls Morkar and Edwin surrendered. Waltheof did as well. But just when the white flag was raised, Hereward the Wake, as agreed upon beforehand, signaled a handpicked group of men. They ran with lightning speed to the south end of the city, dove into the river Foss, and swam across its frigid waters. The forest on the other side absorbed them quickly and entirely as if they never existed at all. They were ensuring the rebellion did not die. Simon and Ebb were among them. Griffin, too.

The city wall stood several hundred yards before them. Their feet pounded the turf, their breath rushed out in intermittent puffs, as close behind them a group of blood-thirsty Normans followed in red-eyed pursuit. Griffin could feel them, envision them as they yelled out their ghastly cry.

And for the first time, Simon's smaller stature and quicker feet possessed the advantage. The two of them would never escape this motley group behind them—not with Griffin holding them back.

*Take my sword. And use it someday if you must to defend your family and those you love.*

The words of King Edward echoed mistily, a call to arms, and Griffin slowed his pace, shouting, "Go, Simon. Run! I'll give you the time you need."

Simon, almost at the wall, looked back and hesitated, but Griffin waved his sword. "Go! I shall be all right!"

*My life for yours.*

He turned to face the foe as Simon surmounted the wall.

There were four of them—four men who experienced the wrath of Griffin Eadricson and the sword of King Edward.

273

Simon's last vision before he jumped into the river was that of his friend standing amid carnage, his blond hair shining pale in the winter sun, his face streaked with the blood of men from across the sea. That familiar cry blew from between his lips as more men fell beneath the terror of his blade. Seeking to destroy the stonemason's son, others approached him.

The white flag was raised.

Griffin lay down his sword when Earl Morkar surrendered. Symbolically, the grass was soaked with the mingled blood of English and Norman. Fires burned throughout the city. Men died all about him. And yet it wasn't until his sword, King Edward's sword, was taken up by the hand of a Norman, that Griffin experienced a perfect hatred. His body shook as he tried to control the rage.

He was bound and led away.

Camped in a large cave with the remainder of the rebel forces, Simon huddled by a fire, seeking warmth to overcome the chill of the icy swim. Griffin's body would swing lifeless from the gallows of William the Conqueror. The thought brought on another series of shivers to the disconsolate Englishman.

He imagined the dome of the heavens where the ceiling of the cave hovered. And in a simple, solemn prayer, Simon Leofricson prayed for his childhood friend.

ক্ষ্ন ক্ষ্ন ক্ষ্ন

Just before the surrender was made, William's keen eye lighted upon the blond berserker. He watched the dance of death Griffin was performing, and immediately his Norse ancestors came to mind. A strange affinity developed inside of him in regard to the Saxon warrior.

"He would serve me well."

But even more intriguing—the sword. He remembered it vividly. But who was its wielder now? And how did he come to possess the sword of a king?

274

He could only be one man, the Conqueror realized, as he remembered the tale of a night in Westminster.

⋙ ⋙ ⋙

All that day hammers pounded nails into wooden planks, the erratic staccato heavily denting the air. Norman carpenters hastily constructed a towering gallows. William would leave no captured rebel alive who refused to swear fealty. His justice was swift, sure, and permanent. Already the north had become a wasteland on his march to York.

In a holding pen near the ruined castle the surrendered outlaws, chained together by their feet, sat on the frozen ground, awaiting their demise. Each thud of the hammers battered their hearts, bringing to mind their wives and their children, mothers and fathers. How easy it would be to swear allegiance to William and go home. Many did. And though he was a man of fortitude, it was only when he looked into Leofwine's weary eyes that Griffin refused to bow the knee to the Conqueror. *Besides, Lilla would have wanted it that way*, he convinced himself.

She carried his child.

The thought made his heart a wretched, twisted thing. The child would grow to maturity without his father. How easy it was to imagine the two of them walking down a sunlit lane, Lilla and a small blond boy. As they continued on, one grew taller, the other older. Griffin winced against the pain and swallowed it down.

The waiting became interminable. But Griffin and Leofwine were chained together, so affording them a bit of company in their final hours.

Leofwine's voice was dull. "So today we die." The noise of the carpenters bore a strange consolation after three years of fighting in one form or another.

"Aye, my lord." Griffin picked at a piece of winter grass, a light, chilly breeze blowing through his hair. He pulled the amulet from beneath his leather hauberk and stared at the golden eye in the center of the disc. "Today we hang." He murmured as though it was the tail-end of a longer, more complex thought.

Leofwine looked on the younger man kindly, mistaking the statement as a reflection of fear. "As a soldier, I've been through worse pain. Hanging is a relatively quick death, son."

"Perhaps. Feelings of sadness—such complete sadness at leaving Lilla and the coming child—eclipse any other emotion I might feel. Fear is the least of it." He continued to toy with the necklace. "And Mother, to be sure, will grieve most handily when the news of my death reaches her ears."

Leofwine grasped an opportunity and why not, they were dead men both. "Your mother. Tell me about her."

Griffin couldn't help but smile. "She's very devout. But she knows how to laugh. Her heart is soft and giving. And after I am gone, I can only hope that Lilla will find her. Lilla has no one. I'm sure my parents would take her as their daughter, help her to raise the child." He sighed deeply, yet without apology. "I never really believed that when Edmund and I rode off, it would be the last time I would talk with her, the last time I would hear her voice."

"At least you got to see her once," Leofwine encouraged.

"Yes, at least there was that."

Silence buffeted them for several minutes. Leofwine stared hypnotically at the amulet which still hung from Griffin's fingers.

"Griffin, there's something I wish to tell you. It's important."

"Speak, my lord."

"Edmund wanted me to tell you before he died. And I suppose it was selfish to wait. But now . . . it matters not. We are to enter the vale of death soon. I'm sure this will all come as a surprise. Yet you have the right to die knowing who you truly are, just what blood flows through your veins."

Griffin was puzzled, and Leofwine continued.

"The amulet you wear bears the mark of our family. We have always thought of ourselves as strong people. Hence the bear and the dragon. This amulet was given to your grandmother many years ago by my father."

Griffin leaned forward.

"My father, Lord Uhtred, is your grandfather. I am your uncle, Griffin." Leofwine felt a sudden thrill rush into his heart as the secret was finally told. "Your grandfather did not die before your mother was born, Griffin. She was the result of a three-month love affair between my father and a simple maiden of Oxneford. After my mother died, he told us the tale. For years after that, he tried to find his daughter, but all he could uncover was that her mother—"

"Bronwyn," Griffin interrupted.

"Yes, Bronwyn . . . left Oxneford before she had the child."

"She must have moved to Bath," Griffin surmised.

"Is that where your mother grew to womanhood?"

Griffin nodded. "She must have known. She handed me the amulet and bade me ride for Oxneford." His head was spinning.

"So you are my uncle," he stated with joy and regret.

"Yes, as was Edmund. He was proud of you. Proud that you shared our blood. For you are of noble blood, Griffin. And you must know it gives me great comfort that Uhtred's seed will not die with me."

"I die today as well."

"Yes, but Lilla lives. And so does the babe. The line of the lords of Oxneford will not go down to dust."

*The line of the lords of Oxneford.*

Through his veins flowed the blood of a warrior house. Griffin thrilled. The lords of Oxneford, ready in battle, clearwitted in the heat of skirmish. Evident it became that he had never been destined to be a stonemason, for in him was Lord Uhtred. Relief cleansed his conscience as a battle long fought in a foggy confusion of years was decided. The victory was clear, and all the doubts and misgivings he had carried into battle with him that morning dissipated with the heated rays of truth. Always he had been meant to fight against the Conqueror, even as his grandfather and his uncle, too, had fought against him at Hastings three years previous.

"Do we all appear like unto Uhtred?" he asked a minute later.

"Ah, so you noticed the resemblance we bear. 'Tis true, we do resemble my father. But what startles me the most is the resemblance you bear to Edmund."

"Edmund?"

"Aye. Before he was overcome with illness. He looked much like you, especially when he was young. Of course, he wasn't as broad as you are. But then, he didn't grow up building a church."

"No, but he grew up loving it just the same."

"Edmund and I were always so different. I often wondered how he could give up his inheritance so easily. But I didn't question him. I wanted it all for myself. I still do."

Griffin said nothing to the futile proclamation. The hammers still pounded, and he clung to the sound, knowing when they stopped, it was that much sooner until the nooses would be thrown over the crossbeam.

"Why didn't you tell me before?"

"I didn't know if I could trust you, Griffin, not to betray me for your own gain."

"Even after I risked my life to free Edmund?"

"Yes. Even then."

Griffin sat back against the wood fence once more, listening as the carpenters erected their monument to death and domination. The hammers ceased and all was still. Breathlessly so. Wulf began to pray, his voice strong and clear. The words of stalwart Englishmen reached the Conqueror's ears as he waited near his pavilion for the execution to begin.

"Our Father, which art in heaven . . ."

## TWENTY-SIX

Robert Montgomery bowed before his king. "The gallows are finished, my liege. Shall the executions begin?"

"Yes. Have all been given another chance to swear fealty?"

"Yes. And all but two remained as before."

The Conqueror nodded, his mouth a grim line. "Proceed then."

"As you wish, sire."

Montgomery gave the orders, and ten prisoners were led single file outside the city walls. Like geometric skeletons, the gallows bared their shaven bones against the British sky as the wind whistled through the cold abscesses between each post, under each crossbar.

Five minutes later, ten more took their place.

The Conqueror carefully studied the proud Englishmen, and as much as he despised the trouble they created for him, he respected their zeal and knew that if he wore such a stole of oppression upon his shoulders, he would act much the same. Many caught his eye as they bravely marched to meet their fate, heads proudly raised, shoulders back. But two, in particular, standing taller than the others, caught his attention. And he remembered the commoner, valiant fighter though he was, who wielded the personal sword of King Edward.

He pointed to Griffin. "Bring that one to me, Montgomery, before he is forever claimed by the noose."

⋖⋗ ⋖⋗ ⋖⋗

Griffin craned his neck back to see the top of the crossbar. Already ten men had been hung. Already their lifeless bodies were removed from the abrasive, strangling nooses which now swung in the breeze. He walked forward, Leofwine in front of him, and stood beneath a noose. Their hands were now tied behind their backs.

"Our Father," he began to repeat the Pater Noster, and his eyes closed against the terror which forced the breath from his lungs, making him feel light and not altogether earthly. But as he had done so many times, he forgot the words he had repeated over and over again all his life.

Though trying to be brave, the young bard Edwin sobbed out in anguish.

Leofwine's voice rang strong above the deathly silence. "Be of courage! We die for England this day!"

An answering cry rose up. "For England!"

The final cry of freedom.

The nooses were shoved over their heads, encircling their necks tightly.

Griffin felt the rough hemp claw abrasively at his neck.

"Oh, Jesu," he prayed once more—once more before seeing his Lord face-to-face." Keep me strong, brave, and faithful to the end. Help me to play the man."

Robert Montgomery strode quickly toward the gallows. The Conqueror wanted to meet the rebel, whoever he was, and he knew he must hurry before the ropes were pulled.

Once Griffin closed his eyes, he dare not open them again. His soul cried out to God, and mercifully the only vision he saw as he waited for the signal, waited for the pressure of the rope, was the face of Lilla. Her soft curls, heavy in his hand, the smoothness of her lips—he could feel them.

The executioner called out.

Griffin fixed his mind on their first time of love before the small fire of the hut. Her silky skin, her smile, the love in her eyes.

The rope tightened.

The vision of Lilla grew stronger, more detailed. Her laughing green eyes. Strong hands reaching out to him. Only him. Only . . .

His feet no longer touched the ground. Soon the blood would cease to flow to the brain, the world would blacken around him, and death would take him from all that he loved best. Yet Griffin didn't fight against the pressure of the noose. Rather, he gave himself up to a clean, honorable, manly passing.

A man shouted, feet scuffled, and Griffin dared not look as consciousness was gratefully lost.

"Wait!" Robert Montgomery raced forward with a yell, up the wooden steps and onto the platform. His sword slipped from its scabbard and in one sweeping arc severed the rope from which Griffin was suspended.

The two-foot fall immediately pulled Griffin from the one-dimensional world of death. His throat burned from the extreme pressure of the rope, his blue eyes took in his rescuer through a haze of confusion.

"Your name, lad," the Norman said. "What is your name?"

He couldn't speak. Montgomery repeated the question, shaking Griffin by the shoulders. "What is your name?"

"Griffin Eadricson," Griffin rasped between coughs, hardly able to breathe, even less so to speak.

"Guards, bind his hands," Montgomery ordered and hurried up to the royal pavilion. As he ran, the king raised a hand and shouted, "Who is he?"

"Griffin Eadricson!" Robert Montgomery shouted back.

"Just as I thought." William said the words to himself. Griffin Eadricson, King Edward's godson, the son of the royal mason. Now that he had seen with his own eyes the way the man could fight, he knew that night in Westminster could not have carried any other outcome.

Just then, Odo de Chauliac ran forward and bent the knee before the king. His face was whiter than usual. "Sire, I would ask that you would put Griffin Eadricson into my care."

Montgomery returned with Griffin.

"What is the reason for your request?"

"He aided Leofwine Uhtredson in freeing Edmund from my prison."

William's eyebrows raised. "Did he? How?"

"Through a well."

"He is young, Odo, and would be a good warrior for your king. I've seen him fight now. Even you are not so ferocious, Odo. But he knows the whereabouts of Hereward the Wake, of that I am certain. It was reported to me that he was running for the wall with the others, but turned to fight off the pursuers. He sacrificed himself for them. Very noble."

"Very stupid," Odo snorted.

The king looked at him sharply. "He bears a strength, an honor you know nothing about, sir knight! All you do, you do for reward. For a guerdon."

The Conqueror turned to Griffin. "You are Griffin Eadricson."

"I am."

"You're speaking to the king!" one of the guards growled, and threw Griffin face down at William's feet. "Show the proper respect!"

"Enough, Rollo," the king said, surprised to hear the rebel speak in his own native language. "Help him to his feet. This man was the godson of King Edward."

Griffin was yanked to his feet, but he said nothing, merely staring stonily at King William.

"Your godfather was my cousin." He reached behind him and pulled Edward's sword off the table. "I remember this well. Did he give it to you?"

In response, Griffin gave only a nod.

"Sir Odo here wants you for himself. What have you to say about that? You can tell us the whereabouts of the rebels now and be a free man."

Griffin still said nothing.

"All right, de Chauliac, I see no good reason why I should not grant your request. You have been a loyal knight for years, despite the reasons why. I'm sure you seek him to make of him an example to the people of Oxneford. But know this: In return for the favor I am extending, I wish for you to find the whereabouts of Hereward the Wake and the others who escaped. This man knows to where they fled and where their final destination was to be should any of them become separated."

Griffin said nothing, for the king was right.

"Thank you, my liege." Griffin would soon be in Odo's clutches. "I will do my best, sire, to find out the whereabouts of the rebels."

The Conqueror's eyes were steely. "I'm counting on that."

Odo bowed and was gone at the subsequent dismissal.

"Put him back into the pen, Montgomery! This one shall not hang today."

At the hand of a gruff Norman soldier, Griffin was led away.

Back in the corral, he lay on his back. The sky had darkened, and the evening's first stars began to illumine the velvet expanse. The coldness of the dark seeped through to the gritty marrow of his bones. For the first time since he had come to know Jesu intimately, Griffin felt completely alone. Where was the Savior now?

Leofwine was dead. Ebb and Simon were gone. And he had fallen into the hands of none other than Odo de Chauliac.

Desolation overtook him.

Along the Roman road, a group of travelers proceeded southward. One Englishman, a rope tied round his throat, struggled to keep up with the horse he was tied behind. His green tunic was an accumulation of tatters, his gray hosen torn in many places. From him his shoes had been taken, leaving his feet blue with cold. A score of gashes and cuts transfigured his face into a mask of pain. Bruises were in evidence under his eyes and flowered in purple profusion over his white limbs.

"Hurry, dog!" the Norman called over his shoulder. "We will make it to Oxneford tonight! And I'm sure you don't wish to be dragged the entire way by your neck!"

Odo de Chauliac clutched the amulet in his hand, looking upon the necklace with a stony face. Griffin faltered again, his exhausted legs obstinately failing to observe the pace of the horse in front of him. He fell facedown into the road, the hemp reopening the scabs which had collected from the hanging. Quickly, his bloody hands reached up to grab the rope, loosing its strangling hold.

"Halt!" Odo called to his retinue. The garrison of Castle Chauliac was returning to their ill-gotten home. They obeyed, reining in their horses to a stop.

De Chauliac jumped down from his horse, straightened his tunic beneath his mantle, pulled a whip from his saddlebag, and strode quickly to his prisoner, who now stood with head bowed, trying to gain a clear enough vision to look at his captor. "Hurry your pace! We must get back. Your lady awaits."

Griffin's head snapped up, his blue eyes sparked with anger, but he spoke not yet through his cracked, swollen lips. He couldn't tell how long they had been traveling thus. Each afternoon he was hoisted into the back of the provisions cart, but only because he was slowing down the group. That frightened him more than anything. Because he knew that de Chauliac wanted him alive—alive yet broken. And each time he pondered that, he remembered the machines in the bottom of the prison tower of Beam-Dune Maur. Surely stronger men than himself had crumpled beneath the pressure of such devices. Better death than to betray Simon, Ebb, and Hereward and his band, he had decided days before. But those thoughts were suddenly cast aside at de Chauliac's reference to Lilla.

"If she is harmed . . ." Griffin grated painfully.

"No. No. She is fine—most beautiful in the goodly garments I have bestowed upon her. She lives the life of a queen. She lives in my castle."

Griffin said nothing.

"She is a special woman, your wife. Once you are dead and I offer her love and care in exchange, she will be freed from her cage. Unless, of course, you reveal the whereabouts of the Wake and his forces."

"She'll know I'm alive. In her heart she'll know that I am not dead."

"Romantic drivel, good man. Now . . . you will hurry your pace. Or must I give you incentive?" He held up the silver-trimmed ebon handle of the whip. Already Griffin's back oozed with festering wounds from the glass-nubbed implement. Griffin squared his shoulders and, drawing strength from the noble blood which ran through him, he said, "Proceed."

De Chauliac mounted his horse, and the journey of agony began again. Yet hope arrived. Lilla was still at Castle Chauliac.

⚜ ⚜ ⚜

"The garrison returns!" a shout was heard from the walls of the castle. The night was black, but with her bedspread wrapped around her, Lilla limped to the window. Pulling back the hide, she peered outside to the courtyard.

Cheers of victory resounded as the victorious troop made their way through the raised portcullis. Torches inefficiently threw their writhing, dancing light against the stone walls. Nothing could be seen in the darkness but vague outlines and large, swaying shadows cast in the flickering illumination.

Lilla watched in horror. Her hand flew to her mouth as her stomach lurched.

The English had fallen at York.

Lord Stephen, his mantle pulled tightly around his nightclothes, rushed outside, and immediately Odo's cry of "We were victorious. Long live King William!" was heard.

"Long live the king!" the unified voice of the garrison roared.

"What happened?" Stephen de Chauliac called with concern above the din. "Did we lose many men?"

"The losses were heavy, yes . . . but the day was ours."

In the back of the cart, Griffin lay, pale and exhausted. But Stephen didn't notice. "After you've seen to your horses," the baron called, "come into the hall and fill your bellies!" He turned to his steward. "Rouse the servants and make the necessary preparations."

"Father," Odo laid a hand on Stephen's sleeve, "the day was ours. Are you not glad?"

"Well done, son," he said, then called out to all the men, "Well done, everyone! Hopefully now both Normans and English will live in peace."

He walked into the keep and up to his solar.

Odo looked up. Lilla's silhouette was clearly seen in her window.

Around the cart he walked, pulling Griffin to his feet.

"Griffin!" she shouted from the tower, remembering Odo's promise to bring him back. "My love! Are you there?"

The stonemason's son opened his mouth to yell. Odo slid his gauntleted hand over his mouth. The cold steel of a dagger was tipped against his jugular. "If you say anything, I promise you, it will be your last word." He yelled cruelly up to Lilla, remembering again her attempt to escape from him, "You proclaim your love to a phantom. Go to sleep, my dear Lilla, and dream of your Griffin."

Griffin was invested into the bottom of the prison tower, a small cell just off the torture chamber. Odo de Chauliac then strode into the keep, seeking nothing more than a good night's sleep.

# ❧ TWENTY-SEVEN ❧

**D**e Chauliac enjoyed the unperturbed sleep of a conscienceless human.

Griffin was tossed upon a sparse pile of decaying straw in the midst of the small cell. The tiny room wasn't long enough for him to stretch out completely, nor high enough for him to stand. He curled himself up tightly—his only means of warmth. *When spring comes it should be better in here,* he thought hopefully as he drifted off into an exhausted sleep. But his eyes opened up wide again. *When spring came?* Had he already committed himself to a long imprisonment? What did de Chauliac have planned for him? And why would Odo think for even a moment that Griffin, who had placed himself between Simon and the Normans, would betray his friend now?

A rat scurried over his torso, but Griffin didn't feel the little clawed paws snag on the wool of his tunic. He had fallen into a deep sleep. A gift from above, for the Savior had not left him at all. The road ahead was long, hard, and ugly, but one that others had trod before him, and when Griffin had completed his journey, he would walk with head held high.

The lock rattled in a way Lilla hadn't heard for over two months. It was just dawning, and already Odo de Chauliac had come.

Her misery was great. Sleep had not come, and she grieved . . . and grieved, till tears refused to refresh her.

He walked into the room. "Lilla."

"My lord." Lilla pulled her bedclothes up around her neck. "You were victorious." The words were an indictment.

"Yes."

"And Griffin?"

"He was hung later that afternoon."

Lilla's shoulders lurched forward as her lungs heaved, and her eyes filled and overflowed once more. But she forced down the urge and turned her face to look at him in accusation. "You promised me you'd bring him back."

"I said I would try, Lilla. There was nothing I could do. King William wanted no lives spared." Odo placed his hand on her shoulder in a tender manner. "He died honorably, Lilla. There were no cries, no protestations. He went silently and with strength. He was given the opportunity thrice to swear fealty to William. But he chose not to."

"Good," Lilla whispered.

"Yes," Odo drew an emotional knife, "'tis a strong man who looks beyond his wife and dies for the sake of freedom."

"And what of Leofwine and Ebb?"

"They were both hung," he lied. There must be no hope left to germinate in Lilla's mind.

Lilla's hands shielded her face. "Leave me, my lord." She would not cry in front of this man.

"As you wish. I'm off to London . . . at father's request. I will return in a week's time."

"It matters not."

De Chauliac raised her hand to his lips and squeezed her fingers gently, an expression of compassion in his black eyes. But Lilla didn't notice. She didn't hear the door click shut.

Didn't hear the bolt thrown into place.

Griffin was dead.

And she was left to carry on without him.

Pleased with his performance, Odo de Chauliac walked down the steps and out into the courtyard. He had made Griffin a hero. His death was clean and honorable in Lilla's mind, with just enough doubt to taint his memory. It was a chapter closed with a tidy finality. Lilla would be his, and the fact that he wanted her at all was most disconcerting. But want her he did. She had sorely softened a spot within his heart.

"I love her," he whispered painfully. "God help me, but I love her."

❧ ❧ ❧

Desolate.

Chilled.

Confined. Griffin awaited Odo de Chauliac's return.

His wounds were healing, his body reconstituting itself. But not in a mighty way. There wasn't enough food for that. The brackish water was hardly a boon to his health either. But Lilla awaited him. Someday.

❧ ❧ ❧

Odo returned bearing all the miseries of hell.

Griffin resisted at first. Shouting against the burning pain of the pokers against his flesh, cursing through his teeth the Normans who had stolen his country.

The interrogations were only directed at one purpose, one goal: the whereabouts of Hereward the Wake. And once when the pain was heinously great, the stress unbelievably overpowering, Griffin had to choke down his screams for fear that in them the coveted information would be found.

Day turned into night. Again and again. Each day a different misery was forced upon him. His beard was plucked out, and on other days he was forced to stand motionless for hours or be beaten senseless. And always he would be thrown back into his cell, wet from the waters of revival which had tumbled upon him many times. How long had it gone on—how many days had he been forced to endure? He couldn't tell. But as long as he spoke not, screamed not, he would remain alive. In the dank, stale air of the chamber, he could not tell when day ended and night began. And always that same torch burned. The torch which lit the brazier in the middle of the floor, its smoke blackening further the suffocating gloom.

A desperation coated his will for survival, for Griffin knew the day he divulged the whereabouts of the rebel camp was the day he would surely die. Odo had no other need for his prisoner in the dungeon. And so his tongue became a useless thing. For whilst his tongue was mute, his mind was far from silent. All was gone from him. His body was burned and scarred. Lilla was unreachable. England was lost.

*Where are You?*

Doubts and fear filled his mind as anger at the Almighty shook his racked body. All was gone, gone. Even God's peace had fled in the hour he needed it most. He never expected life to be a series of joys without heartache, but this? There was no comfort to be found. Nothing but burning physical pain, starvation, cold, loneliness, and darkness. It was as if he was in hell itself.

He likened himself to Job. For although he felt as if God had indeed forsaken him, had given him over to the foul mercies of the prince of darkness, he could not forsake Him. At times he wanted to. Desperately. And that he couldn't make himself do so angered him yet more.

Curse God and die!

It wasn't as easy as it sounded.

But in the desolate darkness of his cell, Griffin would raise his fist in the air anyway, and pretend he was doing just that. To die. To die. To die.

Curse God and die.

❧ ❧ ❧

A month had gone by since Lilla had imparted the news of Griffin's death to Sylvia.

"I have some dreadful news, Lilla," Sylvia began. The late afternoon sun slanted through the window, the atmosphere exhaling the first breath of spring into the room.

"Ida is dead."

"What?"

"Yes. I am afraid it is true."

Lilla leaned forward on her chair. Death . . . so much death. "What happened?"

"She took her own life."

Lilla gasped. "How?"

"They found her by the banks of the river, broken and distorted. She was in her nightclothes and cloak. Apparently, she couldn't sleep and was walking up on the walls. She must have slipped and fallen over."

"And now she and Sir Odo will never make amends."

"No. But their marriage was doomed before they ever said their vows, Lilla."

Lilla nodded. Sylvia was right. But that didn't make the tidings any brighter. Someone else had died. First it was her own child, then Griffin, now Ida.

"Who will go next?" she muttered to herself.

"What did you say, Lilla?"

"Nothing. But tell me, what do you think I should do, Sylvia?" She turned in her chair toward her loom. Automatically, her fingers began to thread the apparatus with a deep-purple silk.

"What do you mean?"

"Griffin is . . . gone. There is no reason for me to stay here. Perhaps I can find a way to escape. More successfully this time."

Sylvia frowned. "Where will you go?"

"I don't know. Surely now that Griffin is dead, Sir Odo has no more need to keep me here."

"Indeed, he does."

Lilla turned back around to look at Sylvia. "What reason could he possibly have?"

"You are most comely, and your spirit is filled with a genuine loveliness. It would call to even Odo, rendering hope of some sort."

"If he truly loves me, he will let me go home."

Sylvia smoothed Lilla's wayward curls. "Odo's love cannot be confused with Griffin's. How he may love, how he may express it, is something we may not be able to predict."

Sylvia lifted an apple off the tray of fruit she had brought with her. "I have an idea, Lilla. Perhaps I should talk to Odo. Maybe the sight of a pleading, pregnant woman will be too much for even him to argue with!"

"Why not, my lady? I cannot stay in this tower forever."

"I may not be able to do it right away. It's best to catch Odo when he is in a good mood."

❧ ❧ ❧

It was a happy homecoming that early April day in the village of Oxneford. One of the inhabitants had served his time in the prison tower of Castle Chauliac. Poaching was his offense.

His wife and children gathered round him and ushered him back to their dwelling. But later that evening, when the little ones were sleeping before the fire, he spoke to his wife in hushed tones, answering her questions regarding his confinement.

She grew angry as he told her of the conditions under which he had lived, saw the weight he had lost when he lifted up his frayed tunic. But he held up a hand.

"My imprisonment was nothing compared to another man who was there."

"Who?"

"I don't know. He was kept down even lower in the tower than I, in rooms which must be far underground. But I heard his screams. At least at the beginning. What happened to him, I know not." He shuddered. "But doors down there were always opening and closing, pounding was going on, thumping. Horrible noises from which I could figure nothing. An Englishman, no doubt."

"God bless him, whoever he is," the good wife whispered as she prayed a brief prayer.

The only prayer which heaven heard on behalf of Griffin Eadricson.

❦ ❦ ❦

"No." Odo's eyes snapped at his sister-in-law.

"What do you mean 'no'?" Sylvia bit back. "You can't keep her prisoner. She grieves her husband, her lost child. Why must you add to her afflictions, Odo?"

"Lost child?" Odo looked sharply in her direction. "I *knew* she had been carrying!" He paused beneath an elm tree. He wondered why Sylvia had invited him for a walk. Now he knew. More than a month had passed since Ida's funeral, and although Lilla was kind and courteous to him, he knew he had made no progress. It was time to change tactics, but he wasn't sure where to go from here. Certainly, he wasn't going to agree to Sylvia's proposal.

"Her husband is dead, Sylvia. Being free won't make any difference. It won't give her succor in her time of need. Only human warmth can do that."

"Of which you have an abundance," Sylvia said sarcastically.

Odo leaned forward, grabbed Sylvia's chin in an iron grip, and bore his eyes into hers. "Hell is the hottest place in existence, dear girl."

"I'll find a way, Odo," Sylvia promised.

He reached out and traced a gentle hand across her belly, which was starting to swell with the coming child. His words were quiet, yet menacing. "If you know what's good for you, for your babe, Sylvia, you'll leave well enough alone. Lilla aided in the escape of Leofwine Uhtredson. She deserves more than what I am giving her."

Sylvia pushed his hand away. "You don't scare me, Odo."

"If you were wise, sister, I would scare the very breath out of your body."

Sylvia knew she was beaten. Odo was right: Lilla was a rebel. "Sweet Mary, Lilla's been locked up for months now, Odo! Give her the chance to at least roam the bailey. She doesn't say so, but her leg grows worse from lack of exercise."

Odo was quiet for a moment as he thought of Sylvia's proposition. "Perhaps you are right, Sylvia." His mouth smiled widely. "If she was in a healthier state, she might turn to me more easily."

"May she take some of her meals with us in the hall?"

"Surely. But she is still a prisoner of Castle Chauliac. That status must be maintained."

Sylvia turned to go, thinking she must be mistaken that a tinge of desperation laced his tones. "Thank you, Odo." And claiming a small victory, she hurried back to the castle to inform Lilla of her success.

Odo allowed Sylvia the feeling of preeminence. What she didn't know was that her demand perfected his plan. If he had seen the genius of it beforehand, he would have instituted the changes himself. Griffin, almost broken from the devices of torture, would crack completely when he saw Lilla on his enemy's arm as she walked the courtyard in her fine gowns.

The Norman had racked the prisoner's body, burned it with pokers and scalding water. Now he would torture Griffin in a different, far more debilitating manner. Pain of the flesh was but a soft caress when compared to pain of the heart.

Ah, the rebels were sure to be his soon. And Lilla. Maybe not soon, but she would be his nonetheless.

Across the field, Odo de Chauliac's laugh echoed.

## TWENTY-EIGHT

M eekly, Griffin allowed himself to be pulled from his cell. Pain had become relative. It was constant now—the only thing that reminded him he was a living human being. All that kept him from becoming a beast.

"Get along, swine!" The jailer pushed him up the steps. "Up you go."

No questions formed in Griffin's mind. He merely did as he was told and stumbled up the steep circular stone staircase.

The room he was shoved into was starkly familiar. Edmund's room. The April breeze freshened the stale air. Odo stepped into the room. "Your days of bodily torture are over, mon amie. You've proved yourself brave and strong."

Griffin kept his head bowed, his chin almost resting on his chest.

"Oui. From this day onward, your life will be spent in this room. 'Tis better than your old one, eh?"

Still he spoke not.

"Come, come," de Chauliac chided, "can we not speak? It's amazing what a man can live through, isn't it, Englishman? But that is no matter. I brought you here for a reason. Tomorrow you shall see Lilla."

Griffin's heart sped its beating, but he made no response, his eyes remained listless.

"That's right. You will look out your window tomorrow morning. Rest now, Englishman. Tomorrow will be the worst day you've ever lived. By the way, she lost the baby months ago," he reported cruelly.

He turned and left, the heavy door closing with a thud. Griffin laid his weary body on the same straw Edward had lain upon, sinking his drastically reduced frame onto the rough woolen blanket.

*Lilla.*

Her face was the last thing he saw before his eyes. He fell asleep planning not to awaken until dawn should arrive. Odo de Chauliac was right: Pain of the body was but flotsam when compared to pain of the heart.

❧ ❧ ❧

It rained the next morning. Driving gales blew up a spring storm, and nature's melee obstinately refused to abate for four days. The great hall was aglow, a massive fire leaping in the center of the room. Its smoke rose through a vent in the ceiling. A flood of lamps and candles added yet more glory to the bustling, celebratory scene. The food was spectacularly served and prepared by Lord Stephen's order to help dispel the shadow of boredom in the hearts of those who inhabited his castle. Lilla sat in between Sylvia and Lord Stephen. Being beside the great man gave her a joy she hadn't known since the news of Griffin's death had come to her. His presence was overwhelming, imparting a sense of warmth and importance to each who sat at his table.

Benevolent and intuitive, his eyes—the color of freshly turned spring soil—smiled into hers. "Did Sylvia tell you that you may have free rein of the grounds inside the palisades?"

"Yes, my lord, and well I would have used them but for these past days of rain."

"You've shown yourself highly respectable, madam—a woman of propriety—and proven to be a loyal friend to Sylvia."

"Thank you, Lord Stephen."

"I would that you could be set free, but Odo says your village is restless. He believes that if we allow you back to your home, it will be seen as a weakness on the part of the de Chauliacs."

Lilla smiled. "What do you think, my lord?"

Stephen smiled back. "I think my daughter-in-law would be most displeased if I set her Lilla free."

"I know. But I so yearn to go, to find a life I can live in peace."

His eyes were kind. "Can you not do so here?"

"No, my lord. Just knowing I am a prisoner, 'tis enough to make my soul yearn."

"And yet you did aid in Leofwine's escape. It's a light punishment you are receiving. Others have been hanged for far less."

"'Tis true, my lord. But even if I were set free, I would stay until your grandchild is birthed."

"Then you care for Sylvia?"

"Yes."

Sylvia, shamelessly eavesdropping on the conversation, placed a warm hand on top of Lilla's.

"Then you are pardoned," Lord Stephen said suddenly. Lilla's eyes widened, but he continued, "On the condition that you stay here until Sylvia gives birth. And perhaps by that time you will wish to stay with us indefinitely."

"May I wander the fields and the town? And may Soot be allowed into my room?"

"Of course. I believe you are a woman true to your word."

"My lord, might I ask of you a question or two?"

"Certainly."

"From all I've seen of Normans before you came, sir, I believed all of you to be a cruel, ruthless people. But upon meeting you and Sir Hugh, and Sylvia, of course, I must confess that I see another side to those from your homeland. But there is something I fail to understand."

Lord Stephen took a drink of red wine from his ornate, gilt drinking horn. "What is that, Lilla?"

"Please do not take this question as disrespectful, my lord. But how did you justify in your own soul the subjugation of an entire nation?"

A sigh escaped Stephen's lips. "My child, there are many opinions as to who should have laid claim to the throne. But when all was said and done, King William's great-aunt was Emma, the mother of King Edward."

"But Edgar Ethling . . . does not he have as great a claim?"

"Yes, he does. But, barring the fact that he is a child, he was never named by Edward to be his successor. King William was. Long ago. True it is that Harold was named by Edward on his deathbed, but one cannot be sure what happened. Was Edward coerced? Was he out of his mind at the end of his life? The events of that day are obscure. Harold was not of royal blood, Lilla. Even the happenings surrounding his coronation are heavily veiled and not altogether clear. William believes the crown was stolen from him by the Godwinson. The pope sided with William as well."

"But," Lilla shook her head in anguish, "so many have died."

"'Tis the way of kings, Lilla. Since the dawn of history, leaders have used up the lives of others for the sake of their own position, their own thirst for power, for immortality. I wish it wasn't so, but we must accept the fact that mankind has always lived as such and always will."

"Until Jesu comes again," Lilla whispered to herself.

Odo walked into the room just then.

"Odo!" Lord Stephen called. "Come here, I've something to tell you."

Sir Odo walked across the bustling hall, climbed the steps of the dais and stood beside his father. "Yes, Father?"

"I've given Lilla her freedom."

"What!"

The lordly Norman held up a hand. "On the condition that she stay until your sister-in-law gives birth to my grandchild."

Odo quickly calculated. "As you will, father," he bowed stiffly. He laid a warm hand upon Lilla's shoulder. "But we certainly will miss the pleasantness of her countenance at Castle Chauliac, will we not?"

"To be sure we will, Odo."

"By the way, father, I am leaving tomorrow for Normandy," Odo announced.

"Good!" Lord Stephen's brows raised in pleasure. "Seeing to the estates?"

"Naturally."

"Well, Odo. That is a relief and a lightening of the mind. I'm enjoying England so greatly I hated the thought of making that trip myself. Thank you."

Odo bowed and went to take his seat. Yes, he was leaving, but not for long, and there was one final matter of business to be taken care of before he left.

Lord Stephen de Chauliac sat back in his chair and looked about him. Cruel and ruthless. Lilla's words haunted him. Surely the only Normans she had come in contact with were his men. His own garrison under Odo's leadership.

For years Stephen de Chauliac had put off the disciplining of his son. He had failed as a father where Odo's character was concerned, and he would readily admit that. But Odo's mother had died only a few years after his birth. The affairs of state had called. And by the time Stephen married again years later the mother of Hugh, it was too late to try and bring Odo into the family. Odo wasn't raised—he merely grew up. Because of that, Stephen had extended great allowances regarding his son's behavior. But no more. If indeed his son had produced a reign of terror in Oxneford, Lord Stephen de Chauliac would uncover it. And for the first time in his life, Odo de Chauliac would be made to answer for his actions.

꙳ ꙳ ꙳

By the time Lilla returned to her room from dinner, the guard was gone and the only lock that could be found upon her door was inside the room. She breathed a sigh of relief. When a knock sounded from the hallway, she answered gladly—thinking, of course, that it was Sylvia.

"May I come in?" Odo stood before her, dressed in a tunic of parti-colored silk. His dark hair curled endearingly around his face and, without warning, Lilla felt her heart open wide with pity. Showing him in, she made sure to leave the door to the hallway open.

"So you've won a victory today, Lilla," he conceded, picking up the wide length of braid she had been weaving that afternoon and running his sensitive fingertips over the nubby thread.

"Of sorts, Sir Odo. 'Twas but a matter of time before I would be viewed as less than threatening."

"Ah," his voice was a soft whisper, "but you are threatening. To me."

Lilla stiffened when he took her hand in his. "You are turning fanciful on the eve of your departure, my lord," she laughed nervously.

He shrugged in that Parisian manner. "That could be. But I think not. You see, my heart has fallen under assault, and you threaten to wrest it from me altogether."

Lilla saw a familiar fire in his eyes. "Surely it is not I, my lord, that threatens, but your own desire."

"My desire is but a reflection of my soul, Lilla. And you are not altogether undesirable."

"Why do you tell me this, Sir Odo?"

Odo sighed. "Because you are different. So unlike Ida and the others! If I had been arranged to marry someone like you, someone so good and kind, who's to say in which direction I might have gone? Instead, I was betrothed to someone just like me."

Lilla's kind heart yearned, and she remembered the compassion of Jesu upon sinners. "Do you want to be good, Sir Odo?"

His eyes beseeched her, their brown depths seeming to open up under her compassionate gaze. "I know not where to begin."

"What would you have me do, my lord? The ways of Jesu are vast, impossible to comprehend, even more burdensome to live unless the heart has been changed."

"Do not forsake me now that freedom is yours. Show me the way."

"But you are leaving tomorrow," she reasoned.

"I shall be back soon enough." Excitement rang through the words. "And then I shall come back to you . . . oh, Lilla . . . do you realize that this might well be the turning point of my life?"

"I pray that it is." Lilla's gentle eyes shone with compassion. "What time are you leaving in the morning?"

"I was going to leave at first light. But just an hour ago the rain stopped. Would you perhaps take some exercise upon my arm tomorrow morning in the courtyard? Sylvia tells me your leg has become most wearisome for lack of exercise."

Lilla nodded. "All right. I shall meet you downstairs just after daybreak."

Odo de Chauliac looked years younger as his brow suddenly cleared and his eyes shone with excitement. "Thank you, Lilla. I shall retire to my bed this night with much anticipation for the morrow."

When her door was shut and locked by her own hand, Lilla lay down on the bed. She cried futile tears, fearing that she had no life anymore but that here at Castle Chauliac. It was a dreadful thought, and desolation accompanied it.

"Oh, Griffin," she whispered, "would that you were alive and with me now."

To those around her, Lilla acted as though she was carrying on, carving out a new existance. But only she knew that deep inside a segment of herself had died with her husband. She would continue to live, thrilling in the love of her Savior now that the rage had abated. But the portion that made her a woman was buried by a Norman spade somewhere in the regions of York.

The last rumblings of the storm faded in the distance. And all was quiet.

❧ ❧ ❧

Out of a deep sleep the sudden silence had aroused Griffin, and automatically, for the first time since York, his hand reached for his sword. He had stopped thinking about God, and prayers had ceased over a month before.

Numbness was his no longer. And the need to be free would soon be available for him to claim.

❧ ❧ ❧

Painstakingly, Lilla made her way down the steps from her tower room. The main doors to the keep were thrown wide open, and a renewing breeze blew off the Thames and the river Cherwell none too distant. She drew in her breath when she stepped into the fresh air. The orchards bloomed to the north of the castle. The perfume, so strong after the dampering of the rain, lit her face up in a celestial smile.

❧ ❧ ❧

Griffin strained against his bonds. He tried to call out, but the gag in his mouth forbade him such liberty.

*Lilla!*

She was standing on the top step of the keep looking so fresh and cherry-cheeked in the wind. Her curls had already escaped their braids, just as he remembered. Each curve of her face, the exact shade of her skin had not been forgotten. Yet she looked different, healthier, not so painfully thin. The hair was more lustrous, the skin rosy and luminous. Obviously the de Chauliacs had been feeding her well. A life of ease seemed to suit her beautifully, he thought with self-regret. And a healthy fullness was hers. Gone was the skinny maiden who had toiled excessively during every daylight hour.

The jailer kept a tight hold on him, his cruel fingers pulling the hair on the back of Griffin's head. "Look, dog! Look upon her, and know that she'll never be yours again."

*How can I not look?* Griffin asked himself. *If she merely came each day to take a bit of air, that would make my life worth living. To watch her grow old.* Is she still a prisoner? he wondered. Lilla remained where she was, looking around her in hopes of seeing someone.

He saw her brow clear and her eyes light up in a sparkle. She lifted her hand in a greeting as from the new stables strode Odo de Chauliac dressed entirely in black.

"Mon cherie!" he called. "You came!"

"I said I would, my lord."

Griffin strained to hear the words, but they were carried away on the wind.

Odo's smile was dazzling. "Walk with me, will you, Lilla?"

"For a bit. It would fare me well, as Sylvia rightly surmised." She leaned down on her walking stick and began to take the first step.

"No. No," de Chauliac smiled, "let me help you." Odo lifted Lilla into his arms and carried her down the steps to set her softly down on the verdant bailey.

Griffin fought against the ropes, but his eyes were bonded to the scene before him. His struggle soon ended.

"Thank you, my lord." Inside she felt uneasy at de Chauliac's familiarity, but he was leaving soon.

They walked slowly, Odo tucking her hand into the crook of his arm. "Lilla, you must already be exercising a bit of influence over me."

"What mean you, Sir Odo?"

"So soon I have a confession to humbly lay at your feet."

"Speak then, my lord. What is it?" *A confession? From Odo de Chauliac?* Lilla shuddered at the sudden conjuring of his possible sins.

He stopped and turned toward her, making sure his back was facing Griffin's cell, hiding Lilla from her husband's view. Reaching into his purse he pulled out an object and pressed it into her hand.

Lilla gasped, fighting back tears. The amulet warmed immediately in her palm as she held it to her lips, then her breast. "Where did you find this?" she asked, biting down the spasms that threatened to erupt.

"I've possessed it ever since I returned from York. That is what I must confess, dear Lilla. I had hoped to turn your heart from your husband to myself. But now I see that you will be tied to him forever." He didn't believe the words for a moment, but Lilla did . . . with all her being.

She threw her arms around his neck, so grateful to have a part of Griffin returned to her, no matter the source. A kiss she placed upon his cheek. "Thank you! Thank you for giving this back to me!" She held the chain and was about to put it over her neck, but Odo stopped her, being sure to keep her hands hidden from Griffin's view. "Put it in your purse," he commanded with a genial smile, lifting the small leather bag from where it hung around her waist, dangling next to Sylvia's cross, "and when you get back to your room you'll find a carven box waiting to keep it in."

Lilla's face was radiant.

They continued their slow stroll until they reached the stables. A quick good-bye was said, and Odo was gone.

After Lilla had returned to the keep, Griffin was untied, ungagged, and thrown onto his straw-filled pallet. The jailor laughed. "Funny how quick a woman can change her mind, eh? But then, my master has that effect on all women. Thought your wench was cut of a different cloth, I'll wager. Ha!"

Griffin responded not. All the fight that he had quelled during the days of pain he summoned forth. For at that very moment, Odo de Chauliac became more than a foul Norman—he became a personal enemy, and Griffin hated him utterly.

Odo entered the room. "She's mine now, Englishman. But you have only to tell me the whereabouts of Hereward the Wake, and she will be yours once again."

Griffin said nothing.

"Still silent? I leave for Normandy. But I shall return."

Griffin knew that Odo would never give Lilla over to his prisoner. He knew that Odo loved her as well. What man wouldn't?

The sun arched over the sky that day, and each position it took in the heavens brought no change to Griffin's expression. Deep in thought the young Englishman was. He would escape, he decided, and he would win back Lilla's heart. Odo would not decimate his will or grind to dust his heart and soul. Griffin Eadricson still possessed the strenth of the abbey. He would survive days, months, even years in the tower. When the time was right, he would take his chances, make his move. Odo would fall, and Lilla would be his once again.

Resolve gripped hard his heart, mind, soul, and spirit. And Griffin found he had so much to live for, the least of which was seeing that Odo de Chauliac never laid another finger on his wife.

It was evident that she thought him dead, that he had left her to carry on alone.

*Lilla, Lilla.* His heart groaned in silence for all that might have been had the Normans not landed at Pevensey. But within the spring zephyr that stirred his dirty, sweaty hair, hope was contained, and Griffin planned until the sun forced a rosy backdrop over the night sky.

That night at supper, Lilla told Sylvia of the walk with Odo.

"If I didn't see it hanging about your neck, Lilla, I'd refuse to believe it."

"I'm as surprised as you are. But it leads me to think that maybe underneath Odo's hardened shell may be a man who knows how to love. Perhaps he was never taught."

Sylvia wasn't convinced. So she changed the subject.

# ⤙❧ TWENTY-NINE ❧⤚

L illa watched from her window as soldiers were summoned into the presence of their lord. Men at arms
filed into the great hall, one by one. Even the five knights in
Lord Stephen's employ were required to answer his questions.

The interrogations lasted for fully a week. April was now
in mid-course, and those wretched days of intensified questioning actually took place amid weather fair and sunny. To
feel the warmth of the spring sun on her eyelids gave Lilla the
emotional boost she needed. Winter was hard enough to mud-
dle through. But a winter of grief is too sore for even the
strongest of souls, the bravest of hearts to emerge unscathed.

During that week, Lilla ventured outside at every opportunity. Each morning as the sun rose, she stood upon the ancient
Roman walls, looking out over the lively countryside, always
in the same direction—eyes following the road which led to
the great gatehouse. Did she see the cottagers harrowing and
sowing in the distance? Did she notice the stripes of land turning green, first a light mist, then filling up with tender shoots?
No.

She saw only Griffin, completely aware of the amulet
which hung between her breasts. The thought of a box to keep
it in had been a kind one, she thought, but unnecessary. Inas-
much as its emptiness mirrored the state of her heart, she was

beginning to heal, and the remembrance of her beloved's face brought not only pain, but a warm fondness.

She recalled the thrill of loving him. Yes, she had chosen to love him after counting the costs. And all the warnings given by Griffin before they wed predicted painful events which eventually took place. But it had been worth it to have been loved by his great heart, caressed by his strong hands, kissed by his perfect mouth.

The road which led away from the castle called to her. For she would leave these walls someday. Perhaps she would return to her cottage, perhaps to Westminster to meet Griffin's parents. But whatever she would do, wherever she chose to go, it would only be by that very road that she would venture to freedom.

Griffin, bound and gagged by the vigilant jailer whenever Lilla ventured forth, watched from his window. Her silhouette was still the same: proud, regal, and forthright. The brown hair hung in loose tendrils this day, and he couldn't help but admit that she had always been meant to wear such fine garb.

Why did she watch the road? Was she waiting for the return of Odo de Chauliac? He refused to ponder the possibility. And when the jailer left him and the door was bolted tight, he began his daily regimen, strengthening his muscles, building up his stamina and the capacity of his lungs.

వ్రై వ్రై వ్రై

Robert Shortpants, son and heir of William the Conqueror, shared a cup of wine and congenial conversation with Odo de Chauliac. To be sure, de Chauliac was a master at wordplay. He was witty, charming, and made the Conqueror's son feel as if he could conquer the world himself.

"You amuse me, de Chauliac," Robert chuckled, signaling for the minstrels to continue the song they had just ended. "Would that you could stay in Normandy, here at my court."

"But, my lord, surely there are many such amusing men to be found in Normandy. I'd like to think our lordly race has produced more than one man such as I!"

Robert laughed again—a clear, guileless laugh. And de Chauliac's mind began to turn. Lilla would have to wait. "Perhaps I will stay on for a bit longer, my lord."

"Good, de Chauliac, good." He slapped the older man on the back with a familiarity that pleased Odo for many reasons. William still refused to give him the guerdon he so deserved. Father, old as he was, was in fine fettle. If his life was to have any purpose at all, it would be found through this genial young man. Through Robert Shortpants he could gain the riches and the position he so truly deserved.

And what of Lilla?

He smiled. Yes, she could wait. Griffin was firmly entrenched within the prison tower. The common rebel could die there now for all he cared. It was obvious he wasn't going to talk. No Hereward . . . no guerdon. That was clear enough. Yet, for some reason, Odo de Chauliac could not bring himself to order Griffin's death.

❧ ❧ ❧

The atrocities were piling up. Lord Stephen felt an oppressive guilt infusing his soul. He could blame Odo all he wanted for the deaths, the hangings, the blindings, but ultimately, he was responsible.

Hugh sat by his father's side, filled with grief. *If only I had been born the eldest,* he thought, *such indulgent barbarity would never have occurred.*

Stephen grew paler with each report. Finding out the truth was easier than he had thought it would be. Each man was more than willing to relieve his conscience.

Hugh, noticing his father's despair, leaned over to whisper, "Father, I'll continue. Why don't you repair to your solar and rest for a bit? You'll receive a report after I'm done."

311

Stephen gratefully was soon sitting by his window looking at the town of Oxneford in the distance. In the solitude of his room—the violent deaths so many of his subjects were forced to endure at the hand of his son piling up in his conscience—the stalwart, righteous Norman wept fiercely.

"The rebellion had to be quelled," he reasoned. But such blackhearted cruelty could not be tolerated. Excessive punishments that caused untold heartache. Years ago he remembered feeling the zeal, the hot ardor that his son experienced. And most disconcerting were the shades of himself as a younger man that were now exhibited in Odo. A man of Stephen's influence didn't get where he was without employing ruthlessness of some form.

God had moved within the heart of Baron Stephen de Chauliac years ago. But so far, Odo had exhibited no spiritual inclinations. Under more than the testimonies' cruelty did Stephen's heart shift and twist painfully. Before his very eyes, his eldest son, evidenced by these very deeds, was trodding the path to hell.

"God, forgive me," he whispered.

❧ ❧ ❧

"'Tis true, your lordship," a humble cottager bowed. "Since the forests have been closed for your personal hunting grounds, the people have been hard-pressed. 'Twas the reason most hung from the walls of Beam-Dune Maur, as a reminder to all whose children cried with hunger not to feed them from the bounty of the woods."

"What of your hide? Does that not grow ample grain for cereals and bread?"

The suntanned man, his cap held respectfully between two hands sporting soil-encrusted fingernails, tried to explain. "It would if we had ample time to farm it, my lord, yes. But, most respectfully speaking, my lord, your son worked us from sunup to sundown five days out of seven building this very keep in which I stand."

Hugh's eyes were filled with rage from where he sat on the dais next to his father. "Is it any wonder, then, that they have resorted to poaching your forests? Does this happen in other regions?" he asked the peasant, already knowing the answer. William meant to subdue the people through any means.

"Yes, m'lord. Sir Odo's behavior is not unusual."

The cottager's wife, a toothless hag with wrinkles carved by days in the fields, spoke up with a surprisingly musical voice. "Indeed, it is so. And blessed we do feel, eh Godric, to know that your lordship is truly a kind and just man. All the people want to do, lord, is feed their children and have a little left over for themselves."

"And that is what they should be doing." Stephen was disturbed, but he maintained a strong appearance.

All morning the citizens of Oxneford and the surrounding region came, at the invitation of Stephen de Chauliac, to wage their complaints. Lilla sat in a corner of the hall and listened. How gracious and understanding the new lord of Oxneford was, but even he could do nothing when shown deep scars from a Norman lash or blade. And even more helpless he was during the tearful recountings of a number of malicious, unnecessary deaths.

Finally, she left, unable to listen any further. And once more she sought solace on the castle walls.

That night, dinner was a solemn affair. Lilla pleaded weariness and stayed in her room. Stephen ate in preoccupied silence. And Hugh leaned heavily upon Sylvia, looking up, as if in a trance, at the round chandelier which hung over the table. "How can I have played so heavy a hand in all of this, my bride?"

She smoothed his red curls soothingly. "What's done is done, my sweet. Now all you can do is make sure these atrocities are not repeated."

He sat up, obviously agitated. "How? When father is dead, Odo will assume the inheritance. For these people, father's kind rulership is but a respite. Because when Odo descends upon them with all the forces of hell at his heels, the past three years will seem like days of sunshine."

Sylvia shared her husband's frustration. "I'm surprised he hasn't done something to get his inheritance sooner."

Hugh nodded side to side. "Odo has his own code of honor. He would never kill his father."

"Why?"

"Oh, years ago a traveling soothsayer happened upon Castle de Chauliac in Normandy. Haven't I told you of this?"

Sylvia nodded from side to side. "Go on."

"His name was Joseph, a grizzled old Jew. He told of many of the events which happened around the death of Christ with a startling amount of detail, almost as if he had been there himself. Which, incidentally, he claimed he was. After answering many of father's questions, he suddenly turned upon Odo as he was leaving and pointed at him with a knobby finger. 'The Lord knows each thought of your blackened heart in regard to the man from whose loins you sprang. The day you carry out its evil commands, you will surely die as well, and by the hand of an enemy whose holy head is illumined like unto a halo.'"

A shudder ran through Sylvia. "So he believed the wandering Jew?"

"He still does, obviously. It's not as if he hasn't killed anyone before." His own matter-of-factness regarding his brother's evilness shocked him.

Hugh became silent once more. The meal was finished, and the minstrels were playing quite some time before Sylvia deigned to break into his quiet musing.

"What is it, Hugh? What has you troubled?"

Hugh shook his head, his features perplexed. "It's something that several who had been imprisoned spoke of. They were all contained in the prison tower at one time or another. All three men spoke of screams coming from far below."

"What does this mean?"

"I don't know. Maybe I'll talk to the jailer again. But I do believe I should investigate the tower myself."

"Are there prisoners still within the tower?"

"Not presently. For grievous offenses, most assuredly, they will be thrown in the tower. But father chooses different methods of discipline. Mostly hard labor."

"Then what shall we find?"

"I'm just planning to take a look. I've never even been in the tower, you know. And to be quite frank with you, my dear, if there's even more evidence against Odo to be found, I want to do just that!"

Apparently, Hugh de Chauliac had ambitions of his own.

❧ ❧ ❧

An extravagant moon shone through Griffin's window—a silver path to freedom. With longing eyes he gazed out over the bailey, then to the keep. To leave here would mean to leave Lilla.

Time was his friend, he knew. There was much of the stuff to be had, and when the moment for him to move ripened, he would be ready. If he had resumed his ways of prayer, he might have realized that Jesu was still in control of his life. But just then, Griffin felt that he was the one who must make all the moves.

He wondered what had happened to Simon. And to Ebb the Silent, who had fled with Hereward and his gang. Why hadn't he come to free his sister? That was a situation he had stopped trying to comprehend. The small, dark man wouldn't even speak his sister's name. Why would he come to her rescue?

❧ ❧ ❧

"Hand me your keys!" Hugh ordered the jailer angrily.

"I'm sorry," he protested with a moldering grin, "but I've got orders from your brother."

315

"I fail to comprehend the problem," Sylvia interjected, "if no one is imprisoned here."

"Why should it matter whether or not you give me the keys?" Hugh finished. "Come, good fellow, I just want to take a look around."

The jailer refused to be coerced. "I'm sorry, sir."

Hugh's russet temper rose high. "Leave us, my dear," he said to Sylvia without looking at her. "Go back to the keep."

Sylvia did as she was bid, but she heard the sound of sliding steel as she walk quickly outside while Hugh pulled out his sword. She hurried across the bailey.

"Now, one final time shall I make this request."

The jailer slid his sword from the scabbard as well. "No."

Hugh swung, and the jailer blocked the sweeping blade with his own. "Would you actually rather die than hand them over?" Hugh asked as the fight ensued.

"Better die at your hand than your brother's." The jailer dodged the sword again and again. "You're not as likely to drag the thing out."

Their swords flew, flickering in the light of the two torches chained to the wall. After several minutes the jailer's breathing became labored, but he fought on with the strength of a bear. Hugh's youthful stamina worked against the grizzled fellow, and soon his back was facing the steps. "Come, man! Give me the keys!"

"Never!" He could not willingly give entrance to the room far below. Lord Stephen would never forgive his participation. Surely, he would hang. He rushed forward, sword positioned to plunge deep within the heart of Hugh de Chauliac.

Hugh easily dodged the blade, and the jailer crashed into the wall, the rough stone lacerating his scalp. Immediately, he rose to his feet to repeat the maneuver. Only Hugh's death stood between himself and his own demise. With a heave of his lungs and baring of teeth, the jailer made a desperate charge. But Hugh, valiant and brave upon the field of Hastings, was ready. The charge was deadly.

With a quick turn of his wrist, the jailer's sword was thrown off course, and with an even quicker twist of his body, Hugh thrust the dagger he had drawn moments before up under his adversary's rib cage.

A look of surprise crossed the older man's face, then an eerie smile of relief. Yet before his eyes closed forever, Hugh watched in morbid fascination an awesome fear twisting the jailer's features as though the flames of hell were licking at his chin. Then his eyes closed, and Hugh crossed himself—not to benefit the jailer's soul, but in feeble prayer for his own.

Several of the soldiers who had been finishing their meal in the great hall when Sylvia came rushing in hurried into the tower. Louis, the captain, was a personal friend of Hugh's, and had come with him from Normandy.

"What's going on here?" Hugh asked one of them angrily.

"Don't know, sir," Louis held his hands wide. "We had strict orders not to impede upon the business that took place in the prison tower."

"My brother's order?"

The four soldiers nodded.

"Have any of you been in here?"

"No, sir," the captain answered, and the other three concurred.

"Get me that torch," he ordered. "Captain, you go downstairs and see if there is indeed no one there. I'll go upstairs. The rest of you, remove this body and arrange for a proper burial. Then stay nearby."

"Shall I send a man to Lord Stephen?" the captain asked.

"Not yet. I would have walked in and thought nothing was amiss if it hadn't been for the overprotective nature of the jailer."

"Jailer?" Louis' brow creased, and he pointed to the huddled mass of humanity on the floor. "That man?"

"Yes."

"He's no jailer. He's a torturer, sir. You can tell by his garb. Too bad you dispatched him so quickly, my lord."

"I agree. Wait here while I search upstairs." His sparkling eyes held an excitement at what he might find. Obviously, something was here—or someone—that Odo had sought to hide. Hugh bounded up the steps, keys out and ready to throw open as many doors as that tower of misery held. Two soldiers followed behind him at Louis' silent command.

ও ও ও

Griffin heard footfalls.

A look of dismay turned down the corners of his mouth. Only one man came at this time of the evening. Odo de Chauliac must have returned.

Immediately, a vivid picture of the torture machines, their chains and ropes, cranks and stones, lit up his mind's eye with violent clarity. *This time*, he promised himself, *Odo will not deal with me thus.*

This time he will die.

Griffin became a desperate man.

The key was thrust into the lock. The mechanism inside began to slide, and Griffin calculated how long it would take for Odo to draw his sword from the time he opened the door. He knew that waiting in the shadows would afford him the element of surprise. Odo was quick, yes, but Griffin was mad with desperation. This was his last chance. If he could but encircle the Norman's neck with his large hands . . . or better yet, knock him out with a single blow.

Torchlight slid across the floor as the door was pushed ajar.

Just as the intruder stepped in the door, Griffin pulled back and jabbed with all his might, his fist connecting with Hugh's jaw.

The momentum pushed Hugh back out the door and sent him reeling onto the floor, and he looked up at the begrimed, yellow-haired, wild-eyed fiend who started to run toward the steps.

A soldier crested the stairs with a torch and drawn sword. Two more were ascending close behind him. Griffin was

318

trapped between the guards and the now seething Hugh de Chauliac.

He was quickly bound and thrown back into the room.

Hugh walked angrily inside. "Who are you?" He had trouble controlling the volume of his voice. And his red-haired temper flared to its highest proportions. He rubbed his jaw.

Griffin refused to answer. He heard the man's accent.

"Why are you here?" Hugh stood directly in front of Griffin now. Hardly eye to eye, but his fiery eyes forced Griffin's defiant ones to look into them.

Griffin didn't respond verbally, but the shift of his pale-blue eyes and the single angry blink told Hugh the answer. Louis hurried into the room, his skin a wan sheet of ice though the room had become stuffy. "My lord," he choked, the thought of what he had just seen making him want to vomit. "Downstairs . . ."

"What is it?" Hugh laid his hand on the man's shoulder.

"'Tis something I cannot describe. Come and see."

"I'll tell you what is down there," Griffin spoke in perfect Norman-French. "I know well what machinations of pain have been spawned in the mind of a de Chauliac."

Hugh wheeled around. "I am a de Chauliac."

Griffin spat on Hugh's brogues.

Pure reaction lifted the red-haired Norman's fist, bringing it in contact with Griffin's jaw. "I'll teach you not to do that again," he said haughtily.

"I'm sure you will. If you are anything like your father," Griffin incorrectly assumed. But the point was well-taken, and Hugh suddenly felt ashamed.

"My brother," he corrected Griffin. "Odo de Chauliac is my brother." He sighed deeply, angrily, without apology, then turned on his heel and ordered the soldier who saved his life, "Watch him until I return from below."

## ❧ THIRTY ❧

ugh choked down the inclination to retch. Not one man of Oxneford had spoken of the machines. Not one man of Oxneford had lived to tell the tale. The gruesome, bloodstained implements screamed of pain amid the smothering silence of the dank, baleful chamber. How many other Englishman had Odo taken down to the subterranean chamber?

The brazier was cold.

"How did he live through it?" Hugh whispered to Louis, the only other occupant of the room.

"I don't know, my friend. A strong man he must be to remain unbroken by such evildoing."

"To think we came from the same man." Hugh wondered how he would ever look upon his brother again. "My brother . . ." The two simple words were a premature eulogy. Premature . . . but final. Louis stirred beside him. "Let's leave this room, my friend. You can decide later what to do with these things."

The captain followed Hugh up the steps and back into Griffin's chamber.

"How did you survive?" the nobleman asked simply.

"How could I not? Because we are English, does that mean we have nothing for which to live? Do we not love our hearth and our wives? Do we not seek to survive for the sake of our children?"

"Truly, you are a brave man," Hugh said softly, then turned back to the soldiers. "I know not when my brother returns from Normandy. Remove those horrid machines, all the implements as well, and burn them at first light. What doesn't burn is to be thrown into the middle of the river. I want that room to be completely empty by noon. Scrub it well."

"Yes, sir," they replied and set to work.

Hugh's attention was once again given to the prisoner. "Who are you?" he asked Griffin again.

"Why is it so important for you to know the name of a simpleminded Englishman such as myself?"

"My brother is a cruel, merciless fellow, as you have no doubt learned firsthand. The fact that he kept you a secret tells me there is much I don't know about his dealings with the English. Tell me who you are. At least let me contact your wife and children for you."

"I have no children now. Just one wife. And your brother has taken her away from me."

"Is she dead?"

"No. In fact, you must know her quite well."

"I doubt that."

"Lilla."

Hugh's eyes grew wide. "You are the stonemason's son!"

Griffin said nothing, but once again his eyes gave way to the truth.

"So you're not dead! How happy Lilla will be when she finds out. I must go and report these things to my father immediately."

"Do as you must," Griffin replied. "But do not tell my wife of these things. "

Hugh looked genuinely confused. Griffin nodded and jerked his head toward the window. "She looks over the ramparts for your brother every morning, waiting for his return.

The day he left he departed with the remembrance of her soft lips upon his scarred cheek."

"No. No. I believe you've misjudged the lady in question. Do you wish for me to bring her to you so that she might speak for her actions?" Hugh asked.

"Not with me looking like this."

"Or smelling like this," Hugh joked. He examined the prisoner closely. Dirty and foul-smelling, Griffin's hair, grown now well past his shoulders, stuck together in matted clumps. What was once his tunic hung in rags. The undergown likewise followed suit. Dried blood, weeks old, stained much of the exposed skin, and what could be seen of his neck, back, and chest showed hideous welts. His legs and arms bore the marks of Odo's cruelty as well. How curious that Odo left his face alone.

"I'll have a tub brought up and some hot water."

"Go, Monsieur de Chauliac. Take care of your jaw and your wife. I've seen you walk together often."

"Yes, she's a good woman. And my head begins to ache."

Hugh turned and left. His jaw was throbbing painfully. But back in his bedchamber, Sylvia ministered to his needs. When he told her of his findings, her cry of joy was so loud the castle community bolted into action, thinking her time of delivery had come.

❧ ❧ ❧

Griffin lowered himself into the round wooden tub. Had he been asked even an hour ago if he would have rather seen Lilla or taken a bath, he wouldn't have hesitated in his answer. All he had wanted was to be with Lilla. But now that the hot water rose higher and higher on his skin with each jug that was poured, he felt a supreme sense of relief.

Months of grime were washed away. The tub was emptied two times before Griffin could scour the dirt from his hair. By the fourth tubful, he was perfectly clean and his face was shaven smooth. He stood to his feet, naked and pale—much thinner, to be sure. The once-smooth skin would never be the same, as countless scars slickly crisscrossed the surface.

Hugh walked in. In his hand he held a saffron-colored tunic, an undergown the color of cream, and a saffron sash. Both were of the softest combed merino wool. Attached to the sleeves, hem, and neckline of the tunic was Lilla's handiwork.

"Here!" Hugh casually threw a pair of holly-green hosen to the giant Englishman, silently noting the network of scars. Griffin caught them and put them on. Next, he took the clothes from Hugh, fingering the delicate threadwork. Without a thought to the company, he lifted them to his face and brushed the trim against his lips. His eyes closed, and Hugh knew without a doubt that he had spoken the truth. The man was Lilla's husband, indeed.

The blue eyes opened, and he looked down thoughtfully at Hugh de Chauliac before dressing. "What is the status of Beam-Dune Maur? What has happened since Lilla was taken prisoner? Sir Odo was in charge, last I knew. You said he was in Normandy?"

"Yes. Beam-Dune Maur is now named Castle Chauliac. Since Lilla was taken prisoner by my nefarious brother, she has been treated most respectfully. My father, Lord Stephen de Chauliac, my wife, and myself did not arrive from Normandy until almost six months ago. Your wife's presence was kept a secret from most of us until Sylvia found out by happenstance that she was being held by my brother in the southwest tower of the keep. She miscarried the child, I'm loathe to tell you."

"Odo told me." But he motioned Hugh to continue while he donned the remainder of his garb.

"Odo arrived home with the sad news that you had been hung at York. Naturally, your wife has been in despair. But she puts on a brave face, as you might well expect."

He pulled the long-sleeved undergown over his head. "She is a woman of great fortitude. Her leg attests to that."

The tunic went on next, its wide sleeves ending just below his elbow. Griffin twisted the sash, then tied it round his slim waist. "Anyway, before Odo left, he gave her your amulet. Perhaps that was when you saw her kiss him."

"So is she still being kept a prisoner?"

"No. Father freed her just before Odo's departure, on the condition that she stay with us until Sylvia births our babe. It is our first, you know, and Sylvia has come to rely heavily on your wife's friendship and caring."

"She is the most kind, caring person I have ever met," Griffin said frankly. "So, what is my status here at Beam-Dune Maur?" He overtly refused to call it Castle Chauliac.

"You are still a prisoner. But you will find my father an altogether different sort of jailer than Odo. Are you ready to walk with me to the keep? He wants to meet you. Guard!" he called for one of his men. "Bind his hands."

"No!" Griffin was adamant. "I am a man of honor, Sir Hugh. You have my word that I will not seek to escape the confines of the castle tonight. Pray preserve my dignity. I have surely earned that privilege at the hands of your brother."

Hugh motioned to the guard to leave the room. "As you wish."

The walk to the castle was glorious. Griffin's legs felt longer than before as they were allowed full stride after extensive confinement. And the wide expanse of breathable air filled his lungs with a fresh satisfaction. Lights glimmered in several of the narrow windows of the keep, and he wondered which window was Lilla's. His eyes scanned the southwest tower. Hugh noted the direction of his gaze and kindly pointed out the darkened hole.

"So she sleeps," Griffin stated.

"Yes. She did not come to supper tonight. I believe there are times that her grief encompasses her so greatly she cannot bear to look upon the faces of others."

By the time they entered the keep, the central fire was a low-burning mass of coals. The minstrels had ceased their playing, and the soldiers were in their barracks down below. Many of the servants had now begun to take their repose on benches. The less-fortunate slept on the rush-strewn floor. Griffin looked about him, and deep into his nostrils he breathed the residual smells of dinner: the perfume of roasted meat, the vegetables, the brown bread. His stomach felt hollow.

"Where is your father?"

"Upstairs in his solar. He will expect of you a full accounting of Odo's atrocities."

Hugh watched Griffin thoughtfully as he followed him up the circular staircase. The man was proud and a force to be reckoned with. He wondered why he hadn't tried to overpower Odo sooner. Knowing his brother, he had been meticulously careful when dealing with the rebel warrior.

"There," Hugh said, "on the left. I will tell him of your arrival." He knocked on the new polished surface of the door. Lord Stephen motioned him with a wave to bring in the prisoner.

Griffin entered the room before Hugh. And Stephen stood up from his chair. "Welcome, Griffin Eadricson," he said, inviting him to sit on a bench which stood against the far wall. He pulled up his chair as Griffin and Hugh sat facing him.

For a full minute Stephen studied the young man before him.

"I'm sorry for Odo's deplorable behavior toward you."

Griffin said nothing.

"When did you fall into my son's hands?"

"After the battle of York, my lord."

"Tell me everything."

Griffin spared nothing. The journey back, the physical torture, the squalid conditions, the meager food allowance. Each horrid event, each memory of pain he gladly shared, for they were badges of honor. In that he survived the most horrifying machinations of the Norman mind, he attested to English bravery.

"So you would have hung rather than swear fealty to King William?"

"Yes."

Lord Stephen de Chauliac sighed. "Then I have no choice but to keep you prisoner."

"May I see my wife?"

"For Lilla's sake."

"You are most gracious. I truly believed all Normans were like your son."

"Normans are not the only ones who can be cruel," Stephen replied, remembering his friend Alfred.

"'Tis true," Griffin conceded, "that before William landed at Pevensy we were a house divided. Happy was many an Englishman when Earl Tosty finally met his fate. 'Tis a shame he wasn't a good man like his brother King Harold was."

"One Godwin is very much like another to me. But no matter—Lilla has told me that you are an educated man."

"Of sorts. I learned from the monks at Westminster Abbey. Particularly Brother Adam. He was a Norman."

"Hence his knowledge of our language," Hugh pointed out. Just then a servant appeared with a trencher of cold mutton, cheese, dried fruit, and bread. A flagon of wine accompanied the repast. "I assumed you weren't given the choicest of dainties in your former abode." Hugh motioned to Griffin to eat.

He fell to, biting off a piece of mutton and downing it with a swallow of wine.

Lord Stephen was still of a mind to question. "So you grew up as the son of Edward's royal stonemason?"

"Eadric of Bath is my father, yes."

"I have seen the new church of St. Peter's at Westminster. It is truly beautiful, a masterpiece."

Griffin looked up, talk of the abbey suddenly sending a thrill into his weary soul. It was his first remembrance of God's majesty in a very long time. "I have heard the church at Jumieges is quite similar and just as beautiful."

"Yes. They are quite similar, it is true. Jumieges should be finished shortly."

"Is it as beautiful as Westminster?" Griffin ate a piece of bread.

Hugh poured Stephen a horn of wine, and the lord sat back thoughtfully in his chair. "Honestly? No. But I don't think it is because of its architecture. I believe it has something to do with the man who built it. Robert of Jumieges is a proud man, and his church has somehow absorbed it into the very stones. King Edward, whom I called friend before he ever took the throne, was a man committed to the cause of Christ. For that reason alone, Westminster shines above Jumieges. Perhaps it is a fanciful interpretation, but nevertheless, it seems to me to be an accurate one."

Griffin looked into Stephen's eyes, and in a fleeting moment the two men shared eternity. Nothing needed to be said; their eyes told all. They were spiritual brothers. Stephen was strong in his faith, trying to reckon with a violent past. Griffin was groping after God, still confused, angry. But that seed of faith planted in his heart had not died.

"So you knew my godfather as a child?"

"King Edward was your godfather?" Lord Stephen de Chauliac looked surprised.

"Yes. Hence my education. He had plans for me, my lord. I was to someday be his royal stonemason."

"Ah. What happened?"

"I had not the inclination for masonry. So, after he died I entered the monastery. I hadn't taken any vows but cloistered myself with the brothers, thinking that perhaps this was the path to spiritual service that God had for me to tread. They needed extra help, to be sure, and I worked many days in the fields on the estates Edward provided outside of Westminster. I was there for almost three years after the invasion. Then, I'm sure you remember hearing about it, my father was maimed by Norman soldiers."

"Yes. I heard. Most regrettably. The news was given me by William himself when I arrived in London last fall. He has taken care of your parents, I'm sure you'd like to know. Your father is given a pension each year, and they are well provided for."

"That is good news." Griffin was on the fruit now, having tasted nothing sweet for far too long. "But it truly is the least he could have done."

Lord Stephen conceded with a nod. "And he now has a large say in the design of a white tower William is proposing to build in London."

Griffin knew that was the best news of all concerning his father. Eadric was a man who needed to keep busy. Sitting at home, receiving money from the king's hand, would have constituted a life of misery. "Have you heard any news regarding the rebel forces?" Stephen nodded. "Yes. They are wreaking all manner of havoc, but on a smaller scale now. Their hideout is still unknown, but it is somewhere in the fenlands."

Finally Griffin finished his meal.

"Are you ready?" Hugh asked softly, his eyes glowing at the thought of Lilla's reaction. For truly, the Englishwoman had become like a sister to him.

Deeply breathing in, Griffin nodded and rose from the bench.

Hugh led him down a corridor, and soon they were standing in front of her door. "You will not try and escape tonight?" he asked.

"You have my word. Besides," he placed his hand on the latch, "there's no place in the world right now that I'd rather be."

## THIRTY-ONE

Lilla slept deeply, so deeply. But the dream she had, it was so lifelike, so intensified in its reality, that she made herself stay asleep.

The dream started out much on a day like any other before she met Griffin. In her cart she was traveling to Oxneford for market day. She came upon Griffin, but this time he was not clad in a monk's robe. His frame was clothed in a fine tunic, and he stood with a smile on his face.

His eyes. They were bluer than she remembered, and his hands lightly touched her all over as if he had never touched her before. Fingertips skimming lightly the flesh on her forehead, eyes, cheeks, chin, neck. Setting her free. Free to remember their days of pleasure, their nights of passion before the fire.

Do not waken, Lilla. Do not waken.

She ordered herself over and over, and in the dream Griffin smiled lovingly at her command. His mouth. It was more beautiful than she could have remembered. And when it descended to hers, it did not demand passion and response. It lightly caressed in a dance of reacquaintance. Was she reacquainting herself with him, or he with her? In the dream it did not matter.

She thrilled.

For it was like having him with her once again. Griffin was alive, and her mind was affording her the feeling of physical touch. Each muscle, each bump of bone on his arms and shoulders she wanted to remember forever. Was this wonderful experience the workings of her mind, or was it a gift from Jesu Himself—a gift of sunshine in the midnight landscape that had become her life? Her hands slid over his arms and back, feeling new hills and valleys, and she wondered in the misty world of dreams from whence the scars had come.

*I love you. I love you.*

Did he say it? Or did she? And were the words uttered out loud in the forest? Or were they back in the hut now?

Then Griffin's arms wound around her, his fingers reached up and slowly undid her braid. A cascading curtain of curls covered them both. But soon after, she realized she was now looking at his face above her, and Lilla gave herself up to the final reality of the making of a love so strong and true that death itself could not keep it chained.

Do not awaken. Do not awaken. Do not awaken.

꙳ ꙳ ꙳

"Lilla!" Griffin whispered more loudly than he had before. "Wake up!"

His voice echoed in the darkness. "Lilla!" Her sleep was so deep, so dense. And he regarded her with pity, knowing it was her grief which rendered her thus. Lightly he kissed her on the cheek. As lightly as the down from a swan, he traced a finger along the sweet line of her cheek. In her sleep she smiled, and he wanted to cry when he saw the dimples appear in her cheeks.

Her hand immediately brushed his fingers away. "Simon . . . Peter . . . go away . . ." she mumbled in her sleep.

Griffin's need to see her became urgent. "Lilla, wake up!" He shook her lightly. "Wake up, Lily. It is I. It is Griffin!"

Green eyes opened at the sound of his name. "Griffin?" She was still befuddled, but she reached to the face which hovered only inches from hers.

"Griffin!" she sprang up to a sitting position. "Griffin! You're alive . . . you're not . . . dead . . . oh my, you're alive! I can't believe it! Griffin! Oh, my Griffin!"

She pulled herself against him so tightly and with such strength he thought his back would break. "You're here! You're here!" She repeated the words over and over again.

"Yes, Lily. I'm here. I'm here," he muttered into her hair. Crushing her against him even more closely. "Oh Lilla, my Lilla," he breathed, feeling overawed, unable to make sense of the feelings assaulting him, let alone give voice to them.

She pulled back a bit to look at him through the darkness. "You're alive! I can't believe it! Are you really here? With me? Now? Or are you a benevolent spirit sent to minister to me in these darkest of hours?"

Griffin pulled her against him. "No, my Lily, I am here."

"You're not dead." It was almost too much to comprehend, and the fact filled her with joy, relief, and a sea of questions. Her brain pounded, but her heart pounded more. "How did you get here? What happened? You'll be captured! We must hide you!"

"It is all right, Lily. Lord Stephen knows I am here. All present worries do not exist. We have only to be with one another."

Having him with her, knowing flesh and bone, reality of presence, overwhelmed her all of a sudden, and Lilla wept until Griffin's lips, soothing and loving, swept all thoughts from her mind but those of love and a commitment that had stood the test of time, war, and death.

"I love you, Lilla," he said hoarsely against her lips.

And Lilla's dream of minutes before became a shining reality.

The morning sun strewed in the window and across the bed where they lay, warmly cuddled together under the blankets. They had awakened only minutes earlier, kissing over and over again inside their warm cocoon. Lilla sat up once she fully opened her eyes.

"Oh, Griffin!" She raised her hand up to her mouth in shock as she rubbed gentle fingers over the numerous scars on his neck. It had been a favorite area of the torturer to place the red-hot pokers against. "Does that hurt?" she asked.

"Your touch can only soothe, my lamb," he said so softly she wanted to weep.

"How did you bear the pain?"

"How did you?"

"What are you talking about?"

"You understand pain. And I had every reason to withstand, Lilla. You and the child."

Lilla opened her mouth to explain, but Griffin held up a hand. "Odo already informed me, gentle lady." He put his arms around her. "It was just another act of cruelty on his part to bear such tidings. I'm so sorry. Sorry most that you had to go through it alone."

"Yes," Lilla sighed, "perhaps that was the most difficult part of it. But I always had faith that surely God had a reason. I still don't know what it could be," she shrugged, "but I know He is wise. Of course, I had to feel much anger to come to such conclusions." Griffin understood the anger, but not the assurance. He changed the subject.

"Do you still love me now that my body bears such hideous marks?" His eyes twinkled.

"As if something like that would matter when my heart loves only you!"

"Now you understand, don't you?"

"Yes. Forgive me for belittling your love when we first declared it."

"I do. For I never doubted once that you would love me anyway."

They continued their conversation, imparting the many details of their lives since they parted company last fall. Finally, a knock sounded on the other side of the chamber door.

"That's Sylvia's knock," Lilla announced, rising from the bed. "Just a minute, Sylvia," she called.

"Don't hurry on my account, you lazy slugabeds!" Sylvia called back. "Lord Stephen wishes to see both of you as soon as possible in his solar. I will seek out the pleasure of your company there. I was just hoping to get a peek at Griffin before then."

"All right," Lilla answered. "We'll be right there."

Quickly they donned their undergowns and tunics. Lilla slid her feet into the fine slippers Odo had brought for her. "Griffin," she began hesitantly, "these clothes . . ."

He took both of her hands in his. "It's all right. You're beautiful in them. It was good of Odo to expend a great many denarii to make you even more beautiful for your husband!" His smile was broad, confident, and mischievous as he pulled her close to him and gave her a quick, soft kiss on her neck.

Lilla pulled back and looked deeply into his eyes. "You astound me, Griffin."

"I astound myself sometimes," he laughed. "But, my Lily, I can only feel such confidence because your love for me is so powerful. Your strength has become my own." He kissed her hair. "Come, let us be going down. It wouldn't be wise to keep Lord Stephen waiting."

"He has been most kind to me, Griffin."

"Aye, Lilla. And for that I wish to thank him."

*⋇ ⋇ ⋇*

"In good conscience, I cannot promise such, my lord." Griffin leaned forward upon the bench and took a piece of bread from the hand of Sylvia, who presided over the small meal that Griffin, Hugh, and Lord Stephen were sharing.

Stephen expected as much, and he said so. "What do you propose we do regarding your imprisonment? Truly, I seek to be as magnanimous a jailer as I can be. But a jailer I am, and I will be responsible to my king."

"I would expect no less, my lord," Griffin answered.

Sylvia whispered something in Hugh's ear. "Father," he began, "Lilla was kept prisoner in her tower room for months. What if we reinstall the lock on the outside of the door and post a guard?"

"No," Stephen said. "Lilla is free. And as much as we have grown to love your wife, trusting her to be your jailer might be somewhat foolish on our part. We cannot keep her locked up in there with you as well." Stephen rubbed his chin. "I suppose I shall have to send you back to the prison tower."

"Father!" Sylvia gasped, unable to keep silent.

"Quiet, daughter!" Stephen ordered.

Griffin spoke. "If that is your wish, I have no choice but to concede. Would my wife be allowed to visit me?"

"Of course."

"That suits me well, my lord. So she will still be extended her freedom?"

"Yes. My word is good. I set her free weeks ago."

"Thank you, my lord."

"So," Stephen finished the discussion, "I trust you will find it in your heart to sup with us in the great hall each evening. With guards posted nearby, of course."

"Of course. As you wish, my lord." Griffin stood to his feet and bowed as Lord Stephen called for the guards. This time Griffin's hands were bound as he was led back to the prison tower.

Stephen turned to his son. "Hugh, hasten to the prison tower and make arrangements for Griffin's comfort. Put in a decent pallet, a table, and a bench. Have some reading material sent up as well. It should help him to fill the hours. Some parchment and ink would be thoughtful, too. Do you think he will wish to send a message to his parents?"

"Yes, father."

Stephen sat in silence for a moment while Hugh left the room to attend to his father's bidding. The noble lord turned to Lilla. "Have you seen the abbey at Westminster?"

"No, my lord."

His voice turned wistful, and a faint yearning quality softened the brown of his eyes. "'Magnificent. I wish to discuss its building at length with your husband. He grew up in its shadow, did he not?"

"Yes, my lord."

Lord Stephen sat in silent reflection, as if his heart were searching for something that was just beyond its present scope of understanding. When Lilla quietly shut the door behind her, he heard not a sound.

ৰূ ৰূ ৰূ

"Ha! Ha!"

Odo de Chauliac threw back his head in laughter. Robert Shortpants beamed at his recounting of the previous night's exploits.

"De Chauliac, I have nary a clue as to where you find the wenches you do, but last night's was a lamb."

"Yes," de Chauliac snickered, "a lamb to be sure, but within a lioness makes her abode."

"Too true. Too true. For the life of me, I wonder how I existed in such a dull fashion before you arrived, sir knight." The Conqueror's son reached for his goblet of wine and drank a long draught of the heady perfumed vintage from Burgundy. He called to the players who had arrived yesterday, and the comedy began.

Before the end, it turned to tragedy. All the players were dead but one.

Odo de Chauliac smiled.

"How does your father fare?" Robert Shortpants asked the next day.

337

"I know not," Odo replied. "I live only for myself."

The bait was set before the Conqueror's son. Robert looked at Odo from the sides of his eyes. And far down in his soul, unbeknownst to him, his own personal tragedy had begun. A tragedy where only the strongest man survived.

# ❧ THIRTY-TWO ❧

The summer passed through the region of Oxneford as a bride weaves through a crowd on her wedding day, leaving touches of beauty with each step of the foot, but gone all too soon. As he promised, Lord Stephen de Chauliac was a kind jailer. In fact, he found himself in Griffin's tower room whenever time afforded him the pleasure. They chatted over backgammon—a Saxon game that Griffin was teaching the Norman. And Lord Stephen was teaching Griffin the game of chess.

Yet Stephen had a separate agenda: to understand the mind of the English, especially someone who had warred against the Normans and was still committed to their overthrow. If he could understand what set fire to Griffin's soul, perhaps he could understand the rebels still on the loose. Perhaps he could help the king in putting a more humane halt to the resistance.

The two had grown to respect one another deeply, and Griffin remarked several times to Lilla, "It's quite impossible for me to believe that I have come to care so much for a Norman."

"It goes beyond nationality, my love," she responded. "For in truth, we are the citizens of heaven before we are Saxon, or English, or Norman, or Italian, or . . ."

Griffin pressed his fingertips against her lips. "I understand your point, my Lily." They laughed together, but deep in his heart he knew it was true. He had not a doubt that Lord Stephen loved God with all his heart. He knew that one day they would meet in the heaven that Jesu had prepared. And indeed, Lilla was right: They were citizens of heaven first. In all things that mattered the most, Griffin was of like mind and similar experience to Stephen de Chauliac.

And Stephen's strong faith, as well as Lilla's, was aiding Griffin in returning to the acceptance of the love of God. There were many things he still failed to understand, however.

"Will you ever swear fealty to William?" Lord Stephen asked on a July afternoon. It was quite hot that day, and he allowed Griffin to roam with him in the bailey. A guard followed them the entire time, but their low voices could be heard by no one but themselves.

"I don't see how I can betray my heart," Griffin answered honestly.

"He would accept you most graciously, Griffin. Truly, he was most regretful that your father was done such a ghastly turn."

"So I've been told," Griffin said with a wry laugh. It was at least the third time Lord Stephen had mentioned it. The nobleman laughed as well.

"What is it, then? What is it that keeps you from swearing your loyalty, from bowing your knee before the Conqueror?"

Griffin looked up at the swallows which swooped overhead. "It was King Edward's wish that Harold Godwinson be crowned king. Sir," he looked straightforward into the eyes of his captor, "I don't know if you can understand this, but I owed King Edward more than I could ever try to express. He was my benefactor. My confessor sometimes, and my friend at all times. I don't mean that in a sentimental way, my lord. But truly, he cared for me, and that is what a friend does, is it not?"

340

"Truly. Edward was known throughout Europe as an amiable man."

"How well did you know him?"

Stephen stopped walking and stood in front of the stables. They watched the grooms care for the large, velvet-nosed beasts. "I knew Edward quite well, actually. He was more devout than his brother. But he was considerably well-liked and highly respected by all the nobles of Normandy. It's easy to see why your devotion to him remains intact well after his passing. Edward did not really wish for Harold Godwinson to inherit his throne, the throne of England."

"How so? Harold was his most consistent source of counsel. He was brave, honorable, and generous. A true Saxon. Besides, Edward proclaimed Harold his successor on his deathbed. He was crowned at the abbey itself shortly thereafter."

The Norman lord chose his words carefully, not wanting to offend but seeking to provoke. "What is your opinion of the house of Godwin in general?"

Griffin smiled and answered craftily. "'Tis not for me to judge, my lord, the comings and goings of those in a higher station than mine own."

Stephen chuckled and rubbed a hand over his bald head. "Truly, you are an educated man. And you surely didn't spend all of your time away from court, for indeed, this isn't the first time I've heard an answer most diplomatic speed from your mouth with all haste!"

"Thank you, my lord."

A serious expression settled in Lord Stephen's brown eyes. "I'm serious when I ask you that, Griffin. Feel free to speak your mind—answer truthfully the question, as you do when you converse with me regarding other matters."

"All right. I have no respect for the Godwins, my lord. Tosty and his father were a constant open sore in the foot of Edward. If it hadn't been for the revolt which sprang forward in Northumberland due to Tosty's irresponsible behavior, most certainly my godfather would have been well enough to have leastwise been at the consecration of the abbey he so loved. He would have heard a Mass within its sacred walls. Nay, I had no respect for the Godwins then or now."

Stephen's voice raised in passion. "Then why do you persist in your refusal to swear to William? I cannot understand this Saxon stubbornness!"

Griffin couldn't help but laugh out loud. "Pardon me if I seem disrespectful, my lord. But the only people I've known that match our Germanic stubbornness are the Normans!"

But Stephen would not be thrown off course. "William is coming to Castle Chauliac, my son. He will arrive in one week's time?"

All humor was instantly eradicated. Griffin's eyes grew wide. "So I have a choice, do I?"

Stephen laid a firm hand upon his prisoner's shoulder. "Yes. William is aware that you are here. He is aware of your plight. He is an understanding man in situations that he understands, but when he cannot make sense of a man, he is equally as unforgiving and sometimes twice as cruel."

"So what you are telling me is that if I do not swear fealty upon the Conqueror's arrival, I will most surely hang?"

"Yes."

"Then I will hang."

"Why?" Stephen's voice was raised even further. "What must I do to make you see sense?"

"Prove to me King Edward wanted William for his predecessor."

"That is not difficult. King Edward sent Harold over to swear fealty to William. I was there myself. Why would he make England a vassal to Normandy when he could just leave his throne to Harold?"

"Forgive me, Lord Stephen, but I've heard many lies from a variety of Normans. When it comes to giving my allegiance to a man who has slaughtered many of my countrymen, I want solid evidence."

Truly, Stephen was exasperated. "I don't know what more I can do." He studied the horse in front of him. Another death. He was tired of these years of conquest. Griffin put a steadying hand upon his shoulder and squeezed comfortingly.

"Do you believe a man must follow his conscience?" he asked.

"Certainly."

"Do you also believe a man's conscience is directed by God to guide him in whatever works He has prepared for him?"

Lord Stephen de Chauliac nodded. "Yes."

"Well then. Do not fear. Perhaps William himself will extend proof."

"Then will you at least willingly go before him? Converse with him?"

"Yes."

"Praise be to Jesu." Stephen was washed with the cool waters of relief. "I'll send a dispatch to him in all haste."

He was out of the stables and up in his solar before Griffin had set one foot on the circular stairs which led up to his chamber. When the guard opened the door, Griffin was most delighted to see that Lilla was waiting for him.

He kissed her soundly and made no mention of the Conqueror's visit.

❧ ❧ ❧

Lord Stephen was a haunted man. He had warred and battled all of his life. And the violence had taken its toll, leaving him sleepless during the broad hours of darkness. In the loneliness of his room, having survived two wives and lived for the whims of his rulers, the memories played out before his eyes like a theatrical painting, and the voices—whispers really— echoed, caught in the passages of his mind and thrown down to echo loudly in the most remote recesses of his subconscious. He thought of the battles he had fought, the men he had killed, and he could almost feel the shell that had hardened around his heart, which allowed him not to recall the faces of those he had sent into the eternal abyss.

He knew the end of his life was near.

Maybe not in the next few months, but Lord Stephen couldn't shake off the still, damning voice which whispered his time on earth was coming to a close. There was much restitution to be made, he had decided, when the feeling of doom had inexorably settled in.

✥ ✥ ✥

Two nights before William was to arrive, the meal was brought into the hall. A trencher of food was set in front of Stephen. The rest of the guests at the raised table shared a trencher between two people. And down at the trestle tables which lined the room, four men shared one platter. Servants passed out fresh flat bread upon which the diners placed their food. The used bread from the previous course would be given to the poor.

Hugh leaned over and asked his father, "When is Odo to return?"

"I'm not sure," Stephen sighed. "I'm loathe to say that if I had a choice, I'd hope it wasn't anytime soon."

"Have you heard from him since he left?" Sylvia asked, then delicately lifted a piece of pheasant to her mouth. As a nursing mother, her appetite had become voracious, and it was clear to see that she was overcompensating for the baby's nutrition. But whether or not Sylvia's waistline was expanding was not pondered or even noticed by anyone, for the glow of motherhood outshone all imperfections. Hugh's eyes shone more brightly when he now looked at his wife. How thankful he was that she had borne him a healthy, beautiful girl.

Stephen shook his head. "No. Not directly. Gossip is circulating that he is doing quite well as the favored companion of Robert."

"I'd heard that," Hugh said. "Surely it bodes no good."

"How can anything concerning Odo bode good?" Sylvia asked.

❧ ❧ ❧

The Conqueror was coming.

And Griffin knew what must be done.

The plan was firmly etched in his mind. All he had to do was tell Lilla. She stood in the middle of his room, her hands clasped tightly together. The look on his face bespoke change, that not all was like it was the day before.

"I'm leaving tonight," he said simply.

"What?"

"Here. Come and sit on the bed while I explain it all."

She complied, but an alarm sounded in her brain. "Are you considering escaping?"

"Aye. King William comes."

"But didn't you tell Lord Stephen you would at least appear before him?"

"Yes, I did. But think of it, Lilla: If the William has no real proof, then I will hang."

"But you gave your word!"

Griffin dragged his stool over beside the bed and sat down. "Lilla, would you lie to save my life?"

"Of course. I will not portray a false righteousness and say I wouldn't."

"Then can you not see that I am lying to save my own life?"

She leaned forward, and their faces were only inches from each other. "What is your plan?"

"Do you remember Leofwine speaking of the well which leads into the bottom of this tower?"

"Yes. The one you and Ebb swam through."

"Exactly. I will overpower the guard tonight when he checks on me last."

345

"How will you get him to come in?"

"That will not be difficult. I'll feign illness. Knowing my place in Lord Stephen's heart, he will not wish ill to befall me. Then I shall lock him here in the room after gagging him and tying him up."

"What will you use for rope?"

"That is where I'll need your help. Will you bring me some of your trim? Do you have a goodly length in your room?"

"Aye."

"That is what I shall use to tie up the guard. Then I shall escape through the tunnel, out into the Thames. You'll leave your room early in the morning. We'll meet in Oxneford, and from thence make our way into hiding. "

"But I haven't a length as long as you need!"

"Then bring two."

"But—"

"We've got to do this, Lilla!"

Lilla's mind was turning furiously. "So you appear to have it all figured out. Why did you not do this before?"

"I was not moved before by desperation. But my life hangs in the balance."

Tears formed in the corners of Lilla's eyes. "I don't understand why you cannot swear fealty. What is most important to you: King Edward's wish or Lilla's? The months I thought you dead were horrifying, Griffin. How can you be willing to put me through that again?"

"You'd be with me, Lilla, soon enough," he said in earnest.

"Oh? And what happens when the Normans give chase and I hinder you? We'll both be slain. Griffin . . . I've been pardoned. I don't wish to live as an outlaw. Don't you see the winds of change are blowing across England for good? The Normans will not leave, and we can either choose to live in peace, love each other, and raise a family, or we can run for the rest of our lives. And I promise you, our lives will be considerably shortened if we dare to take the latter course."

"What am I to do?" Griffin argued. "I am chained to my own promises. If William cannot convince me that he is the rightful king, I am bound by honor to hang!"

"And what of your promises to me? Do you care more for honor in regard to other men or in regard to your wife?"

"You do not understand the ways of a man!"

"Nay, I do not! You're all more stubborn than a pack of jackasses! But, I do believe, there is something you've overlooked."

"That can't possibly be, Lilla."

"What about your responsibility to your people?"

"The people of Oxneford?"

"Yes. Leofwine told me before he went north the secret of the amulet. I, too, know who you are, my Griffin."

"But what does that have to do with the matter at hand?"

"You are the only male descendant of Lord Uhtred. I can see you do not wish to take back Beam-Dune Maur from Lord Stephen. But unless you are alive, you cannot help the people when Odo finally grasps his inheritance. If you will not swear for me, Griffin, swear for them. Because this one thing is true: Uhtred's blood flowed in your veins before King Edward's wishes for you or Harold Godwinson were ever uttered. That is what you must honor, my love. On the graves of Leofwine and Edmund, and even Uhtred, you owe it to them to care for their sheep."

Silence lay heavy on the air between them, and Griffin, his forehead in his hands, sat motionless. Finally, he looked up, the blue of his eyes absorbing Lilla's green.

"Lay down, Lilla," he commanded.

And when she did he reclined beside her, curling his long body around hers, his chin resting on the top of her head.

"You are a wise woman, wife."

"Thank you, husband."

"I will do as you ask. I will swear fealty to William. For you. For Edmund and Leofwine. But, in most ways, for the people

of Oxneford. Odo will prove a formidable menace, and someone must be there to stop him."

"Hugh won't," she stated.

"No. Hugh hasn't the longevity of spirit. Indeed, his heart
is as far away from Jesu's as Odo's is."

"Aye." Lilla turned over and looked up into his eyes. "I
love you, Griffin. And I know that somewhere there's a purpose to all of this."

Griffin wanted to know what it possibly could be.

They lay still for many minutes, enjoying the beating of
each other's heart, the smell of their hair, and the breath on
their cheeks. Lilla suddenly sat up.

"What is William like?"

"He's a mighty man, oftentimes cruel, sometimes merciful.
Lord Stephen assures me he will extend the hand of friendship
to me if I but swear."

"Then so be it," Lilla declared.

"Aye, love. So be it."

William arrived the next day.

## THIRTY-THREE

T he first portion of the entourage crested the horizon shortly after daybreak. Dust was hefted up from the roadbed by the asses' hooves which pulled the achingly full carts heavily laden with the king's household wares. Each person the procession passed could not help but feel sorry for the little beasts of burden. They also felt a weary kinship.

Servants walked alongside the animals. Both genders. All ages. They were invariably the first to arrive. Ensuring the king's comfort, seeing he was well taken care of and felt utterly at home in his foreign surroundings—that was their duty.

Lord Stephen de Chauliac's servants helped the others unload the furniture, the rugs, the clothes, and the various foodstuffs King William's cook believed his lord could not possibly survive without. But after a bit, the residents of Castle Chauliac stood aside and surveyed in awe the well-oiled mechanism that was the king's household do its job. Lilla watched with Griffin from the small window of his tower room.

"To think Lord Stephen has spent the last three weeks in preparation! I'd wager he needed to do naught now that I've observed the way the king's servants have descended upon the castle."

Griffin laughed. "Worry not over vain preparations, my lamb. Not just the king and his queen are on their way. His court is following as well. It was the same in the days of Edward. Believe me well: Stephen de Chauliac's larders will become yawning holes and will be found entirely wanting after the procession you see before you reverses its direction."

Several hours later, the courtiers began to arrive. Lilla gasped at the splendor by which the various earls, barons, and their ladies were surrounded. Their horses were fine, prancing animals, with long manes and thin, muscle-carved legs. The decorated litters which held the ladies attested to the sumptuous garb of the noblewomen inside. Personal servants preceded them, their carts laden with all sorts of garments, jewels, and personal fancies. Brightly colored banners flew, and the nobles rode in pairs or threesomes, their laughter echoing up over the walls and into the ears of Lilla and Griffin.

"You could do worse than aligning yourself with men such as these," Lilla stated.

Inside, Griffin winced. The decision he had made had rubbed his soul raw. And he knew that deeming himself a man of honor would only be done through a constant self-reminding of the real reason he had chosen to swear fealty.

Finally, an hour later, trumpets blared strangled blasts from their skinny necks. The Conqueror was just over the rise. Lilla and Griffin hurried back over to the window. She grabbed his hand and clasped it tightly as the russet-haired king, sitting proudly upon his white stallion, crested the hill. Rays of sun were streaming down through the clouds in lines of light. They caught at his hair, causing it to blaze an even more glorious red. Lord Stephen, who stood atop the wall, lifted his hand in greeting. The King of England did the same.

*Hail the conquering king*, Lilla thought, and at that moment was impressed with not only the majesty and strength of the man who was coming toward her, but also with his entourage—the likes of which she had never before observed.

"Had I been Edward," she looked out and pressed herself closer into Griffin's side, "I would have chosen such a one to inherit my throne."

Under the weight of his wife's awestruck statement, Griffin saw William the Conqueror in a new light. And new thoughts shuttled in his brain. Under a strong king such as William, England would become truly united. No more warring between power-hungry earls. None would dare to challenge the authority of the Conqueror. Surely, he would keep the Scots and the Welsh silent as well. With no evidence in his hand, Griffin knew that Lilla's thought would have been Edward's. The throne of England had always belonged to William, the Duke of Normandy. If Harold Godwinson had honored his vow of fealty, had not sought a deathbed proclamation, King William would have assumed the throne in peace, not as Conqueror but as heir.

At that moment, Griffin knew it was true: The winds of change would never shift back upon themselves. The island of Britain had been conquered again, men had died, and blood was spilled over the verdant plains, in huts, and over castle walls. But when the last arrow flew, the last fortress was conquered, and Norman and English settled together, intermarrying and coexisting peacefully, it would be true then what was true now and had always been true.

England rested in the hands of God.

He would move the hearts and minds of the men in leadership, and if that was William the Conqueror, then let it be so. Griffin recognized that the time had come most certainly to be subject to the higher powers.

"There is no power but of God," he quoted, remembering the passage in Romans that Brother Adam had taught him.

"What?" Lilla turned to him.

"It's from the book of Romans, Lilla."

"You must teach it to me. I haven't learned a new passage of Scripture in years. My heart aches for such knowledge."

"All right, my love. I'll teach you all that I know. Perhaps we'll be able to make it back to the abbey someday, and I'll copy other passages for you to learn."

"Thank you, Griffin." She turned and placed her arms around his neck. They remained in the embrace, lost in their own thoughts—one overcome in her relief, the other wary of the future but trusting the God who made him for guidance.

So much had begun to make sense to Griffin. Being the true lord of Oxneford, his responsibilities lay clearly before him. All the events through which he had been brought were illuminated as necessary by the light of God's providence.

❧ ❧ ❧

All day they waited. But the Conqueror did not send forth a summons.

Lilla had her tablet loom brought up to Griffin's chamber, and she steadily worked, her fingers negotiating the threads in quick time to her rapidly beating heart. The braid was especially fine, commissioned by Lord Stephen himself. The diamond pattern reminded her of the markings along the back of a snake. The burnished orange and gold threads were the foundation of a warm palette of colors, the dark brown and smoky green added contrast, throwing the warm hues forward, visually closer to the eye which beheld them. She reached over and turned the tablets, then passed the shuttle of thread back through. And she repeated the process, first one way, then the other, over and over, the activity so automatic she didn't need to think or even consciously count.

Griffin paced. His long legs crossed the chamber in only four paces. And back he went again.

"How is it that you are so calm, wife?" he asked finally, laying down on his bed with an agitated sigh.

"'Tis not serenity I feel right now, Griffin. To be sure, my stomach has more twists and turns in it than does this braid."

"Will you accompany me?"

"I don't believe you really want me to, my love."

He raised himself up on his elbow. "Why do you say that?"

"Oh, call it intuition. Or perhaps I really do understand the ways of a man more than you think. No. I shall await your return in my own room, for surely, my love, that is where you'll sleep tonight," she said hopefully.

Already the evening shadows had turned to the black of a country night. Griffin's head nodded from side to side. "Why don't you go then? Prepare our bed, my Lily, and when the deed is done I shall lay down beside you, a free man."

"Truly free?"

His eyes looked deeply into hers. "There are always chains to the past under whose bondage we will never escape."

"Not until Jesu comes again," she reminded him with a smile.

He returned it. "How good you are for me. You pull me from my world of self-examination and shed the light of the spiritual upon my temporal nature. Maybe someday I will do the same for you."

Lilla rose to her feet, leaned down, and placed a firm kiss on his lips. "I shall await your return to me, husband. Be not afraid of the task set before you. You believe, don't you, that this is what Jesu is requiring of you?"

"Yes."

"Well, then, what more assurance is needed?"

He stood up. "Having William call me to his presence would help. Lionel!" he yelled for the guard.

A minute later, Lilla was gone, and Griffin waited alone, his impatience churning inside him like an unpolished stone.

❧ ❧ ❧

The red moon was a dim crescent in the sky, a reflection of a deadly scimitar, shedding little light and even less comfort. Across the bailey a lone figure strode from the direction of the keep. His figure exuded strength of muscle, the tilt to his chin, strength of character. His stride told a thousand tales of a man who could do anything, a man whose goals were always achieved.

William the Conqueror took the key from Lionel and trod the steps to the tower room.

Griffin sat at his table, drumming his fingers, rubbing their tips against the fading calluses of his sword hand. His beautiful sword—the only object he had to remember King Edward by—was gone. And though it was a cause for regret, he had decided long ago to delegate the realm of the past to a remote, infrequently summoned place. Instead, he concentrated on the present, anticipating all possible avenues down which the conversation might progress, and readying himself accordingly. He pictured himself visually, over and over, bending his knee to the Conqueror, hoping that the more he conjured the scene in his mind, the easier it would be.

Footsteps echoed in the corridor.

The moon hung low, burning down the midnight even as the tallow candle on the table did likewise. Griffin stood to his feet as the key, shaped much like an ankh, was inserted into the lock.

Slowly the door opened. "Have I been sent for, Lion . . . ?" Griffin asked, but could not finish the question. For even in the dimness he recognized the stance he had seen so many times from the walls of York. The majesty. The strength. And when William the Conqueror entered the room, he remembered well the intense eyes, the wide, regal bearing.

Immediately, without thinking, Griffin bowed the knee. "My liege," he said in the true humility of a vassal recognizing his king. King William felt a glow of satisfaction at the giant kneeling before him, but he knew better than most men that every man possessed an inherent pride.

"Rise, Griffin Eadricson," he said right away in his own language. "You're obeisance is duly noted."

A bit surprised at his automatic reaction, Griffin did as the Conqueror bid, then brought over his stool on which the king sat. Saying nothing, William rubbed his chin, examining the prisoner thoughtfully for what seemed many minutes. Finally, he rested his hands on his knees.

"You were Edward's godson. I knew Edward well and loved him well. As did you."

"Yes. I owe everything I am to King Edward, my lord."

"As do I."

Griffin looked up quickly.

"Well, not everything," William said with a brief smile, "but most certainly, England."

"Then King Edward truly chose you to inherit the throne?"

The king reached into a purse which hung from his belt. "Here," he pulled out a piece of parchment. "Stephen tells me that Edward had you educated. Read this. I myself was not afforded the benefits of higher learning," the Conqueror stated matter-of-factly, remotely referring to his illegitimate birth.

Quickly, Griffin's eyes scanned the personal letter proclaiming Edward's wishes. It was signed in that delicate script he had seen before and sealed with King Edward's own seal.

"You kept this all these years, my lord?"

The king's dark eyes sparkled. "Of course. You are not the only one who wished to see this. Although I must say that you are indeed fortunate, Griffin, in that I wouldn't have proved myself to you at all but for the pleadings of my good friend Stephen de Chauliac. Your life is given you because of him, and even more so because of Edward's love for you."

"Thank you, my king."

"And it pleases me much that you bowed the knee before reading this. Tomorrow morning you will swear fealty to me in the presence of my court."

"Yes, your highness."

The king rose to his feet, as did Griffin. "You may consider your imprisonment over. I understand you have a wife here at Castle Chauliac?"

Griffin nodded.

"Then go to her." In a rare apocalyptic moment, his face cleared of all kingly pretense. "Do you love her, son?"

"More than my own honor."

"I love my Matilda, you know. Never once have I strayed from her. I've found that to be good counsel."

"Thank you, your highness."

Then the Conqueror walked away, gave word to the guard, and proceeded to his chambers. Griffin gathered his few belongings, walked past Lionel who congratulated him in his native language, and went to be with his wife.

Lilla was still weaving when he opened their door.

Book III
The Knight

## THIRTY-FOUR

# Emma

Griffin came home. And with him, his bride.
Both Eadric and I loved her well.

Lilla was tender and kind, and all that we could have asked in a mate for our only son. It didn't take long for her to become a part of our family. Having Griffin return was miraculous enough, for over a year we had recalled only visions of his parting. But the fact that he had lived what seemed an entire lifetime proved to us most handily that he had become a man.

Sir Griffin Eadricson.

Yes, King William had knighted him after Griffin had passed the night in prayer in the abbey two months after swearing fealty. It was fitting that in the presence of his godfather's remains he should prepare for the mantle God was evidently placing around his shoulders. The morning he emerged, ready for the ceremony, he had indeed changed.

He was at peace. Finally and most assuredly, his calling had come upon him in the abbey itself.

At the ceremony, Eadric and I proudly watched as Edward's sword descended upon both of his broad shoulders. His head was bowed respectfully, his knee was bent before the single man who had conquered a nation. I cried. As did Lilla beside me. We held hands tightly throughout the ceremony, and

I realized I had most definitely gained another daughter. One cannot have too many daughters.

And so the son of the royal stonemason, the son of the abbey, became a knight in the service of the king, under the care of Lord Stephen de Chauliac. King William magnanimously returned the sword to Griffin, who was careful never to lose hold of it again.

When they left to go back to Oxneford, my heart was heavy, for I had always known who Griffin really was. Lilla told me of my half-brothers, both of us weeping for their deaths as the tale unfolded. How appropriate it was that my son should return to the castle of his grandfather, my own father, whom I never knew.

Though I never told Eadric the truth, I took a certain pride in the fact that I was the mother of the true lord of Oxneford.

## THIRTY-FIVE

On his way home, Sir Griffin Eadricson walked the spring countryside. The apple orchards were slowly unveiled in the retreating mists after the sudden rainstorm. The fields and meadows were colorful quilts, bedecked with eyebright and forget-me-not. And the hedgerows were alive with blooms: blackberry, hawthorn, and wild roses. Cottagers worked their strips of land in between and chopped down trees for fencing or to clear more farmland. The smell of freshly turned earth filtered pleasingly through the atmosphere. Often enough the sheriff was seen, taking the king's share. But the cottagers, small holders, and villeins did not complain overmuch. For truly, Lord Stephen was kind.

The Eadricsons were temporarily ensconced within the vast hulk of Castle Chauliac. Griffin hurried up to their small solar. A comely serving wench had just laid a platter of cheese and bread upon the blanket chest. The young knight looked hungrily at the offerings, and the girl slipped quietly out of the room.

Lilla, clad in an ivory linen kirtle, finely embroidered with green thread, came in from the bedchamber. Her white silk veil fluttered around her curls as she walked slowly forward with her hands upon her hips. "I never shall worry about you having a wandering eye as long as a plate of food lies in the girl's hands!"

He took her into his arms and kissed her. "How are you feeling, today, Lily? Any better?"

"Yes, dear husband." She rubbed her bulging belly with a sigh. "I told you once the sickness was gone I would concentrate on getting fat. And I never break my word!"

"No, Lily. You never do."

"How did your day progress? Is our new house coming along beautifully?"

"Yes. Father is building us a small palace, I'll warrant. He's tackling the job as if it were more important to him than even the abbey was."

"Surely not!"

"No. Not really. But he told me it should be done by spring."

"Lord Stephen is most taken with him. I'm sure he'll be putting him to work himself!"

"'Tis true, my lamb. Lord Stephen will be building a chapel here at the castle. Father will begin work on it as soon as he is done with our home."

"Then your mother and father will be staying on with us for a while longer?"

"Aye. Mother's certainly enjoying the de Chauliacs' hospitality. And father . . . well, my Lily, as long as he's planning what to do with a block of stone, he's most happy."

Lilla nodded warmly. "It's been so nice having your mother here with us. Will they stay with us at the house while the chapel is being built?"

"I think so."

"So . . . what else did your day hold?"

"Most of the morning was spent here. We have been busy training the new recruits that Odo has sent over from Normandy."

"I'll wager you're glad now you had to learn to speak their language so many years ago."

He absentmindedly rubbed his hand across her protruding stomach. "Yes. Although, at the time I'm sure Brother Adam received more than enough glares from my direction!"

"Sylvia told me Odo was magnificent when it came to training soldiers. Do you think he will ever return?"

"I don't know. When Lord Stephen decided that he would never gain the English estates, I'm sure he wasn't excited about the idea."

"At least he has taken over the Normandy estates now. And better there than here." Lilla's brows wrinkled. "Did he ever receive his guerdon from William?"

"No. In fact, when William got word of Lord Stephen's decision, he said that he would honor his friend's decision and do likewise."

"He fought well for William at Hastings, did he not?"

"Yes. From all I've heard, Odo de Chauliac fought with the strength of ten men. They say he's also handy with a bow."

Lilla nodded her head. "He used to practice quite regularly when he was here. I suppose Odo will never come back to England now. According to Sylvia, it was quite a scene the last time he was home and Lord Stephen shared the ill tidings of his future. Perhaps he will return someday. After all, Lord Stephen's health seems to be worsening."

"That's for certain, my love. Besides, Odo still is the favorite of Robert Shortpants."

"It's amazing to me the Conqueror hasn't put a stop to that."

Reaching out, he put his arm around her and drew her close into his side as they sat. "I imagine Queen Matilda has something to do with that. Robert is her favorite. And, as you fully know, women can sometimes have a profound effect on their husbands!"

"Well, then, why don't you take a bit of food and rest before dinner?" she suggested.

"See what I mean?" his eyes sparkled. But he did as she bid and was soon fast asleep on their bed, his head against her heartbeat.

"I don't blame you for hating Hugh, mon chere," Odo's mistress, Countess Elaine de Valois, soothed, playing with his curls as he lay with his head in her lap. Gray hairs now littered the black, and puffy bags rested under his black eyes—a reflection of the day his inheritance was taken from him, the day Griffin entered his life.

Odo had changed for the worse even as Griffin had changed for the better.

"After all," the wife of Odo's childhood friend complained, "if he was any true, loyal brother, he would have said no to your father. Pah! They do such wickedness."

"Do not concern yourself with my affairs, good woman. You should know me well enough by now to realize that I have plans of my own." A vengeful fire burned red inside his eyes—a reflection of the hatred that was consuming even ambition itself, was consuming him, rendering him fit only for the fires of hell itself. And yet, Lilla remained foremost in his consciousness. And the more he thought of her, the more angry at the outlaw he became. When he came back to Castle Chauliac after Griffin had been knighted, the sight of her by his youthful side, gazing up at him with such blatant adoration . . . it caused him to experience a pain of the heart he yet writhed under. How accurate had been his brash statement that night when he told Griffin Eadricson that pain of the body is nothing when compared to the pain suffered by the heart. The words haunted him yet.

"Will you share your plot with me?" the countess asked playfully, stealing his thoughts from the only woman he had ever loved.

He ignored the question, arose, and put on his undergown, then his tunic. "You'd best be going, Elaine."

"But it's only 11 o'clock!"

"I have no further need of your services tonight." He had turned cold. The conversation brought a certain matter of business to mind—business which needed immediate attention. Clearly the short affair was being conducted only upon terms that were his.

A knock vibrated the door to his chamber.

"Come!" he called, without regard for his mistress' propriety.

His manservant entered with a written summons.

*King William requests your presence at court immediately.*

The note was thrown to the floor as soon as Odo read it. "Hah! I'll bet it's a request!"

Dressed now, Odo left Elaine and hurried to the moonlit stables. Many small tasks must be finished before the sail on his ship was raised to face the breeze of the channel.

⁕ ⁕ ⁕

"Sylvia!"

Lilla rushed to the door as her dearest friend alighted from the carriage.

"Lilla!" She handed her baby Eleanor, who was no longer really a baby at almost a year and a half of age.

The two women hugged. Sylvia had been in Normandy visiting her parents at their estates near Evreux. Two months had passed since they had last seen one another.

Lilla tucked her arm through Sylvia's. "Come inside and refresh yourself. I heard the call, and there's cider and cheese waiting in your chamber."

"Oh, Lilla, you are precious. Thank you."

Sylvia was in much the same state as Lilla. Another child was expected only two months after Lilla's. Of course, at six months along, Sylvia looked as if her pregnancy was considerably further advanced.

Inside the coolness of the keep, Lilla and Sylvia ascended the steps to the living quarters on the top floor. They sat at the table together, glad to be in one another's company after so long an absence. Lilla grabbed Sylvia's hand and squeezed it warmly. "How were your parents?"

"Old and wise, and so glad to see us."

Lilla smiled. "Did Sir Odo perchance visit you while were there?"

"Ha! Odo? I should think not! He is much too busy in Rouen with Robert." Sylvia leaned forward and spoke softly. "There's talk that Robert is unhappy with his father, the king."

Lilla's eyebrows peaked with intrigue. "Truly? What have your parents heard?"

"He wishes to take Normandy completely for his own."

Lilla drew in her breath sharply. "You jest!"

"Surely not! And I doubt not for a single minute that the instigator of Robert Shorthose's ill affections is none other than my brother-in-law."

"Does the king know?"

"Of course he knows. He seems to know everything. And I have another piece of news regarding the odious Odo."

"Tell me." Lilla leaned forward even further.

"William has summoned him to his court. Odo left for England just before I did. Clearly, it is a reprimand. It reminds me of the many times in childhood I had to stay close by the chateau because my wanderings took me to too many dangerous places."

Lilla waved the topic of Odo away with a graceful hand. "Oh, Sylvia, it's so wonderful to have you back. Truly, God is merciful, having given us each other."

Sylvia reached across the table and hugged Lilla impulsively. "Sometimes I wonder if we're not the only women in the world with such a friendship."

A servant came running in. He bowed to Lilla. "There's someone to see you, my lady. A stranger. He'll only talk to you."

"I'll be right there."

Sylvia stayed put, looking forward to just a minute of solitude whilst her friend repaired downstairs.

By the time Lilla returned, the bread and cheese were gone.

"Who was it?" Sylvia asked, then reached for a blackberry from the wooden bowl on the table.

Lilla shrugged. "A traveler, requesting a place to bide the night."

"Awfully early in the day to be seeking cover, isn't it?"

"Aye. He said he had traveled all night. So I told him to bed down in the stables and, if the cook was in a felicitous mood, he could perchance refresh himself with some broth and meat."

Both women tired quickly, and when Sylvia declared a nap was in order, Lilla escorted her friend to her bed, tucked her in, and shut the door quietly. She gave Baby Eleanor over to a nurse, and hurried down to the stables where the mysterious stranger waited her audience.

ho are you?" Lilla's eyes sparkled with curiosity. And if her words came out harshly, it was only due to the fact that this man was the filthiest vagabond she had seen since coming to the castle. His hair—a mat of long black curls—grew beneath a brown cap dubiously adorned by a bedraggled gray feather. Not having bathed in what seemed to her sensitive nose like years, it was difficult to discern his coloring. He was not overly tall, but he appeared to possess, beneath his grimy skin, muscles wiry and strong.

"My name is not important. But what I've come to request of you is."

"How about bathing before you do so?" She wrinkled her nose fastidiously.

"No!" The stranger was adamant. "How long until your husband returns?"

"What is that to you?"

"I must be well on my way. I wouldn't be here at all, at this Norman sty talking to a traitor's wench, if it wasn't at the request of a dying man."

"What do you mean 'traitor'?"

"You heard me. He licked the boots of the Bastard."

Lilla pushed her anger aside for a moment. "Have you ever loved a woman, sir?"

"No," he said too quickly. "And I thank God for it."

"Then do not be so quick to judge a man whose love for a woman is so great, whose love for his family runs foremost in his heart. For you cannot understand why Griffin Eadricson bowed the knee. But those reasons were not, ultimately, why he chose to swear fealty. That, however, would be for him to tell you and not myself. And if you knew that, perhaps you would not be so quick to pass judgment on a man you know nothing about. Besides, after he was taken at York not once did anyone come to his rescue, not even his best friend." By the end of the speech, her eyes were back to angry. It didn't put off the stranger at all.

"So . . . now that you've handed me such a pretty parcel of words, my lady, will you listen to my request? For most assuredly, I did not come to hear proclaimed the virtues of your mate."

"As you wish," she agreed. "But please, let us walk outside. The smell of you and the horses is too much for me to take at one time."

They ventured into the late-afternoon sunshine.

"Who is the dying man of which you spoke?" She looked directly into his face.

"He bides not far from here, my lady. In fact, it is just a simple walk. Maybe two miles."

She smiled. "No walk is simple for me, stranger."

"I can lead you there by horse, if you prefer." He had noticed her severe limp straightaway. But had forgotten her infirmity in the course of their conversation.

"All right. Bring a beast then, and we shall begin our journey. But first you must tell me who it is."

"That I cannot do . . . at his request. But certainly, if you will not accompany me, I will rouse him from his deathbed and bring him to you."

"Heavens, no! You will not do such a thing to a dying man. I shall accompany you forthwith. Go and get your horse.

Although I must say, when my husband returns and hears of my madness, he will surely not be pleased!"

The stranger let out a disgusted snort as he turned back to the stables. Lilla folded her hands into her lap and waited.

❧ ❧ ❧

Into the forest the stranger led the horse. It was an intriguing journey, most certainly, for she had made it many times on her way home from market at Oxneford. Indeed, the path looked remarkably the same, and when the horse stopped at the door to her now-dilapidated hut, Lilla became most confused.

"Why have you brought me back here?" she asked, leaning forward to let the stranger bear the bulk of her weight as she slid off the brown mare.

"If a man is not afforded the honor of death in battle, he wishes to die at home."

The jays called loudly to one another, and the tops of the elm trees whispered their fluttering words. The sounds of the forest were amplified as the wanderer's words became clear.

"Ebb!"

Lilla cried in anguish and awkwardly ran inside.

❧ ❧ ❧

The small hut was already in a state of disrepair. Her table was overturned, the floor was not swept, and a corner of the thatch was giving away overhead, making the floor beneath it a muddy mess.

He lay on her pallet.

The hearth was cold.

"Ebb." It was a whisper.

He said nothing. But merely held out his icy hand.

Lilla took it in both of hers. She looked imploringly at him, bidding him speak. He could not.

"They cut out his tongue." The vagabond volunteered the information.

371

Tears pooled in her eyes. Ebb looked at his friend and nodded barely.

"He wanted to ask for your forgiveness."

Lilla threw herself across her brother's dying form. She cried. Her hot tears and kisses raining down on his frigid, wan features. She wept for the time he had wasted, but she would not tell him that.

"It's all right, brother. You couldn't have known I would fall from that tree."

Ebb's eyes still held their tortured stare at the ceiling.

"Look at me, Ebb," she said.

He refused and continued his iron gaze at the thatch.

"Look at me, brother," she commanded again, and turned his face to hers. "I love you. I always have. Shall I summon a priest?"

Ebb nodded but closed his eyes.

Lilla felt a tap on her shoulder.

"Come," said Simon, "it is time to go back. Let the man die as he lived." He kindly helped her to her feet.

"Good-bye, brother," she said, gathering her tears and stowing them away for later.

Ebb remained motionless.

Lilla mounted the horse and was led back to the castle. As the horse's hooves softly thumped down the path, Ebb the Silent lay still. And when the noise of his sister's departure ceased, he breathed his last.

## THIRTY-SEVEN

A raw March wind buffeted the castle. It increased in strength even as Lilla's labor increased in intensity. She fought hard against the pain, refusing to cry out, to let the tears come forth.

Fourteen hours it had been going on thus.

The midwife seemed worried but gave no voice to her fears. Holding Lilla's hand, Sylvia sat at the side of the bed. Griffin waited in the hallway, his face pale and worn. He had never felt so helpless in his life. And his fervent prayers reached a pace most frantic.

Sylvia slipped from the room, shutting the door behind her.

"What's happening in there?"

She shook her head as she rubbed her own large belly. "The baby is just not coming. The midwife thought at first it was just a difficult birth, Lilla is so slender and small. But I can see the worry lines increasing on her brow."

"I want to go in."

"Oh, Griffin, you can't."

"I can't bear it. If only she'd scream or something. But to think she's bearing such pain without a sound. . . ."

"She just needs your prayers now."

"Well, she has them. I've been doing nothing else."

Just then the midwife's voice was heard. "My lady, come quick, I can finally see the top of the head!"

Sylvia rushed back in, and Griffin was again left to wait.

Lilla was now squatting on the bed.

"Push, my lady! Push!" the midwife yelled, sweat streaming down her wrinkled face. "Push!"

Lilla summoned up all the energy she had left, which was surprisingly more than she would have guessed. And she pushed, every muscle in her body straining.

After the contraction was over with, Sylvia extricated her hand from Lilla's severe grasp and dipped a cloth in cool water. "There, there, dearest one. Let me cool your brow."

"Thank . . . you," Lilla gasped gratefully. And then winced as another contraction came upon her.

The pushing began again. "Come, girl!" the midwife yelled again. "Harder! Push harder!"

Lilla tried with all her might, forgetting her leg which throbbed from the position in which she found herself. But it was all turning into some kind of eerie dream world as the contractions and pushing ebbed on and on.

An hour went by.

Finally, the midwife reached inside yelling, "Push, girl! Push with all of your might!"

Lilla did, screaming with pain and a violent need.

At the sound of his wife's only cry, Griffin ran into the room, just as the baby slipped into the world.

"It's a boy!" the midwife cried joyfully as she slapped the baby's bottom.

The babe cried.

Lilla fell back onto the bed, covered in sweat, spent completely.

He gasped air into his tiny lungs and let out a loud wail of utter indignation.

Griffin took his son, held him to his chest, and cried for the first time since he was a child.

❦ ❦ ❦

It was a foul segment of London in which Odo de Chauliac had found himself. The stench of the decaying garbage and waste which lay in soppy heaps in the streets was overpowering, and yet he barely noticed it as he made his way to his final destination.

A small house with a steep-pitched roof, huddled at the end of a narrow lane. It was misshapen, its angles all askew, the door unable to shut properly. He walked inside without knocking.

A prophecy was forgotten.

A deal was made.

And Odo de Chauliac emerged with a smile upon his face.

❦ ❦ ❦

"Are you sure you feel well enough to travel?" Griffin asked Lilla.

"Certainly. It has been a month since Edward was born. I'll be fine. Besides, I don't want to bid you good-bye ever again. And if King William has invited you to London for Easter, 'tis only natural that I accompany you."

"All right, Lily. If you feel able to travel all day, I will take you. For your sake, I'd rather you stayed here. But as for me, I'm of the same mind. I never want to say good-bye to you either."

And so they were on their way.

Eadric and Emma bid them stay at the house in Westminster, and they gratefully accepted the invitation. After all, Milly—maiden Milly—was still living there, keeping house until her parents' return.

"Come in! Come in!" she bustled them all inside, immediately taking the baby from Lilla's arms. "Let's get you a fresh nappy, and I'm sure you're hungry after such a journey!" She looked up at her brother with a smile. "Oh, Griffin, I knew he would look like you! I changed more of your nappies than Mother did. Lilla, he's beautiful."

"Thank you, Mildred," Lilla smiled warmly. "But you really don't have to change him."

"Nonsense! Griffin, don't just stand there looking lost. Take Lilla into Mother and Father's room. You must be exhausted after your long day. I'll change Edward and bring him to you for his feeding. I'm sure you both could do with a nice cup of broth as well. Those litters get chilly, even in the springtime! By the way, Mary is coming with her brood in about an hour. We'll sup together."

Griffin's and Lilla's eyes met in laughter. "You'd best do as she says and show me the bedchamber, husband. Milly's right—I am quite tired."

Minutes later she was lying comfortably on the bed, nursing the baby. Griffin's and Mildred's voices were heard in mumbling tones from outside the door, and contentment was hers. She and Edward drifted off into a peaceful sleep.

❦ ❦ ❦

Supper was quite a spectacle. Lilla sat back and enjoyed the display of Mary and Mildred waiting on Griffin's every need. If Milly was overpowering, Mary was doubly so. The eldest sister had come with her four children, ranging from 16 down to two. Her husband smiled cheerfully under his burden of various foodstuffs cooked that day amidst much ado in their household.

After the fancy meals she had been served at Castle Chauliac for well over a year, Lilla enjoyed the crusty brown bread, hearty soup, roasted pig, and potatoes. Mary's husband had even caught some fish fresh that morning, and the smell of it grilling over the fire had succeeded in making Lilla mad with hunger.

After praying for God's blessing upon the meal, the family fell heartily to consuming the wonderful offerings. Laughter beautified the setting even further, and Lilla's heart swelled to grand proportions when she realized that once again she was part of a family.

There was a knock at the door.

Milly set down her knife and quickly stood to her feet. "I'll see who it is."

She opened the door, and Lilla heard her name issue from the caller's lips. The voice was so familiar that it made her heart turn.

"Lilla? Someone for you. He will not tell me his name."

Griffin had recognized the voice and he stood up, his eyes suddenly filled with a blazing anger. "I'll tell him to go."

"No!" Lilla placed a hand on his arm. "Don't do that, Griffin. Let me talk to him just for a moment. You know I can get through to Odo in a way no one else can. There must be a good reason why he's come."

"Lilla, I don't trust him."

"Oh, love, he won't hurt me. I promise you. Odo would never hurt me."

He handed her the walking stick. "Stay right by the door, Lilla, and I'll let you speak with him. I want to be able to see you at all times."

"Your request is fair. I shall do as you ask."

She took the stick from Griffin and slowly walked across the room. She stepped just outside the door.

"Lilla." Odo's eyes shone at the sight of her. "You're even more beautiful than I remembered."

"Odo. It has been a long time. And you look your same handsome self," she said brightly, her manner friendly and easy. "What brings you to Westminster?"

"I'm biding in London at the present. I'm sure you heard that William called me to court."

"Becoming a little too ambitious, were we?" she laughed, knowing she could get away with it.

"Oh, Lilla, you know me too well. Yes, I suppose I was a tad too influential upon Robert Shortpants."

"Why have you come?"

"I had to see you again, knowing you're close by."

"You don't give up easily, do you?"

"You can't tell me if Griffin had truly been dead I would have stood no chance of gaining your favor."

Lilla sighed. "No, I can't. But Griffin is alive, Sir Odo. And that makes all the difference. No thanks to you! You certainly made my life more of an adventure, Odo!"

Odo smiled a rare grin and lifted his hand to softly caress her cheek.

"I must get back in," she said, looking into his eyes with regret—not for what might have been between them, but that this man could only love in futility.

"Good night, dearest Lilla." He turned and walked down the street, a solitary figure in the chilly strands of the moonlight.

Lilla went back inside.

"What did he want?" Griffin asked, helping her back down onto the bench.

"I don't know, Griffin. It was all so very strange."

"What did he say?"

"Only that he wanted to see me . . . being in the neighborhood and all!" Lilla joked.

"Well, 'tis a good thing he didn't seek to hurt you or take you from me. It's been my secret dream to have just cause to rid England of Odo de Chauliac once and for all."

# ❧ THIRTY-EIGHT ❧

ood Friday dawned the next day. A thick mass of
clouds covered the land, and a typical March breeze
brushed over town and country. The sky was dark, and it
seemed as if the earth recollected that today was the day all of
Christendom remembered the passion of Christ, and so set the
tone accordingly.

Little Edward awoke with a light fever.

"You go on to Mass without me," Lilla said to Griffin. "I'll
go later."

"But, Lilla, I hate to leave you here by yourself."

"Nonsense, husband," she laughed. "I lived by myself for
years! Go! As you said yourself, the king will be there this
morning. I insist, Griffin."

"You've got that 'don't cross me' look on your face."

"You're learning, my love."

He leaned over where she lay on the bed and kissed
Edward first, then Lilla. "Saved the best for the last," he
whispered.

"The baby's asleep," she said invitingly. "Are you sure you
have to go?"

"Don't tempt me, Lily." He sat down on the edge of the
bed and kissed her—a lingering, deep exchange. "You're right.
Perhaps I should stay."

She pushed him away from her playfully. "I just convinced you to go without me. Do you really think I'd let you stay now?"

"But didn't you just invite me to—"

"Your closeness made me a bit befuddled, that's all. Take it as a compliment and hasten. The bells will be tolling any minute."

"You are beguiling, Lilla. Do you know that?" He softly ran his hand through her curls.

"And you are much too distracting, even dressed up in your fine clothes."

He learned forward and whispered in her ear. "That's because you know what's underneath."

"Come back to me soon," she whispered huskily as she pressed her mouth against his. "You'll have me soon enough."

"I want you now."

Just then Milly called in. "Griffin, come brother. 'Tis time we leave!"

"Wait anxiously, Lilla. I'll be returning to you soon."

"I should hope so."

Griffin walked to the door.

"Griffin?" Lilla called urgently.

"What is it, my Lily?"

"Be careful."

He looked at her quizzically and left the room.

⚜ ⚜ ⚜

"Behold the Lamb of God which taketh away the sins of the world. Happy are we who are called to His supper." The abbot held high the wine and bread.

Griffin bowed his head in respect as he repeated the response with the others. "Lord, I'm not worthy to receive You. Only say the word and I shall be—" He looked back up. He had seen a movement before he bowed his head. Yes, he was sure of it.

Up high, in the triforium.

"—healed," he finished the response.

Quietly he left his seat.

ᴥᴥ ᴥᴥ ᴥᴥ

Sylvia pleaded fatigue when Hugh asked if she would like to go for a stroll. Her time of delivery was imminent, and as large as she had been with her first child, she was even larger with this pregnancy.

"Why don't you and your father go for a ride after Mass? Certainly it would be good for him."

"Yes, he does seem to be experiencing a bit of melancholy these days. Perhaps the fresh air will do him good." Hugh kissed Sylvia soundly. "How is it that you're always so unbelievably practical?"

"Just fortunate, I guess," she responded wryly. "Most women wish to be thought of as spontaneous, delightful, amusing. But I get practical," she sighed with a grin. "I suppose it will just have to do."

Hugh laughed.

An hour later, Hugh and Lord Stephen were riding across the open fields.

"Look, father." Hugh pointed at the thick belt of trees which spread out to their left. "Do you see that smoke coming up from the woods there?"

"Yes. Those are my hunting grounds, are they not?"

"It is as you say. Poachers, no doubt."

They spurred their horses to a faster pace and were soon entering the woods.

"Maybe we should go back and bring a few men with us," Hugh suggested, but Lord Stephen held up his hand and nodded no.

"It's Good Friday, son. Today these men will be shown that even as Jesu was merciful in dying, Stephen de Chauliac can show mercy as well."

381

Hugh just shrugged and they continued, at last coming upon the source of the fire.

Two strangers sat before the small blaze, the flames of which licked at the belly of a small wild boar. *Poachers indeed*, Hugh thought. *Stupid poachers.* The intruders looked at each other, a pleasant surprise found in their expressions.

"Ah," Stephen said as he dismounted, "not only have you hunted my supper for me, it seems as if you've cooked it as well."

One said with a smirk, "Aye, but we hunt more than just boar, m'lord."

Unexpectedly and horrifyingly quick, the two men reached behind them for the crossbows they had previously loaded. Before there was time even to react, Hugh and Lord Stephen were taken down by the forceful projectiles.

One of the assassins looked pleased. "That was easier than we thought it would be," he remarked to his compatriot.

"So much easier than scaling walls in the middle of the night. And here we thought we were just getting a bit to eat before doing the job. Maybe we should start to lure our prey to us instead of serving them in their own quarters!"

They laughed together and quickly broke camp.

ٮ۞ ٮ۞ ٮ۞

Griffin hurriedly negotiated the stone staircase which led up to the triforium—the upper passageways which overlooked the interior of the church. His feet knew well the way, and for once he was as silent as even Ebb would have been.

Down below, the abbot and several monks were preparing to distribute communion. A hymn was being sung in Latin by several of the brothers, their unwavering voices bouncing in clear reverberation against the stonework. William the Conqueror arose from his seat near the front of the nave when Griffin topped the stairs. He stayed within the shadow of the walls.

The triforium was not blessed with windows. It was dimly lit at best, and oddly hushed though the service down below continued. Approximately 30 feet in front of Griffin, a monk stood motionless, his black habit contrasting little against the darkness.

He breathed a sigh of relief that all was as it should be. Then alarm vanquished his ease when he examined the man more closely. The shoes were too good. No monk he had ever seen wore such expensive brogues.

Inching closer, Griffin saw that the monk intentionally hid in a dark shadow. Nor was he attending to the service, but with the slightest of movements scanned the abbey. Griffin, at the ringing of altar bells, moved even closer, pressed against the wall.

One arm was hidden, and underneath his robe the monk seemed to be holding something.

And when the intruder leaned forward and lifted a crossbow, Griffin knew that surely this was no man of God.

His heart pounded in his ears.

The bowman aimed it directly at the king, who was just about to receive the host.

Stifling his cry, Griffin rushed at the man, throwing him off balance the moment the arrow was released from the bow. He wrapped his arms around the man, restraining him tightly. Time suspended itself as Griffin watched in horror, his voice caught in his throat, for the arrow moved so quickly there was no time to warn those below. Yet the deadly bolt seemed to inch along, almost suspended, slicing wickedly through the air. But it had been thrown off course. And it barely missed the king, lodging itself in the abbot's shoulder instead. One of the monks dove to catch the host before it fell to the ground as the abbot stumbled to his knees, his hand against the wound, the shaft protruding from between his fingers.

The assassin struggled free and instinctively reached for his sword, but the folds of his robe hampered him. Griffin quickly drew his own sword and, without a word, he thrust it into the would-be assassin. The man crumpled to the floor.

Pandemonium had already erupted down below. There were shouts and cries, the monks had stopped their singing. King William's mighty voice was heard above the din. "Continue with the distribution of the host," he commanded. Communion began again as the abbot was helped to his abode to have the arrow extracted.

The Conqueror hurried up to the triforium, where Griffin stood over the wounded man. "My liege, the arrow was aimed at you. I barely made it in time."

"Pity for the abbot."

The assassin moaned in pain, but the wound inflicted by Griffin was not mortal. He could still live, provided the king saw fit to allow him the luxury.

"Who are you?" William growled, crouching down next to the man. "What cause is there against me?"

"None, sire. I'm merely a hired man."

"Who hired you?"

"I cannot tell you that. I would rather die," the assassin said through clenched teeth.

"So be it." The king stood back to his feet, oblivious to his surroundings. "Sir Griffin, throw him over the edge."

"My king?" Griffin's eyes opened in surprise.

"You heard me. Do it. Now!"

Griffin obeyed, lifting the man who cried out first in pain and then screamed as he was hefted further into the air, "No! No! I will tell you . . . please, I will tell you!"

The king motioned for Griffin to set him down. "Tell me." His eyes cut through the frightened stare of the man.

"Odo de Chauliac!"

William the Conqueror looked at the man dispassionately, then said to one of his barons, "Hang him straightaway. Find Odo de Chauliac and bring him to me."

## THIRTY-NINE

# Emma

T he people of Westminster talked of nothing else for days. Many supposed the king's failure to give Odo his guerdon was the reason, others speculated it was Robert Shortpants' doing. William's son denied any knowledge of the plot, and for Matilda's sake, William believed him.

Contrary to the prophecy of the wandering Jew, Odo de Chauliac did not die at the hand of a blond-haired man. He was never found after that day. No one at any port towns had seen a man fitting his unique, scarred description. Some say he stayed in England, waiting to carry out his plan when the time was right. Griffin believed it and waited patiently for Odo to return to Lilla one last time. In all of his dark, unhappy life, Lilla was Odo's only ray of light. And though a man will love darkness better than light, light is what he needs to live.

We were all anxious for many a day when we found out what had happened near Castle Chauliac to Lord Stephen and Hugh. When his gamekeeper found them, Lord Stephen was dead. Hugh, though grievously wounded, was not. For over a week he fought to live, Sylvia by his side every minute, holding his hand, blessing him with healing tears shed on behalf of herself and her children. Lilla and Griffin returned to Castle Chauliac as soon as they heard the news, but not before being summoned before the king.

"Griffin, you saved my life."

"It was an honor, my liege." Griffin bowed his knee.

"I will reward you."

"'Tis not necessary."

"Oh, but it is. I never let a debt of such magnitude go unpaid. The life of Hugh de Chauliac even now hangs tenuously between heaven and earth. If he should leave us, I wish for you to be the lord of Oxneford."

Griffin hesitated, for he and Hugh had become friends. He wanted only for Hugh to live. "Then, my king, I can but pray that I receive not such a reward from your hand."

The king, his elbow on the arm of his chair, rested his chin on his fist. He stared hard at the stonemason's son. "You are an odd man, Griffin Eadricson. I mean what I say. Everything has come so easy for you. You've not the need for ambition or gain at the expense of others."

"'Tis true that I've no need for more than I have right now, sire. But that is because the road to where I now stand has been difficult, and not a little painful. Yet if I might serve my king and my God well because of it, it has been worth it."

William smiled. A rare occurrence. "I bless the day you bowed the knee to me, son. You are a man of honor, a true knight."

It was a dismissal.

Griffin hastened to Oxneford.

Happily enough, Hugh lived and assumed the lordship of Oxneford. Griffin was summoned yet again to William's presence and offered a barony. He refused. The king sat back in surprise.

"And why would you refuse a gift such as this, Griffin? Before God and the saints, you've earned it outright."

"I mean no disrespect, sire. But in place of the barony, I have a simple request. I wish to be invested as a knight for the Monastery of St. Peter's."

The king's brows raised. "Westminster? Surely it is a request which I can easily fulfill. But son, being a knight of the abbey will not afford you the riches and the glory you will receive as one of my barons."

"It matters not, sire. The abbey is where my heart is found, where I wish to be most near. She represents my quest for a purpose, my quest for God. To serve her with the talents God has given me would be an honor and a privilege that all the riches England has to offer could not supply. Please, sire," he knelt before William, "'tis my only wish."

"Then you shall have it, Griffin Eadricson. Westminster surely is not one of the wealthier, more important religious houses of the land. What they will be able to give in recompense for your services will not be nearly enough to meet the needs of your family. But, as the other monasteries do, they must contribute to the security of England. I will do this, Griffin. In gratitude to you and to God that my life was spared, I will bestow upon you a small manor just outside of Westminster across the Thames. You should be able to rent out a goodly portion of it to some villeins and cottagers. In this way, you will not be beholden to one of my barons or earls, but will answer only to me. I will commission a house for you as well. Built by your father, of course."

Griffin bowed deeply. "Thank you, sire."

"Rise and go. From this day forward, you will protect and serve the abbey, and when I need your services you will serve me as well."

"Truly, my lord, I shall serve you well with all my strength and a full heart."

Griffin became a knight of the abbey, and King William was true to his promises. He was given an ample manor just across the Thames. Lilla bore him four more children, two of them girls. The boys were educated at the abbey. Edward, the eldest, firmly knew his calling as a child. The abbey graciously showed him the way, affording him an easy destiny. A destiny where God would be served and he would be fulfilled. Was he of stronger character than his father? I don't think so. It was Griffin who cleared the path for Edward's future, even as Eadric built Griffin's, stone by stone, and with loving hands. For some a destiny is paved, for others it is carved—sometimes through pain, sometimes through simple dedication, but always by faith.

And so ends my tale.

*When we build, let us think that we build for ever.*
*— John Ruskin*

# ❧ EPILOGUE ❧

*Many years later.*

**O**h glorious, glorious day. The sun shone hot and soared free in its heavens. Sweetly the air was perfumed with the many blossoms of spring. Griffin, riding on horseback, shielded his eyes against the bright light as his small entourage drove by the fields behind Widow Urfried's hut.

Lilla called to him from her seat in the carriage. "Look, my dearest, at the field. It is filled with daffodils!"

He smiled tenderly over at her and commanded the driver to stop the carriage so that they might relish the beauty of spring for just a while.

"Poor Simon," Lilla sighed, pushing a tendril of gray hair away from her eyes, remembering Griffin's tales of their childhood play.

"Aye," Griffin said, his voice far away. "God rest his soul. Perhaps he finally knows peace. And he died as he would have wanted to die . . . at the last stand of England the way it was. The way it should have been, really. 'Tis good Hereward the Wake had Simon with him at the end. He probably never understood why I chose to swear fealty."

"Well, you wrote him a letter of explanation. You did what you could do. Do you have any regrets?"

"No. We've loved well together all these years. It was God's will."

"'Tis true. It was God's will."

"And what of you—any regrets on your part?"

She looked surprised at the question. "Me? How could there be, my husband? You're all I ever dreamed a man could be. You've taken care of me, given me wonderful children, and have loved me all of your life with all of your heart."

"I had no choice, my lamb. Even as William conquered England, so did you vanquish my heart."

Her eyes smiled intimately into his. "I love you, Griffin."

"And I love you, my Lily."

The small procession moved forward, over the Tyburn, and into Westminster. The abbey rose before them, shining splendorous in the sun. The great middle tower hovered over the structure, guarding the residents of its monastery with a benevolent eye.

Griffin helped her out of the carriage, then scooped her up in his yet-strong arms. At the age of 50, Lilla was almost completely crippled by arthritis, but Griffin was a kind, considerate gentleman, carrying her where she could not walk, and taking her on leisurely trips in their carriage all around the southernmost portions of England. It had been her idea to come to the abbey today. They seemed to find themselves here quite often because Lilla knew that this place fed her husband's soul. He needed to come back and feast upon that which delighted not only himself, but had delighted his father and his godfather so completely.

"King Edward had great plans for this place, Lily," he remarked, looking up. "Had he lived, there probably would be more than the 12 or so monks that are here now."

"Perhaps someday, Griffin," her arms were around his sturdy neck, "it will become an illustrious place which people will journey from afar to visit."

"Already I've heard tales that miracles have happened at the grave of King Edward."

"Truly?"

"'Tis what they say. One can't be quite certain about such matters."

By this time they had entered the nave. "Can you stand here?" Griffin asked Lilla.

"Yes, my darling. Set me by one of the pillars, and I'll lean against it. Oh look, Griffin, here comes the esteemed cellarer!" Her eyes twinkled in the direction of the monk who was in charge of all the monastery provisions.

An important-looking young man, who wore his authority most comfortably yet in utmost humility, walked toward them. Several times along the way he was detained by men wishing to speak with him, and always he would stop and listen carefully to their pleas and requests. His face was serene, yet determined, and the mouth that could smile so easily was also made to administer others. Dedicated to God, yet shrewd in business and administration for a younger man, this monk they prayed would someday usher the Monastery of St. Peter's at Westminster into the greater glory that its founder had planned for it since before the day the cornerstone was laid.

He held his arms wide. "Mother! Father!"

And Griffin and Lilla took Brother Edward into the loving circle of their arms and prayed in thankfulness to the God of the abbey. Their God. The One who had loved them, kept them, and conquered their hearts, securing a firm foundation for them, their children, and their children's children.

The bell tolled for high Mass. It was 11 o'clock.

Edward hurried over to the other monks who filed into the church, and Lilla and Griffin stood where they were as Mass was said. Their hearts lifted in praise to God.

"Blessed are they who hunger and thirst after righteousness, for they shall be filled," Lilla whispered, and Griffin smiled, placing his arm tightly around her shoulders, supporting her with his strength.

# Also by Lisa Samson

## The Highlanders

- *The Highlander and His Lady*
- *The Legend of Robin Brodie*
- *The Temptation of Aaron Campbell*

# Harvest House Publishers

For the Best in Inspirational Fiction

### Lori Wick
## A PLACE CALLED HOME
A Place Called Home
A Song for Silas
The Long Road Home
A Gathering of Memories

## THE CALIFORNIANS
Whatever Tomorrow Brings
As Time Goes By
Sean Donovan
Donovan's Daughter

## KENSINGTON CHRONICLES
The Hawk and the Jewel
Wings of the Morning
Who Brings Forth the Wind
The Knight and the Dove

## ROCKY MOUNTAIN MEMORIES
Where the Wild Rose Blooms

## CONTEMPORARY FICTION
Sophie's Heart

### MaryAnn Minatra
## THE ALCOTT LEGACY
The Tapestry
The Masterpiece
The Heirloom

*Ellen Gunderson Traylor*
BIBLICAL NOVELS
Esther
Joseph
Joshua
Moses
Samson
Jerusalem—the City of God

*June Masters Bacher*
PIONEER ROMANCE NOVELS

*Series 1*
Love Is a Gentle Stranger
Love's Silent Song
Diary of a Loving Heart
Love Leads Home
Love Follows the Heart
*Series 2*
Journey to Love
Dreams Beyond Tomorrow
Seasons of Love

*Series 3*
Love's Beautiful Dream
When Hearts Awaken
Another Spring
Gently Love Beckons

HEARTLAND HERITAGE SERIES
No Time for Tears
Songs in the Whirlwind

*Other Novels*
Rumors of Angels, *John Coniglio*
Unforgiven Sins, *Joe Dallas*
The South Wind Blew Softly, *Ruth Livingston Hill*
The Reckoning, *Huggins*
A Wolf Story, *James Byron Huggins*